ALSO BY JONATHAN STROUD

LOCKWOOD & CO.
The Screaming Staircase

THE BARTIMAEUS BOOKS
The Amulet of Samarkand
The Golem's Eye
Ptolemy's Gate
The Ring of Solomon
The Amulet of Samarkand: The Graphic Novel

Buried Fire
The Leap
The Last Siege
Heroes of the Valley

Lockwood & Co.

BOOK TWO

The Whispering Skull

Lockwood & Co.

BOOK TWO

The Whispering Skull

JONATHAN STROUD

Disney • HYPERION

LOS ANGELES   NEW YORK

First Edition

Printed in the United States of America

1 3 5 7 9 10 8 6 4 2

G475-5664-5-14182

Library of Congress Cataloging-in-Publication Data
Stroud, Jonathan.
The whispering skull/by Jonathan Stroud.
pages cm.—(Lockwood & Co.; book 2)
Summary: "Lockwood & Co. are hired to investigate Edmund Bickerstaff, a Victorian doctor who reportedly tried to communicate with the dead, while Lucy is distracted by urgent whispers coming from the skull in a ghost jar"
—Provided by publisher.
ISBN 978-1-4231-6492-0 (hardback)
[1. Ghosts—Fiction. 2. Supernatural—Fiction. 3. Psychic ability—Fiction. 4. London (England)—Fiction. 5. England—Fiction. 6. Mystery and detective stories.] I. Title.
PZ7.S92475Whi 2014
[Fic]—dc23   2014014683

Reinforced binding

Visit www.DisneyBooks.com

SUSTAINABLE FORESTRY INITIATIVE   Certified Sourcing
www.sfiprogram.org
SFI-00993

THIS LABEL APPLIES TO TEXT STOCK

For Laura and Georgia

Contents

I

The Wimbledon Wraiths

Chapter 1

"Don't look now," Lockwood said. "There's two of them."

I snatched a glance behind me and saw that he was right. Not far off, on the other side of the glade, a *second* ghost had risen from the earth. Like the first, it was a pale, man-shaped curtain of mist that hovered above the dark, wet grass. Its head, too, seemed oddly skewed, as if broken at the neck.

I glared at it, not so much terrified as annoyed. For twelve months I'd been working for Lockwood & Co. as a Junior Field Operative, tackling spectral Visitors of every horrific shape and size. Broken necks didn't bother me the way they used to. "Oh, that's brilliant," I said. "Where did *he* spring from?"

There was a rasp of Velcro as Lockwood pulled his rapier clear of his belt. "Doesn't matter. I'll keep an eye on him. You keep watching yours."

I turned back to my position. The original apparition still floated about ten feet from the edge of the iron chain. It had been with us for almost five minutes now, and was growing in clarity all the time. I could see the bones on the arms and legs, and the connecting knots of gristle. The wispy edges of the shape had solidified into flecks of rotted clothing: a loose white shirt, dark tattered breeches ending at the knee.

Waves of cold radiated from the ghost. Despite the warm summer night, the dew below the dangling toe bones had frozen into glittering shards of frost.

"Makes sense," Lockwood called over his shoulder. "If you're going to hang one criminal and bury him near a crossroads, you might as well hang two. We should have anticipated this."

"Well, how come we *didn't*, then?" I said.

"Better ask George that one."

My fingers were slippery with sweat. I adjusted the sword grip in my hand. "George?"

"What?"

"How come we didn't know there'd be two of them?"

I heard the wet crunch of a spade slicing into mud. A shovelful of soil spattered against my boots. From the depths of the earth a voice spoke grumpily. "I can only follow the historical records, Lucy. They show that one man was executed and buried here. Who this other fellow is, I haven't a clue. Who else wants to dig?"

"Not me," Lockwood said. "You're good at it, George. It suits you. How's the excavation going?"

"I'm tired, I'm filthy, and I've found precisely zip. Aside from that, quite well."

"No bones?"

"Not even a kneecap."

"Keep going. The Source must be there. You're looking for *two* corpses now."

A Source is an object to which a ghost is tied. Locate that, and you soon have your haunting under control. Trouble is—it isn't always easy to find.

Muttering under his breath, George bent to his work again. In the low light of the lanterns we'd set up by the bags, he looked like some giant, bespectacled mole. He was chest deep in the hole now, and the pile of earth he'd created almost filled the space inside the iron chains. The big, squared mossy stone, which we were sure marked the burial site, had long ago been upended and cast aside.

"Lockwood," I said suddenly, "mine's moving closer."

"Don't panic. Just ward it off gently. Simple moves, like we do at home with Floating Joe. It'll sense the iron and keep well clear."

"You're sure about that?"

"Oh, yes. Nothing to worry about at all."

That was easy enough for him to say. But it's one thing practicing sword moves on a straw dummy named Joe in your office on a sunny afternoon, and quite another warding off a Wraith in the middle of a haunted wood. I flourished my rapier without conviction. The ghost drifted steadily forward.

It had come fully into focus now. Long black hair flapped around the skull. Remnants of one eye showed in the left-hand orbit, but the other was a void. Curls of rotting skin clung to spars of bone on the cheeks, and the lower jaw dangled at a rakish angle above the collar. The body was rigid, the arms clamped to the sides as if tied there. A pale haze of other-light hung around the apparition; every now and then the figure quivered, as if it still dangled on the gibbet, buffeted by wind and rain.

"It's getting close to the barrier," I said.

"So's mine."

"It's *really* horrible."

"Well, mine's lost both hands. Beat that."

Lockwood sounded relaxed, but that was nothing new. Lockwood *always* sounds relaxed. Or almost always: that time we opened Mrs. Barrett's tomb—he was definitely flustered then, though that was mainly due to the claw marks on his nice new coat. I stole a quick sidelong glance at him now. He was standing with his sword held ready: tall, slim, as nonchalant as ever, watching the slow approach of the second Visitor. The lantern light played on his thin, pale face, catching the elegant outline of his nose, and his flop of ruffled hair. He wore that slight half-smile he reserved for dangerous situations: the kind of smile that suggests complete command. His coat flapped slightly in the night breeze. As usual, just looking at him gave me confidence. I gripped my sword tightly and turned back to watch my ghost.

And found it right there beside the chains. Soundless, swift as thinking, it had darted in as soon as I'd looked away.

I swung the rapier up.

The mouth gaped, the sockets flared with greenish fire. With terrible speed, it flung itself forward. I screamed, jumped back. The ghost collided with the barrier a few inches from my face. A bang, a splash of ectoplasm. Burning flecks rained down on the muddy grass outside the circle. Now the pale figure was ten feet farther off, quivering and steaming.

"Watch it, Lucy," George said. "You just stepped on my head."

Lockwood's voice was hard and anxious. "What happened? What just happened back there?"

"I'm fine," I said. "It attacked, but the iron drove it off. Next time, I'll use a flare."

"Don't waste one yet. The sword and chains are more than enough for now. George—give us good news. You must have found something, surely."

In response, the spade was flung aside. A mud-caked figure struggled from the hole. "It's no good," George said. "This is the wrong spot. I've been digging for hours. No burial. We've made a mistake somehow."

"No," I said. "This is *definitely* the place. I heard the voice right here."

"Sorry, Luce. There's no one down there."

"Well, whose fault is that? You're the one who said there would be!"

George rubbed his glasses on the last clean portion of his T-shirt. He casually surveyed my ghost. "Ooh, yours is a looker," he said. "What's she done with her eye?"

"It's a man," I snapped. "They wore their hair long back then, as everyone knows. And don't change the subject! It's your research that led us here!"

"My research, and your Talent," George said shortly. "*I* didn't hear the voice. Now, why don't you put a cork in it, and let's decide what we need to do."

Okay, maybe I'd been a little ratty, but there's something about rotting corpses leaping at my face that puts me a bit on edge. And I was right, by the way: George *had* promised us a body here. He'd found a record of a murderer and sheep-stealer: one John Mallory, hanged at Wimbledon Goose Fair in 1744. Mallory's execution had been celebrated in a popular chapbook of the time. He had been taken on a wagon to a place near Earlsfield crossroads and strung up on a gibbet, thirty feet high. Afterward, he'd been left "to the attention of the crowes and carrion birds" before his tattered remains were buried near the spot. This all tied in nicely with the current haunting, in which the sudden appearance of a Wraith on the Common had slightly tarnished the popularity of the local toddler playground. The ghost had been seen close to a patch of scrubby trees; when we discovered that this wood had once been known as "Mallory's End," we felt we were on the right track. All we had to do now was pinpoint the exact location of the grave.

There had been an oddly unpleasant atmosphere in the wood that night. Its trees, mainly oaks and birches, were crabbed and twisted, their trunks suffocated by skins of gray-green moss. Not one of them seemed quite a normal shape. We'd each used our particular Talents—the psychic senses that are specially tuned to ghostly things. I'd heard strange whisperings, and creaks of timber close enough to make me jump, but neither Lockwood nor George heard anything at all. Lockwood, who has the best Sight, said he glimpsed the silhouette of someone standing far off among the trees. Whenever he turned to look directly, however, the shape was gone.

In the middle of the wood we found a little open space where no trees grew, and here the whispering sound was loud. I traced it carefully back and forth through the long wet grass until I discovered a mossy stone half buried at the center of the glade. A cold spot hung above the stone, and spiderwebs were strung across it. A clammy sensation of unnatural dread affected all three of us; once or twice I heard a disembodied voice muttering close by.

Everything fit. We guessed the stone marked Mallory's burial spot. So we laid out our iron chains and set to work, fully expecting to complete the case in half an hour.

Two hours later, this was the score: *two* ghosts, no bones. Things hadn't quite gone according to plan.

"We all need to simmer down," Lockwood said, interrupting a short pause in which George and I had been glaring at each other. "We're on the wrong track somehow, and there's no point continuing. We'll pack up and come back another time. The only thing to do now is deal with these Wraiths. What do you think would do it? Flares?"

He moved around to join us, keeping a watchful eye on the second of the two ghosts, which had also drifted near the circle. Like mine, it wore the guise of a decaying corpse, this time sporting a long frock coat and rather jaunty scarlet breeches. Part of its skull appeared to have fallen away, and naked arm bones protruded from frilly sleeves. As Lockwood had said, it had no hands.

"Flares are best," I said. "Salt-bombs won't do it for Type Twos."

"Seems a shame to use up two good magnesium flares when we haven't even found the Source," George said. "You know how pricey they are."

"We could fend them off with our rapiers," Lockwood said.

"That's chancy with two Wraiths."

"We could chuck some iron filings at them."

"I still say it has to be the flares."

All this while the handless ghost had been inching closer and closer to the iron chains, half-head tilted querulously, as if listening to our conversation. Now it pressed gently up against the barrier. A fountain of other-light burst skyward; particles of plasm hissed and spat into the soil. We all took a half step farther away.

Not far off, my ghost was also drawing close again. That's the thing about Wraiths: they're hungry, they're malevolent, and they simply don't give up.

"Go on, then, Luce," Lockwood sighed. "Flares it is. You do yours, I'll do mine, and we'll call it a night."

I nodded grimly. "Now you're talking." There's always something satisfying about using Greek Fire outdoors. You can blow things up without fear of repercussion. And since Wraiths are such a repulsive type of Visitor (rivaled only by Raw-bones and the Limbless), it's an extra pleasure to deal with them this way. I pulled a metal canister from my belt and threw it hard on the ground beneath my ghost. The glass seal broke; the blast of iron, salt, and magnesium lit the surface of the trees around us for a single white-hot instant— then the night went black again. The Wraith was gone, replaced by clouds of brightly slumping smoke, like strange flowers dying in the darkness of the glade. Small magnesium fires dwindled here and there across the grass.

"Nice," Lockwood said. He took his flare from his belt. "So that's one down, and one to— What is it, George?"

It was only then that I noticed George's mouth was hanging open in a grotesque and vacuous manner. That in itself isn't unusual and wouldn't normally bother me. Also, his eyes were goggling against his spectacles, as if someone were squeezing them from inside; but this too is a familiar expression. What *was* concerning was the way his hand was raised, his pudgy finger pointing so unsteadily at the woods.

Lockwood and I followed the direction of the finger—and saw.

Away in the darkness, among the twisting trunks and branches, a spectral light was drifting. At its center hung a rigid, man-shaped form. Its neck was broken; its head lolled sideways. It moved steadily toward us through the trees.

"Impossible," I said. "I just blew it up. It can't have re-formed already."

"Must have," Lockwood said. "I mean, how many gallows Wraiths can there be?"

George made an incoherent noise. His finger rotated; it pointed at another section of the wood. My heart gave a jolt, my stomach turned. *Another* faint and greenish glow was moving there. And beyond it, almost out of eyeshot, another. And farther off . . .

"Five of them," Lockwood said. "Five more Wraiths."

"Six," George said. "There's a little one over there."

I swallowed. "Where can they be coming from?"

Lockwood's voice remained calm. "We're cut off. What about behind us?"

George's mound of earth was just beside me. I scrambled to the top and spun three hundred sixty nervous degrees.

From where I stood I could see the little pool of lantern light, surrounded by the faithful iron chain. Beyond its silvery links, the remaining ghost still bunted at the barrier like a cat outside an aviary. And all around, the night stretched smooth and black and infinite beneath the stars, and through the softness of the midnight wood a host of silent shapes was moving. Six, nine, a dozen, even more . . . each one a thing of rags and bones and glowing other-light, heading in our direction.

"On every side," I said. "They're coming for us on every side. . . ."

There was a short silence.

"Anyone got tea left in their thermos?" George asked. "My mouth's a little dry."

Chapter 2

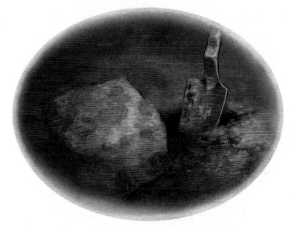

Now, we don't panic in tight situations. That's part of our training. We're psychic investigation agents, and I can tell you it takes more than fifteen Visitors suddenly showing up to make us snap.

Doesn't mean we don't get irritable, though.

"*One man*, George!" I said, sliding down the mound of earth and jumping over the mossy stone. "You said *one man* was buried here! A bloke called Mallory. Care to point him out? Or do you find it hard to spot him in all this crowd?"

George scowled up from where he was checking his belt-clips, adjusting the straps around each canister and flare. "I went by the historical account! You can't blame me."

"I could give it a try."

"No one," Lockwood said, "blames anyone." He had been standing very still, his narrowed eyes flicking around the glade. Making his decision, he swung into action. "Plan F," he said. "We follow Plan F, right now."

I looked at him. "Is that the one where we run away?"

"Not at all. It's the one where we beat a dignified emergency retreat."

"You're thinking of Plan G, Luce," George grunted. "They're similar."

"Listen to me," Lockwood said. "We can't stay in the circle all night—besides, it may not hold. There are fewest Visitors to the east; I can only see two there. So that's the way we head. We sprint to that tall elm, then break through the woods and out across the Common. If we go fast, they should have trouble catching us. George and I still have our flares; if they get close, we use them. Sound good?"

It didn't sound exactly *great*, but it was sure better than any alternative I could see. I unclipped a salt-bomb from my belt. George readied his flare. We waited for the word.

The handless ghost had wandered to the eastern side of the circle. It had lost a lot of ectoplasm in its attempts to get past the iron and was even more sorry-looking and pathetic than before. What *is* it with Wraiths and their hideous appearance? Why don't they manifest as the men or women they once were? There are plenty of theories, but as with so much about the ghostly epidemic that besets us, no one knows the answer. That's why it's called the Problem.

"Okay," Lockwood said. He stepped out of the circle.

I threw the salt-bomb at the ghost.

It burst; salt erupted, blazing emerald as it connected with the plasm. The Wraith fractured like a reflection in stirred water.

Streams of pale light arched back, away from the salt, away from the circle, pooling at a distance to become a tattered form again.

We didn't hang around to watch. We were already off and running across the black, uneven ground.

Wet grass slapped against my legs; my rapier jolted in my hand. Pale forms moved among the trees, changing direction to pursue us. The nearest two drifted into the open, snapped necks jerking, heads lolling up toward the stars.

They were fast, but we were faster. We were almost across the glade. The elm tree was straight ahead. Lockwood, having the longest legs, was some distance out in front. I was next, George on my heels. Another few seconds and we'd be into the dark part of the wood, where no ghosts moved.

It was going to be all right.

I tripped. My foot caught, I went down hard. Grass crushed cold against my face, dew splashed against my skin. Something struck my leg, and then George was sprawling over me, landing with a curse, and rolling clear.

I looked up: Lockwood, already at the tree, was turning. Only now did he realize we weren't with him. He gave a cry of warning, began to run toward us.

Cold air moved against me. I glanced to the side: a Wraith stood there.

Give it credit for originality: no skull or hollow sockets here, no stubs of bone. This one wore the shape of the corpse *before* it rotted. The face was whole; the glazed eyes wide and gleaming. The skin had a dull, white luster, like those fish you see piled in market stalls. The clarity was startling. I could see every last fiber in the rope around the neck, the glints of moisture on the bright, white teeth. . . .

And I was still on my front; I couldn't raise my sword, or reach my belt.

The Visitor bent toward me, reaching out its faint white hand. . . .

Then it was gone. Searing brightness jetted out above me. A rain of salt and ash and burning iron pattered on my clothes and stung my face.

The surge of the flare died back. I began to rise. "Thanks, George—" I said.

"Wasn't me." He pulled me up. "Look."

The wood and glade were filled with moving lights: the narrow beams of white magnesium flashlights, designed to cut through spectral flesh. Bustling forms charged through undergrowth, solid, dark, and noisy. Boots crunched on twigs and leaves, branches snapped as they were shoved aside. Muttered commands were given; sharp replies sounded, alert and keen and watchful. The Wraiths' advance was broken. As if bewildered, they flitted purposelessly in all directions. Salt flared, explosions of Greek Fire burst among the trees. Nets of silhouetted branches blazed briefly, burned bright against my retinas. One after the other, the Wraiths were speedily cut down.

Lockwood had reached us; now, like George and me, he stopped in shock at the sudden interruption. As we watched, figures broke free into the glade and marched over the grass toward us. In the glow of the flashlights and explosions, their rapiers and jackets shone an unreal silver, perfect and pristine.

"Fittes agents," I said.

"Oh *great*," George growled. "I think I preferred the Wraiths."

It was worse than we thought. It wasn't *any* old bunch of Fittes agents. It was Kipps's team.

Not that we discovered this immediately, since for the first ten seconds the newcomers insisted on shining their flashlights directly into our faces, so that we were rendered blind. At last they lowered their beams, and by a combination of their feral chuckling and their foul deodorant, we realized who they were.

"Tony Lockwood," said an amused voice. "With George Cubbins and . . . er . . . is it Julie? Sorry, I can never remember the girl's name. What on earth are you playing at here?"

Someone switched on a night lantern, which is softer than the mag-lights, and everyone's face was illuminated. There were three of them standing next to us. Other gray-jacketed agents moved to and fro across the glade, scattering salt and iron. Silvery smoke hung between the trees.

"You do look a sight," Quill Kipps said.

Have I mentioned Kipps before? He's a Team Leader for the Fittes Agency's London Division. Fittes, of course, is the oldest and most prestigious psychic investigation agency in the country. It has more than three hundred operatives working from a massive office on the Strand. Most of its operatives are under sixteen, and some are as young as eight. They're grouped into teams, each led by an adult supervisor. Quill Kipps is one of these.

Being diplomatic, I'd say Kipps was a slightly built young man in his early twenties, with close-cut reddish hair and a narrow, freckled face. Being undiplomatic (but more precise), I'd say he's a pint-sized, pug-nosed, carrot-topped inadequate with a chip the size of Big Ben on his weedy shoulder. A sneer on legs. A malevolent buffoon. He's too old to be any good with ghosts, but that doesn't stop him from wearing the blingiest rapier you'll ever see, weighed down to the pommel with cheap plastic jewels.

Anyway, where was I? Kipps. He loathes Lockwood & Co. big-time.

"You *do* look a sight," Kipps said again. "Even scruffier than usual."

I realized then that all three of us had been caught in the blast of the flare. The front of Lockwood's clothes was singed, his face laced with stripes of burnt salt. Black dust fell from my coat and leggings as I moved. My hair was disordered, and there was a faint smell of burning leather coming from my boots. George was sooty too, but otherwise less affected—perhaps because of the thick coating of mud all over him.

Lockwood spoke casually, brushing ash from his shirt cuffs. "Thanks for the help, Kipps," he said. "We were in a tightish spot there. We had it under control, but still"—he took a deep breath—"that flare came in handy."

Kipps grinned. "Don't mention it. We just saw three clueless locals running for their lives. Kat here had to throw first and ask questions later. We never guessed the idiots were you."

The girl beside him said, unsmilingly, "They've completely botched this operation. There's no way I can listen here. Too much psychic noise."

"Well, we're clearly close to the Source," Kipps said. "It should be easy to find. Perhaps Lockwood's team can help *us* now."

"Doubt it," the girl said, shrugging.

Kat Godwin, Kipps's right-hand operative, was a Listener like me, but that was about all we had in common. She was blond, slim, and pouty, which would have given me three good reasons to dislike her even if she'd been a sweet lass who spent her free time tending sick hedgehogs. In fact, she was flintily ambitious and cool-natured and had less capacity for humor than a tortoise. Jokes made her irritable, as if she sensed something was going on around her that she couldn't understand. She was good-looking, though her jaw was a bit too sharp. If she'd repeatedly fallen over while crossing soft ground, you could have sown a crop of beans in the chin holes she left behind. The back of her hair was cut short, but the front hung angled across her brow in the manner of a horse's flick. Her gray Fittes jacket, skirt, and leggings always seemed spotless, which made me doubt she'd ever had to climb up inside a chimney to escape a Specter, or battle a Poltergeist in the Bridewell sewers (officially the Worst Job Ever), as I had. Annoyingly, I always seemed to meet her after precisely that kind of incident. Like now.

"What are you hunting tonight?" Lockwood asked. Unlike George and me, both wrapped in sullen silence, he was doing his best to be polite.

"The Source of this cluster-haunting," Kipps said. He gestured at the trees, where the last Visitor had just evaporated in a burst of emerald light. "It's quite a major operation."

Lockwood glanced at the lines of child agents streaming out across the glade. They carried salt guns, hand catapults, and flare throwers. Apprentices loped along with chain reels strapped to their backs; others dragged portable arc lamps, and tea urns, and wheeled caskets containing silver seals. "So I see. . . ." he said. "Sure you have *quite* enough protection?"

"Unlike you," Kipps said, "we knew what we were getting into." He cast his eyes over the meager contents of our belts. "How you thought you'd survive a host of Wraiths with *that* little bit, I don't know. Yes, Gladys?"

A pigtailed girl, maybe eight years old, had scampered up. She saluted smartly. "Please, Mr. Kipps—we've found a possible psychic nexus in the middle of the glade. There's a pile of earth and a big hole—"

"I'll have to stop you there," Lockwood said. "That's where *we're* working. In fact, this whole thing is *our* assignment. The mayor of Wimbledon gave us the job two days ago."

Kipps raised a ginger eyebrow. "Sorry, Tony, he's given it to us, too. It's an open commission. Anyone can take it. And whoever finds the Source first gets the money."

"Well, that'll be *us*, then," George said stonily. He'd cleaned his glasses, but the rest of his face was still brown with mud. He looked like some kind of owl.

"If you've found it," Kat Godwin said, "how come you haven't sealed it? Why are all the ghosts still running around?" This, despite her chin and hairstyle, was a fair point.

"We found the burial spot," Lockwood said. "We're just digging for the remains now."

There was a silence. "Burial spot?" Kipps said.

Lockwood hesitated. "Obviously. Where all these executed criminals were put . . ." He looked at them.

The blond girl laughed. Imagine an upper-class horse neighing contemptuously from a chaise lounge at three passing donkeys, and you'd have her down perfectly.

"You total and absolute bunch of duffers," Kipps said.

"That's rich," Kat Godwin snorted. "That's priceless."

"Meaning what?" Lockwood said stiffly.

Kipps wiped his eye with a finger. "Meaning this clearing isn't the *burial site*, you idiots. This is the *execution ground*. It's where the gallows stood. Hold on. . . ." He turned and called out across the glade. "Hey, Bobby! Over here!"

"Yes, sir, Mr. Kipps, sir!" A tiny figure trotted over from the center of the glade, where he'd been supervising operations. I groaned inwardly. Bobby Vernon was the newest and most annoying of Kipps's agents. He'd only been with him for a month or two. Vernon was very short and possibly also very young, though there was something oddly middle-aged about him, so that I wouldn't have been surprised if it turned out he was secretly a fifty-year-old man. Even compared to his leader, who was diminutive, Vernon was small. Standing next to Kipps, his head came up to his shoulders; standing next to Godwin, he came up to her chest. Where he came up to on Lockwood I dread to think; fortunately I never saw them close together. He wore short gray pants from which tiny legs like hairy bamboo canes protruded. His feet were almost nonexistent. His face shone pale and featureless beneath a swirl of gelled-back hair.

Vernon was clever. Like George, he specialized in research.

Tonight he carried a small clipboard with a penlight attached to it, and by its glow surveyed a laminated map of Wimbledon Common.

Kipps said, "Our friends seem a bit confused about the nature of this site, Bobby. I was just telling them about the gallows. Care to fill them in?"

Vernon wore a smirk so self-satisfied, it practically circled his head and hugged itself. "Certainly, sir. I took the trouble to visit Wimbledon Library," he said, "looking into the history of local crime. There I discovered an account of a man called Mallory, who—"

"Was hanged and buried on the Common," George snapped. "Exactly. I found that too."

"Ah, but did you also visit the library in Wimbledon All Saints' Church?" Vernon said. "I found an interesting local chronicle there. Turns out Mallory's remains were rediscovered when the road was widened at the crossroads—1824, I think it was. They were removed and reinterred elsewhere. So it's not his *bones* that his ghost is tied to, but the *place he died*. And the same goes for all the other people executed on this spot. Mallory was just the first, you see. The chronicle listed *dozens* more victims over the years, all strung up on the gallows here." Vernon tapped his clipboard and simpered at us. "That's it, really. The records are easy enough to find—*if* you look in the right place."

Lockwood and I glanced sidelong at George, who said nothing.

"The gallows itself is, of course, long gone," Vernon went on. "So what we're after is probably some kind of post, or prominent stone that marks where the gallows once stood. In all likelihood this is the Source that controls all the ghosts we've just seen."

"Well, Tony?" Kipps demanded. "Any of you seen a stone?"

"There was *one*," Lockwood said reluctantly. "In the center of the glade."

Bobby Vernon clicked his tongue. "Ah! Good! Don't tell me . . . Squared, slanting on one side, with a wide, deep groove, just like so?"

None of us had bothered to study the mossy stone. "Er . . . might have been."

"Yes! That's the gallows mark, where the wooden post was driven. It was above that stone that the executed bodies would have swung until they fell apart." He blinked at us. "Don't tell me you disturbed it at all?"

"No, no," Lockwood said. "We left it well alone."

There was a shout from one of the agents in the center of the hollow. "Found a squared stone! Obvious gallows mark. Looks like someone just dug it up and chucked it over here."

Lockwood winced. Vernon gave a complacent laugh. "Oh dear. Sounds like you uprooted the prime Source of the cluster, and then ignored it. No wonder so many Visitors began to return. It's a bit like leaving the tap on when filling the sink . . . soon gets messy! Well, I'll just go and supervise the sealing of this important relic. Nice talking to you." He skipped off across the grass. We watched him with dark eyes.

"Talented fellow, that," Kipps remarked. "Bet you wish you had him."

Lockwood shook his head. "No, I'd always be tripping over him, or losing him down the back of the sofa. Now, Quill, since we clearly found the Source, and your agents are sealing it, it's obvious we should share the commission. I propose a sixty/forty split, in our favor. Shall we both visit the mayor tomorrow to make that suggestion?"

Kipps and Godwin laughed, not very kindly. Kipps patted Lockwood on the shoulder. "Tony, Tony—I'd love to help, but you know perfectly well it's only the agents who actually *seal* the Source that get the fee. DEPRAC rules, I'm afraid."

Lockwood stepped back, put his hand to the hilt of his sword. "You're taking the Source?"

"We are."

"I can't allow that."

"I'm afraid you haven't any choice." Kipps gave a whistle; at once, four enormous operatives, each one clearly a close cousin of a mountain ape, stalked out of the darkness, rapiers drawn. They arranged themselves beside him.

Lockwood slowly took his hand away from his belt; George and I, who had been about to draw our weapons, subsided too.

"That's better," Quill Kipps said. "Face it, Tony. You're not really a proper agency at all. Three agents? Scarcely a single flare to call your own? You're a flea-pit shambles! You can't even afford a uniform! Anytime you come up against a real organization, you end up a sorry second best. Now, do you think you can find your way back across the Common, or shall I send Gladys here to hold your hand?"

With supreme effort, Lockwood had regained his composure. "Thank you, no escort will be necessary," he said. "George, Lucy—come on."

I was already walking, but George, eyes flashing behind the round discs of his spectacles, didn't move.

"George," Lockwood repeated.

"Yeah, but this is the Fittes Agency all over," George muttered. "Just because they're bigger and more powerful, they think they can strong-arm anyone who stands in their way. Well, I'm sick of it. If it was a level playing field, we'd thrash them."

"I know we would," Lockwood said softly, "but it isn't. Let's go."

Kipps chuckled. "Sounds like sour grapes to me, Cubbins. That's not like you."

"I'm surprised you can even hear me behind your wall of hired flunkies, Kipps," George said. "You just keep yourself safe there. Maybe one day we'll have a fair contest with you. We'll see who wins out then." He turned to go.

"Is that a challenge?" Kipps called.

"George," Lockwood said, "come on."

"No, no, Tony . . ." Kipps pushed his way past his agents; he was grinning. "I like the sound of this! Cubbins has had a decent idea for once in his life. A contest! You lot against the pick of my team! This might be quite amusing. What do you say, Tony—or does the idea alarm you?"

It hadn't struck me before, but when Kipps smiled, he rather mirrored Lockwood—a smaller, showier, more aggressive version, a spotted hyena to Lockwood's wolf. Lockwood wasn't smiling now. He'd drawn himself up, facing Kipps, and his eyes glittered. "Oh, I *like* the idea well enough," he said. "George is right. In a fair fight we'd beat you, hands down. There'd have to be no strong-arming, no funny business; just a test of all the agency disciplines—research, the range of Talents, ghost-suppression and removal. But what are the stakes? There'd need to be something riding on it. Something that makes it worth our while."

Kipps nodded. "True. And there's nothing you've got that I could possibly want."

"Well, actually, I disagree." Lockwood smoothed down his coat. "What about this? If we ever get a joint case again, the team that solves it wins the day. The loser then places an ad in the *Times*, publicly admitting defeat and declaring that the other's team is infinitely superior to his own. How's that? You'd find that highly amusing, wouldn't you, Kipps? *If* you won." He raised an eyebrow at his rival, who hadn't answered immediately. "Of course, if you're nervous at all . . ."

"Nervous?" Kipps snorted. "Not likely! It's a deal. Kat and Julie are witness to it. If our paths cross again, we'll go head-to-head. Meanwhile, Tony—*do* try to keep your team alive."

He walked away. Kat Godwin and the others followed him across the glade.

"Er . . . the name's Lucy," I said.

No one heard me. They had work to do. In the glow of arc lights, agents under Bobby Vernon's direction were placing silver chain nets over the mossy stone. Others pulled a dolly over the grass, ready to carry the stone away. Cheers sounded; also clapping and sporadic laughter. It was another triumph for the great Fittes Agency. Another case stolen from under the noses of Lockwood & Co. The three of us stood silently in darkness for a time.

"I had to speak out," George said. "Sorry. It was either that or punch him, and I've got sensitive hands."

"No need to apologize," Lockwood said.

"If we can't beat Kipps's gang in a fair fight," I said heartily, "we may as well give up now."

"Right!" George clapped his fist into his palm; bits of mud dropped away from him onto the grass. "We're the best agents in London, aren't we?"

"Exactly," Lockwood said. "None better. Now, Lucy's shirt is rather burnt, and I think my trousers are disintegrating. How about we go on home?"

II

The Unexpected

Grave

Chapter 3

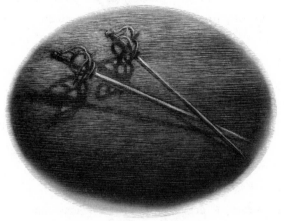

Next morning, like every morning that fine, hot summer, the sky was blue and clear. The parked cars lining the street were glittering like jewels. I walked to Arif's corner store in a T-shirt, shorts, and flip-flops, squinting at the light, listening to the city's busy, breathless hum. The days were long, the nights short; ghosts were at their weakest. It was the time of year when most people tried to ignore the Problem. Not agents, though. We never stop. Look at us go. I bought milk and Swiss rolls for our breakfast, and flip-flopped my slow way home.

Thirty-five Portland Row, shimmering in the sunlight, was its usual unpainted self. As always, the sign on the railing that read

A. J. Lockwood & Co., Investigators
After dark, ring bell and wait beyond the iron line

was wonky; as always, the bell on its post showed signs of rust; as always, three of the iron tiles halfway up the path were loose thanks to the activity of garden ants, and one was missing completely. I ignored it all, went in, put the rolls on a plate, and made the tea. Then I headed for the basement.

As I descended the spiral stairs, I could hear the shuffling of shoes on a polished floor, and the *whip, whip, whip*ping of a blade through air. Soft, crisp impacts told me the sword was finding its target. Lockwood, as was his habit after an unsatisfactory job, was ridding himself of his frustrations.

The rapier room, where we go to practice swordplay, is mostly empty of furniture. There's a rack of old rapiers; a chalk dust stand; a long, low table; and three rickety wooden chairs against one wall. In the center of the room, two life-size straw dummies hang suspended from hooks in the ceiling. Both have crude faces drawn on with ink. One wears a grubby lace bonnet; the other an ancient, stained top hat; and their stuffed cotton torsos are pricked and torn with dozens of little holes. The names of these targets are Lady Esmeralda and Floating Joe.

Today, Esmeralda was receiving the full force of Lockwood's attentions. She was spinning on her chain, and her bonnet was askew. Lockwood circled her at a distance, rapier held ready. He wore sharp fencing slacks and loafers; he'd removed his jacket and rolled up his shirtsleeves a little way. The dust danced up around his gliding feet as he moved back and forth, rapier swaying, left hand held out behind for balance. He cut patterns in the air, feinted, shimmied to the side, and struck a sudden blow to the dummy's ragged shoulder, sending the tip right through the straw and out the other side. His face was serene, his hair glistened; his eyes shone with dark intent. I watched him from the door.

"Yes, I'll have a slice, thanks," George said. "If you can tear yourself away."

I crossed over to the table. George was sitting there, reading a comic book. He wore distressingly loose tracksuit bottoms and an accurately named sweatshirt. His hands were white with chalk dust, and his face was flushed. Two bottles of water sat on the table; a rapier was propped beside him.

Lockwood looked up as I passed. "Swiss rolls and tea," I said.

"Come and join me first!" He indicated a long, torn-open cardboard box lying by the rapier rack. "Italian rapiers, just arrived from Mullet's. New lighter steel and silver enameling on the point. Feel really good. They're worth a try."

I hesitated. "That means leaving the cakes alone with George. . . ."

Lockwood just grinned at me, flicking his blade to and fro so that the air sang.

It was hard to say no to him. It always is. Besides, I wanted to try the new rapier. I drew one from the box and held it loosely across my palms. It was lighter than I'd expected, and balanced differently from my usual French-style épée. I gripped the handle, looking at the complex coils of silvery metal surrounding my fingers in a protective mesh.

"The guard has silver filigree on it," Lockwood said. "Should keep you safe from spurts of ectoplasm. What do you think?"

"Bit fancy," I said doubtfully. "It's the kind of thing Kipps would use."

"Oh, don't say that. This has class. Give it a try."

A sword in the hand always makes you feel good. Even before breakfast, even when wearing flip-flops, it gives you a feeling of power. I turned toward Floating Joe and cut a standard ward knot around him, the kind that keeps a Visitor penned in.

"Don't lean in so much," Lockwood advised. "You were a bit off balance there. Try holding your arm forward a little more. Like this. . . ." He turned my wrist, and altered my stance by gently adjusting the position of my waist. "See? Is that better?"

"Yes."

"I think these rapiers will suit you." He gave Floating Joe a nudge with his shoe so that he swung back and forth, and I had to skip aside to avoid him. "Imagine he's a hungry Type Two," Lockwood said. "He wants human contact and is coming at you in a rush. . . . You need to keep the plasm in one place, so it doesn't break free and threaten fellow agents. Try doing a double ward knot, like this. . . ." His rapier darted around the dummy in a complex blur.

"I'll never learn that," I said. "I couldn't follow it at all."

Lockwood smiled. "Oh, it's just a Kuriashi turn. I can take you through the positions sometime."

"Okay."

"Tea's getting cold," George remarked. "And I'm on the penultimate slice."

He was lying. The rolls were still there. But it *was* time to eat something. I had a fluttery feeling in my tummy and my legs felt weak. It was probably the late night catching up with me. I ducked between Joe and Esmeralda and went over to the table. Lockwood did a few more exercises: swift, elegant, and flawless. George and I watched him as we chewed.

"So, what do you think of the rolls?" I said, with my mouth full.

"They're all right. It's things like Kuriashi turns that I can't stomach," George said. "Nothing but trendy claptrap, invented by the big agencies to make themselves look fancy. In my book, you thwack a Visitor, avoid being ghost-touched, and make it home. That's all you need to know."

"You're still sore about last night," I said. "Well, I am too."

"I'll get over it. It's my fault for not researching properly. But we shouldn't have missed that stone. We could have had the case done and dusted before that Fittes rabble showed up." He shook his head. "Bunch of stuck-up snobs, they are. I used to work there, so I know. They look down on anyone who hasn't got a posh jacket or neatly ironed trousers. As if appearance is all that counts. . . ." He stuck a hand inside his tracksuit bottoms and had an indignant scratch.

"Oh, most of the Fittes crowd are all right." Despite his exertions, Lockwood was scarcely out of breath. He dropped his rapier into the rack with a clatter and dusted the chalk from his hands. "They're just kids like us, risking their lives. It's the supervisors who cause the trouble. They're the ones who think themselves untouchable, just because they've got cushy jobs at one of the oldest, biggest agencies."

"Tell me about it," George said heavily. "They used to drive me mad."

I nodded. "Kipps is the worst, though. He *really* hates us, doesn't he?"

"Not us," Lockwood said. "*Me*. He really hates me."

"But why? What's he got against you?"

Lockwood picked up one of the bottles of water and sighed reflectively. "Who knows? Maybe it's my natural style he envies, maybe my boyish charm. Perhaps it's my setup here—having my own agency, no one to answer to, with fine companions at my side." He caught my eye and smiled.

George looked up from his comic. "Or it could be the fact you once stabbed him in the bottom with a sword."

"Yes, well there is that." Lockwood took a sip of water.

I looked back and forth between them. "What?" I said. "When did this happen?"

Lockwood flung himself into a chair. "It was before your time, Luce," he said. "When I was a kid. DEPRAC holds an annual fencing competition for young agents here in London. Down at the Albert Hall. Fittes and Rotwell always dominate it, but my old master, Gravedigger Sykes, thought I was good enough, so I entered too. Drew Kipps in the quarter final. Being a few years older, he was a lot taller than me then, and he was the hot favorite going in. Made all sorts of silly boasts about it, as you can imagine. Anyway, I bamboozled him with a couple of Winchester half-lunges, and the long and short of it was, he ended up tripping over his own feet. I just gave him a quick prod while he was sprawling on all fours, nothing to get upset about. The crowd rather liked it, of course. Oddly, he's been insanely vindictive toward me ever since."

"How strange," I said. "So . . . did you go on to win the competition?"

"No." Lockwood inspected the bottle. "No . . . I made the final, as it happens, but I didn't win. Is that the time? We're sluggish today. I should go and wash."

He sprang up, seized two slices of Swiss roll and, before I could say anything more, was out of the room and up the stairs.

George glanced at me. "You know he doesn't like opening up too much," he said.

"Yeah."

"It's just the way he is. I'm surprised he told you as much as he did."

I nodded. George was right. Small anecdotes here and there were all you got from Lockwood; if you questioned him further he shut tight, like a clam. It was infuriating—but intriguing, too. It always gave me a pleasant tug of curiosity. One full year after my arrival at the agency, the unrevealed details of my employer's early life remained an important part of his mystery and fascination.

All things considered, that summer—and leaving the Wimbledon debacle aside—Lockwood & Co. *was* doing okay. Not *super* okay— we hadn't gotten rich or anything. We weren't building swanky mansions for ourselves with ghost-lamps in the grounds and electrically powered streams of water running along the driveway (as Steve Rotwell, head of the giant Rotwell Agency, was said to have done). But we *were* managing a little better than before.

Seven months had passed since the Screaming Staircase affair had brought us so much publicity. Our widely reported success at Combe Carey Hall, one of the most haunted houses in England, had immediately resulted in a spate of prominent new cases. We exorcised a Dark Specter that was laying waste to a remote portion of Epping Forest; we cleansed a rectory in Upminster that was being troubled by a Shining Boy. And of course, though it nearly cost all of us our lives, our investigation of Mrs. Barrett's tomb led to the company's being short-listed for *True Hauntings*' "Agency of the Month" for the second time. As a result, our appointment book was almost full. Lockwood had even mentioned hiring an office assistant.

For the moment, though, we were still a small outfit, the smallest in London. Anthony Lockwood, George Cubbins, and Lucy Carlyle: just the three of us rubbing along together at 35 Portland Row. Living and working side by side.

George? The last seven months hadn't changed him much. With regard to his general scruffiness, sharp tongue, and fondness for bottom-hugging puffer jackets, this was obviously a matter for regret. But he was still a tireless researcher, capable of unearthing vital facts about each and every haunted location. He was the most careful of us too, the least likely to jump headlong into danger; this quality had kept us all alive more than once. George also retained his habit of taking off his glasses and polishing them on his sweater whenever he was (a) utterly sure of himself, (b) irritated, or (c) bored rigid by my company, which, one way or another, seemed pretty much all the time. But he and I were getting along better now. In fact, we'd only had one full-on, foot-stamping, saucepan-hurling row that month, which was itself some kind of record.

George was very interested in the science and philosophy of Visitors: he wanted to understand their nature, and the reasons for their return. To this end he conducted a series of experiments on our collection of spectral Sources—old bones or other fragments that retained some ghostly charge. This hobby of his was sometimes a little annoying. I'd lost track of the number of times I'd tripped over electric cables clamped to some relic, or been startled by a severed limb while rummaging in the deep freeze for fish fingers and frozen peas.

But at least George *had* hobbies (comic books and cooking were two of the others). Anthony Lockwood was quite another matter. He had few interests outside his work. On our rare days off, he would lie late in bed, riffling through the newspapers, or re-reading tattered novels from the shelves about the house. At last he'd fling them aside, do some moody rapier practice, then begin preparing for our next assignment. Little else seemed to interest him.

He never discussed old cases. Something propelled him ever onward. At times an almost obsessive quality to his energy could be glimpsed beneath the urbane exterior. But he never gave a clue as to what drove him, and I was forced to develop my own speculations.

Outwardly he was just as energetic and mercurial as ever, passionate and restless, a continual inspiration. He still wore his hair dashingly swept back, still had a fondness for too-tight suits; was just as courteous to me as he'd been the day we met. But he also remained—and I had become increasingly aware of this fact the longer I observed him—ever-so-slightly detached: from the ghosts we discovered, from the clients we took on, perhaps even (though I didn't find this easy to admit) from his colleagues, George and me.

The clearest evidence of this lay in the personal details we each revealed. It had taken me months to summon up the courage, but in the end I'd told them both a good deal about my childhood, my unhappy experiences in my first apprenticeship, and the reasons I'd had for leaving home. George, too, was full of stories—which I seldom listened to—mostly about his upbringing in north London. It had been unexcitingly normal; his family was well-balanced and no one seemed to have died or disappeared. He'd even once introduced us to his mother, a small, plump, smiley woman who had called Lockwood *ducks*, me *darling*, and given us all a homemade cake. But Lockwood? No. He rarely spoke about himself and certainly *never* about his past or family. After a year of living with him in his childhood home, I still knew nothing about his parents at all.

This was particularly frustrating, because the whole of 35 Portland Row was filled to overflowing with their artifacts and heirlooms, their books and furniture. The walls of the living room and stairwell were covered with strange objects: masks, weapons, and what seemed to be ghost-hunting equipment from faraway cultures. It seemed obvious that Lockwood's parents had been researchers or collectors of some kind, with a special interest in lands beyond Europe. But where they were (or more likely, what had happened to them), Lockwood never said. And there seemed to be no photographs or personal mementos of them anywhere.

At least, not in any of the rooms *I* visited.

Because I thought I knew where the answers to Lockwood's past might be.

There was a certain door on the first-floor landing of the house. Unlike every other door in 35 Portland Row, this one was never opened. When I'd arrived, Lockwood had requested that it remained closed, and George and I had always obeyed him. The door had no lock that I could see and, as I passed it every day, its plain exterior (blank, except for a rough rectangle where some label or sticker had been removed) presented an almost insolent challenge. It dared me to guess what was behind it, defied me to peek inside. So far, I'd resisted the temptation—more out of prudence than simple nicety. The one or two occasions when I'd even *mentioned* the room to Lockwood had not gone down too well.

And what about me, Lucy Carlyle, still the newest member of the company? How had *I* altered, that first year?

Outwardly, not so much. My hair remained in a multipurpose, ectoplasm-avoiding bob; I wasn't any sleeker or better-looking than before. Height-wise, I hadn't grown any. I was still more eager than skillful when it came to fighting, and too impatient to be an excellent researcher like George.

But things *had* changed for me. My time with Lockwood & Co. had given me a confidence I'd previously been lacking. When I walked down the street with my rapier swinging at my side, and the little kids gawping, and the adults giving me deferential nods, I not only knew I had a special status in society, I honestly believed I'd begun to *earn* it too.

My Talents were fast developing. My skill at inner Listening, which had always been good, was growing ever sharper. I heard the whispers of Type Ones, the fragments of speech emitted by Type Twos; few apparitions were entirely silent to me now. My sense of psychic Touch had also deepened. Holding certain objects gave me strong echoes of the past. More and more, I found I had an intuitive feel for the intentions of each ghost; sometimes I could even predict their actions.

All these were rare enough abilities, but they were overshadowed by something deeper—a mystery that hung over all of us at 35 Portland Row, but particularly over me. Seven months before, something had happened that had set me apart from Lockwood and George, and all the other agents we competed with. Ever since, my Talent had been the focus of George's experiments, and our major topic of conversation. Lockwood even believed it might be the foundation of our fortunes, and make us the most celebrated agency in London.

First, though, we had to solve one particular problem.

That problem was sitting on George's desk, inside a thick glass jar, beneath a jet-black cloth.

It was dangerous and evil, and had the potential to change my life forever.

It was a skull.

Chapter 4

George had left the rapier room now and gone into the main office. I followed him in, taking my tea with me, winding my way among the debris of our business: piles of old newspapers, bags of salt, neatly stacked chains, and boxes of silver seals. Sunlight streamed through the window that looked out onto the little yard, igniting dust particles in the air. On Lockwood's desk, between the mummified heart and the bottle of gobstoppers, sat our black leather casebook, containing records of every job we'd undertaken. Soon we'd have to write up the Wimbledon Wraiths in there.

George was standing by his desk, staring at it in a glum sort of way. My desktop gets messy fairly often, but this morning George's was something else. It was a scene of devastation. Burnt matches, lavender candles, and pools of melted wax littered the surface. A chaos of tangled wires and naked elements spilled forth from a disemboweled space heater. In one corner, a blowtorch lay on its side.

At the other end of the desk, something else sat hidden under a black satin cloth.

"Heating it up didn't work, I take it?" I said.

"No," George said. "Hopeless. Couldn't get it hot enough. I'm going to try putting it in daylight today, see if that spurs him on a bit."

I regarded the shrouded object. "You sure? It didn't do anything before."

"Wasn't so bright then. I'll take him out into the garden when the noonday sun comes around."

I tapped my fingers on the desk. Something that I'd been meaning to say for a while, something that had been on my mind, finally came out. "You know that sunlight hurts it," I said slowly. "You know it burns the plasm."

George nodded. "Yep. . . . Obviously. That's the idea."

"Yeah, but that's hardly going to get the thing to talk, is it?" I said. "I mean, don't you think it'll be counterproductive? All your methods seem to involve inflicting pain."

"So what? It's a Visitor. Anyway, do Visitors actually *feel* pain?" George pulled the cloth away, revealing a glass jar, cylindrical and slightly larger than the average wastebasket. It was sealed at the top with a complex plastic stopper, from which a number of knobs and flanges protruded. George bent close to the jar and flipped a lever, revealing a small rectangular grille within the plastic. He spoke into the grille. "Hello in there! Lucy thinks you feel discomfort! I disagree! Care to tell us who's right?"

He waited. The substance in the jar was dark and still. Something sat motionless in the center of the murk.

"It's daytime," I said. "Of course it won't answer."

George flicked the lever back. "It's not answering out of spite. It's got a wicked nature. You said as much yourself, after it spoke to you."

"We don't really know, to be honest." I stared at the shadow behind the glass. "We don't know anything about it."

"Well, we know it told you we were all going to die."

"It said *Death is coming*, George. That's not quite the same thing."

"It's hardly a term of endearment." George heaved the tangle of electrical equipment off his desk and dumped it in a box beside his chair. "No, it's hostile to us, Luce. Mustn't go soft on it now."

"I'm not going soft. I just think torturing it isn't necessarily the way forward. We may need to focus more on its connection with me."

George gave a noncommittal grunt. "Mm. Yes. Your mysterious connection."

We stood surveying the jar. In ordinary sunlight, like today's, the glass looked thick and slightly bluish; under moonlight, or artificial illumination, it glinted with a silvery tinge, for this was silver-glass, a ghost-proof material manufactured by the Sunrise Corporation.

And sure enough, within the glass prison was a ghost.

The identity of this spirit was unknown. All that could be certain was that it belonged to the human skull now bolted to the base of the jar. The skull was yellowish-brown and battered, but otherwise unexceptional. It was adult size, but whether a man's or woman's, we could not tell. The ghost, being tethered to the skull, was trapped inside the ghost-jar. Most of the time, it manifested as a murky greenish plasm that drifted disconsolately behind the glass. Occasionally, and usually at inconvenient moments, such as when you were going past with a hot drink or a full bladder, it congealed violently into a grotesque transparent face, with a bulbous nose, goggling eyes, and a rubbery mouth of excessive size. This shocking visage would then leer and gape at whoever was in the room. Allegedly George had once seen it blow kisses. Often it seemed to be trying to speak. And it was this apparent ability to communicate that was its central mystery, and why George kept it on his desk.

Visitors, as a rule, don't talk—at least, not in a very meaningful way. Most of them—the Shades and Lurkers, the Cold Maidens, the Stalkers and other Type Ones—are practically silent, except for a limited repertoire of moans and sighs. Type Twos, more powerful and more dangerous, *can* sometimes deliver a few half-intelligible words that Listeners like me are able to pick up. These, too, are often repetitious—imprints on the air that seldom alter, and that are often connected to the key emotion that binds the spirit to the earth: terror, anger, or desire for vengeance. What ghosts don't do, as a rule, is talk *properly*, except for the legendary Type Threes.

Long ago, Marissa Fittes—one of the first two psychic investigators in Britain—claimed to have encountered certain spirits with which she held full conversations. She mentioned this in several books, and implied (she was never very forthcoming about the *details*) that they had told her certain secrets: about death, about the soul, about its passage to a place beyond. After her *own* demise, others had tried to achieve similar results; a few even claimed to have done so, but their accounts were never verified. It became a point of faith among most agents that Type Threes existed, but that they remained almost impossible to find. That's certainly what *I'd* believed.

Then the spirit in the jar—that same one with the horrid, goggly face—had talked to *me.*

I had been alone in the basement at the time. I'd knocked over the ghost-jar, twisting one of the levers in its stopper, so that the hidden grille was exposed. And all at once I heard the ghost's voice talking in my head—*really* talking, I mean; addressing me by name. It told me things, too—vague, unpleasant things of the *death's coming* variety—until I turned the lever and shut it up.

Which may have been a mistake, because it had never spoken again.

Lockwood and George, when I told them about my encounter, had reacted at first with vast excitement. They raced to the basement, took out the jar, and swung the lever; the face in the jar said nothing. We tried a series of experiments, turning the lever differing degrees, trying at different times of day and night, sitting expectantly beside the jar, even hiding out of sight. Still the ghost was silent. Occasionally it materialized as before, and glared at us in a resentful, truculent manner, but it never spoke or seemed inclined to do so.

It was a disappointment to us all, for different reasons. Lockwood was acutely aware of the prestige our agency would have gained from the event, if it could be proved. George thought of the fascinating insights that might be gained from someone speaking from beyond the grave. To me it was more personal, a sudden revelation of the terrifying potential of my Talent. It frightened me and filled me with foreboding, and there was a part of me that was relieved when it didn't happen again. But I was annoyed, too. Just that one fleeting incident, and both Lockwood and George had looked at me with new respect. If it could be repeated, if it could be confirmed for all to see, I would in one fell swoop become the most celebrated operative in London. But the ghost remained stubbornly silent, and as the months passed, I almost began to doubt that anything significant had occurred at all.

Lockwood, in his practical fashion, had finally turned his attention to other things, though in every new case, he made sure to double check what voices, if any, I could hear. But George had persisted with his investigations into the skull, attempting ever more fanciful methods to get the ghost to respond. Failure hadn't discouraged him. If anything, it had increased his passion.

I could see his eyes gleaming now behind his glasses as he studied the silent jar.

"Clearly it's aware of us," he mused. "In some way it's definitely conscious of what's going on around it. It knew your name. It knew mine, too—you told me. It must be able to hear things through the glass."

"Or lip-read," I pointed out. "We *do* quite often have it uncovered."

"I suppose. . . ." He shook his head. "Who knows? So many questions! Why is it here? What does it want? Why talk to you? I've had it for years, and it never even *tried* to talk to me."

"Well, there wouldn't have been much point, would there? You don't have that Talent." I tapped the bottle glass with a fingernail.

"How long have you actually had this jar, George? You stole it, didn't you? I forget how."

George sat heavily in his chair, making the wood creak. "It was back when I was at the Fittes Agency, before I got kicked out for insubordination. I was working at Fittes House on the Strand. You ever been in there?"

"Only for an interview. It didn't last long."

"Well, it's a vast place," George said. "You've got the famous public rooms, where people come for help—all those glass booths with receptionists taking down their details. Then there're the conference halls, where they display all their famous relics, and the mahogany boardroom overlooking the Thames. But there's a lot of secret stuff, too, which most of the agents can't access. The Black Library, for instance, where Marissa's original collection of books is kept under lock and key. I always wanted to browse in there. But the bit that *really* interested me was underground. There are basements that go deep down, and some of them stretch back out under the Thames, they say. I used to see supervisors going down in special service elevators, and sometimes I'd see jars like this being wheeled into the elevators on carts. I often asked what all this was about. Safe storage, they said; there were vaults where they kept dangerous Visitors safe until they could be incinerated in furnaces on the lowest level."

"Furnaces?" I said. "The Fittes furnaces are over in Clerkenwell, aren't they? Everyone uses them. Why'd they need more down underground?"

"I wondered that," George said. "I wondered about a lot of things. It used to annoy me that I got no answers. Anyway, in the end I asked so many questions that they fired me. My supervisor—a woman called Sweeny, face like a sock soaked in vinegar—gave me an hour to clear out my desk. And as I was standing there, gathering a few things up in a cardboard box, I saw a cart with two or three jars being pushed toward the elevator. The porter got called away. So what did I do? Only slipped over and swiped the nearest jar. I put it in my box, hid it under an old sweater, and carried it away right under Sweeny's nose." He grinned in triumph at the memory. "And that's why we've got our very own haunted skull. Who'd have thought it would turn out to be a genuine Type Three?"

"If it actually *is* one," I said doubtfully. "It hasn't done anything much for ages."

"Don't worry. We'll find a way to get it to speak again." George was polishing his glasses on his T-shirt. "We've got to. The stakes are so high, Luce. Fifty years since the Problem began, and we've hardly scratched the surface understanding ghosts. There are mysteries all around us, everywhere we look."

I nodded absently. Riveting as George was, my mind had flitted elsewhere. I was staring at Lockwood's empty desk. One of his jackets hung over the back of his old, cracked chair.

"Speaking of a mystery slightly closer to home," I said slowly, "don't you ever wonder about Lockwood's door upstairs? That one on the landing."

George shrugged. "No."

"You must."

He blew out his cheeks. "Of course I wonder. But it's his business. Not ours."

"I mean, what can be in there? He's just so touchy about it. I asked him about it last week, and he nearly snapped my head off again."

"Which probably tells you that it's best to forget all about it," George said. "This isn't our house, and if Lockwood wants to keep something private, then that's entirely up to him. I'd drop it, if I were you."

"I just think it's a pity that he's so secretive," I said simply. "It's a shame."

George gave a skeptical snort. "Oh, come on. You love all that mystery about him. Just like you love that pensive, far-off look he does sometimes, as if he's brooding about important matters, or contemplating a tricky bowel movement. Don't try to deny it. *I* know."

I looked at him. "What's that supposed to mean?"

"Nothing."

"All I'm saying," I said, "is that it's not right the way he keeps everything to himself. I mean, we're his friends, aren't we? He should open up to us. It makes me think that—"

"Think what, Lucy?"

I spun around. Lockwood was at the door. He'd showered and dressed, and his hair was wet. His dark eyes were on me. I couldn't tell how long he'd been there.

I didn't say anything, but I felt my face go pink. George busied himself with something on his desk.

Lockwood held my gaze a moment, then broke the connection. He held up a small rectangular object. "I came down to show you this," he said. "It's an invitation."

He skimmed the object across the room; it flipped past George's outstretched hand, skidded along his desk, and came to a halt in front of me. It was a card—stiff, silvery-gray, and glittery. Its top was emblazoned with an image of a rearing unicorn holding a lantern in its forehoof. Beneath this logo, it read:

The Fittes Agency

Ms. Penelope Fittes
and the board of the Estimable Fittes Agency invite

Anthony Lockwood, Lucy Carlyle, and George Cubbins

to help celebrate the 50th Anniversary
of the company's founding at
Fittes House
The Strand
on Saturday 19th June at 8.00 p.m.

Black Tie   Carriages at 1.00 a.m.   RSVP

I stared at it blankly, my embarrassment forgotten. "Penelope Fittes? Inviting us to a party?"

"And not just *any* party." Lockwood said. "*The* party. The party of the year. Anybody who's anybody will be there."

"Er, so why have *we* been asked, then?" George gazed over my shoulder at the card.

Lockwood spoke in a slightly huffy voice. "Because we're a very prominent agency. Also because Penelope Fittes is personally friendly to us. You remember. We discovered the body of her childhood friend at Combe Carey Hall. At the bottom of the Screaming Staircase. What was his name? Sam something. She's grateful. She wrote telling us so. And maybe she's kept an eye on our more recent successes, too."

I raised my eyebrows at this. Penelope Fittes, Chairman of the Fittes Agency and granddaughter of the great psychic pioneer Marissa Fittes, was one of the most powerful people in the country. She had government ministers lining up at her door. Her opinions on the Problem were published in all the newspapers and discussed in all the living rooms of the land. She seldom left her apartment above Fittes House, and was said to control her business with an iron fist. I rather doubted she was overly interested in Lockwood & Co., fascinating though we were.

All the same, here was the invitation.

"Nineteeth of June," I mused. "That's this Saturday."

"So . . . are we going?" George asked.

"*Of course* we are!" Lockwood said. "This is the perfect opportunity to make some connections. All the big names will be there, all the agency heads, the big cheeses of DEPRAC, the industrialists who run the salt and iron companies, maybe even the chairman of the Sunrise Corporation. We'll never get another chance to meet them."

"Lovely," George said. "An evening spent in a crowded, sweaty room with dozens of old, fat, boring businesspeople . . . what could be better? Given a choice between that and fighting a Pale Stench, I'd go for the flatulent ghost any time."

"You lack vision, George," Lockwood said disapprovingly, "and you also spend far too much time with *that* thing." He reached out and, just as I had done, tapped his nail on the thick glass of the ghost-jar. It made a faint, discordant sound. The substance in the jar stirred briefly, then hung still. "It isn't healthy, and you're not getting anywhere with it."

George frowned. "I don't agree. There's nothing more important than this. With the correct research, this could be a breakthrough! Just think—if we could get the dead to speak to us *on demand*—"

The buzzer on the wall sounded, signaling that someone had rung the bell upstairs.

Lockwood made a face. "Who can that be? No one's made an appointment."

"Perhaps it's the delivery boy?" George suggested. "Our weekly groceries?"

I shook my head. "No. He comes tomorrow. It'll be new clients."

Lockwood picked up the invitation and tucked it safely in his pocket. "What are we waiting for? Let's go and see."

Chapter 5

The names on the visiting cards were Mr. Paul Saunders and Mr. Albert Joplin, and ten minutes later these two gentlemen were settling themselves in our living room, and accepting cups of tea.

Mr. Saunders, whose card described him as a *Municipal Excavator*, was clearly the dominant personality of the pair. A tall, thin man, all jutting knees and elbows, who had folded himself with difficulty onto the sofa, he wore an ancient gray-green worsted suit, very thin about the sleeves. His face was bony and weather-beaten, his cheekbones broad and high; he smiled around at us complacently with narrow, gleaming eyes half-hidden by lank gray bangs. Before taking his tea, he placed his battered fedora hat carefully on his knees. A silver hatpin was fixed above its brim.

"Very good of you to see us without notice," Mr. Saunders said, nodding to each of us in turn. Lockwood reclined in his usual chair; George and I, pens and notebooks at the ready, sat on upright seats nearby. "Very good, I'm sure. You're the first agency we've tried this morning, and we hardly hoped you'd be available."

"I'm pleased to hear we were top of your list, Mr. Saunders," Lockwood said easily.

"Oh, it's only on account of your place being closest to our warehouse, Mr. Lockwood. I'm a busy man and all for efficiency. Now then, Saunders of Sweet Dreams Excavation and Clearance, that's me, operating out of King's Cross these fifteen years. This here's my associate, Mr. Joplin." He jerked his heavy head at the little man beside him, who'd not yet said a word. He carried an enormous and untidy bundle of documents, and was gazing around at Lockwood's collection of Asian ghost-catchers with wide-eyed curiosity.

"We're hoping you might be able to give us some assistance this evening," Saunders went on. "'Course, I've got a good day team working under me already: spadesmen, backhoe drivers, corpse wranglers, light technicians . . . plus the usual night squad. But tonight we need some *proper* agency firepower as well."

He winked at us, as if that settled the matter, and took a loud slurp of tea. Lockwood's polite smile remained fixed, as if nailed in position. "Indeed. And what exactly would you want us to do? And where?"

"Ah, you're a details man. Very good. I'm one myself." Saunders sat back, stretched a skinny arm along the back of the sofa. "We're working up at Kensal Green, northwest London. Cemetery clearance. Part of the new government policy of eradicating ARs."

Lockwood blinked. "Eradicating what? Sorry, I must have misheard you there."

"ARs. Active Remains. Sources, in other words. Old burials that are becoming unsafe, and might cause danger to the neighborhood."

"Oh, like the Stepney Creeper!" I said. "You remember last year?" The Creeper had been a Phantasm that had issued from a grave in a Stepney churchyard, drifted across the road, and killed five people in nearby houses on two consecutive nights. On the third night Rotwell agents had cornered it, forced it back into its tomb, and destroyed it with a controlled explosion. The incident had caused a lot of anxiety, because the churchyard had previously been declared safe.

Mr. Saunders rewarded me with a toothy grin. "Exactly, girlie! A bad business. But this is the way the Problem is going. New Visitors appearing all the time. That Stepney grave was three hundred years old. Had it caused trouble before? No! But afterward they discovered that the person in that grave had been murdered all that time ago, and of course *those* are the spirits most likely to become restless, as we know—murder victims, suicides, and so on. So government policy now is to monitor all cemeteries, and that's what Sweet Dreams Excavation and Clearance is doing up at Kensal Green."

"It's a massive cemetery," George said. "How many graves are you digging up?"

Saunders scratched the bristles on his chin. "A few plots each day. Trick is to weed out the ones that are likely to give us trouble. We do the assessment work after dark, as that's when psychic emanations are strongest. We've got night teams pinpointing suspect graves. They mark 'em with yellow paint. Next morning we dig 'em up and remove the bones."

"Sounds dangerous, the night work," Lockwood said. "Who's on that team?"

"Bunch of night-watch kids, some freelance sensitives. A few adult males to keep the relic men at bay. They get well paid. Mostly it's just small-time stuff: Shades, Lurkers, other Type Ones. Type Twos are rare. Anything *really* iffy, we hire agents in advance."

Lockwood frowned. "But how *can* you assess this danger in advance? I don't understand."

"Ah, *that's* up to Joplin here." Mr. Saunders dug his companion roughly in the ribs with a bony elbow. The little man gave a start, and dropped half his documents on the floor; Saunders glared impatiently as he scrabbled to retrieve them. "He's invaluable, Albert is, when we can find him. . . . Well, go on, then. Tell 'em what you do."

Mr. Albert Joplin straightened and blinked at us amiably. He was younger than Saunders—early forties, I guessed—but equally disheveled. His curly brown hair hadn't seen a comb in weeks, perhaps years. He had a pleasant, rather weak face: round and ruddy in the cheeks, and tapering to an undershot jaw. His apologetic, smiling eyes were framed by a pair of small, round glasses, not dissimilar to George's. He wore a crumpled linen jacket, rather dusted with dandruff, a checked shirt, and a pair of dark slacks that were ever so slightly too short for him. He sat stoop-shouldered, hands drawn protectively over his papers in the manner of a shy and studious dormouse.

"I'm the project's archivist," he said. "I provide assistance to the operation."

Lockwood nodded encouragingly. "I see. In what way?"

"Digging!" Mr. Saunders cried, before Joplin could continue. "He's the best excavator in the business, aren't you, Albert, eh?" He reached over and squeezed one of the small man's puny biceps in theatrical fashion, then winked at us again. "You wouldn't think so, to look at him, would you? But I'm serious. Thing is, though, while the rest of us dig for bones, Joplin here digs for *stories*. Well, come on man, don't just *sit* there like a melon. Fill them in."

"Yes, well . . ." Joplin, flustered, adjusted his spectacles nervously. "I'm a scholar, really. I look through the historical burial records and cross-reference them with old newspaper reports to find what you might call the really 'risky' interments: you know, people who came to nasty or tragic ends. I then alert Mr. Saunders, and he takes whatever action he thinks necessary."

"Usually we clear the grave without problems," Saunders said. "But not always."

The scholar nodded. "Yes. We were working in Maida Vale Cemetery two months ago. I'd pinpointed the grave of an Edwardian murder victim—all overgrown it was, the stone had been quite forgotten. One of those night-watch boys was busy clearing the brambles away, getting it ready for the digging, when up popped the ghost, right out of the ground, and tried to drag him into it! Horrid gray woman, apparently, with her throat hanging open and eyes staring out of their sockets. Poor little chap let out a squeal like a dying rabbit. He was ghost-touched, of course. Agents got to him and gave him boosters, so I believe he may recover. . . ." Mr. Joplin's voice ebbed away; he smiled sadly. "Anyway," he said, "that's what I do."

"Excuse me," George said, "but are you the same Albert Joplin who wrote the chapter on medieval burials in Pooter's *History of London's Graveyards?*"

The little man blinked. His eyes brightened. "Why . . . yes. Yes, I am!"

"Good article, that," George said. "A real page-turner."

"How extraordinary that you should have read it!"

"I thought your speculation about the tethering of the soul was very interesting."

"Did you? Well, it's *such* a fascinating theory. It seems to me—"

I stifled a yawn; I was beginning to wish I'd brought my pillow. But Lockwood was impatient too. He held up a hand. "It seems to *me* we should hear why you need our help. Mr. Saunders, if you could please get to the point."

"Quite right, Mr. Lockwood!" The excavator cleared his throat, adjusted the hat on his knee. "You're a man of business, like myself. Good. Well, the last few nights we've been surveying the southeast area of the cemetery. Kensal Green's an important burial ground. Established in 1833. Covers seventy acres of prestige land."

"Got many fine tombs and mausoleums," Joplin added. "*Lovely* Portland stone."

"Aren't there catacombs there too?" George asked.

Saunders nodded. "Indeed. There's a chapel in the center, with catacombs beneath. They've been closed off now—it's too dangerous with all those exposed coffins. But up top, the burial plots are laid out around gently curving avenues between Harrow Road and the Grand Union Canal. Mid-Victorian burials, common folk mostly.

The avenues are shaded by rows of old linden trees. It's all peaceful enough, and relatively few Visitors have been reported, even in the last few years."

Mr. Joplin had been rifling through the papers in his arms, pulling out sheets and stuffing them back again. "If I could just . . . ah, here are the plans of the southeast corner!" He drew out a map showing two or three looping paths, with tiny numbered boxes marking the grave plots in between. Stapled to this was a grid filled with spidery handwriting—a list of names. "I've been checking the recorded burials in this zone," he said, "and found nothing for anyone to fear. . . . Or so I thought."

"Well," Saunders said, "as I say, my teams have been walking the avenues, hunting for psychic disturbances. All went smoothly until last night, when they were exploring the plots just east of this aisle here." He jabbed at the map with a dirty finger.

Lockwood had been tapping his own fingers impatiently on his knee. "Yes, *and* . . ."

"And we found an unexpected headstone in the grass."

There was a silence. "How d'you mean, *unexpected?*" I asked.

Mr. Joplin flourished the handwritten grid. "It's a burial that's not recorded in the official lists," he said. "It shouldn't be there."

"One of our sensitives found it," Saunders said. His face had grown suddenly serious. "She immediately became ill and couldn't continue with her work. Two other psychics investigated the headstone. They each complained of dizziness, of piercing headaches. One said that she sensed something watching her, something so wicked that she could hardly move. None of them wanted to go within ten feet of that little stone." He sniffed. "'Course, it's hard to know just how seriously to take all that. You know what psychics are like."

"Indeed," Lockwood said drily. "Being one myself."

"Now *me*," Saunders went on, "I haven't a psychic bone in my body. And I've got my silver charm here too, to keep me safe." He patted the hatpin on his fedora. "So what do I do? I nip over to the stone, bend down, have a look. And when I scrape the moss and lichen off, I find two words cut deep into the granite." His voice had dropped to a throaty whisper. "Two words."

Lockwood waited. "Well, what were they?"

Mr. Saunders moistened his narrow lips. He swallowed audibly; he seemed reluctant to speak. "A name," he whispered. "But not just *any* name." He hunched forward on the sofa, his long bony legs jutting precariously over the teacups. Lockwood, George, and I leaned in close. A curious atmosphere of dread had invaded the room. Mr. Joplin, all a-flutter, lost control of his papers again and dropped several on the carpet. Outside the windows, a cloud seemed to have passed over the sun; the light was drab and cold.

The excavator took a deep breath. His whisper rose to a sudden terrible crescendo. "Does *Edmund Bickerstaff* mean anything to you?" The words echoed around us, bouncing off the ghost-goads and spirit-charms that lined the walls. We sat there. The echoes faded.

"In all honesty, no," Lockwood said.

Mr. Saunders sat back on the sofa. "No, to be fair, I'd never heard of him either. But Joplin here, whose speciality it is to poke his nose down odd and unsavory byways of the past, *he'd* heard the name. Hadn't you, eh?" He nudged the small man. "And it makes him nervous."

Mr. Joplin laughed weakly, made a great business of readjusting the mess of papers on his lap. "Well, I wouldn't *quite* say that, Mr. Saunders. I'm *cautious*, Mr. Lockwood. Cautious, is all. And I know enough about Dr. Edmund Bickerstaff to recommend we get agency help before disinterring this mystery burial."

"You intend to dig it up, then?" Lockwood said.

"There are *strong* psychic phenomena associated with the site," Saunders said. "It *must* be made safe as soon as possible. Preferably tonight."

"Excuse me," I said. Something had been bothering me. "If you know it's dangerous, why not excavate it during the day, like you do the others? Why do you need to bring us in?"

"New DEPRAC guidelines. We have a legal obligation to bring in agents for all graves that may contain a Type Two Visitor, and since the government funds this extra cost, these agents must carry out their work at night, so they can confirm our claims."

"Yes, but who is this Bickerstaff?" George asked. "What's so frightening about him?"

In response, Joplin rummaged among his papers again. He brought out a yellowed sheet, unfolded it, and turned it toward us. It was an enlarged photocopy of part of a nineteenth-century newspaper, all narrow columns and closely printed text. In the center was a smudged engraving of a thickset man with upright collar, heavy sideburns, and a large handlebar mustache. Aside from a slightly brutish quality about the mouth, it could have been any typical mid-Victorian gentleman. Underneath were the words:

HAMPSTEAD HORROR
Terrible Discovery at Sanatorium

"*That's* Edmund Bickerstaff," Joplin said. "And as you'll discover from this article in the *Hampstead Gazette*, dated 1877, he's been dead and gone a long time. Now it seems he's reappeared."

"Please tell us all." Up until now Lockwood's body language had been one of polite disinterest. I could tell he was repelled by Saunders and bored by Joplin. Now, suddenly, his posture had changed. "Take some more tea, Mr. Joplin? Try a piece of Swiss roll, Mr. Saunders? Homemade, they are. Lucy baked them."

"Thank you, I will." Mr. Joplin nibbled a slice. "I'm afraid many details about Dr. Bickerstaff are sketchy. I have not had time to research him. But it seems he was a medical practitioner, treating nervous disorders at Green Gates Sanatorium on the edge of Hampstead Heath. Previously he'd been an ordinary family doctor, but his practice went south. There was some scandal, and he had to shut it down."

"Scandal?" I said. "What kind of scandal?"

"It's not clear. Apparently he gained a reputation for certain unwholesome activities. There were whispers of witchcraft, of dabbling in forbidden arts. Even talk of grave robbing. The police were involved, but nothing was ever proved. Bickerstaff was able to go on working at this private sanatorium. He lived in a house in the hospital grounds—until one winter night, late in 1877."

Joplin smoothed the paper out with his small, white hands, and consulted it a moment.

"It seems that Bickerstaff had certain associates," he went on, "like-minded men and women who gathered at his house at night. It was rumored that they dressed in hooded robes, lit candles, and performed—well, we do not know *what* they were up to. On such occasions, the doctor's servants were ordered to leave the house, which they were only too pleased to do. Bickerstaff apparently had a ferocious temper, and no one dared cross him. Well, on December thirteenth, 1877, just such a meeting took place; the servants were dismissed, with pay, and told to return two days later. As they departed, the carriages of Bickerstaff's guests were seen arriving."

"Two days off work?" Lockwood said. "That's a long time."

"Yes, the meeting was intended to last the full weekend." Joplin looked down at the paper. "But something happened. According to the *Gazette*, the following night some of the attendants at the sanatorium passed the house. It was quiet and dark. They assumed Bickerstaff must have gone away. Then one of them noticed movement in an upstairs window: the net curtains were twitching; there were all sorts of little shudders and ripples, as if someone—or something—was feebly tugging at them from below."

"Ooh," I breathed. "We're not going to like this, are we?"

"No, girlie. You're not." Mr. Saunders had been munching another slice of cake, but he spoke up now. "Well," he added, "depends on your state of mind. Albert here loves it. He's fascinated by this old stuff." He brushed crumbs off his lap and onto the carpet.

"Go on, Mr. Joplin," Lockwood said.

"Some of the attendants," Joplin said, "were all for breaking into the house there and then; others—recalling the stories surrounding Dr. Bickerstaff—were all for minding their own business. And while they were standing outside arguing about it, they noticed that the movement in the curtains had redoubled, and suddenly they saw long, dark shapes running along the windowsill on the inside."

"Long, dark shapes?" I said. "What were they?"

"They were rats," Mr. Joplin said. He took a sip of tea. "And now they saw that it was the *rats* that were making the curtains move. There were lots of them, darting back and forth along the sill, and hanging off the curtains, and jumping down into the dark, and they reasoned that the pack of them must be in that room for some particular reason, which you can maybe guess. So they put together a group of the bravest men and gave them candles, and these men broke into the house and went upstairs. And while they were still on the stairs, they began to hear terrible wet rustling noises from up ahead, and ripping sounds, and also the click of teeth. Well, perhaps you can picture what they found." He pushed his glasses up his nose and shuddered. "I don't want to give the details. Suffice it to say that what they saw would have stayed with them for the rest of their days. Dr. Bickerstaff, or what was left of him, lay on the floor of his study. There were fragments of robe, but little else. The rats had eaten him."

There was a silence. Mr. Saunders gave a short sniff and wiped a finger under his nose. "So that's how Dr. Bickerstaff ended up," he said. "As a pile of bloody bones and sinew. Nasty. That last slice of Swiss roll, now—anyone want it?"

George and I spoke together. "No, no, please—be our guest."

"Ooh, it's a gooey one." Saunders took a bite.

"As you can imagine," Joplin said, "the authorities were very anxious to speak to the doctor's associates. But they could not be found. And that really was the end of Edmund Bickerstaff's story. Despite the horrible circumstances of his death, despite the rumors that hung about him, he wasn't long remembered. Green Gates Sanatorium burned down in the early twentieth century, and his name faded into obscurity. Even the fate of his bones was lost."

"Well," Lockwood said, "we know where they are now. And you want us to make them safe."

Mr. Saunders nodded; he finished eating and wiped his fingers on his trouser leg.

"It's all very strange," I said. "How come no one knew where he'd been buried? Why wasn't it in the records?"

George nodded. "And what exactly killed him? Was it the rats, or something else? There are *so* many loose ends here. This article is clearly just the tip of the iceberg. It's crying out for further research."

Albert Joplin chuckled. "Couldn't agree more. You're a lad right after my own heart."

"*Research* isn't the point," Mr. Saunders said. "Whatever is in that grave is getting restless, and I want it out of that cemetery tonight. If you could oblige me by supervising the excavation, Mr. Lockwood, I'd be grateful to you. What do you say?"

Lockwood glanced at me; he glanced at George. We returned his gaze with shining eyes. "Mr. Saunders," he said, "we'd be delighted."

Chapter 6

When Lockwood, George, and I arrived at the West Gate of Kensal Green Cemetery at dusk that evening, we had our new silver-tipped Italian rapiers hanging at our belts, and our largest duffel bags in our hands. Behind us the sun was setting against a few puffy, pink-flecked clouds—it was the end of a perfect summer's day. Despite the beauty of the scene, our mood was somber, our tension high. This was not a job we were undertaking lightly.

The great cemeteries of London, of which Kensal Green was the oldest and the finest, were relics of an age when people had a gentler relationship with the deceased. Back in Victorian times, their pleasant trees and landscaped paths made them places of respite from the metropolitan whirl. Stonemasons vied with one another to produce attractive headstones; roses grew in bowers, wildlife flourished. On Sundays families came to wander there, and muse upon mortality.

Well, not anymore, they didn't. The Problem had changed all that. Today the cemeteries were overgrown, the bowers wild and laced with thorns. Few adults ventured there by daylight; at night they were places of terror to be avoided at all costs. While it was true that the vast majority of the dead still slept quietly in their graves, even agents were reluctant to spend much time among them. It was like entering enemy territory. We were not welcome there.

The West Gate had once been wide enough for two carriages at a time to pass through to the Harrow Road. Now it was rudely blocked by a rough-hewn fence, laced with strips of iron, and thickly pasted with faded posters and flyers. The most common poster showed a wide-eyed smiling woman in a chaste knee-length skirt and T-shirt, standing with hands outstretched in greeting. Beneath her, radiant letters read: THE OPEN ARMS FELLOWSHIP: WE WELCOME OUR FRIENDS FROM THE OTHER SIDE.

"Personally," I said, "I like to welcome them with a magnesium flare." I had that knot in my stomach I always get before a case. The woman's smile offended me.

"These ghost cults contain some idiots," agreed George.

In the center of the fence a narrow entrance door hung open, and beside this stood a shabby hut made of corrugated iron. It contained a deck chair, a collection of empty soda cans, and a small boy reading a newspaper.

The boy wore an enormous flat cap, colored with rather sporty yellow checks and almost entirely shading his face. Otherwise he was decked out in the usual drab brown uniform of the night watch. His iron-tipped watch-stick was propped in a corner of the hut. He regarded us from the depths of the deck chair as we approached.

"Lockwood and Company, here to meet Mr. Saunders," Lockwood said. "Don't get up."

"I won't," the boy said. "Who are you? Sensitives, I suppose?"

George tapped the pommel of his rapier. "See these swords? We're agents."

The boy seemed doubtful. "Could've fooled me. Why ain't you got uniforms, then?"

"We don't need them," Lockwood replied. "A rapier's the true mark of an agent."

"Codswallop," the boy said. "*Proper* agents have fancy jackets, like that hoity-toity Fittes crowd. I reckon you're another drippy bunch of sensitives, who'll pass out cold at the first sign of a Lurker." He turned back to his paper and snapped it open. "Anyways, in you go."

Lockwood blinked. George took a half step forward. "Agents' swords aren't just good for ghosts," he said. "They can also be used for whipping cheeky night-watch kids. Want us to show you?"

"Oh, how terrifying. See me tremble." The boy pushed his cap farther over his eyes and made himself comfy in his chair. He jerked his thumb over his shoulder. "Straight up the main avenue, make for the chapel in the center of the site. You'll find everyone camped there. Now, move along, please. You're standing in my light."

For a moment it was touch and go whether another small ghost might soon be haunting the margins of the Harrow Road, but I resisted the temptation. Lockwood motioned us on. We passed through the gate and entered the burial grounds.

Instinctively, as soon as we were in, we stopped and used our hidden senses. The others looked, I listened. All was peaceful; there wasn't any sudden upsurge in psychic pressure. I heard nothing except for blackbirds calling sweetly, a few crickets in the grass. Gravel paths, shining dimly in the half-light, radiated away between dark ranks of memorials and tombs. Trees overhung the walkways, casting them into deeper shadow. Overhead, the sky was a fathomless dark blue, punctured by the risen moon's bright disc.

We took the main avenue between rows of spreading linden trees. Dim triangles of moonlight cut between the trees, frosting the black grass. Our boots crunched on gravel; the chains in our bags chinked faintly as we marched along.

"Should be fairly straightforward," Lockwood said, breaking our silence. "We stand by while they dig down to the coffin. When that's done, we open it up, seal Dr. Bickerstaff's bones with a bit of silver, and head on our way. Easy."

I made a skeptical noise. "Coffin opening's never that simple," I said. "Something always goes wrong."

"Oh, not *always*."

"Name a single one that went well."

"I agree with Lucy," George said. "You're assuming Edmund Bickerstaff won't cause trouble. I bet he does."

"You're both such worriers," Lockwood exclaimed. "Look on the bright side. We know the exact position of the Source tonight, plus we don't have Kipps to fret about, do we? I think it's going to be an excellent evening. As for Bickerstaff, just because he had an unfortunate end doesn't mean he'll necessarily be an aggressive spirit now."

"Maybe . . ." George muttered. "But if I was eaten by rats, I know I'd be fairly upset."

After five minutes' walk we saw the heavy white roof of a building rise among the trees like a whale breaching a dark sea. This was the Anglican chapel in the center of the cemetery. At the front, four great pillars supported a Grecian portico. A broad flight of steps led to its double doors. They were open; electric light shone warmly from within. Below, half lit by giant hydraulic floodlights, sat two prefabricated work cabins. There were mechanical excavators, small dump trucks, piles of earth. Twists of lavender smoke rose from buckets of coal burning at the edges of the camp.

Evidently we had reached the operations center for Sweet Dreams Excavations and Clearance. A number of figures stood at the top of the chapel stairs, silhouetted against the open doors. We heard raised voices; fear crackled like static in the air.

Lockwood, George, and I dropped our bags on the ground beside one of the smoking buckets. We climbed the steps, hands resting on our sword hilts. The crowd's noise quieted; people moved aside, silently regarding us as we drew near.

At the top of the steps, the angular figure of Mr. Saunders broke free of the throng and bustled over to make us welcome. "Just in time!" he cried. "There's been a small incident, and these fools are refusing to stay! I keep telling them we have top agents arriving— but no, they want their pay now. You're not getting a penny!" he roared over his shoulder. "Risk's what I employ you for!"

"Not after what they've seen," a big man said. He was aggressively stubbled, with skeleton tattoos on his neck and arm, and a chunky iron necklace hung over his shirt. Several other burly workmen stood in the crowd, along with a few frightened night-watch kids, clutching their watch-sticks to them like comforters. I also noted a posse of teenage girls, whose shapelessly floaty dresses, black eyeliner, outsized bangles, and lank armpit-length hair marked them out as sensitives. Sensitives do psychic work, but they refuse to ever actually *fight* ghosts, for reasons of pacifist principle. They're generally as drippy as a summer cold and as irritating as hives. We don't normally get along.

Saunders glared at the man who'd spoken. "You should be ashamed, Norris. What's next, jumping at Shades and Glimmers?"

"*This* thing's no Shade," Norris said.

"Bring us some *proper* agents!" someone shouted. "Not these fly-by-nights! Look at them—they don't even have nice uniforms!"

With a clatter of bangles, the floatiest and wettest-looking of the sensitives stepped forward. "Mr. Saunders! Miranda, Tricia, and I refuse to work in any sector near *that grave* until it's been made safe! I wish to make that clear."

There was a general chorus of agreement; several of the men shouted insults, while Saunders struggled to be heard. The crowd pressed inward threateningly.

Lockwood raised a friendly hand. "Hello, everyone," he said. He flashed them all his widest smile; the hubbub was stilled. "I'm Anthony Lockwood of Lockwood and Company. You may have heard of us. Combe Carey Hall? Mrs. Barrett's tomb? That's us. We're here to help you tonight, and I'd very much like to hear what problems you've experienced. You, miss"—he turned his smile upon the sensitive—"you've clearly had a *terrible* experience. Are you able to tell me about it?"

This was classic Lockwood. Friendly, considerate, empathetic. My personal impulse would have been to slap the girl soundly around the face and boot her moaning backside out into the night. Which is why he's the leader, and I'm not. Also why I have no female friends.

True to type, she batted big, moist eyes in his direction. "I felt like . . . like something was rushing up beneath me," she breathed. "It was about to . . . to grab me and swallow me. Such baleful energy! Such malice! I'm never going near that place again!"

"That's nothing!" one of the other girls cried. "Claire only felt it. I *saw* it, just as dusk was falling! I swear it turned its hood and looked at me! A moment's glimpse was all it took. Ah, it made me swoon!"

"A hood?" Lockwood began. "So can you tell me what it looked like—?"

But the girl's squeaks had reignited the passions of the throng; everyone began talking now, clutching at us. They pressed forward, pushing us against the door. We were the center of a ring of frightened spotlit faces. Beyond the chapel steps, the last red light drained away across the endless ranks of headstones.

Saunders gave a bellow of renewed rage. "All right, you cowards! Joplin can put you on another sector tonight! Far away from that grave! Satisfied? Now, get out of our way—go on, move!" Grasping Lockwood by the arm, he shouldered his way inside the building. George and I followed, bumped and buffeted, squeezing through the closing doors. "And no severance pay!" Saunders yelled through the crack. "You all still work for me!" The doors slammed shut, silencing the clamor of the crowd.

"What a palaver," Saunders growled. "It's my mistake for trying to speed things up. I got the excavators to begin work digging around the Bickerstaff grave an hour ago. Thought it would help you out. Then all hell broke loose, and it wasn't even dark." He took his hat off and wiped his sleeve across his forehead. "Perhaps we'll get a moment's peace in here."

The chapel was a small, plainly decorated space with walls of whitewashed plaster. There was a smell of damp; and also a persistent underlying chill, which three glowing space heaters arranged across the flagstone floor did little to remove. Two cheap-looking desks, each piled high with a mess of papers, sat near the heaters. Along one wall a dusty altar stood behind a wooden rail, with a small closed door beside it, and a wooden pulpit close at hand. Above our heads rose a scalloped plaster dome.

The most curious object in the room was a great block of black stone, the size and shape of a closed sarcophagus; it rested on a rectangular metal plate set into the floor below the altar rail. I studied it with interest.

"Yes, that's a catafalque, girlie," Saunders said. "An old Victorian lift for transporting coffins to the catacombs below. Uses a hydraulic mechanism. Still works, according to Joplin; they were using it until the Problem got too bad. Where *is* Joplin, anyhow? Damned fool's never at his desk. He's always wandering off when you want him."

"This *small incident* at the Bickerstaff grave," Lockwood prompted. "Please tell us what's happened."

Saunders rolled his eyes. "Heaven only knows. I can't get sense out of them. Some of the sensitives *saw* something, as you heard. Some say it was very tall, others that it wore a cloak or robe. But there's no consistency. One night-watch kid said it had seven heads. Ridiculous! I sent *her* home."

"Night-watchers don't normally make up stories," George said.

This was true. Most children with strong psychic abilities become agents, but if you're not good enough for that, you swallow your pride and join the night watch. It's dangerous, low-paid work, mostly taking guard duties after dark, but those kids are talented enough. We never underestimate them.

Lockwood had his hands in the pockets of his long, dark coat. His eyes glinted with excitement. "It's all getting curiouser and curiouser," he said. "Mr. Saunders, what's the current state of the grave? Is it exposed?"

"The men dug some way down. I believe they struck the coffin."

"Excellent. We can deal with it now. George here is good with a spade—aren't you, George?"

"Well, I certainly get plenty of practice," George said.

The path to the unexpected grave of Edmund Bickerstaff lay along a narrow side aisle just beyond the excavators' camp. Saunders led us there in silence. No one else from the camp followed; they hung back in the circle of light beneath the arc lamps, watching us go.

The burials in this part of the cemetery were modest ones— mostly marked by headstones, crosses, or simple statues. It was dark overhead now. The stones, half hidden by thorns and long wet grass, showed white and stark under the moon; but their shadows were black slots into which a man might fall.

After a few minutes of walking, Saunders slowed. Up ahead, piles of brambles marked where patch of ground had been roughly cleared. Nearby rose a mound of dark, wet earth. A small mech- anized backhoe, scuffed and yellow in the light of Saunders's flashlight, blocked the path at an angle. Its bucket was still full. Spades, picks, and other digging tools lay scattered all around.

"They left in a hurry," Saunders said. His voice was tight and high. "Right, this is where I stop. If you want anything, just call." With undisguised haste, he drifted back into the dark, and we were left alone.

We loosened our rapiers. The night was silent; I was aware of the heavy beating of my heart. Lockwood took a penlight from his belt and shone it into the black space to the left of the path. It was a square plot of open ground, bordered by normal graves and box tombs. In its center, a small discolored slab of stone rose crookedly from the soil. The grass in front of this stone had been scooped away, leaving a broad, gently sloping pit torn in the earth. It was maybe eight feet across and three feet deep. The tooth marks of the backhoe's bucket showed as long grooves in the mud. But we had eyes only for the stone.

We used our senses, quickly, quietly, before we did anything else.

"No death-glows," Lockwood said softly. "That's to be expected, because no one's died here. Got anything?"

"Nope," George said.

"I have," I said. "A faint vibration."

"A noise? Voices?"

It bothered me—I couldn't make it out at all. "Just a . . . disturbance. There's definitely *something* here."

"Keep your eyes and ears open," Lockwood said. "Right, first thing we do, we put a barrier right around. Then I'm checking out the stone. Don't want to miss anything, like we did last night."

George set a lantern on one of the box tombs, and by its light we took out our lengths of chain. We laid them out around the circumference of the pit. When this was finished, Lockwood stepped over the chains and walked toward the stone, hand ready on his sword. George and I waited, watching the shadows.

Lockwood reached the stone; kneeling abruptly, he brushed the grass aside. "Okay," he said. "It's poor quality material, badly weathered. Scarcely a quarter of the height of a standard headstone. Hasn't been laid properly—it's badly tilted. Someone did this *very* hurriedly. . . ."

He switched on the flashlight and ran the beam over the surface. Decades of lichen had crusted it, and built up deeply in the letters carved there. "*Edmund Bickerstaff,*" Lockwood read. "And *this* isn't a proper mason's work. It's hardly even an inscription. It's just been scratched by the first tool that came to hand. So we've got a rushed, illegal, and very amateur burial, which has been here a long time."

He stood up. And as he did so, there was the gentlest of rustlings. From behind the grave a figure broke free of the darkness and lurched forward into the lantern light. George and I cried out; Lockwood leaped to the side, ripping his rapier clear. He twisted as he jumped, landing in the center of the pit, facing the stone.

"Sorry," Mr. Albert Joplin said. "Did I startle anyone?"

I cursed under my breath; George whistled. Lockwood only exhaled sharply. Mr. Joplin stumbled around the edge of the pit. He moved with an awkward, stoop-shouldered gait that reminded me vaguely of a chimp's; small showers of gray dandruff drifted about him as he rolled along. His spindly arms were clasped across his sheaf of papers, which he pressed protectively against his narrow chest as a mother shields a child.

He pushed his glasses apologetically up his nose. "I'm sorry; I got lost coming from the East Gate. Have I missed anything?"

George spoke—and at that moment I was enveloped by a wave of clawing cold. You know when you jump into a swimming pool and find they haven't heated it, and the freezing water hits your body? You feel a smack of pain—awful and all over. This was exactly like that. I let out a gasp of shock. And that wasn't the worst of it—as the cold hit me, my inner ears kicked into life. That vibration I'd sensed before? It was suddenly *loud*. Behind the hum of George's voice and Joplin's chatter, it had become a muffled buzzing, like an approaching cloud of flies.

"Lockwood . . ." I began.

Then it was done. My head cleared. The cold vanished. My skin felt red and raw. The noise shrank into the background once again.

". . . really quite extraordinary church, Mr. Cubbins," Joplin was saying. "The best brass rubbings in London. I must show you sometime."

"Hey!" This was Lockwood, standing in the center of the pit. "Hey!" he called. "Look what I've found! No, not you, please, Mr. Joplin—you'd better stay beyond the iron."

He had his flashlight trained on the mud beside his feet. Moving slowly, my head still ringing, I crossed the chains with George and went down into the hole. Our boots trod on soft, dark mud.

"Here," Lockwood said. "What do you make of this?"

At first I made out nothing in the brightness of the beam. Then, as Lockwood moved his flashlight, I saw it: the long, hard, reddish edge of something, poking from the mud.

"Oh," George said. "That's weird."

"Is it the coffin?" Little Mr. Joplin was hovering beyond the chains, craning his thin neck eagerly. "The coffin, Mr. Lockwood?"

"I don't know. . . ."

"Most coffins I've seen are made of wood," George murmured. "Most Victorian coffins would have long since rotted in the ground. Most are buried at a respectable six feet, with all the proper rites and regulations. . . ."

There was a silence. "And this?" Joplin said.

"Is only four feet down, and has been tipped in at an angle, like they wanted to get rid of it as fast as possible. And it hasn't rotted, because it isn't made of wood at all. This box is made of iron."

"Iron . . ." Lockwood said. "An iron coffin . . ."

"Can you hear it?" I said suddenly. "The buzzing of the flies?"

"But they didn't have the Problem then," George said. "What did they need to trap in there?"

Chapter 7

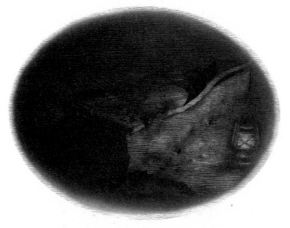

I t took us till midnight to dig the thing out. One of us stood guard, taking readings, while the others labored with the tools. Every ten minutes we swapped. We used the spades and picks that had been discarded on the path to cut away the mud from metal, deepen the pit at its center, and slowly expose the object's lid and sides.

We rarely spoke. Silence enfolded us like a shroud; we heard nothing but the *skrrt, skrrt, skrrt* of the tools in the earth. All was still. Occasionally we scattered salt and iron up and down the center of the pit to keep supernatural forces at bay. It seemed to work. It was ten degrees colder in the pit than on the path beyond, but the temperature remained steady. The buzzing noise I'd heard had gone.

Albert Joplin, for whom the mysterious burial exerted a powerful fascination, remained with us for a while, flitting back and forth among the gravestones in a state of high excitement. Finally, as the night darkened and the coffin rose clear of the earth, even he grew cautious; he remembered something important he had to do back at the chapel, and departed. We were alone.

Skrrt, skrrt, skrrt.

At last we finished. The object stood exposed. Lockwood lit another storm lantern and placed it in the mud near the center of the pit. We stood a short way off, gazing at what we'd found.

An iron box about six feet in length, two feet wide, and just over a foot deep.

Not any old box, in other words. As Lockwood had said—an iron coffin.

The sides were still partially caked with soil, gray and sticky-looking. Where the grunge had come away, the surface of the box showed through. Rust bloomed on it like flowers of coral, the color of dried blood.

Once, presumably, its sides had been clean and straight, but the pressing earth and weight of years had so contorted the box that its vertical edges were skewed, and the top sagged in the middle. I've seen lead coffins, from the Roman burials they find under the city, with the exact same squashed look. One corner of the lid was so warped it had risen away from the side completely, revealing a narrow wedge of darkness.

"Remind me never to get buried in an iron coffin," George said. "It gets so shabby."

"And it's no longer doing its job, either," Lockwood added. "Whatever's inside is finding its way out through that little gap. Are you all right, Lucy?"

I was swaying where I stood. No, I didn't feel great. My head pounded; I felt nauseous. The buzzing noise was back. I had the sensation of invisible insects running up and down my skin. It was a powerful miasma—that feeling of deep discomfort you often get when a Visitor is near. Powerful *despite* all that iron.

"I'm fine," I said briskly. "So. Who's opening it?"

This was the big question. Good agency practice, as set out in the *Fittes Manual*, dictates that only one person be directly in the line of fire when "sealed chambers" (i.e. tombs, coffins, or secret rooms) are opened up. The others stand to the side, weapons at the ready. Rotating this duty fairly is second only to the cookie rule in terms of importance. It's a regular point of contention.

"Not me." Lockwood tapped the mended claw marks on his coat front. "I did Mrs. Barrett's tomb."

"Well, I did that trapdoor in Melmoth House. George?"

"I did that secret room at the Savoy Hotel," George said. "You remember—the one with the ancient plague mark on the door? Ooh, that was eerie."

"No, it wasn't. It wasn't haunted *or* secret. It was a laundry room filled with undies."

"I didn't know that when I went in, did I?" George protested. "Tell you what, we'll toss for it." He rummaged deep in his pants pocket, produced a dirty coin. "What do you think, Luce? Heads or tails?"

"I think—"

"Heads? Interesting choice. Let's see." There was a blur of movement, too fast for the eye to follow. "Ah, it's tails. Unlucky, Luce. Here's the crowbar."

Lockwood grinned. "Nice try, George, but you're doing it. Let's fetch the tools and seals."

Breathing a sigh of relief, I led the way to the duffel bags. George followed with ill grace. Soon the silver seals, the knives and crowbars, and all the rest of our equipment were in position beside the coffin.

"This won't be too tricky," Lockwood said. "Look—the lid's hinged on this side. Opposite that, we've two latches—here and here, but one's already snapped. There's just the one by you, Lucy, still corroded shut. Quick bit of nifty crowbar work from George, and we're home free." He looked at us. "Any questions?"

"Yes," George said. "Several. Where will you be standing? How far away? What weapons will you use to protect me when something horrible comes surging out?"

"Lucy and I have everything covered. Now—"

"Also, if I don't make it back home, I've made a will. I'll tell you where to find it. Under my bed in the far corner, behind the box of tissues."

"Pray to God it won't come to that. Now, if you're ready—"

"Is that some kind of inscription on the lid?" I said. Now we'd come to the point, I was really alert, all my senses firing. "See that bit of scratching there?"

Lockwood shook his head. "Can't tell under all this mud, and I'm not going to start wiping it off now. Come on, let's get this done."

In fact, the lid of the coffin proved harder to force than Lockwood had anticipated. In addition to the corroded latch, the bloom of rust across the surface had bonded the top to the sides in several places, and it took twenty minutes of laborious chipping with pocketknives and chisels before the hinges were loosened and the lid freed.

"Right . . ." Lockwood was taking a final reading. "It's looking good. Temperature's still holding firm, and the miasma isn't any worse. Whatever's in there is keeping surprisingly quiet. Well, there's no time like the present. Lucy—let's take our positions."

He and I went to opposite ends of the coffin. I held our largest, strongest silver chain net, four feet in diameter. I unfolded it, and let it hang ready in my hands. Lockwood unclasped his rapier and held it with an angled Western grip, ready for a quick attack.

"George," he said, "over to you."

George nodded. He closed his eyes and composed himself. Then took up the crowbar. He flexed his fingers, rolled his shoulders, and did something with his neck that made it click. He approached the coffin, bent close, set the end of the crowbar into the crack between the broken clamps. He widened his stance and waggled his bottom like a golfer about to take a swing. He took a deep breath—and pressed down on the bar. Nothing happened. He pressed again. No, the lid was twisted; perhaps its contortions had jammed it shut. George pressed down again.

With a clang, the lid shot up; George's end of the bar shot down. George jerked backward, lost his balance, and landed heavily on his backside in the mud, with his glasses slightly askew. He sat himself up, stared stupidly down into the coffin.

And screamed.

"*Light*, Lucy!" Lockwood had dived forward, shielding George with the blade of his rapier. But nothing had come out. No Visitor, no apparition. The gleam of the lanterns shone on the inside of the lid, and also on something in the coffin below—something reflecting a darkly glittering light.

The flashlight was in my hand. I shone it full into the interior, on what was lying there.

If you're easily icked-out, you might want to skip this paragraph and the next, because the body staring back at me wasn't just bones, but a great deal more. That was the first surprise: there was much that hadn't decayed away. Ever left a banana under a sofa and forgotten about it? Then you'll know that it soon goes black, then black and gooey, then black and shrunk right down. This guy, entombed in iron, was like a banana midway between the second stage and the third. The flashlight beam glimmered on the dried and blackened skin, stretched tight above the cheekbones. In places it had cracked. There was a neat hole in the center of his forehead, around which the skin had entirely peeled away.

Long hanks of white hair, colorless as glass, hung beside the head. The eye sockets were empty. Dried lips had shrunk back, revealing gums and teeth.

He wore the remnants of a purple cloak or cape, and beneath it an old-style black suit, stiff high collar, black Victorian cravat. His hands (bony, these) cradled something shrouded in tattered white cloth. Whether because of the angle of the burial, or because of the movement of the earth in the long years since, the object had slid from beneath the cloth and was peeping out between the skeletal fingers. It was a piece of glass—perhaps the width of a human head, with an irregularly shaped rim. It was quite black with dirt and mold, and yet the glass still glinted—and the glinting caught my eye.

"Look! Look . . ."

What was that voice?

"Lucy! Seal it up!"

Of course. It was Lockwood shouting.

With that I cast the silver chain net, and the contents of the coffin were blotted out.

"So what did you *see*, George?" Lockwood asked. We were standing on the path now, drinking tea and eating sandwiches, which some of Saunders's team had brought. A decent crowd had gathered—Saunders, Joplin, several workmen, and the night-watch kids—some because the fun was over, others possibly in delayed response to George's scream. They all hung about the gravestones, staring at the pit, a safe distance from the chains. We'd shut the coffin lid; just a corner of the chain net could be seen. "I mean, I know Bickerstaff looked bad," Lockwood went on, "but, let's face it, we've seen nastier. Remember Putney Vale?"

George had been very subdued for the past few minutes. He had barely spoken, and there was an odd expression on his face. His eyes showed numb distress, but they also held a yearning, far-off look; he kept gazing back toward the pit as if he thought he had left something there. It worried me. It reminded me a little of ghost-lock, where the victim's willpower is drained by an aggressive spirit; but we had sealed the Source with silver, and there was no ghost present now. Still, George seemed to be improving. The food was fast reviving him. He shook his head at Lockwood. "It wasn't the body," he said slowly. "I've seen worse things in our fridge. It was the mirror that he held."

"You thought it was a mirror, then?" I said. When I closed my eyes, I still saw that piece of glass, glinting, flashing, darker than dark.

"I don't know what it was. But my eyes were drawn to it. I saw in it . . . I don't know *what* I saw. It was all black, basically, but there was something in that blackness, and it was awful. It made me scream—I felt like someone was sucking my insides out through my chest." George shuddered. "But at the same time, it was fascinating, too—I couldn't take my eyes away. I just wanted to gaze at it, even though it was doing me harm." He gave a long, heartfelt sigh. "I'd probably still be staring at it now, if Lucy hadn't covered it with the net."

"Good thing you're not, by the sound of it," Lockwood said. He too had been watching George closely. "Funny sort of mirror. No wonder they kept it in an iron coffin."

"Did they *know* about the properties of iron in Bickerstaff's time?" I asked. It was only with the start of the Problem, fifty years before, that mass production of ghost-proof materials made of iron and silver had begun. And this burial dated from a generation or two earlier than that.

"Most people didn't," Lockwood said. "But silver, salt, and iron have always been used against ghosts, and evil spirits in general. So it *can't* be a coincidence that we've got iron here." He lowered his voice. "Either of you notice anything odd about Dr. Bickerstaff himself, incidentally?"

"Aside from the general mummified corpse angle, you mean?" I said.

"That's just it. According to Joplin's newspaper, Bickerstaff was eaten by rats, wasn't he? That fellow was all in one piece. And did you see the hole in his—" He broke off as Saunders and Joplin approached. The excavator had been barking orders at the night-watch kids, while the archivist lingered by the iron chains, staring at the coffin. Both had big smiles for us; there was a round of back-slapping and congratulations.

"Excellent work, Mr. Lockwood!" Saunders cried. "Very efficiently done. Perhaps we can get on with our proper business here, now all that nonsense is over." He took a swig from a steaming mug of coffee. "People are saying old Bickerstaff held a crystal or some such? Something from one of his weird rituals, maybe. But you've covered it with your net, of course."

Lockwood laughed. "You'll want to keep that net in position, believe me. There's certainly *some* kind of powerful Source in there. We'll need to contact DEPRAC straightaway, so they can arrange for safe disposal."

"First thing tomorrow!" Saunders said. "Right now we need to get on with ordinary business. We've lost half a night's work already. Well, I suppose you'll want me to sign papers for the work done, Mr. Lockwood. Come back to the office, and we'll get that sorted for you."

"Can we move the coffin into the chapel tonight?" Joplin asked. "I don't like leaving it out here. There's the danger of thieves and relic-men . . . you know."

Lockwood frowned. "Well, be sure to keep the net in position. Replace the chains around it when it's moved, and don't let anyone go near it."

Lockwood and Saunders departed. George leaned against a box tomb and began an animated conversation with Joplin. I busied myself gathering our equipment, taking my time. It was early yet, not even midnight; definitely a better evening than the previous one. Strange, though. A *very* strange burial, and impossible to fathom. George had seen something, but there'd been no tangible ghost at all. Yet anything that could create so much psychic disturbance despite all that iron was formidable indeed.

"Miss?"

It was the workman named Norris, the biggest and brawniest of the excavators. His skin was leathery. Whitish stubble extended up to the buzz cut on his scalp. The tattoo on his neck was a wakeful skull with extended wings. "Excuse me, miss," he said. "Did I hear correctly? No one's to go near the coffin?"

"Yes, that's right."

"Better stop your friend, then. Look at him go."

I turned. George and Joplin had crossed the iron chains. They'd approached the coffin. They were talking excitedly, Joplin bunching his papers tighter under his arm.

"George!" I called. "What on earth are you—?"

Then I realized.

The lid. The inscription.

Still chattering blithely, George and Joplin stooped beside the coffin and began chipping mud away from the lid. George had his penknife; he raised the lid slightly to aid his work. The silver net beneath was dislodged. It slipped to one side.

Norris said something to me, but I didn't hear him, because at that moment I'd become aware that a *third* figure was standing alongside Joplin and George.

It was still, silent, very tall and thin, and only partially substantial. The iron coffin passed straight through one corner of its long gray robe. Glistening swirls of plasm, short and stubby like the feelers of anemones, flexed and curled outward from the base of the apparition—but there were no arms or legs, just the plunging robe. Its head, swathed in a long, curled hood, could not be seen. Except for two details: a pale sharp chin, dull white as fish bones, and an open mouth of jagged teeth.

I opened my own mouth and—in the heartbeat that it took to shout a warning—heard a voice speak in my mind.

"*Look! Look!*"

"George . . ."

"*I give you your heart's desire—*"

"George!"

Because he wasn't moving, and neither was Joplin, though the figure was directly in their view. Both of them were still half bent, frozen in the act of brushing mud from the coffin. Their eyes were wide and staring, their faces transfixed.

"*Look . . .*"

The voice was deep and lulling—yet also coldly repellent. It muddled my senses; I longed to obey it, but was desperate to defy it, too.

I forced myself to move.

And the figure also moved. It rose up, a great gray column, faint against the stars.

Behind me, someone shouted. No time. I drew my sword.

The shape loomed over George and Joplin. All at once they seemed to snap out of their trance; their heads jerked up, they started back. I heard George cry out. Joplin dropped his papers. The figure hung there, frozen for an instant. I knew what it would do. I knew it would suddenly arch down, drop like a falling jet of water. It would engulf them. It would consume them both.

I was too far away. Stupid . . . The rapier was useless.

No time to change; no time to reach for anything in my belt. The rapier—

The shape dropped down—the open mouth, the teeth descending in an arc.

I threw the sword; it spun like a wheel against the sky.

Joplin, tripping over his own feet in his panic, knocked George to the side. George, retreating, fumbling in his belt for some defense, lost his balance, began to fall—

"I give you your heart's desire—"

The sword passed directly between George and Joplin, just above their heads. The silver-coated blade sliced point-first through the cowled face.

The figure vanished. The voice in my head cut off. A psychic impact-wave sped out from the center of the circle and knocked me off my feet. Lockwood, hair flying, coat flapping, ran past me down into the pit. He skidded to a halt beside the chains and scanned the scene with glittering eyes. But it was okay. George was okay. Joplin was okay. The coffin was quiet. The summer stars were shining overhead.

The Visitor was gone.

Chapter 8

In the event, Lockwood was fairly restrained. He said nothing at the cemetery. He said nothing on the way home. He waited while we locked the door and reset the ghost-wards and dumped our bags in the corner and visited the facilities. Then his restraint ran out. He marched George straight to the living room and, without so much as a pause for our normal post-case chips and cocoa, gave him the rollocking he deserved.

"I'm surprised at you," he said. "You put your own life—and that stupid Mr. Joplin's—at immediate risk. You were seconds away from being ghost-touched. If it weren't for Lucy, you *would* have been! And *don't* give me any of that guff about how you thought the Source was neutralized. It's against all the rules to let a nonagent anywhere near an active Source in an operative situation. You *know* that! What were you thinking?"

George had parked himself in his favorite chair by the coffee table. His face, usually so inexpressive, showed a mix of contrition, defiance, and attempted unconcern. "We'd been talking about the inscription on the lid," he said sullenly. "Once DEPRAC gets its hands on the coffin today, we know we'll never see it again, so Joplin said—"

"What Joplin said shouldn't have had any effect on you!" Lockwood cried. "You think that's a good excuse for nearly getting killed? Trying to decipher some scratchings on a foul old coffin? I'm surprised at you, George! Honestly surprised."

He wasn't really, and nor was I. One of George's most famous characteristics, aside from sarcasm, wind, and general bloody-mindedness, was his fascination with things unknown. When he wasn't roaming dusty archives researching background stuff on cases, he roamed dusty archives researching Visitor Theory— trying to discover *why* ghosts were returning and *how* precisely this occurred. It wasn't just the skull in our ghost-jar that fascinated him; where possible, he also investigated other objects of psychic power. It figured that the iron coffin fell into that category.

It also figured that the tiresome little scholar Joplin shared George's approach.

Lockwood had fallen silent now. He waited, arms folded, clearly expecting an apology, but George wasn't giving up the argument quite yet. "I agree that the coffin and its contents are dangerous," he said doggedly. "That mirror I saw was horrible. But their powers are entirely unknown. So I think it's a legitimate agency job to dis-cover anything we can about what it is we're dealing with—and that includes the inscription. It could have given us some clues to what Bickerstaff—and his ghost—were up to."

"Who cares?" Lockwood cried. "Who cares about any of that? It's *not part of our job!*" In many ways, Lockwood was the complete opposite of George, and not just in terms of personal hygiene. He had no interest in the mechanics of ghosts, and little in their individual desires or intentions. All he really wanted was to destroy them as efficiently as possible. As much as anything, however, I guessed it was George's careless amateurism that had truly offended him here. "That kind of stuff," he went on more quietly, "is for Barnes and DEPRAC to worry about. Not us. Right, Lucy?"

"Right! Of course it isn't. Absolutely not." I adjusted a corner of my skirt carefully. "Though sometimes it *is* interesting. . . . So did you actually *see* the inscription, George? I never thought to ask."

George nodded. "I did, as it happens."

"What did it say?"

"It said: *As you value your soul, forsake and abjure this cursed box.* Just that."

I hesitated. "'Forsake and abjure'?"

"It means don't open it, basically."

"Well, it's a bit late for that now."

Lockwood had been glaring at us throughout. He cleared his throat. "It doesn't really matter anymore, does it?" he said sweetly. "Because, as I keep telling you, Bickerstaff and his mirror thing are *no longer any of our business.* And, George—"

"Hold on," I said suddenly. "We're talking about this being Edmund Bickerstaff. But how does that square with Joplin's story of how Bickerstaff died? That bloke in the coffin wasn't torn apart by rats, was he? He'd had a bullet through his head."

George nodded. "You're right. Good point, Lucy."

"Though I suppose he might have been shot and then sort of nibbled."

"I guess so. . . . But he seemed in one piece to me."

"*It doesn't matter!*" Lockwood exclaimed. "If the case was open, it would be interesting, as you say. But the job's done. It's over. Forget it! The important thing is that we did what we were paid to do, which was to locate and contain the Source."

"Er, no, we didn't contain the Source, actually," George said. "As I rather conclusively proved. All that iron and silver, and *still* Bickerstaff's ghost was able to get out. *That's* unusual. Surely even you would admit it's worth investigating."

Lockwood uttered an oath. "No! No, I don't! You dislodged the net, George—*that* was how the Visitor was able to escape and ghost-lock you. You could have died! The problem is that, as always, you're too easily distracted. You need to get your priorities straight! Look at this mess in here—"

He stabbed a finger in the direction of the coffee table, where the ghost-jar sat, the skull dully visible, the plasm as blank and greenish as ever. George had conducted further experiments that afternoon. Noonday sun hadn't done anything, and nor had brief exposure to loud bursts of classical music on the radio. The table was strewn with a sea of notebooks and scribbled observations.

"This is a perfect example," Lockwood went on. "You're wasting too much time on that wretched jar. Try spending a bit more time on solid case research—help the company out a little."

George's cheeks flushed. "What's that supposed to mean?"

"I mean that Wimbledon Common business the other day . . ."

The stuff about the history of the gallows, which you completely missed. Even that idiot Bobby Vernon uncovered more useful information than you!"

George sat very still. He opened his mouth as if about to argue, then closed it again. His face lacked all expression. He took off his glasses and rubbed them on his jersey.

Lockwood ran his hands through his hair. "I'm being unfair. I shouldn't have said that. I'm sorry."

"No, no," George said stiffly. "I'll try to do better for you in future."

"Fine."

There was a silence. "How about I make some cocoa?" I said in a bright voice. Hot chocolate helps soothe things in the early hours. The night was growing old. It would soon be dawn.

"I'll make it," George said. He stood abruptly. "See if I can do *that* right. Two sugars, Luce? Lockwood . . . I'll make yours an extra-frothy one."

Lockwood frowned at the closing door. "You know, that last comment makes me uneasy. . . ." He sighed. "Lucy, I've been meaning to say, that was an impressive move back there—what you did with the rapier."

"Thanks."

"You aimed it perfectly, right between their heads. An inch to the left, and you'd have skewered George right between the eyes. Really sensational accuracy there."

I made a casual gesture. "Well . . . sometimes you just do what has to be done."

"You didn't actually aim it at all, did you?" Lockwood said.

"No."

"You just chucked it. In fact it was pure blind luck that George lost his balance and fell out of the way. That's why he wasn't kebabbed by you."

"Yup."

He smiled at me. "Still . . . that doesn't mean it wasn't a great piece of work. You were the only one who reacted in time."

As always, the full warmth of his approval made me feel a little flushed. I cleared my throat. "Lockwood," I said. "Bickerstaff's ghost. What kind *was* it? I've never seen anything like it before. Did you see how it rose up so high? What Visitor *does* that?"

"I don't know, Luce. Hopefully all the rest of the iron we piled on will keep it quiet till dawn. Then, I'm glad to say, it becomes DEPRAC's problem." He sighed, rose from his chair. "I'd better go and help George. I know I've offended him. Also, I'm slightly worried about what he's doing to my cocoa."

After he left, I lay back on the sofa, staring at the ceiling. Whether it was my weariness or the events of the night, the room didn't seem quite still. Images spun before my vision—George and Joplin frozen by the coffin; the blackened grinning face of the Bickerstaff corpse; the terrible ghost in its long gray shroud rising, rising toward the stars. . . . The figures moved slowly around and around in front of me as if I was watching the least child-friendly carousel ride in the world.

Bed; I needed bed. I closed my eyes. It didn't do any good. The images were still there. Plus it made me remember the cold yet wheedling voice I'd heard as I stood there in the pit, urging me to look at . . . To look at what? The ghost? The mirror?

I was glad I didn't know.

"Feeling rough?" someone said softly.

"Yeah. A little." Then something like an elevator shaft opened in my belly, and I felt myself drop through it. I opened my eyes. The door was still closed. Two rooms away I could hear Lockwood and George talking in the kitchen.

There was a greenish light revolving on the ceiling.

"Because you sure as hell look it." It was the lowest, throatiest of whispers; alien, but familiar. I'd heard it once before.

I raised my head slowly and looked at the coffee table, which now shone in emerald ghost-light. The substance in the jar was pulsing outward from the center like boiling water in a pot. There was a face within it, a leering face superimposed upon the plasm. The tip of its bulblike nose pressed hard against the silver-glass; wicked eyes glittered; the lipless mouth champed and grinned.

"You," I said. My throat was dry; I could barely speak.

"Not the greatest welcome I've ever had," the voice said, *"but accurate. Yes, I can't deny it. Me."*

I struggled to my feet, breathing too fast, fierce exultation surging through me. So I'd been right: it *was* a Type Three. Fully conscious, able to communicate! But Lockwood and George weren't here—I *had* to show them, *had* to prove it somehow. I started toward the door.

"Oh, don't bring them into it." The whispering voice sounded pained. *"Let's keep it intimate, you and me."*

That made me pause. Seven months had passed since the skull

had last chosen to speak. I could easily believe it would clam up the moment I opened the door. I swallowed, tried to ignore my heart hammering in my chest. "All right," I said hoarsely, facing it directly for the first time. "If that's how you want it, let's have some answers. What are you, then? Why are you talking to me?"

"*What am I?*" The face split open, the plasm parted, and I had a clear glimpse of the stained brown skull at the bottom of the jar. "This *is what I am*," the voice hissed. "*Look on me well. This fate awaits you, too.*"

"Oh, very sinister," I sneered. "You were just the same last time. What did you say then? *Death is coming?* Well, so much for your predictions. I'm still alive, and you're still just a dribble of luminous slime trapped in a jar. Big deal."

At once the plasm drew together like two elevator doors closing, and the face re-formed. Its reproving look was slightly undermined by the fact that its rejoined halves didn't quite match, giving it a grotesquely lopsided appearance. "*I'm disappointed,*" it whispered, "*that you didn't heed my warning. Death's in Life and Life's in Death— that's what I said. Problem is: you're stupid, Lucy. You're blind to the evidence around you.*"

Far off in the kitchen I could hear the clink of cutlery. I moistened my lips. "That claptrap means nothing to me."

The voice gave a groan. "*What, you want me to draw you a picture? Use your eyes and ears! Use your intelligence, girl. No one else can do it. You're on your own.*"

I shook my head, as much to clear my brain as anything. Here I was, hands on hips, arguing with a face in a jar. "Wrong," I said. "I'm not alone. I have my friends."

"What, fat George? Deceitful Lockwood?" The face crinkled with merriment. "Ooh yes, brilliant. What a team."

"Deceitful . . . ?" Up until then there had been something almost hypnotic about the voice; I'd found it impossible to disregard. All at once the gloating quality of the whisper repulsed me. I backed away across the room.

"Don't look so shocked," the voice said. "Secretive, deceitful. You know it's true."

I laughed at the ludicrousness of it. "I know no such thing."

"So go on, then," came the whisper. "There's a door, it's got hinges. Use them."

That I would. Suddenly I needed company; I needed the others. I didn't want to be alone with the gleeful voice.

I crossed the room. My fingers reached for the handle.

"Speaking of doors, I saw you once on the upstairs landing. Standing outside the forbidden room. You were dying to go through, weren't you?"

I halted. "No . . ."

"Good thing you didn't. You'd never have left alive."

It was as if the floor beneath my feet tilted slightly. "No," I said again. "No." I fumbled for the handle, began to turn it.

"There are other things in this house to fear, besides me."

"Lockwood! George!" I wrenched the door open and found myself roaring the words right into their astonished faces. Lockwood was so surprised, he spilled half his cocoa on the rug in the hall; George, who was carrying a tray, manfully juggled chips and sandwiches. I ushered them both inside.

"It's talking!" I cried. "The jar is! Look! Listen!"

I gestured urgently at the glass. Needless to say, the ghost said nothing. Needless to say, the face was gone; the plasm hung there, dull and still, as interesting and active as muddy rainwater in a jam jar. In the center of the mess, I could see the teeth of the skull grinning dimly between the metal clamps.

My shoulders sagged. I took a deep breath. "It *was* talking," I said limply. "*Really* talking to me. If you'd been here a minute earlier—" I scowled at them, as if it was their fault they'd missed out.

They said nothing, just stood there. With the tip of his little finger, George nudged a sandwich back into position. Finally Lockwood moved across and put the mugs down on the table. He took out a handkerchief and wiped a splash of cocoa from his hand.

"Come and have a drink," he said.

I stared at the grinning skull. Rage filled me. I took a swift step forward. If Lockwood hadn't put out a hand, I believe I would have kicked that jar right across the room.

"It's all right, Luce," he said. "We believe you."

I ran a harassed hand through my hair. "Good."

"Sit down. Have some food and cocoa."

"Okay." I did so. We all did. After a while I said, "It was like the first time, down in the cellar. It just started talking. We had a conversation."

"A real back-and-forth conversation?" Lockwood said. "A real Type Three?"

"Definitely."

"So what was it like?" George asked.

"It was . . . irritating." I glared at the quiescent jar.

He nodded slowly. "Only, Marissa Fittes said that communicating with Type Three ghosts was perilous, that they twisted your words and played with your emotions. She said if you weren't careful, you felt yourself falling slowly under their power, until your actions were not your own. . . ."

"No . . . I'd still say *irritating* about sums it up."

"So what did it tell you?" Lockwood asked. "What searing insights did it give?"

I looked at him. He was sitting back, sipping his cocoa. As always, despite the rigors of the night, he seemed composed. He was fastidious, self-possessed, always in control. . . .

There are other things in this house to fear, besides me.

"Um, nothing very much," I said.

"Well, there must have been something."

"Did it talk about the afterlife?" George said eagerly. His eyes shone bright behind his spectacles. "That's the big one. That's what everyone wants. Old Joplin told me he goes to scholars' conventions about it. What happens after death. Immortality . . . The fate of the human soul . . ."

I took a deep breath. "It said you were fat."

"What?"

"It talked about us, basically. It watches us and knows our names. It said—"

"It said I was fat?"

"Yeah, but—"

"Fat? *Fat?* What kind of otherworldly communication is that?"

"Oh, it was all like that!" I cried. "Just meaningless stuff. It's

evil, I think; it wants to hurt us, get us fighting among ourselves. . . .
It also said I was blind to things around me. . . . I'm sorry, George. I
didn't mean to insult you, and I hope that—"

"I mean, if I was interested in my weight, I'd buy a mirror,"
George said. "This is just so disappointing. No piercing insights
about the other side? Shame." He took a bite of sandwich, slumped
regretfully in his chair.

"What did it say about me?" Lockwood asked, watching me
with his dark, calm eyes.

"Oh . . . stuff."

"Such as?"

I looked away, took a sudden interest in the sandwiches, and
made a big show of pulling out a plump one. I held it fastidiously in
my fingers. "Oh good, ham. That's fine."

"Lucy," Lockwood said, "the last time I saw body language like
yours was when we were chatting to Martine Gray about her missing husband, and afterward found him at the bottom of her freezer.
Don't be so shifty, and spit it out." He smiled easily. "It's honestly
not going to get me upset."

"It's not?"

"Well, I mean, what did it say?" He chuckled. "How bad can it
have been?"

"Okay, so it told me . . . I mean, I didn't *believe* it, obviously, and
it's not something I care about, no matter what the truth may be. . . .
It implied you had something dangerous hidden in that room. You
know, the room upstairs. On the landing," I finished lamely.

Lockwood lowered his mug; he spoke flintily. "Yes, I know the
one. The one you can't stop asking about."

I gave a hoarse cry. "*I* didn't bring it up this time! The ghost in the jar did!"

"The ghost in the jar. Oh yes. Who just happens to have the same obsession as you." Lockwood folded his arms. "So tell me, what exactly did the 'ghost in the jar' say?"

I licked my lips. "It doesn't matter. You obviously don't believe me, so I'm not going to say any more. I'm off to bed."

I got to my feet, but Lockwood got up too. "Oh no, you're not," he said. "You can't just throw out wild assertions and then swan off like a prima donna without backing them up. Tell me what you've seen."

"*I* haven't seen anything. I keep telling you it—" I paused. "So there *is* something."

"I didn't say that."

"You definitely implied there was something to see."

We stood there, glaring at each other. George took another sandwich. At that moment the phone rang, out in the hall. All three of us jumped.

Lockwood swore. "Now what? It's four thirty in the morning." He went out to answer it.

George said, "Looks like Marissa Fittes was right. Type Three ghosts *do* mess with your head and play with your emotions. Look at the two of you now, arguing over nothing."

"It's not nothing," I said. "This is a basic issue of trust, which—"

"Looks like a whopping great zero from where I'm sitting," George said. "This ghost also called me *fat*; do you see me reacting?"

The door opened, Lockwood appeared. The anger in his face had been replaced with puzzlement and some concern.

"This night's getting weirder," he said. "That was Saunders at the cemetery. There's been a break-in at the chapel, where they were keeping the Bickerstaff coffin. One of the night-watch kids was hurt. And you remember that creepy mirror? It's been stolen."

III
The Missing
Mirror

Chapter 9

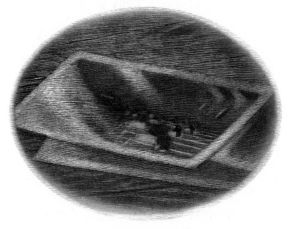

That phone call wasn't the last one we got that morning. Another came four hours later, around eight a.m., when we were trying to get some sleep. Our ordinary response in such circumstances would be to either (a) ignore it (Lockwood); (b) ask them politely to ring back (George); or (c) send them away with a shrill torrent of abuse (me: I get grumpy when I'm tired). However, since it was Inspector Barnes of DEPRAC, summoning us to an urgent meeting, we didn't have these options. Fifteen minutes later, dazed, and breakfastless, we squeezed into a taxi and set off for Scotland Yard.

It was another perfect summer's morning in London, the roads full of sweet gray shadow and sparkling dappled light. Inside the taxi, things were noticeably less sunny. Lockwood was whey-faced and monosyllabic, while two field mice could have made hammocks from the bags under George's eyes. We said little as we drove along.

This suited me. My head was full to bursting. I wound down the window and closed my eyes, letting the fresh air blow cool and clean across my mind. The events of the evening jostled for attention—the apparition at the cemetery, the skull grinning in its jar, my argument with Lockwood—yet at the same time, everything also seemed unreal. The skull's warnings, most of all. Stumbling my way downstairs to the taxi, the sight of the forbidden door on the landing had given me a brief, sharp pang. But the power of the ghost's words shriveled with the sunlight, and I knew I had been wrong to let them affect me. The thing was a liar. It sought to snare me, just as George had said. As a Listener, I had to beware.

Still, the actual conversation had been real enough. And no one else in London—perhaps no one since the great Marissa Fittes—had ever had one like it. The thought gave me a sleepy thrill as I sat there in my fuddled state. Was it the skull that was unique—or was it me?

I realized I was smiling to myself. I opened my eyes abruptly; we'd reached Victoria Street and were almost at our destination. The taxi idled in traffic, just outside the vast offices of the Sunrise Corporation. Ads for their latest products—new lavender grenades; slimmer, lighter magnesium flares—gleamed on billboards above the forecourt.

George and Lockwood sat slumped and silent, gazing out into the day.

I sat up straight, shifted my rapier to a more comfortable position. "So what does Barnes want, Lockwood?" I asked. "Is it Bickerstaff?"

"Yes."

"What have we done wrong *now*?"

He grimaced. "You know Barnes. Does he need a reason?"

The taxi moved on, pulled up outside the shimmering glass facade of Scotland Yard, where DEPRAC had its headquarters. We got out, paid, and trudged inside.

The Department of Psychic Research and Control—or DEPRAC, as it was more conveniently known—existed to monitor the activities of the dozens of agencies now in existence throughout the country. It was also supposed to coordinate the national response to the ongoing epidemic of hauntings, and there apparently existed vast research laboratories in iron bunkers deep below Victoria Street, where DEPRAC scientists wrestled with the conundrums of the Problem. But it was in its incessant attempts to control independent agencies such as ours that the Department most often entered our lives, particularly in the form of its dourly pedantic operational director, Inspector Montagu Barnes.

Barnes instinctively disapproved of Lockwood & Co. He didn't like our methods, he didn't like our manners; he didn't even like the charming clutter of our offices at Portland Row, although he *had* complimented me on the pretty tulips I'd put in the boxes outside the windows this past spring. Any "request" to call in on him at Scotland Yard inevitably led to our standing in front of his desk and being scolded like a row of naughty schoolchildren.

So it was something of a surprise when, instead of being stuck in the usual waiting area, which smelled faintly of ectoplasm wipes, we were taken directly to the main operations room.

It was at its quietest, this hour of the day. The London street map on the wall showed hardly any flashing lights; no one was manning the ranks of telephones. A few neatly dressed men and women sat at a table, sifting through manila folders, collating new incident reports. A bloke with a mop swept up the residue of salt, ash, and iron filings that had been tramped in by DEPRAC agents the night before.

At a meeting table on the far side of the room, a flip chart had been set up. Near this sat Inspector Barnes, staring grimly at a pile of papers.

He wasn't alone. Beside him, as pristine and self-satisfied as ever, sat Quill Kipps and Kat Godwin.

I stiffened. Lockwood made a small noise between his teeth. George groaned audibly. "We've had near-death experiences," he muttered, "we've had domestic fights, we've had a pitiful amount of sleep. But this is going to drive me over the edge. If I leap on the table and start shrieking, don't try to stop me. Just let me howl."

Barnes looked at his watch as we approached. "At last," he said. "Anyone would think you'd had a difficult night. Sit down and pour yourselves some coffee. I see you still can't afford proper uniforms. Is that egg or ectoplasm on your T-shirt, Cubbins? I swear you had that the last time I saw you. Same shirt, same stain."

Kipps smiled; Godwin looked blank. Yet again their outfits were crisp and spotless. You could have eaten your lunch off them, provided their faces didn't spoil your appetite. Yet again I was conscious of my sorry state: my unbrushed hair, still dampish from my shower; my rumpled clothes.

Lockwood smiled around questioningly. "We're happy to wait while you finish your meeting with Kipps, Mr. Barnes. Don't want to butt in."

"If you're firing them, I know of two vacancies," George added. "Toilet attendants needed at Marylebone Station. Could wear those same jackets, and all."

"Mr. Kipps and Ms. Godwin are here at my request," Barnes said. "This is important, and I need more than one set of agents on hand. Now, sit down, and stop glowering at each other. I want your full attention."

We sat. Kipps poured us coffee. Is it possible to pour coffee unctuously? If so, Kipps managed it well.

Barnes said, "I've heard about your efforts at Kensal Green last night. Mr. Paul Saunders of"—he checked his notes, spoke with fastidious distaste—"of Sweet Dreams Excavation has given me a basic summary. I'm going to pass over the fact that you should have contacted us straightaway to dispose of that coffin. In the light of what has happened since, I need all the details you can give me."

"And what *has* happened, Mr. Barnes?" Lockwood asked. "Saunders rang early this morning, but he wasn't in a state to give me details."

Barnes considered us thoughtfully. His face was as lived-in as ever, his pouchy eyes still sharply appraising. As usual, though, it was his impressive mustache that attracted my attention. To me, Barnes's mustache closely resembled some kind of hairily exotic caterpillar, probably from the forests of Sumatra, and certainly previously unknown to science. It had a life of its own, rippling and ruffling in accordance with its owner's mood. Today it seemed fluffed out, bristling with purpose. Barnes said, "Saunders is an idiot, and he *knows* that he's in trouble, which makes him no good for anything. Had him in here an hour ago, blathering and blustering, making every excuse under the sun. The short story is that the iron coffin you found has been ransacked, and the contents stolen."

"Did someone get hurt?" I asked. "I heard that a night-watch kid—"

"First things first," Barnes said. "I need a full account of what happened to you when you opened the coffin. What you saw, what you heard; all the relevant phenomena. Go."

Lockwood gave the story, with George and me pitching in with our impressions too. I noticed that George was hazy about what had happened to him when he and Joplin were in the circle. The way he told it, Bickerstaff's ghost had swept down as soon as they'd approached the coffin. There was nothing about them both standing frozen, helpless, unable to move.

When I mentioned the voice, Lockwood frowned. "You didn't tell me that before."

"Just remembered it now. It was the ghost, I suppose. It badly wanted us to look at something. Said it would bring us *our heart's desire*."

"It was talking to you?"

"I think it was talking to all of us."

Barnes stared at me a moment. "You have impressive Talent, Carlyle. Now, this object that so startled Cubbins—you say it was a mirror or looking glass, with a sort of wooden frame?"

George and I both nodded.

"Is that it?" Quill Kipps asked. "Not much of a description to go on."

"There was no time for a proper look," Lockwood said. "Everything happened very fast, and frankly, it was too dangerous to spend time studying it."

"For once," Barnes said, "I think you acted wisely. So, to sum up—it seems we have had *two* possible Sources in the grave. The body of Dr. Bickerstaff, and the mirror."

"That's right. The apparition must have come from the corpse," Lockwood said, "because our net was still covering the mirror at the time. But from what George experienced, that mirror certainly has some kind of psychic energy of its own."

"Very well, then." From among his papers, Barnes took several glossy black-and-white photographs, which he set facedown in front of him. "I'll now tell you what happened in the early hours of this morning. After you left, this Mr. Saunders had the coffin removed by one of his forklifts; it was taken to the chapel and carried inside. Saunders says they made sure all your silver nets and other seals were kept in place. They put a chain around it, set a night-watch boy to guard the door, and got on with other business."

"Wait a minute," Lockwood said. One of his familiar transformations had come over him. All signs of fatigue had been left in the taxi; now he was alert, interested, radiating concentration. "That chapel is Saunders's office. He and Joplin work in there. Where were they the rest of the night?"

"According to Saunders, he and Mr. Joplin were busy in another sector of the cemetery. Most of the night-watch team was with them, though there were always people coming and going in the camp: fetching equipment, taking breaks, and so on.

"Midway through the night, around two thirty a.m., the guard changed. Saunders supervised it, and took the opportunity to look inside the chapel. Says it was all quiet, the coffin exactly as before. Another lad, name of Terry Morgan, came on watch. Eleven years old, this boy." Barnes glared around at us, and rubbed his mustache with a finger. "Well, dawn came at four thirteen this morning, so that's when the psychic surveys had to stop. Just before four thirty, another kid came to the chapel to take over from Terry Morgan. He found the door hanging open. Just inside was Morgan's body."

My heart gave a jolt. "Not—"

"No, fortunately. Out cold. But he'd been clubbed with something hard. Whoever hit him had then flung open the coffin, thrown all your seals aside, and tipped the contents out onto the floor."

He turned over the top two photographs and spun them along the table. Kipps took one, Lockwood the other. We leaned in to take a look.

The shot had been taken from just inside the chapel door; in the background, I could see one of the desks and a portion of the altar. All across the floor was splashed a mess of agency equipment: our iron chains, our silver net, and several other seals and wards with which we'd secured the coffin. In the center, the iron coffin lay on its side, with the mummified corpse half tumbled out onto the flagstones. Bickerstaff was just as unappetizing as my brief glimpse last night had suggested, a blackened, shrunken thing dressed in a ragged robe and moldy suit. One long, bony arm splayed out at an unnatural angle, as if snapped at the elbow; the other lay palm up, as if reaching for something that had left. Fronds of white hair stretched like the legs of drowned spiders around the naked skull.

"Nasty," George said. "Don't look at that face, Kat."

The blond girl scowled across at us. "I'm used to such things."

"Yes, you work with Kipps here, don't you? I suppose you are."

Kipps was frowning at the picture. "That coffin looks heavy to lift," he said. "Must be more than one thief."

"Excellent point," Barnes said. "And you're right. Terry Morgan woke up in the hospital an hour ago. He's pretty shaken up, but he was able to describe how he was attacked. He heard a noise in the undergrowth beside of the steps. He looked over, saw a man in a dark ski mask fast approaching. Then someone else struck him from behind."

"Poor kid," I said. Kat Godwin, sitting opposite, raised an eyebrow at me. I stared back at her, expressionless. *I* could do the stony-faced look too.

"And so the mirror is gone. . . ." Kipps mused. "They must have done it near dawn, when they thought it was safe to remove the defenses. Still, it was a risky thing to do."

"What's *really* interesting," Barnes said, "is the speed of it. The coffin was opened around midnight. Less than four hours later the thieves were at the door. There wasn't time for word to spread normally. This was a direct order from someone at the scene."

"Or someone who'd recently *left* the scene," Kat Godwin said. She smiled at us.

I glanced at Lockwood. He was staring intently at the photo, as if something in it puzzled him. He hadn't noticed Godwin's jibe. "Who knew about the coffin?" I said.

Barnes shrugged. "The excavators, the sensitives, the night-watch kids . . . and you."

"If you think we did it," I said, "feel free to search the house. Start with George's dirty laundry basket. That's where we always hide the stuff we steal."

The inspector made a dismissive gesture. "I *don't* think you stole it. But I *do* want it found. Mr. Lockwood!"

"He's half asleep," Kipps said.

Lockwood looked up. "What? Sorry." He put the photograph down. "The mirror? Yes, you were saying you want it found. May I ask why?"

"You know why," Barnes said gruffly. "Cubbins only had to glance at the mirror to feel a weird and foul effect. Who knows what it would have done to him? Besides, all psychic artifacts are classified as dangerous materials by the State. Their theft, sale, or dispersal among the population is strictly forbidden. Let me show you something,"

Barnes flicked copies of another black-and-white photograph down the table. This one showed the drab interior of a public hall. The photo had been taken from the back of the room. About ten people sat in wooden pews, facing a raised platform. A policeman stood on the platform, and strips of police tape could be seen stretched across a doorway. Sunlight speared through windows high up by the roof. On the stage was a table, and just visible on this table was an object like a broad glass fruit bowl.

"The Carnaby Street Cult," Barnes said. "Twenty years ago. Obviously before your time, any of you. But *I* was there, a young officer on the case. It was the usual thing. Bunch of people who wanted to 'communicate' with the dead, learn secrets about the afterlife. Only they didn't just *talk* about it; they went about buying objects from the relic-men in the hope they might meet a Visitor one day. See that bowl there? In it they put their precious relics: bones found buried in the yard of Marshalsea Prison, with the iron cuffs still on 'em. Well, often enough the relic-men sold them any old junk, but *this* was the real deal. A Visitor came. And you can see the kind of message that *it* brought them."

We stared at the photo, at the slumped heads of the congregation in the pews. "Hold on," Kat Godwin said. "So those people . . . they're all . . ."

"Dead as doornails, every man jack of them," Barnes said heartily. "Thirteen, all told. I can give you dozens of other instances, could show you the pictures, too, but I daresay it would put you off your breakfast." He sat forward, began prodding the desk with a hairy finger. "The message is this: powerful artifacts are deadly in the wrong hands! They're like bombs waiting to go 6ff. This mirror, or whatever it might be, is no exception. DEPRAC is highly concerned, and we want it found. I've been instructed to give it full priority."

Lockwood pushed his chair back. "Well, good luck to you. If we can be of any further assistance, just let us know."

"Much against my better judgment," Barnes said, "you can. I'm short-staffed this morning. There's a serious outbreak in Ilford, which many DEPRAC teams are working on. Since you're already involved with this case, and since it could be argued that it's *your fault* the thing wasn't handed to us last night, I want you to pursue it. You'll be properly paid."

"You're hiring *us*?" George blinked at the inspector. "Just how desperate can you be?"

The mustache drooped ruefully. "Fortunately, the Fittes Agency has offered Kipps and his team as well. They're also on the case. I want you all to work together."

We stared in dismay across the table. Kipps and Godwin gazed coolly back.

I cleared my throat. "But, Mr. Barnes, it's a big city. There are *so* many agents to choose from. Are you *sure* you need to use them?"

"Pick a madman off the street," George protested. "Go to a rest home and choose a random senior citizen. *Anyone* would be better than Kipps."

Barnes gave us all a baleful glare. "Locate the missing relic. Find out who's stolen it and why. Do it as quickly as possible, before someone else gets hurt. And if you want to keep my good opinion"—the mustache jutted forward; teeth appeared briefly beneath it—"you'll all work well together, without sarcasm, insults or, above all, swordplay. Do you understand?"

Kipps nodded smoothly. "Yes, sir. Of course, sir."

"Mr. Lockwood?"

"Certainly, Inspector. That won't be a problem."

"Here's the way it is," Lockwood said, as we all left the room together. "You keep out of our way, and we'll keep out of yours. No espionage or funny business on either side. But now we come to the little matter of our contest. This is our opportunity to go head-to-head, as we agreed. Are you still up for it, or do you want to back out now?"

Kipps let out a short, barking laugh. "Back out? Not likely! Our agreement is in force as of today. First side to track down the mirror and bring it to Barnes wins the bet. The loser takes out the ad in the paper and eats very public humble pie. Agreed?"

Lockwood had his hands in his pockets; he looked casually around at George and me. "Are you both happy?"

We nodded.

"Then the contest's on as far as we're concerned. Do you want to discuss it with your team?"

"Oh, I'm ready for it," Kat Godwin said.

"What does Bobby Vernon think?" George asked. "I assume he's here." He looked left and right along the empty corridor.

Kipps scowled. "Bobby's not *that* small. We'll fill him in later. But he'll go along with what I say."

"All right, then," Lockwood said. "A race it is. Good luck."

They shook hands. Kipps and Godwin walked away.

"There's a bathroom over there," George said. "You might want to wash that hand."

"No time." Lockwood smiled at us grimly. "We've got a contest to win. Let's go."

Chapter 10

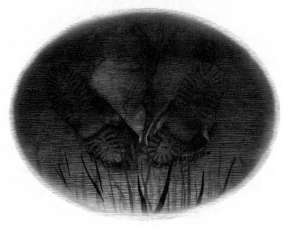

Early afternoon, and the sun was high above the cemetery. Bees buzzed among the crosses, butterflies winked above the mourning angels and ivy-covered urns. It was hot; everything was slow and drowsy. Except for Lockwood—he led us along the gravel path at breakneck speed, talking rapidly all the while.

"The Kipps group will already be there," he said. "We have to ignore them, come what may. Don't rise to any provocation—or give any: especially *you*, George."

"Why especially me?"

"You only have to look at people sometimes to arouse their savage rage. Now listen—we need to work fast. Going back to Portland Row has put us seriously behind."

This, while true, had been unavoidable. We'd all needed to collect our belts and bags, restock our equipment, and eat a proper meal. George had needed to take a shower. These were important considerations.

"Kipps will be doing the obvious thing," Lockwood went on, as the roof of the chapel came into sight between the trees. "He'll be splitting forces to follow two separate lines of inquiry. The first: What *is* the mirror, and what did the mysterious Edmund Bickerstaff use it for? Who *was* Bickerstaff, come to that, beyond all that baloney about sorcery and rats? George, that's your department from now on."

George's glasses sparkled. "I should get over to the Archives straightaway."

"Not yet. I want you to take a look at the scene of the crime with me, and particularly at that coffin. After that you can head off, while Lucy and I pursue the second problem—namely: Who stole the object and where is it now? We'll take a look around, talk to people at the scene. . . ." He broke off, as something occurred to him. "Oh, I've been meaning to ask you. That photo Barnes had. Either of you see anything odd in it?"

We looked at him, shook our heads.

"No? It's just I thought I saw something inside the coffin," he said, "half hidden by the legs of the body. It was very hazy, hard to be sure, but—"

I frowned. "Well, what did you think it was?"

"I don't know. I was probably wrong. Ah, didn't I tell you? Here's Kipps's gang."

We had rounded the chapel and come in sight of the Excavations camp, which was alive with gray-jacketed forms. A host of Fittes agents were at work beside one of the porta-cabins. Some talked to the tattooed workmen who, sitting on folding chairs with plates in their laps, were attempting to finish lunch. Others wandered around taking photographs and staring at footprints in the dirt. A sizeable group had rounded up several small night-watch kids and appeared to be questioning them. One of the agents, a bulky youth with a mop of shaggy hair, was gesticulating fiercely. The children, whom I recognized from the previous evening, looked pale and scared.

"That's Ned Shaw," George murmured. "Recognize him?"

Lockwood nodded. "One of Kipps's enforcers. He's a nasty piece of work. There were accusations that he once beat up a Grimble agent, but nothing was ever proved. Hello, Mr. Saunders, Mr. Joplin! Here we are, then, back again!"

Neither the excavating agent nor the little scholar seemed in very good shape after the events of the night. Saunders was gray-faced and anxious, his chin lined with stubble. He wore the same crumpled clothes as the day before. Joplin was in an even worse state, his eyes red with anger and distress. He scratched worriedly at his hair, blinking at us through his little glasses. His dandruff was more noticeable than ever; it lay on his shoulders like gray snow.

"This is a terrible event!" he wailed. "Unheard of! Who *knows* the value of what's been stolen! It's terrible! Atrocious! Awful!"

"And of course there was that poor night-watch kid getting hurt," I said.

The men ignored me. Saunders was scowling at Joplin. "Hardly *unheard of*, Albert. We've had thefts before. Security on our digs is like a sieve sometimes. What's different now is all the fuss that's being made. DEPRAC getting upset. Agents crawling around like flies."

Joplin sniffed. "I *told* you to place it under proper guard, Paul! Just one child on the door? That was never going to be enough. But no, *you* wouldn't have it! You always overrule me. I wanted to go back to check on him, but you said—"

"Would you mind if we just visit the chapel, gentlemen?" Lockwood was all smiles. "Please don't feel you have to escort us. We know the way."

"Not sure what you'll find that the others didn't," Saunders said sourly. "You do realize it was an inside job? Someone from the night watch tipped off the thieves. Ungrateful little beggars! The amount I pay them!"

Lockwood looked toward the group of night-watch kids, and their interrogation. Even from a distance, Ned Shaw's harassing tones could be heard. "I see they're getting a hard time," he said. "May I ask why?"

Saunders grunted. "No mystery, Mr. Lockwood," he said. "Just look at the layout. Here's the chapel, here's the only entrance up these steps. Right outside we've got the camp. Toward dawn—when the theft took place—most of the night watch were coming back to their cabins. There were always several of them milling about around the fires. It would have been hard for the criminals to slip past without being seen. That's why Kipps believes some or all of the night watch were in on it."

"But why should the thieves go past the cabins?" I said.

"That's the way to the West Gate, girlie, which is the only exit left open at night. All the others are locked, and the boundary wall is far too high to climb over."

Mr. Joplin had seemed distracted until now, biting his lip and staring with hot eyes out across the cemetery, but he suddenly spoke up. "Yes, and if we'd *kept* the gate closed—*as I advised*, Paul— perhaps we wouldn't have had a theft at all!"

"Will you stop going on about it?" Saunders snapped. "It's just a stupid relic!"

George was frowning at the far end of the church where it brushed up against thick bushes. "Kipps's theory makes no sense," he said. "The thieves could have crept around the back of the chapel just as easily as going past the camp, and gotten to the gate that way."

"Not really," Joplin said, "because that was where Saunders and I were working. We were with the night team on that side of the chapel until dawn, assessing another sector. There were dozens of us. It would have been difficult to get by."

"Interesting," Lockwood said. "Well, we'll take a look and see if anything occurs to us. Thank you, gentlemen! Nice to see you!" We walked away. "I hope those two idiots don't follow us," he breathed. "We need some peace and quiet here."

Two strands of black-and-yellow DEPRAC police tape had been stretched across the chapel doors. As we approached, Quill Kipps and his little researcher, Bobby Vernon, emerged from beneath the tape, blinking in the light. Vernon was almost hidden behind a giant clipboard; he wore latex gloves and carried an enormous camera around his neck. As he passed us, he was jotting something carefully onto a notepad strapped to the board.

Kipps nodded to us lazily. "Tony. Cubbins. Julie." They pattered down the stairs.

"Er . . . it's Lucy!" I called after him.

"*Why* did none of us trip him?" George muttered. "It would have been *so* sweet."

Lockwood shook his head. "Be strong, George. Remember—no provocations!"

We stood awhile at the chapel entrance, analyzing the spot where the unfortunate night-watch guard had been attacked. It faced slightly away from the camp, and would have been in darkness. An intruder could certainly have approached sidelong from the bushes, climbed up the steps, and stood there without being seen by anyone below. The lock on the door itself had been broken by something sharp, probably a chisel.

That was all we could make out. We ducked under the tape and out of the day's heat into the cool of the chapel.

Things hadn't changed much since Barnes's photo had been taken. Chains, coffin, and the crumpled corpse of Dr. Bickerstaff: all were as before—except that, rather to my relief, the body had been covered with a piece of dirty burlap.

In the daylight, the iron coffin seemed bigger than I remembered: hefty, thick-walled, and crusted with corrosion. Off to one side, a discarded watch-stick lay amid the scattered salt and iron.

Lockwood bounded over to the chains; he bent low and inspected the flagstones. "The thieves crouched just outside the circle," he said. "You can see the toe prints of their boots here, scuffed into the salt. It was dawn. They were almost safe from Visitors. But they didn't want to bank on it. They'd knocked out the kid and taken his stick. They used that to pry open the lid and pull off the silver net. Then they hung back, waiting to see if anything happened. Nothing did. All was quiet. Now they stepped into the circle and tipped the coffin, so the body tumbled out onto the floor." He narrowed his eyes. "Why do that? Why not just grab the mirror?"

"Maybe they wanted to see if anything else was in there," George said.

"And they didn't want to manhandle Bickerstaff," I added. "*That* part I understand."

"Fair enough," Lockwood said. "So they tipped it over. But *was* there anything else inside . . . ? And is there now?"

He hopped over the body and peered inside the coffin. Taking his rapier from his belt, he poked it into the furthest recesses. Then he straightened.

"Nothing," he said. "Odd. In the photograph, I thought . . ."

"So what *did* you see in the photo?" I asked.

"A bundle of sticks." He brushed his hair irritably back from his face. "I know; doesn't seem likely. Maybe it was a trick of the eyes. Anyway, it's not there now."

For a while we assessed the rest of the chapel. I paid particular attention to the little wooden door behind the altar rail. It had been padlocked and triple-bolted. I pulled at the padlock speculatively.

"Internal door, leading down to the catacombs," I said. "Firmly locked on this side. I did wonder if that was the way the thieves came and went, though I suppose it doesn't square with the night-watch kid's account."

"Looks secure," Lockwood agreed. "Okay, let's go outside."

"So what do you think about Kipps's theory?" George asked, as we set off down the steps. "You think the thieves went past the night-watchers' camp? Think the kids are in on it somehow?"

Lockwood pulled at his long, straight nose. "I very much doubt it. It's far more likely that—" He stopped; we'd heard a cry of pain.

The camp had quietened down since we'd been inside. Saunders, Joplin, and the workmen had gone about their business, and Kipps was nowhere to be seen. Only one final night-watch kid was left, four burly Fittes agents standing over him like a wall. He was just picking up his checked yellow cap from the ground; as he stood up I recognized the surly urchin who'd been stationed at the gate the previous day. The kid put his cap back on. At once the biggest agent, Ned Shaw, leaned over and casually slapped the side of his head. The cap fell off again; the boy stumbled and almost fell.

Six quick strides—and Lockwood was at the scene. He tapped Shaw on his shoulder. "Stop doing that, please. You're twice his size."

Shaw turned around. He was about fifteen, as tall as Lockwood, and hefty with it. He had a bland, strong-jawed face, not unhandsome, except for eyes slightly too narrowly set. Like all the Fittes crowd, his outfit was pristine, but the effect was undermined by his brown shock of hair. It looked like a baby yak had fallen on him from on high.

Shaw blinked; there was uncertainty in his face. "Shove off, Lockwood. This has nothing to do with you."

"I understand your eagerness to clout this kid," Lockwood said. "I've itched to do the same myself. But it's not right. You want to push people around, pick someone taller."

Shaw's lip curled like someone was winding it around a pencil. "I'll push anyone I like."

"Little kids? That makes you a coward."

Shaw smiled briefly; he looked out into the haze of the cemetery. He seemed to be thinking of something peaceful and far away. Then he turned and punched Lockwood hard in the side of the face—or tried to, because Lockwood swayed back and dodged the blow. Shaw's momentum carried him forward; Lockwood took hold of his flailing arm and twisted it sharply to the side and back. At the same time he stuck his boot behind one of Shaw's ankles. Shaw cried out, lost his balance, tripped over his own feet and fell, knocking into one of the other agents and sending them both flailing to the ground.

Shaw's face flushed purple; he instantly sought to rise, but he found the point of my rapier gently resting against his chest.

"Our no-provocation rule is surprisingly flexible," George remarked. "Can I give him a kick too?"

Shaw silently regained his feet. Lockwood watched impassively. I lowered my sword arm, but held it ready. None of the other Fittes agents did anything at all.

"We can continue this whenever you like," Lockwood said. "Just name a time."

"Oh, we'll continue it." Ned Shaw nodded. "Don't you worry about that." He glared at Lockwood and then at me, his fingers twitching.

"Come on, Ned," one of his companions said. "This little runt doesn't know anything anyway."

Ned Shaw hesitated; he gave the night-watch boy a narrow, appraising stare. At last he nodded and gave a signal to the others. Without further words they loped away among the gravestones. The kid watched them go, his eyes wet and shining.

"Pay no attention to him," Lockwood said. "They can't really touch you."

The boy drew himself up to his full, not very considerable height. He adjusted his cap with an angry gesture. "I know that. 'Course they can't."

"They're just bullies throwing their weight around. Some agents do that, I'm afraid."

The boy spat into the cemetery grass. "Yeah. Agents. Stuck-up snobs, the lot of them. Who gives a damn about agents? Not me."

There was a silence. "Yes, actually *we're* agents too," I said, "but we're different from Ned Shaw. We don't use his methods. We respect the night-watch. So if we ask you a few questions, it'll be done differently. No slapping about, for one thing."

I smiled winningly at the boy. The boy stared back at me.

"We're not going to thump you, is what I mean."

The boy sniffed. "That's a laugh. I'd like to see you try."

Lockwood's nostrils twitched slightly. "Okay," he said. "Listen, a dangerous artifact was stolen last night. In the wrong hands, it could do terrible things around London."

The kid looked bored; he stared impassively away at a patch of ground.

"The theft happened while your team was on watch. One of your friends was badly injured, wasn't he?"

"Terry Morgan?" The kid rolled his eyes. "That chinwipe? He ain't my friend."

We all stared at him. "Yeah," George breathed. "*That* statement I can believe."

"You were on the West Gate last night," Lockwood went on in a steely voice. "If you saw anything, if you know anything that can help, it would be well worth you telling us. Anything that might give us the clue we need."

The boy shrugged. "Are we finished? Good, 'cuz I'm missing chowtime." He jerked a thumb toward the prefab cabin. "There'll still be sandwiches in there. See you." He began to swagger away.

Lockwood stood back. He looked up and down the cemetery. No one was coming. He grabbed the boy by the scruff of the neck, lifted him squealing above the grass. "As I say," he said, "we're not like that Fittes crowd. We don't go in for slapping people around. We do have other methods, however, that are equally effective. See that chapel? There's an iron coffin in there. It *was* occupied, but now it's empty. Well, it'll be occupied again in a minute if you don't start answering my civil questions."

The kid flicked a tongue over dry lips. "Get lost. You're bluffing."

"You think so? You know little Bill Jones of the Putney night watch?"

"No! I've never seen him!"

"Exactly. *He* crossed us too. Lucy, George, grab a leg—we're taking him inside."

The boy kicked and squeaked, to no avail. We advanced toward the chapel.

"What do you think?" Lockwood said. "Five minutes in the coffin, see if he talks?"

I considered. "Make it ten."

"All right, all right!" The kid was suddenly frantic. "I'll cooperate! Put me down!"

We lowered him to the ground. "*That's* better," Lockwood said. "Well, then?"

The kid paused to adjust his cap, which now half-covered his face. "I still reckon you're bluffing," he panted, "but I'm missing my sandwiches, so . . ." He rolled his shoulders as if to gear up his tongue. "Yeah, I was on the West Gate all last night. I saw nothing. After you left, no one came through at any time."

"You were there until after dawn?"

"Until after the alarm was raised."

"Excellent." From nowhere, Lockwood brought forth a coin and tossed it to the boy. "There's more of that if you can help me. Think you can?"

The kid looked hard at the coin. "Maybe."

"Then keep talking to me now. Come on! We haven't got time to waste!" With a sudden spring, Lockwood darted aside into the shadow of the chapel steps; he plunged into the bushes. "Come on!" he called again. "This way!"

After a moment's hesitation the kid's greed got the better of him. He followed, despite himself. George and I did, too.

Lockwood moved speedily, ducking under branches, dodging gravestones choked with thorns, following a trail that only he could see. He left the chapel behind, broke out onto a path, crossed it, and plunged into another overgrown section of the cemetery. "You've confirmed exactly what I thought!" he called over his shoulder. "The thieves found another way in. They got to and from the chapel by keeping to the unfrequented areas—like *this* part, for instance, which leads right toward the boundary wall."

He gave a flying leap, landed on a box tomb, and clung to the angel atop it as he surveyed the ground beyond. "The undergrowth's too thick *that* way," he mused. "But what about over there . . . ? Aha! Yes . . . I see a route. We'll try it!" Jumping down, he grinned back at the night-watch kid. "Nothing went past you last night," he said. "But what about *other* nights? You keep your eyes open. Seen any strangers? Relic-men?"

The kid had been scampering to keep up, holding his cap to his head, seemingly mesmerized by the speed and decisiveness of Lockwood's movements. His hostility had entirely vanished; he held the coin tightly in his grubby hand. "I seen some," he panted, as we set off again. "There's always a few hanging around the cemeteries."

"Any in particular?"

"Couple. They're well known, always go around together. Saw them a week or two back. Came in during public hours. Workmen had to chase them from the camp."

"Excellent!" Lockwood cried. He was rushing down a grassy aisle between high stones. "Two together? Good. Can you describe them?"

"One, not so much," the kid said. "Plump bloke, blond hair, scritty mustache. Young, wears black. Name of Duane Neddles."

George made a skeptical noise that sounded like gas escaping from a rhino. "*Duane Neddles?* Oh, he sounds *scary.* Sure you're not making this up?"

"And the other?" Lockwood called.

The kid hesitated. "*He's* got a reputation. A killer. They say he bumped off a rival during a job last year. Maybe I shouldn't . . ."

Lockwood stopped short. "It was a team of two last night that bashed your colleague," he said. "Let's say one was Neddles. Who was the other?"

The kid leaned close, spoke softly. "They call him Jack Carver."

A group of crows rose squalling from the gravestones. Wings cracking, they circled against the sky and flew off over the trees.

Lockwood nodded. He reached inside his coat, brought out a bill and handed it to the disbelieving kid. "I'll make it worth your while every time you give me decent information. If we find Neddles and Carver, I'll give you twice that. Understand me? Now, I want Carver's description."

"Carver?" The boy scratched his chin. "Young man, in his twenties, as tall as you, a little broader in the shoulders, heavier around the belly. He's got light-red hair, long and straggly. Pale skin, long nose. Narrow eyes, can't recall the color. Wears black: black jeans, black biker's jacket. Carries a work belt, a bit like yours, and an orange backpack. Oh yeah, and black lace-up boots, like the ones the skinheads wear."

"Thanks," Lockwood said. "I think we're going to get along well." He set off up the path again. Ahead of us loomed the boundary wall, hidden behind a row of spreading linden trees.

The kid trotted along beside us, busily stuffing the money into some sweatily remote portion of his clothes. George shook his head. "Duane Neddles . . . Jack Carver . . . If you're keen on giving money away so easily, Lockwood, don't give it to random kids. *I* can make up silly names too."

But Lockwood had halted so abruptly we almost bumped into him. "Look!" he cried. "I knew it! We're on the right track!" He pointed ahead of us. There, lying in shadow beside a tree, was something I had only previously seen for a split second, held in a corpse's fist. A ragged white cloth, lying crumpled in the grass.

We clustered close, but of course the mirror it had contained was gone.

"I don't get it," I said. "Why ditch it here?"

"It's a stinking bit of corpse-rag," Lockwood said. "*I* wouldn't hold on to it for long. And it was dawn by that time. Psychic objects lose their power when the sun is up. They knew it'd be safe to touch the mirror then. Maybe they transferred it to a backpack, in preparation for their climb. . . ."

He pointed to the dappled canopy above. Looking up, we saw the spreading branches of the linden, saw the silhouette of the longest branch jutting out against the brightness of the sky. Our eyes ran along it until it reached the boundary wall and disappeared beyond. The rope tied to it could just be seen dangling on the other side.

"That's the Regent's Canal over there," Lockwood said. "They shinned down, landed on the towpath. Then they were away."

George had been staring off among the gravestones. "Nice one, Lockwood. That's great detective work. But you haven't got everything right."

Lockwood looked slightly put out. "Oh, really? In what way?"

"They didn't both climb the tree."

"How d'you know that?"

"One of them's still here."

We looked at him. George stepped aside. Beyond, wedged between two gravestones, was a body, lying on its back. It was a young man, dressed in black: black jeans, boots, a hooded top. A plump young man with an atrocious peach fuzz mustache and pale, acned skin. He was very dead. The early stages of rigor mortis had set in, and his hands were raised up in front of his throat, fingers frozen in an awful defensive clawing pose. That wasn't the worst of it. His eyes were wide open, his face twisted into a paroxysm of such horror that even Lockwood went white, and I had to look away.

The night-watch kid made a choking noise.

"Maybe I owe you an apology, kid," George said. "From your description, this might be Duane Neddles."

"Was it ghost-touch?" I said. "Can't be! It was after dawn!"

"It's not ghost-touch, because he's not swollen or discolored. But *something* killed him, very fast and very horribly."

I thought of the so-called mirror, of its little circle of dark glass. I thought of the way George had looked into it and felt as if his insides were being pulled out. "How, then?" I whispered.

George's voice was surprisingly level, matter-of-fact. "From the way he looks, Luce, I'd have to say he died of fright."

Chapter 11

Fifty years of the Problem have led to many changes in our society, and not all of them are what you'd expect. When the great Tom Rotwell and Marissa Fittes went public with their discoveries, all that time ago, the general reaction was shock and panic. Their first publication, *What Binds the Departed to Us?*, proposed that certain objects, connected to violent deaths or other traumas, might become "psychically charged," and so act as a "source" or "gateway" for supernatural activity. Human remains, precious belongings, or indeed *any* potential object of desire might fall into this category, as might the exact location of a murder or accident. The idea caused a sensation. A public frenzy took over. For a while any object even dimly supposed to have some kind of psychic residue was treated with terror and disgust. Items of old furniture were burned and random antiques smashed or thrown into the Thames. A priceless painting in the National Portrait Gallery was hurled to the floor and trampled on by a vicar, "because it looked at me in a funny way." Anything with a strong connection to the past was considered suspect, and a cult of modern objects grew up, which remains with us even now. The notion that anyone might be *interested* in Sources for their own sake was laughable; they were perilous and needed to be destroyed. It was left to the agencies to deal with them.

Before long, however, it turned out that forbidden things *were* of interest after all, to several different kinds of customer. And where there are customers, people will be found to supply them. A black market in psychic artifacts soon began, with a new category of criminal operating at its heart: the so-called *relic-men*.

During my apprenticeship with Jacobs in the north of England, I was taught that the wicked relic-man was in every respect the moral opposite of what an agent stood for. Both hunted out Sources: the relic-man driven by a desire for profit, the agent driven by a desire for public good. Both had psychic Talent; but while an agent used his to protect society from Visitors, the relic-man gave this no thought at all. An agent disposed of dangerous artifacts carefully—first encasing them in silver or iron, then taking them to the Fittes furnaces in Clerkenwell to be burned. A relic-man, by contrast, sold his prizes to the highest bidder. Rumors abounded of sinister collectors, of wild-eyed cultists and worse, who squirreled away deadly Sources for purposes that ordinary citizens would fear to fathom. Relic-men were thieves, in short—society's bottom-feeders, who skulked in graveyards and charnel houses, looking for unwholesome scraps to trade. Unsurprisingly, they quite often came to bad ends.

Few ends, at least if his expression was anything to go by, were quite as bad as that which had befallen the unfortunate Duane Neddles, and our discovery of his body caused a great stir at Kensal Green. Before the hour was out, Inspector Barnes arrived; soon the place was crawling with DEPRAC forensic scientists, with Kipps and his associates hovering on the sidelines. Kipps, inevitably, reacted to our find with agitation and, being desperate not to miss any clues we might have found, kept getting in the way of the forensic team until Barnes bluntly told him to get lost. In truth, though, there was little more to be learned. A search of the canal bank beyond the wall revealed no sign of Neddles's associate or the missing mirror, and the exact cause of the relic-man's death remained a mystery.

What with all the commotion, it was late afternoon before we could disperse on our different missions. Lockwood and I took a taxi south toward the city. George, crackling with suppressed excitement, set off for the dusty Archives. The night-watch kid (who now seemed to think of himself as an honorary agent, strutting around with an air of great importance, cap set at a rakish angle) was packed off to resume his duties, with strict instructions to call on us at Portland Row if he saw or heard anything further of interest. Whether it was Lockwood's energy and charisma, or (more likely) the money in his pocket, the kid readily agreed. We still didn't know his name.

"So," I said to Lockwood five minutes later, as the taxi moved steadily down Edgware Road, "aren't you going to tell me where we're going?"

The shadows in the street were thin and bathed in gold. The shops had begun their last great flurry of activity before the long, slow, sensual onset of dusk. We agents call this the *borrowed time*:

extra hours of sunlight you only get in midsummer. During these hours, many people seem filled with a strange and feverish energy, a kind of defiance against the looming dark. They do a lot of eating, drinking, and spending; the shops were bright and cheery, the sidewalks thronged. The ghost-lamps were just coming on.

Lockwood's face was lit by traces of the dying sun. He'd been unaccountably silent, deep in thought, but when he turned to me his eyes sparkled with the thrill of the chase. As always, that awoke a similar thrill in me.

"We're going to see a contact of mine," he said. "Someone who might help us find our missing man."

"Who is he? A policeman? Another agent?"

"No. A relic-man. Well, a relic-*woman*, really. Her name's Flo Bones."

I stared at him; my thrill diminished. "A relic-woman?"

"Yes. Just a girl I know. We'll find her down by the river somewhere, once it's dark."

He looked blandly out of the window again, as if he'd suggested a shopping trip or something equally mundane. And again I had that tipping sensation, the slosh of blood inside the head, like I'd had when the skull was whispering to me. It was the feeling of parameters shifting, old certainties becoming misaligned. *Secretive, deceitful*—that's what the skull had said. Obviously I didn't believe that for a moment. Still, I'd lived with Lockwood a full year, and this was the first time I'd heard of Flo Bones.

"This relic-girl," I said. "How did you meet? I've never heard you talk of her before."

"Flo? I met her a long time ago. When I was just starting out."

"But relic-men are . . . well, they operate outside the law, don't they? It's illegal for any agent to fraternize with them."

"Since when have you become a stickler for DEPRAC's rules, Luce? Anyway, we need all the help we can get on this one. We're in a race against time with Kipps. Plus this job is more dangerous and puzzling than I thought."

"You mean the mirror, of course." I could still picture the body in the graveyard: the popping eyes, the mouth drawn back into a slash of horror.

"The mirror, yes; but there's more to it than that. Barnes isn't telling us everything. This isn't any old Source, which is why George's job is so crucial now." Lockwood stretched languidly. "Anyway, Flo's all right. She's not quite as antisocial as the other relic-men. She'll talk to you, though she *is* cranky. You just need to know the right way. . . . Which reminds me—" Lockwood swiveled suddenly in his seat, lifted the swinging lavender crucifix, and spoke through the hatch. "If we could stop by Blackfriars Station, driver. You know that little newsagent there? Yes." He turned to me and grinned. "We need to get some licorice."

Between Blackfriars and Southwark bridges, which connect the City of London to the ancient borough of Southwark, the River Thames turns gradually southeast. Here the current slows slightly, and at low tide a broad expanse of mudflats is exposed beneath the south side of Southwark Bridge, where sediment dropped by the river has built up around the curve. Lockwood pointed this out to me as we walked across the bridge in the glare of the dying sun.

"She'll be down there, most likely," he said. "Unless she's changed her habits, which is about as probable as her changing her underwear. She starts the night at the Southwark Reaches, where stuff's washed up by the tide. Later, she'll move downstream, following the tide line."

"What's she looking for?" I asked, though I guessed already.

"You name it. Bones, relics, drowned things, things scoured up from the river mud."

"She sounds delightful," I said. "Can't wait to meet her." I adjusted the rapier at my belt.

"Don't try any heavy stuff on Flo," Lockwood warned. "In fact, the best thing is to leave the talking to me. We can go down here."

We ducked through a gap in the parapet, and descended some stone steps that hugged the brickwork of the bridge. Its arch soared over us; there was a powerful smell of mud and decay. We alighted on a cobbled lane that ran along the embankment and walked down it a little way. A rusted streetlight clung like a dead tree to the low wall overlooking the river. Behind us were warehouses, dark and clifflike. A faint apricot-pink sphere of light gleamed about the lamp, illuminating nothing except a narrow flight of steps leading below the wall.

Above and all around were space and river mist, and the flowing onset of the night. Lockwood said, "We move carefully now. Don't want to scare her off."

The steps led steeply down toward the river. From the wall we could see the northern bank—a broken snake of lights, with London's great gray mess of spires behind. The tide was fully out; the river's sullen glister hung low and far away.

It was very quiet everywhere.

Lockwood nudged me, pointed. A lantern was moving out on the mudflats, an orange light, held close to the ground. Its reflection, flitting just beneath it, faint as a Shade, swooped wet and pale across the shingle, lighting the stones and weeds and all the river's washed-up flotsam—the wood and plastics, fragments of metal, bottles, drowned and rotting things. A stooped, slow figure walked above the lantern light, cocooning it, as if to shroud it jealously from all sight. It moved with methodical purpose, stopping now and then to pick at something in the debris. A heavy sack, which it dragged behind it, carved an intermittent furrow in the slime. Whether it was the trail it left, or its hunched and rounded shape, this creature seemed more like a giant snail from the bottom of the Thames than a fellow human being.

"You want to talk to *that*?" I whispered.

Lockwood made no answer, but pattered down the river stairs. I followed. Halfway down, the steps became soft and wet with moss. Lockwood reached the last step, but went no farther. He raised a hand and called out over the dark expanse. "Hey, Flo!"

Away across the mud the figure froze. I sensed, rather than saw, the pale face staring at us from afar.

Lockwood raised his voice again. "Flo!"

"What if it is? I haven't done nothing."

The reply, rather high and cracked, didn't carry well; it would have been natural to move closer, but Lockwood was cautious. He remained standing on the bottom step.

"Hey, Flo! It's Lockwood!"

Silence. The figure straightened abruptly; I thought for a

moment it was going to turn and run. But then the voice came again, faint, hostile, and guarded. "You? What the bloody hell do *you* want?"

"Oh, that's fine," Lockwood murmured. "She's in a good mood." He cleared his throat, called out again. "Can you talk?"

The distant person considered; for a few seconds we heard nothing except the sloop and slosh of the river along the shore. "No. I'm busy! Go away."

"I've brought licorice!"

"What, you're trying to bribe me now? Bring money!" More silence; just the sucking of the water. Away in the haze a head was cocked to one side. "What *kind* of licorice?"

"Come and see!"

I watched as the figure began to plow its way rapidly toward us through the mire. It was a limping witch, a night hag from a child's fever dreams. My heart beat fast. "Um . . . what would have happened," I said, "if she *wasn't* in a good mood?"

"Best not to ask," Lockwood said. "I saw her chuck an agent into the river once," he went on reflectively. "Just lifted her up by the leg and tossed her in. Flo was in a good mood *that* day too, as it happens. But she'll like *you*, I'm almost sure. Just don't say much, and stay out of stabbing distance. I'll handle it from here."

The shambling creature drew close, dragging the sack, bearing the light before it. I glimpsed a pale and filthy hand, the crown of a tattered straw hat. Great boots sucked and slurped in the mud and shingle. Lockwood and I instinctively moved up a step. A sudden groan, a curse; the sack was swung up and over to land on the stone below. At last the figure straightened; she stood in the mud beneath the steps and stared up at us. In the light of the lantern I got a proper look at her for the first time.

The first shock, now that she'd rid herself of her burden, was that she was tall—half a head taller than me. It was hard to tell more about her shape (this was fine by me; no sane person would have wanted to look beneath her clothes). She wore an unutterably foul blue puffer jacket that went down almost to her knees; the lower reaches were dark with moisture, caked with river mud. The zipper was open, providing glimpses of a pale expanse of dirty neck, a grimy shirt collar, a patched and shapeless jersey hanging down over ancient and faded jeans. She either had the biggest feet of any female I'd ever met, or was wearing a men's pair of rain boots, or both. The boots, which reached her knees, were splayed outward like a duck's, and were ripple-stained by muck and water.

A length of rope, tied twice around her waist, served as a makeshift belt. Something hung there in the recesses of the coat. I thought it might have been a sword, which is illegal for a nonagent to wear.

From her hobbling approach and shapeless outline, she might have been very elderly, so the second shock came when she pushed back the broad-brimmed hat. From under it a spray of hair, the color and stiffness of old straw, radiated outward from a wide and grubby forehead. Dirt had collected in the creases running across it, and in the lines beside the eyes; in this she was no different from any vagrant lining up for safe quarters overnight. But she was young—still in her teens. She had a small, up-tilted nose, a wide face, pinkish cheeks smeared with gray, and bright blue eyes that sparkled in the lantern light. Her mouth was broad and contemptuous, her head jutting forward aggressively. She took me in with a single glance, then focused her attention on Lockwood. "Well, *you* haven't changed," she said. "Still as la-di-da as ever, I see."

Lockwood grinned. "Hello, Flo. Well, you know me."

"Yeah. See you still can't afford a suit that fits. Don't bend over quick wearing *those* trousers, that's my advice. I thought I said I never wanted to see you again."

"Did you? I don't remember. Did I say I'd brought licorice whirls?"

"Like *that* changes anything. Give them here." A paper bag was produced and delivered to a clawlike hand, which stowed it in some unmentionable recess beneath the coat. The girl sniffed. "So who's this trollop?"

"This is Lucy Carlyle, my associate," Lockwood said. "I should say at once that she has no connection with DEPRAC or the police, or the Rotwell Agency. She's an independent operative, working with me, and I trust her with my life. Lucy, this is Flo."

"Hello, Flo," I said.

"Florence Bonnard to you, I'm sure," the girl said in a hoity-toity voice. "See you've got another posh 'un here, Lockwood."

I blinked indignantly. "Excuse me, I'm working-class northern. And when you say *another*—"

"Listen, Flo, I know you're busy. . . ." It was Lockwood's emollient voice, the one he used in tough corners—with irritable clients and with angry creditors who came knocking on our door. The full gigawatt smile would be coming next, sure as day. "I don't want to bother you," he said, "but I need your assistance. Just a little bit of information, then I'll be gone. A crime's been committed, a kid's been hurt. We've got a lead on the relic-man who did it, but we don't know where to find him. And we were wondering if you could help."

The blue gaze narrowed; the creases around the eyes disappeared into the dirt. "Don't flash that smile at me. This relic-man. He got a name?"

"Jack Carver."

A cold breeze blew across the river, rippling the matted stalks of Flo Bones's hair. "Sorry. There's a code of silence among our kind. We can't rat on each other. That's just the way it is."

"First I've heard of it," Lockwood said. "I thought you were famous for your cutthroat rivalry, and happy to sell each other's grandmother for sixpence."

The girl shrugged. "The two things ain't mutually exclusive, if you want to stay healthy." She grabbed the neck of her canvas bag. "And I don't want to be washed up by the dawn tide, so that's the end of it. Good-bye."

"Flo, I gave you licorice whirls."

"It's not enough."

"No good, Lockwood," I said. "She's scared. Come on."

I touched his arm, made as if to climb the steps. The girl's face was a sudden white oval staring up at me. "What did you say?"

"Lucy, it's probably not wise—"

But I'd had enough of keeping quiet. Flo Bones annoyed me, and I was going to let her know it. Sometimes politeness only gets you so far. "It's all right," I said. "She can go back to scrabbling gently in the mud, while we get on with hunting the guy who bashed a kid and robbed a grave, and now has a vicious artifact that probably threatens London. Each to their own. Come on."

A hop, a skip; a stench that made my toenails curl. A puffer jacket crackling against my coat, a jutting face pressed into mine. I was thrust back against the stonework of the steps. "I don't like what you're saying," Flo Bones said.

"It's okay," I said sweetly. "I'm not blaming you. People have to know their limitations. Most avoid danger, no matter what. It's just the way things are. Now, I don't want you to scuff your coat. . . ."

"You think I avoid danger? You think there's no danger in what I do?" A series of emotions probably passed across the girl's face at this point—anger, outrage, followed by a long, slow dawn of cunning realization—but what with all the darkness and the dirt, and her sheer stomach-turning proximity, it was impossible to be sure. "Tell you what," she said, and suddenly she was away from me and dancing down the steps again, light-footed and nimble beneath her cumbersome boots and coat. "Tell you what, I'll make you a deal. You do something for me, *I'll* do something for you." With a crunch, she landed back on the shingle and took up the lantern. "Come out onto the reaches with me, unless you're 'fraid of getting your feet wet. Afterward I'll tell you all about him."

"You know Jack Carver, then?" Lockwood said. "You'll tell us what you know?"

"Yes." Her eyes glittered; her mouth grinned broadly. "First, just a little gentle scrabbling in the mud. Something you can help me with, what I ain't been able to do."

Lockwood and I glanced at each other. Speaking personally, the girl's insane grin didn't inspire enormous confidence. But we didn't

have much choice, if this line of inquiry was to proceed. We jumped
down onto the sand.

Twenty minutes later my boots were sopping, my leggings soaked
as high as my calves. Three times I'd stumbled, and the side of one
arm was caked in mud and sand. Lockwood was in a similar state,
but he bore it without complaint. We followed Flo Bones's lantern
as it leaped and swung ahead of us like a will-o'-the-wisp, darting
from side to side as she picked her way across the mire. Under the
sodden blackness beneath the bridge we went, and out onto the
Southwark Reaches, with the tide wall of the embankment curling
steadily away from us to the right. River mists had risen. On the
opposite bank, the wharves rose from the water like rotting black
cliffs, soft and formless. Faint red and orange lights pulsed on the
tips of the crane masts and the jib ends.

"Here we are," Flo Bones said.

She raised the lantern. Two rows of great black wooden posts
emerged from the muck, twelve feet tall or more, tracing the line of
a long-lost wharf or pier. Their sides were thick with weeds, mostly
black, in places faintly luminous; barnacles and shells clung to them
too, rising above our heads to the high-tide line. In places, rotten
spars still spanned the posts. To our left the farthest posts rose from
the water, but where we stood, the muck was soft and granular with
millions of tiny stones.

Flo Bones seemed energized; she tossed her sack aside and
bounded up to us. "Here," she said again. "There's something here
I want, only I've never been able to get it."

Lockwood took his flashlight out and shone it around. "Show us where. If it's heavy, I've got rope in my pack."

Flo chuckled. "Oh, it's not *heavy*. I'm sure it's very small. No, right now you've got to wait. Stand tight. We won't be long."

With this, she skipped away toward the nearest post, rounded it, and zigzagged to another, chuckling throatily the while.

I leaned in close to Lockwood. "You realize," I whispered, "that she's *completely* mad."

"She's certainly a bit odd."

"And *so* disgusting. Gaaah! Have you gotten *close* to her? That smell . . ."

"I know," Lockwood said mildly. "It's a little intense."

"Intense? I can feel my nose hairs shriveling. And if—" I stopped, suddenly alert.

"What is it, Lucy?"

"Do you feel that?" I said. "Something's starting." I pulled up my sleeve; my skin was peppered with goose bumps. My heart had given a double beat; the back of my neck was tingling. As an agent, you learn to listen to these signs: early warnings of a manifestation. "Creeping fear," I said, "and chill. Also"—I wrinkled my nose—"you smell that? There's a miasma building."

Lockwood sniffed. "To be frank, I thought that was Flo."

"No. It's Visitors. . . ."

As one, we drew our swords, stood watchful and alert. Away among the posts, Flo's bobbing light grew stilled; we heard her fretful crooning. Mists swirled, the new night darkened around us. Ghosts came.

Chapter 12

Lockwood saw the apparition first; he's got better Sight than me.

"Over there," he breathed. "See that post on the other side, the second one along?"

I squinted through the darkness and the swirling river mist. If I stared directly at the spot he indicated, I saw nothing. If I looked slightly away from it, out toward the middle of the river, I could just make out something whitish hanging high in the air beside the post. It was extremely frail; it hung there bothersomely, like a smudge on a lens, a trick of the eyes.

"I see it," I said. "Looks like a Shade to me."

"Agreed." He made a noise of faint perplexity. "It's weird, though. We're right by the Thames. . . . How much running water do you need?"

The Problem, the great mystery, is itself composed of numberless small mysteries, and one of the oddest is the undeniable fact that Visitors, of all types and temperaments, *hate* fresh running water. They can't abide it, even in small amounts, and won't cross its flow. This is a precious fact, which every agent has relied on at one time or another. George claims he once escaped a Specter by turning on a garden hose and standing safe behind its little spurting stream. It's also why so many shops in central London have runnels by them, and why so much trade is done by boat, up and down the Thames.

Yet here was the river, only twenty yards away, and here was the glowing haze.

"Low tide," I said. "The water's drawn back. The Source must be dry."

"Must be." He whistled. "Well, I didn't expect *this*."

"*Flo* did," I said. "She's tricked us. This is some kind of trap."

"'S'not." The voice spoke loudly in my ear. I gave a jump, knocked into Lockwood; swung my rapier around to find Flo Bones leering at my side. She'd lowered the covers on her lantern; her face seemed to float in darkness, a grubby disembodied head. "Trap?" she hissed. "This is your side of the bargain. This is the three of us scrabbling happily in the dirt. What's the matter? You're an agent. You're not afraid."

"Of this? One Shade?"

"Oh, you see just *one* up there, do you?" She pursed up her mouth, all tight and crinkly, then snorted in disapproval. "*Very* good. Well done. Have a cigar and join a proper agency. There are *two*, you daft dollop. There's a little one beside her."

I scowled into the darkness. "Don't see it. You're making it up."

"No, she's right. . . ." Lockwood had his hand cupped over his eyes; he was clearly concentrating hard. "Faint and formless, like a cloud. The tall one's a woman, wearing a hat or shawl . . . a hooped skirt . . . Victorian or Edwardian, maybe."

"That's it: old, *old*," Flo Bones said. "I expect a mother and child what jumped in the Thames together. Suicide and murder, an ancient tragedy. Their bones must be under that wharf, I reckon. And you don't see it?" she said to me. "Well, well."

"Sight's not really my area," I said stiffly.

"Ain't it? Shame." Her head jerked close. "So, enough of this nattering. I want your 'elp now. Here's how it goes. We all of us creep near the post, slowly, quietly, no sudden moves that might make 'em suspect nothing. Then, it's easy. You keep an eye on 'em, making sure they don't get agitated, while I go a-ferreting with my trusty marsh-knife, here." She pushed back the noxious coat, and I saw the blade at her belt for the first time—a short, wickedly curved weapon with an odd double prong at the point, like a giant can-opener or those little wooden forks you get with jellied eels. "Just watch my back," she said. "That's all you have to do. It won't be deep. I won't take long."

I made an exclamation of disgust. "So the idea is: we're to stand guard while you go digging for a dead kid's bones? Which you then hope to sell on the black market?"

Flo nodded. "That's about the size of it, yeah."

"Absolutely no way. Lockwood—"

He grasped my arm, squeezed it. "Come on, Luce. Flo's wise. Flo's clever. She's got information. If we want it, we have to help her. Simple as that." Another sharp squeeze.

A fond, rather fatuous grin had spread over Flo's face. "Ah,

Lockwood, you always *was* sweet-talking. One of your best qualities. Not like this sour mare. So, come on then. Up and at 'em! Let's go for glory and get this done!"

Without further words, Lockwood and I checked our belts. We readied the rapiers in our hands. Shades are *usually* very passive and unresponsive; they're too caught up in the replay or remembrance of the past to pay attention to the living. But it's not something to rely on, and clearly Flo had reason to be cautious here. Slowly, setting our boots down with utmost deliberation on the shingle, we approached the tall black post.

High above us, the white thing hung in the night sky; it might have been a puff of smoke, framed against the stars.

"Why's it up *there*?" I whispered. Flo was just ahead, humming jauntily to herself.

"It's the old level of the wharf. Where she stood before jumping in. Hear anything?"

"Hard to tell. Could be a woman sighing. Could be the wind. What about you?"

"No death-glows. We wouldn't expect to see them, if they died in fresh water. But I *do* feel"—Lockwood breathed deep to steady himself—"a strong weight pressing down on me. You get it? Such grief . . ."

"Yeah, I've got it. Powerful malaise for a Shade."

He stopped short. "Hold on. Did you see it move, Lucy? I thought I saw it quiver there."

"No. No, I missed that. Ugh, *look* at Flo! Where's her self-respect?"

The relic-girl had reached the base of the post; setting the lantern down, she squatted on her haunches, and began scooping up gouts of mud and pebbles with her long curved knife.

Lockwood motioned me back a little way. Keeping his eyes fixed on the shape hanging directly above, he stationed himself behind Flo's crouching form.

Now that we were close, the malaise had intensified. A fearsome melancholy stole over me. I felt my shoulders droop, my knees begin to buckle. Tears pricked at my eyes, a vile hopelessness swirled in my gut. I shook it off—it was a false emotion. I opened a belt pouch and took out some gum, chewing furiously to distract myself. One time, long ago, this had been real, one person's sorrow turned to insanity or despair. Now it was just an echo—a blank and mindless force, expending itself on anyone who came near.

Not that Flo Bones seemed particularly affected. She was digging at a furious rate, casting aside great lumps of slime; periodically she stopped to peer at some foul fragment she'd unearthed, before tossing it away.

A ripple of sound against my eardrums, a quiver in the air. The sighing I could hear grew louder. Up by the post top, the patch of whiteness deepened, as if substance had been drawn into it.

Lockwood had noticed this too. "We've got movement above us, Flo."

The relic-girl's bottom was high; her head practically in the hole. She didn't look up. "Good. Means I'm getting warm."

The pressure in the air grew stronger. All trace of the river breeze was gone. The weight in my heart was painful, wedged there like a stone. Gum snapped in my mouth; I listened to the knife scratching in the foul, wet ground, watched the hanging whiteness. Even from the corner of my eye it stayed stubbornly unformed, though for the first time I thought I saw a smaller discoloration beside it: the faint shape of a child.

A shudder ran through the larger cloud. My eye jerked to it. Lockwood took a slow step farther away.

"Getting warm," Flo said again. "I can feel it."

"It's moving, Flo. We've got signs of agitation. . . ."

"Getting warm . . ."

A screech of sound, a sudden crack of air. I jerked back sharply, swallowing my ball of gum. The white shape dropped straight down beside the post, directly toward Flo's head. Lockwood darted inward, slicing his rapier across its path. The shape jerked up, avoiding the slashing silver-coated blade; I had the briefest sensation of wide, billowing skirts and a coil of smoke-like hair as it somersaulted silently over our heads and came to a halt a few feet from me, hovering just above the ground.

Rage had given the apparition solid form. A tall, thin woman in an old-fashioned dress—tight up top, with a spreading crinoline skirt. She wore a pale bonnet, with long strands of dark hair half obscuring her face, and she had a necklace of spring flowers at her throat. Curls of other-light spun about her like river weeds flexing in a current. At her side a tiny figure huddled close against her skirts. They were holding hands.

I stepped back, dry-throated, trying to recall the stance I'd used with Esmeralda in the rapier room. This wasn't a Shade, but a Cold Maiden—a female ghost that persists because of ancient loss.

Most Cold Maidens are melancholy, passive things that don't put up much of a fight when you're hunting for their Source. But not this one.

With a rush, she swept toward me. Her hair blew back; her face was a bone-white horror, a frozen, black-eyed mask of scowling madness. I whirled the sword in a desperate defense. For a moment I seemed surrounded by palely clawing hands; a shrieking beat upon my ears. But the ward-knot held firm; the rapier's blade protected me. And all at once the air was clear, and far across the mud two faint, translucent shapes were streaming away—a tiny child, a weeping woman in a trailing dress.

"Back to the post, Lucy," Lockwood called. "You take one side; I take the other. Flo! Talk to us! How's it going down there?"

"And if you say *getting warm* again," I snarled, as I drew close, "I'll bury you in the hole myself."

"Warm*er*," Flo said promptly. "Warm*ish*. You might say, almost hot. I got a few little pieces up for consideration here. Which, though? What's the Source?"

I looked out across the Southwark Reaches, where the Visitors sped, lit by their own faint glow. Now, without breaking pace, they arced around, came racing back.

"Whichever it is, they *really* don't want you to take it," I said. "Please hurry up, Flo."

Flo squatted by the hole, cupping a set of tiny objects in her hands. "Is it these bones? If so, this one or that? Or not the bones at all? This little thing, this funny metal horse?"

"Tell you what," Lockwood said. "How about you take them

all?" The glowing shapes were getting nearer, nearer, flying above the stones.

"I don't want to take *any* old rubbish," Flo Bones said, in an aggrieved voice. "I've got standards. My customers have expectations."

The shapes were tilted forward in their hate and fury. Again I saw the woman's face—the thin, dark mouth, the gaping eyes.

"*Flo* . . ."

"Oh, *very* well."

She took up the sack, tore it open, and a sweet and cleansing scent burst forth. Flo shoved the fragments inside. At once the glowing forms blinked out; a rush of wind burst harmlessly against us. The corners of Lockwood's coat flicked back, and softly subsided. The night was dark. When I looked up at the top of the post, I saw nothing but stars.

Flo pulled the strings tight. I sank down on the sand, and rested my sword across my knee.

"In the bag," Lockwood said. He was leaning against the post. "Is it—?"

"Lavender. Yeah. Stuffed with it. Stronger than silver, lavender is, while the fragrance lasts. It'll keep *them* quiet for a bit." She grinned at me. "Anything happen just now? I was busy, couldn't take a look-see."

"You *knew* they would attack," I said. "Didn't you? You'd had a go at this before."

Flo Bones took off her hat and scratched at her matted blond scalp. "Seems you're not as dumb as you look. . . . Well," she said. "I guess that's that."

"Not quite," Lockwood said grimly. "That's *our* side of the bargain. Now we get to *yours*."

Few London eating establishments are open during the night, and fewest of all in the dark hours before the dawn. Still, certain places *do* exist for agents or night-watch kids to break their fast, and it seemed relic-men had their favored venues too. The Hare and Horsewhip— an inn situated in the dingiest back alley in Southwark—was Flo's first choice, and we proceeded there at speed.

We soon discovered, however, that it was not a place for us that night. Three silver-gray vans, painted with the rearing unicorn, had parked at dramatic angles outside the inn. A score of adult Fittes agents, accompanied by armed police and DEPRAC dog-handlers, were bundling people out of the pub and into the vans. Scuffles had broken out. Some men tried to flee; they were pursued by dogs, seized, and dragged to the ground. From where we skulked at the far end of the street, we could just make out Kipps, Ned Shaw, and Kat Godwin standing aloof beside the door.

Lockwood drew us back into the dark. "They're rounding up the relic-men," he murmured. "Kipps is spreading his net wide."

"Think he knows about Jack Carver?" I said. "The kid wouldn't have told him, surely."

"Someone else might know the connection between Carver and Neddles. . . . Well, we can't do much about it. Anywhere else we can go, Flo?"

The relic-girl had been unusually silent. "Yeah," she said softly. "Not far."

Her second choice turned out to be a café close to Limehouse

Station, a small-hours joint catering mainly to off-shift night-watch kids. The doors and windows were laced with iron grilles, and over-hung by battered ghost-lamps. Inside, a row of plastic tubs displayed the sweets and toffees favored by the youngest clients. A corkboard near the door was pinned with ads, job offers, Lost and Found notices, and other scraps of paper. A few stained magazines and comic books were scattered on the Formica tabletops; five gray-faced children sat at separate tables, eating, drinking, staring into space. Their watch-sticks waited in the weapon racks beside the door.

Lockwood and I ordered scrambled eggs, kippers, and tea. Flo wanted coffee and jam on toast. We found a table in the corner and got down to business.

Under the café's strong light, Flo looked even grubbier. She accepted her coffee, black, and proceeded to fill it, slowly, methodi-cally, with eight teaspoons of sugar.

"So, Flo," Lockwood said, as the goo was stirred, "Jack Carver. Tell us all."

She nodded, sniffed, took the mug in dirty fingers. "Yes, I know Carver."

"Excellent. So you know where he lives?"

She shook her head shortly. "No."

"Where he hangs out?"

"No."

"The people he associates with?"

"No. Aside from Duane Neddles, and you say he's dead."

"His hobbies, the kinds of thing he does in his spare time?"

"No."

"But you do know where we might find him?"

Her eyes brightened. She took a sip of coffee, frowned, and tipped another spoon-load of sugar into the black syrup. A frenzy of stirring followed while we watched and waited; at last the ritual was complete. Finally, she regarded us both levelly. "No."

I made a movement in the direction of my rapier. Lockwood adjusted a napkin on the table. "Right," he said. "So when you claim to *know* Carver, you mean this in quite a generalized, limited, and in fact completely useless way?"

Flo Bones raised her cup, drank the mixture in a gulp. "I know the nature of his reputation, I know what he does with the artifacts he steals, and I know how a message could be got to him, all of which might be of some interest to you."

Lockwood sat back, hands flat on the table. "Ah, yes. They would, if true. But how could you get a message to him when you don't know him from Adam?"

"Don't tell me," I said. "You'd put it in a moldy skull and leave it at midnight in an open grave."

"Nope, I'd pin a notice over there." She pointed at the corkboard beside the door. "That's how people of my profession keep in touch. It's not done often, mind, we as a rule being solitary types. But there's several boards that serve a certain function." She wiped her nose on her fingers, and her fingers on her coat. "The Hare and Horsewhip has one, but we can't use that."

I frowned, but Lockwood seemed to think it plausible enough. "Interesting. I might just do that. How would I address it?"

"Mark it for the attention of the Graveyard Fellowship. That's relic-men, to you and me. Carver might not see it himself, but someone else might, and pass word on."

"This is no good to us," I snapped. "We need something concrete. What does Carver do with his relics when he's stolen them?"

"He takes 'em to Winkman. Can I have another coffee?"

"No, you bloody can't. Not until you've given us the details. Then, all the coffee you want."

"Or we can just pour you a bowl of sugar and you can drizzle a teaspoonful of coffee on top," Lockwood said. "Might be simpler that way."

"Hilarious," Flo said, unsmilingly. "You always was a regular comedian. All right, I'll tell you about Carver. There's two types of relic-collector. Those such as *moi*, who make our way quietly in the world, looking for forgotten things of psychic significance. We don't give no trouble, and we don't look for it neither. Then there's the others. They're too impatient to mess about with shore combing. They like things that give quick profit, notwithstanding they might be another's property. So these boys haunt the cemeteries, stealing what they can; and they aren't above robbing the *living*, too, even if it means . . ."

I looked at her. "Means what?"

"Killing 'em dead." She looked at us with contemptuous satisfaction. "Knocking a person on the head, slitting their throat from ear to ear; or throttling them slow, if they've a fancy. Then they nick their goods. That's their game. 'Spect it shocks you—what with your soft hands and lily-white faces." She grinned at us. "Anyhow, this Carver," she went on, "he's one of the lean and hungry ones. He's a killer. I've seen him in places much like this, and I can tell you he wears the threat of violence around him like a cloak."

"The threat of violence?" Lockwood said. "How d'you mean?"

"It's hard to say. Maybe it's the gleam in his eye, the cruel thinness of his lips . . . even something in the way he stands. Plus, I saw him beat a man almost to death once just for looking at him funny."

We absorbed this in silence. "We heard he's red-haired, pale-skinned, always wears black," I said.

"Yeah. And he's tattooed, they say. Remarkable tattoos."

I blinked. "Why remarkable? What are they of?"

"Can't tell you. You're too young."

"But we fight murderous phantoms every night. How can we be too young?"

"If you can't guess, you're *definitely* not old enough," Flo said. "Look, here's your kippers. Another coffee—thanks, love—and this sugar bowl needs filling."

"So it's all thieves, scavengers, and thugs, is it?" I said, once the waitress had departed. "Seems relic-collecting's a real savory business all around."

Flo Bones stared at me. "Really? Worse than what you do, is it? You'd rather I got a legal job like these kids here?" She nodded over at the night-watchers, all slumped in various attitudes of weariness and dejection. "No, thanks. Be taken advantage of by big corporations? Be paid peanuts and given a bloody stick and told to stand in the cold all night, watching for Specters? I'd rather walk the tide line. Scratch my bum and look at the stars, and do it on my own terms."

"I know exactly what you mean," Lockwood said. "The stars bit, anyway."

"Yeah, because you were Gravedigger Sykes's lad. You got taught right. Keep yourself independent. Be a maverick. Dance to your own drum."

"You know about Lockwood's old master?" My surprise (and mild resentment) was evident in my voice. Flo clearly knew a whole lot more than I did about Lockwood's past and education.

"Yeah," Flo said. "I keep myself informed. I like to read the papers, before I wipe myself with 'em."

I paused with a forkful of kipper halfway to my mouth. Lockwood's toast visibly wilted in his hand.

"Pity poor Sykes went the way he did," Flo went on imperturbably. "Still, from what I hear, your company's successes continue to drive DEPRAC up the wall. That's what's made me inclined to help you out tonight."

"You mean you'd have helped us anyway?" I asked. "Without us going to the marsh?"

"Oh, surely."

"Well, that's good to know."

"Tell us about this Winkman," Lockwood said. "I've heard rumors of the name, but—"

Flo took her second coffee, and a new bowl of sugar. "Winkman, Julius Winkman. He's one of the most important receivers of stolen goods in London, and a very dangerous man. Runs a little shop in Bloomsbury. Outwardly *very* respectable, but if you've something dug up in a graveyard, or pinched from a Mayfair town house, or acquired in some intermediate hush-hush way, he's the man to see. Highest offers, quickest sale, and farthest reach. Has clientele all over the city, people with cash who don't ask questions. If Jack Carver has this object that you're after, it'll be Winkman he'll talk to first. And if Winkman buys it, he'll organize a secret auction, get his best customers together. Won't have done that yet, I shouldn't think. He'll want to maximize his earnings."

Lockwood had cleared his plate. "Okay. Now we're getting somewhere. This Bloomsbury shop, where is it?"

Flo shrugged. "Hey, Locky, you don't want to mess with Winkman, any more than you do with Carver. There's people tried to double-cross him—their remains have never been found. His wife's almost as bad, and their son's a holy terror. Stay clear of the whole family, that's my advice."

"All the same, I need the address." Lockwood tapped his fingers on the tabletop. "Where do these secret auctions take place?"

"I don't know. They're secret, see? Changes every time. But I can find out, maybe, assuming your Fittes friends have left any relic-men on the streets."

"That would be superb. Thanks, Flo—you've done us proud. Luce, you always carry money. Mind going up and paying? And while you're there"—he glanced toward the corkboard—"see if they could lend us a piece of paper and a pencil."

Chapter 13

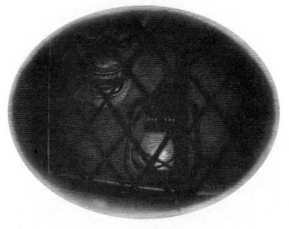

The Bloomsbury Antiques Emporium, also known as Winkman's Stores, stands on Owl Place, a narrow lane running between Coptic and Museum Streets in central London. It is a dowdy, uneven little side street, with only three commercial establishments: a pizza place on the corner with Coptic; a Chinese Psychic Healer, whose narrow glass door is shadowed beneath bamboo-and-paper awnings; and a broad-fronted building with two bay windows, which is the Bloomsbury Antiques Emporium.

The windows of this shop are low-slung and hatched with diamond leading. The interior is always dark. Nevertheless, a variety of objects can be glimpsed within: an equestrian statue in the Greek style, with one fore-hoof broken off; a Roman vase; a cabinet in red mahogany; a Japanese ghost-mask, grinning from ear to ear. Stickers on the door announce the types of credit cards accepted; and the hours of business, which extend to after Curfew. There are no ghost-bars on the door, and no obvious defenses. Mr. and Mrs. Winkman, who live above the shop, seem to have no need of them.

At a quarter past three on the afternoon following our encounter with Flo Bones, two young teenaged tourists, slurping iced Cokes from giant paper flagons, turned out of Museum Street's hot sunlight and entered the shady alley. The girl wore a *True Hauntings* T-shirt, a floaty knee-length skirt, and sandals. The boy wore a blue cotton shirt, an enormously baggy pair of shorts, and sneakers. Both had large sunglasses; they laughed and joked loudly as they strolled along.

Three doors down, they stopped as if on impulse outside the windows of the Bloomsbury Antiques Emporium and spent a little while staring at its array of dusty exhibits. The boy nudged the girl playfully in the ribs; he gestured at the store. The girl nodded. They walked to the doorway and went inside.

In setting out on our undercover investigation, Lockwood and I knew very well that we were taking risks. Flo had made that perfectly clear. The previous night, as her final favor, she had shown us the shop, pointing it out from the corner of the lane. Then she'd stolen away into the dark, leaving only a faintly unwashed smell behind. This had been as close as she wanted to get to Winkman's.

We, however, had slipped a little nearer, until we could make out a gas lantern flickering in the left-hand bay window, with the ghost-mask hanging above it like the gory head of a Floating Bride. Lockwood guessed that the light was some kind of signal; he'd been sorely tempted to keep watch, but we were far too weary. The night was halfway over, and we'd had very little sleep the night before. We left Bloomsbury and walked back home, where we slept in late, and came downstairs with the sunlight angled steeply through the windows.

George had already gone out. In the kitchen we'd found a note scrawled on the white paper tablecloth draped over the kitchen table. This is our thinking cloth. We always have some pens lying there, and we use it for memos, shopping lists, messages and doodles, as well as sketches of Visitors we've seen. Wedged in a space between an empty doughnut tray, a burger box, and two dirty teacups was the following message:

Out on hunt! Developments! Be here later. G

Nearby was a series of obscure scribblings:

150 °F	*15 mins*	*No response*
200 °F	*15 mins*	*No*
250 °F	*15 mins*	*No*
300 °F	*6 mins*	*Plasm stirs. Face forms*
	12 mins	*Mouth moves. Expressions (rude)*

BUY MORE CHIPS

We'd considered the cryptic notes in silence for a few moments. Then Lockwood crossed to the oven. He opened it slowly to discover the ghost-jar jammed inside. In places, the surface of the glass was slightly blackened. The plasm was almost translucent, the skull at its heart clearly exposed. You could see the little fissures in the bone, the brown staining on the teeth.

This was the first time we'd seen the skull since our squabble over its comments two nights before. I glanced nervously at Lockwood, who was making a fleeting effort to pry the jar out of the oven, but he didn't look at me. Instead he stood back and passed his hand across his face. "I don't have the strength to think about this now. George's experiments are getting slightly out of control. Remind me to have a word with him this evening."

First, however, we had other things to attend to, and Lockwood had already come to his decision. As far as tracking down Jack Carver went, there was little more that we could presently do. The previous night he had left a note at the café carefully addressed to the Graveyard Fellowship. It requested that anyone with information concerning "a recent incident" at Kensal Green Cemetery should get in touch with us, and offered a small reward. Carver himself would clearly not respond, but since half the relic-men seemed to be at each other's throats, it was possible someone else might bring us information. Meanwhile, Flo had promised to let us know if word got out about a special black market auction in the next few days; and we would hear the results of George's research later. Everything, in other words, was well in hand.

That just left Winkman's Stores.

Since it was likely Carver had already passed the mirror to Winkman, Lockwood reasoned it was worth at least investigating the antique shop. At best, we might get a clue to the mirror's whereabouts; at worst—well, given the black marketeer's reputation, it was sensible not to think about that. But we would go disguised, and not try anything too dangerous. It would be okay. We dressed ourselves as summer tourists, and took the tube to Bloomsbury.

A small bell, dangling from a D-shaped spindle above the door, danced and tinkled madly as we stepped inside the shop. The interior was dim, cool, and smelled of dust and herbal polish. The ceiling was low. Behind us, sunlight glistened against the diamond panes, passed through stained net curtains, and stretched in broken shards across the old scuffed floor. The room was a forest of stacked tables, display cabinets, chairs, and random objects. Straight ahead was a counter, behind which a woman stood, as massive, tall, and ominous as a statue of some long-forgotten god. She was polishing a small glass figurine with a tiny cloth. The top of her bouffant hairdo brushed the ceiling as she straightened to regard us.

"Can I help you?"

"Just looking, thanks," I said.

I took her in with a quick look: she was a strong, big-boned person in her early fifties. What with her size and pink skin, she reminded me of my mother. She had long hair, dyed very blond; plucked eyebrows; a thin-lipped mouth; and gray-blue eyes. She wore a bosomy, flowery dress with matching belt. At first glance she seemed soft and fleshy; at second glance the aura of hard competence that radiated from her was clear.

We knew who she was. Flo had given us the description. She was Mrs. Adelaide Winkman; she and her husband had owned the place for twenty years, since their predecessor had been accidentally crushed beneath a piece of Indian erotic statuary.

"Say, this is a cool shop you've got here," Lockwood said. He blew out a small pink bubble of gum. It popped loudly; he drew it back into his mouth and grinned.

The woman said, "You'll want to take your sunglasses off. We keep the lights low, on account of the artifacts, their delicate nature."

"Sure," Lockwood said. "Thanks." He didn't remove his glasses, and nor did I. "So all this is for sale?"

"For those with money," the woman said. She looked back down; her big pink fingers rubbed slowly with the cloth at the contours of the figurine.

Lockwood and I drifted around the shop, trying to look aimless, drinking in the details. We found a weird variety of paraphernalia: things of value, stuff that was evidently just junk. An Appaloosa rocking horse, dappled white flanks stained yellow with age; a tailor's dummy, head and shoulders of moth-eaten cloth, sitting atop a wormy wooden pole; an early washing machine with a hose coiled on its top; a Bakelite radio; three weird Victorian dolls with glassy, staring eyes. Those dolls made me shudder. You'd think even Victorian kids would have gotten the creeps from them.

Away to the left, a black curtain hung half concertinaed across a doorway. Beyond it was some kind of annex, or smaller room. I caught a glimpse of a wing chair there, and in it—dark and shiny—the crown of someone's head.

"Hey, are these haunted?" Lockwood pointed to the dolls.

The big woman didn't look up. "No. . . ."

"Man, they ought to be."

"There are shops on Coptic Street that have a wide selection of cheap gifts," the woman said. "You may find them more suitable for your means than . . ." She let the sentence trail away.

"Thanks. We're not looking to buy, are we, Suse?"

"No." I giggled, sucked noisily on my straw.

We wandered here and there a little longer, staring at objects, casing the joint. My snap survey told me there were two exits from the shop floor: an open door behind the counter that led to the domestic apartments (I could see a narrow hallway with a faded Persian rug and sepia photos on the wall), and the room behind the black curtain. It was still occupied—I heard a rustle of papers, and a man's sudden sniff.

Also, as I always do, I listened to the inner things. And there *was* something there; not strong, not a *noise*, exactly. Perhaps the faintest hum, coiled up, waiting to be let out. Was it the mirror? I remembered the sound I'd heard in the cemetery—like the buzzing of countless flies. It didn't sound quite like that. Whatever it was, it was very close.

Lockwood and I rendezvoused at the corner of the room farthest from the curtain. Our eyes met. We didn't say anything, but Lockwood raised his fingers to me, making sure his body blocked the view of the woman at the counter. We'd arranged the code beforehand. One finger: we were going to leave. Two fingers: he'd found something. Three fingers: he needed a distraction.

Wouldn't you know it? It was three. I had to put on a show. He winked, drifted away to the opposite end of the shop.

I glanced at the woman. The cloth moved in little circles, around and around and around.

I put my hand casually in the pocket of my skirt.

It's amazing how much noise a dozen coins can make, dropped on a hardwood floor. That sudden crash, that scattering reverberation . . . It even took me by surprise.

Coins spilled under tables, between chair legs, and away behind the bases of statues. Over at the counter, the woman's head jerked up. "What's going on?"

"My change! My pocket's ripped!"

Without waiting, I ducked down and wriggled my way under the nearest table. I did it clumsily, knocking the table so that the jewelry stands on it swayed and tinkled. Flicking a couple of coins farther in, I squeezed between two African bird sculptures. They were flamingos or something: tall, beaky, a bit top-heavy. Above me, the heads swung precariously from side to side.

"Stop that! Get out of there now!" The woman had left the counter. From behind the tables I saw her fat pink calves and heavy shoes approach at speed.

"Yeah, in a sec. Just getting my money."

There was an Oriental paper lantern ahead of me. It looked old, fragile, perhaps quite valuable. Since it was theoretically possible that a coin might have fallen inside it, I gave it an industrious shake, ignoring the gasps of Mrs. Winkman, who was bobbing anxiously beyond the tables, trying to get close to me. Putting the lantern down, I reversed sharply, so that my bottom collided with a plaster column displaying some kind of Roman vase. The vase toppled, began to fall. Mrs. Winkman, demonstrating greater dexterity than I'd have expected for someone so large, reached out a hamlike hand and seized it as it went.

"Julius!" she screeched. "Leopold!"

Away across the room, the curtains were flung aside. Someone emerged, moved with stately tread along the aisles. I saw a pair of short and stocky legs, tightly clad in cotton trousers. I saw old leather sandals on the feet. I saw no socks; the feet were hairy, the yellowed toenails long and cracked.

A moment later a second pair of legs—markedly smaller than the first, but identical in shape and attire—emerged from the back room and came trotting after.

I made a pretense of scrabbling deeper under the table, gathering a few coins in my shaking hands, but I knew the game was up. I was already inching back toward the aisle when I heard a deep, soft voice say, "What's all this, then, Adelaide? Silly children playing games?"

"She won't come out," Mrs. Winkman said.

"Oh, I'm sure she can be persuaded," the voice said.

"I'm coming," I called. "Just had to get my coins."

I emerged, dusty, red-faced and puffing, stood, and turned to face them. The woman had her massive arms folded; she was gazing at me with an expression that would ordinarily have been enough to turn my bowels to water. But not this time. It was the man beside her I had to worry about now. Julius Winkman.

My first impression was of a big man made short by some quirk of genetics, or by an elevator falling on him, or both. He had a squat, endomorphic body, with an enormous head, a thick neck, and powerful shoulders resting on a barrel-shaped chest. His arms were vast and hairy, his legs stubby and bowed. His black hair was cut very short and oiled back against the surface of his scalp. He wore a gray suit with the sleeves rolled up to the elbows, a white shirt, and no tie. Thick hairs protruded at the collar of his shirt. He had a broad nose and a wide, expressive mouth. A pair of golden pince-nez was balanced incongruously on his nose. Though clearly a person of considerable strength, he was little taller than me. I could look him directly in the eyes, which were big and dark, with long, sensuous lashes. The rest of his face was heavy, swarthy; the notched chin dark with stubble.

Beside him was a boy who seemed in many ways a smaller replica of the man. He too had the physique of an upturned pear, the slicked-back hair and toadlike mouth. He wore similar gray trousers and a tight white shirt. There were *some* differences: no pince-nez, and mercifully less body hair; also his eyes were like his mother's, blue and piercing. He stood at his father's shoulder, staring at me coolly.

"What do you think you're doing," Julius Winkman said, "crawling around my shop?"

Far away across the room, behind them all, the curtain leading to the back room twitched once, briefly, and hung still.

"I didn't mean any harm," I said. "I dropped my money." I flourished the evidence in my palm. "It's okay, though. I got most of it. You can keep the rest. . . ." Under their collective gaze my feeble grin grew sickly and crawled away to die. "Um, it's a nice shop," I went on. "So much cool stuff. Bet it's pricey, though, isn't it? That rocking horse now—what is that, couple of hundred at a guess? Lovely. . . ." The important thing was to keep them talking, keep their attention on me. "What about that vase there? How much would *that* set me back, if I wanted it? Um . . . is it Greek? Roman? Fake?"

"No. Let me tell you something." Julius Winkman moved close suddenly, raised a hairy finger, as if he were about to prod me on the chest. His fingers, like his toes, had long, ragged nails. I smelled peppermint on his breath. "Let me tell you this. This is a respectable establishment. We have respectable customers. Delinquent kids who mess about, cause damage, they're not welcome here."

"I quite understand that," I said hastily. Bloody Lockwood— next time *he* could do the distraction. I made a move for the exit. "Good-bye."

"Wait," Mrs. Winkman said. "There were two of them. Where's the other one?"

"Oh, I guess he left," I said. "He gets *so* embarrassed when I drop things."

"I didn't hear the door."

Julius Winkman glanced back across the room. He was so thick-necked he had to turn sideways to do so, rotating his torso at the hips. He smiled faintly. There was a curiously feminine quality to his eyes and mouth that sat oddly with his hirsute frame. He said, "Thirty seconds, maybe forty. Then we'll see."

I hesitated. "Sorry. I don't understand."

"Look at her hand, Dad." The boy spoke eagerly. "Look at her right hand."

That puzzled me. "You want to see the coins?"

"Not the coins," Julius Winkman said. "Your hand. Good boy, Leopold. Show it to me now, you lying little tramp, or I'll snap your wrist."

My skin crawled. Wordlessly I extended my hand. He took it, held it still. The softness of his touch appalled me. He adjusted the pince-nez slightly and bent close. With his free hand he ran his fingers lightly across the surface of my palm.

"As I thought," he said. "Agent."

"Didn't I tell you, Dad?" the boy said. "Didn't I say?"

I could feel tears pricking my eyes. Furiously I blinked them back. Yes, I *was* an agent. I would *not* be intimidated. I pulled my hand away. "I don't know what you're talking about. I've just come in to take a look at your stupid store and you're not being very nice to me at all. Leave me alone."

"You're a hopeless actor," Winkman said. "But even if you were a theatrical genius, your hand would still betray you. No one but an agent has those two calluses on the palm. Rapier marks, I call them. Come from all that practicing you do; all that silly little swordplay. Yes? Should have thought of that, shouldn't you? And so we're just waiting for your little friend to come out." He looked at the watch strapped to his hairy wrist. "I'd guess, any time now. . . ."

A flash of light from beyond the curtain; a yelp of pain. A moment passed, then the curtain twitched aside; in came Lockwood, white-faced, grimacing, clutching the fingers of his right hand. He took a deep breath, mastered himself. He walked slowly down the aisle, came to a halt before the waiting Winkmans.

"I must say," Lockwood said, "it's not very customer-friendly here. I was just looking around that little showroom of yours, when some kind of electric shock—"

"Silly children, playing silly games," Julius Winkman said in his soft, deep voice. "Which did you try, boy, the bureau or the safe?"

Lockwood smoothed back his hair. "The safe."

"Which is wired to administer a mild electric punishment to anyone who fails to disarm the circuitry before touching the door. The bureau has a similar mechanism. But you were wasting your time, since there's nothing of any possible interest to you in either. Who are you, and who are you working for?"

I said nothing. Lockwood looked as dismissively contemptuous as was possible for someone wearing a colorful pair of vacation shorts and with a lightly steaming hand.

Mrs. Winkman shook her head. She seemed taller than ever, standing in front of the mullioned windows. Her looming form blocked the light. "Julius? I could lock the door."

"Cut 'em into pieces, Dad," the boy said.

"Not necessary, my dears." Winkman gazed at us. The smile was still present, but behind the fluttering lashes the gaze was hard as stone. "I don't need to know who you are," he said. "It doesn't matter. I can guess what you want, but you won't get it. Let me tell you something: in all my establishments, I have certain defenses to deal with people who are not welcome. An electric shock is just the least of them—crude, but useful during the day. By night, should anyone be foolish enough to break in, I have other methods. They are most effective; sometimes my enemies are dead even *before* I come downstairs. Do you understand?"

Lockwood nodded. "You've been very clear. Come on, Suse."

"No," Julius Winkman said. "Not like that. You don't get to walk out of here." Bearlike hands shot out and seized us, me by the forearm, Lockwood by the collar; without effort he pulled us both inward, close to him, then lifted us off the floor. The grip was tight; I cried out in pain. Lockwood struggled, but could do nothing. "Look at you," Winkman said. "Without your silly uniforms and fancy swords, you're nothing but kids. Kids! This is the first time, so you get off lightly. Next time, I won't be so restrained. Leopold—the door!"

The boy hopped over, swung the door aside. Light spilled in, the doorbell tinkled sweetly. Julius Winkman lifted me up and back, then flung me out into the sunlight. The muscles in my arm wrenched; I landed heavily and fell forward onto my knees. A moment later Lockwood landed beside me, bounced once upon his backside, and skidded to a dusty halt. Behind us, we heard the door to the Bloomsbury Antiques Emporium being softly, but firmly, closed.

Chapter 14

An hour later, two bruised tourist kids arrived home. We trudged through the gate and up the path, past the hanging bell and the broken line of iron tiles that I still hadn't gotten around to mending. I leaned against the wall while Lockwood felt for the keys.

"How's your hand?" I said.

"Sore."

"Bottom?"

"Sorer."

"That didn't go so well, did it?"

Lockwood opened the door. "I had to see what was in his private room. There was just a chance the mirror might have been back there. But it was all racing forms and account books—and a half-finished jigsaw that his revolting son must've been doing. Winkman keeps the hot stuff somewhere else, of course." He sighed, and hitched up his enormous Bermuda shorts as we proceeded down the hall. "Still, I suppose the afternoon wasn't entirely wasted. We've seen what sort of fellow Mr. Winkman is firsthand, and we won't underestimate him again. I wonder if George has had better luck."

"I certainly have!" The kitchen door swung open. George was sitting at the table, aglow with vitality, a pencil and a breadstick protruding from his mouth. His eyes widened as he saw our outfits. "Blimey. Are those shorts you're wearing, Lockwood, or are you trying to take flight?"

Lockwood didn't answer, but stood in the doorway, casting morose eyes over the chip bags, teacups, photocopied sheets, and open notebooks littering the table. I went to put the kettle on. "They're shorts," I said. "We've been undercover, but we've not had a very good day. I see *you've* been busy, though. Any progress?"

"Yeah, I've been getting somewhere at last," George said. "Heat. Proper heat might just be the answer. Not solar heat, mind; that just makes the plasm shrink. I'm talking thermal. I popped that skull in the oven last night, and I tell you it soon got that ghost nicely worked up. The plasm started twirling and coiling at three hundred degrees. Turns out *that's* the magic number. Soon the face appeared, and then I honestly think it started talking! Couldn't actually hear it, of course—I needed *you* there for that, Luce—but if my lipreading's anything to go by, it knows some pretty ripe language. Anyway, it's a giant leap, and I'm rather chuffed with myself." He leaned triumphantly back in his chair.

I felt a flash of irritation. The skull had recently spoken with me—and at room temperature, no less. These endless experiments seemed suddenly tiresome.

Lockwood was gazing at George. I could sense the pressure building in the room. I said, "Yeah, we found the skull-jar in the oven this morning. We were a *little* surprised. . . . What I was really talking about was the whole Bickerstaff thing."

"Oh, don't worry, I've got news for you on that score, too." George took a complacent crunch on his breadstick. "Tell you what about ovens. They don't make them big enough. I could barely get the jar in—and now it's stuck! I mean, it's pathetic. What if it had been a whopping Christmas roast?"

"Yes," I said coolly. "How strange would *that* be?" I found some mugs, plonked tea bags in.

"Ah, but this could be such a breakthrough," George was saying. "Just think, if we could get the dead to speak to us *on demand*. Joplin was saying it's been the dream of scholars throughout history, and if all it actually took was getting a couple of big ovens and—"

Lockwood gave a sudden cry; he strode forward into the room. "Will you *stop* going on about that stupid skull! That's *not* our priority, George. Are we getting paid for it? No! Is it an imminent danger to people in London? No! Are we racing against Quill Kipps and his team to solve its mystery, and so prevent our public humiliation? No, we aren't! But all those very things are happening while you bumble about with jars and ovens! Lucy and I have risked our lives today, if it's of any interest to you." He took a deep breath; George was staring at him as if mesmerized. "All I ask," Lockwood said, "is that you *please* try to focus on the job at hand. . . . Well? What do you say?"

George pushed his glasses up his nose. "Sorry, can you repeat that? It's those shorts. I couldn't concentrate on what you were saying."

The kettle boiled loudly, drowning Lockwood's brief response. I made three hasty cups of tea, banging the spoon about, rattling the fridge door, trying to fill the ensuing silence. It didn't really work. The atmosphere wasn't fast improving. So I doled out the tea like a sullen waitress and went upstairs to get changed.

I took my time about it too. It had been a difficult afternoon, and our encounter with the Winkmans had left me more shaken than I'd admitted to Lockwood. The soft touch of the man's hand, the implicit violence in his movements. . . . I suddenly viewed my silly tourist outfit with extreme dislike. Up in my attic bedroom I dressed swiftly in my usual dark top, skirt, and leggings; the heavy-duty boots, too. An agent's clothes. Clothes you didn't mess with. It was a small thing, but it made me feel a little better. I stood at the window looking out at the dusk, and the silence of Portland Row.

I wasn't the only one who seemed unsettled. Lockwood's irritability was unusual. The urgent need to beat Kipps to the mirror was clearly preying on his mind.

Or was it? Maybe it was something else that bothered him. Maybe it was the skull. The skull and its whispered insinuations. . . .

On my way downstairs I paused on the first-floor landing. Polynesian spirit-chasers and ghost-wards hung shadowed on the walls. I was alone; I could hear Lockwood's and George's voices below me in the kitchen.

Yes, there it was: the door that must never be opened.

There are other things in the house to fear, besides me.

An impulse overtook me. I tiptoed over and pressed my hands

and ear to the wood of the door. I let my inner senses take control, *listening, listening. . . .*

No. There was nothing. Really I should just open the door and take a look inside. It was unlocked. What could possibly happen?

Or I could just mind my own business and forget the lying, wheedling words of the foul thing in the jar! I tore myself away, set off down the stairs. Yes, I *did* want to delve a little deeper into Lockwood's past, but there were other ways to do it than by snooping. Flo had mentioned an old master of Lockwood's, who had seemingly come to some nasty end. Perhaps I could follow George's example and visit the Archives one day. . . .

They were still in the kitchen, still at the table, nursing cups of tea. Something must have happened while I was gone, however, because ham and mustard sandwiches were now piled high in the center of the table, together with bowls of cherry tomatoes, pickles, and crinkly lettuce. And chips. It looked pretty good. I sat. We ate.

"All better now?" I said after a while.

Lockwood grunted. "I've apologized."

George said, "Lockwood's been drawing that missing object from the Bickerstaff coffin. You know, the thing he saw in the photo. What do you think?"

I took a look at the thinking cloth. It wasn't a very good sketch, since Lockwood can't really draw: three or four parallel lines, with sharp ends. "Looks like a bundle of pencils," I said.

"Bigger than pencils," Lockwood said. "More like sticks. Reminded me of those fold-up tripods the *Times* photographers used when they took pictures in Mrs. Barrett's tomb." He had a bite of sandwich. "Doesn't explain where they disappeared to, though. Anyway, let's talk business. I've filled George in, more or less, on what we've been doing the last twenty-four hours. And he's not happy."

George nodded. "That's right. I can't *believe* you went blundering into Winkman's shop like that. If he's the man you say he is, that was a terribly rash thing to do."

"We had to make a snap decision," Lockwood said with his mouth full. "Okay, it didn't work out, but it could have. Sometimes, George, we have to act on the spur of the moment. Life's not all fiddling around with ghost-jars and paperwork. Oh, don't get mad at me again. I'm just saying."

"Listen, I'm in the front line too," George growled. "Who was it that got a faceful of that haunted mirror the other night? I can still feel the effects now. It's like something's tugging on my mind, calling to me. I reckon I wasn't far from meeting the same end as that relic-man we found, and that's not a nice sensation." There were two small red points on his cheeks; he looked away. "Anyway, my *fiddling around* has rounded up plenty of good stuff, so I don't think you'll be disappointed. We've made more progress than Kipps and Bobby Vernon have, I'm sure."

Night had fallen. Lockwood got up and closed the kitchen blinds, blocking out the darkness in the garden. He switched on a second light and sank back in his chair. "George is right. I phoned Barnes while you were upstairs, Luce, and Kipps isn't doing well. He hasn't got a lead on either Jack Carver or the mirror. DEPRAC's holding cells are filled to bursting with half the relic-men of London, but Carver isn't among them. There's no clue as to his whereabouts.

Barnes is a little frustrated. I told him we were following a hopeful lead."

"Did you tell him about Winkman?" I said.

"No. I don't want Kipps muscling in on that. It's our best hope of success, the secret auction, as long as Flo can get us news of it in time."

"Where've you been hiding this Flo Bones?" George asked. "She sounds like a useful contact. What's she like?"

"Soft-spoken, mild-mannered, and gentle," I said. "Classy. You know the type. I think you'd get along well with her."

George pushed his spectacles up his nose. "Really? Good."

"So then, George," Lockwood said, "it's over to you. What did you find out about Bickerstaff and the mirror?"

George tidied his papers and stacked them neatly beside the remaining sandwiches. His annoyance had subsided; he now had a keen and businesslike air.

"Okay," he said. "As expected, the National Archives didn't let me down. My first port of call was the *Hampstead Gazette* article Albert Joplin showed us, the one about the rats. I found that and made a copy; I've got it here. Well, you'll remember the basics. Our Edmund Bickerstaff works at a sanatorium—that's a kind of hospital for people with chronic illnesses—on Hampstead Heath. He has something of a bad reputation, though the details are hazy. One night he has a private party with friends; when his body's discovered, it's been almost entirely devoured by rats. Yeech, even thinking about it makes me reluctant to chomp on one of these cherry tomatoes. But I will anyway."

"So it doesn't mention him being shot, then?" I said, remembering the corpse in the iron coffin, and the round hole in its forehead. "Not shot and *then* eaten?"

"Nothing about that at all. But it's quite possible the newspaper didn't get the story entirely right. Some of the specifics may have been missed or left out."

Lockwood nodded. "That whole rats story sounds daft to me. Find any other newspaper accounts?"

"Not as many as you might expect. You'd think the rats would have made all the front pages, but there's very little. It's almost as if the story was being deliberately suppressed. But I did find a few references, some extra details. One theme that keeps coming up is that Bickerstaff had a nasty habit of hanging around graveyards after dark."

"No shame in that," I said, crunching on a pickle. "We do that too."

"*We* aren't seen creeping home after midnight with a bulging bag over our shoulders and grave dirt dripping from our shovels. One paper says he'd sometimes have a servant lad with him, poor kid dragging heaven knows what behind him in a heavy sack."

"Hard to believe no one arrested him," I said. "If there were witnesses . . ."

"It may be that he had friends in highish places," George went on. "I'll get to that in a minute. Anyway, a couple of years later, the *Gazette* reports that someone went into Bickerstaff's house—it had been standing empty, I guess no one wanted to buy it—and discovered a secret panel in the living room. And behind that panel they found . . ." He chuckled, paused dramatically. "You'll never guess."

"A body," I said.

"Bones." Lockwood took some chips.

George's face fell. "Yeah. Oh, I suppose I gave you the clue. Anyway, yes, they found all sorts of body parts stacked in a hidden room. Some of them seemed very old. This confirmed that the good doctor had been going around digging up things he shouldn't, but precisely *why* he should do so wasn't clear."

"And *this* didn't make the headlines, either?" Lockwood said. "I've got to admit that's odd."

"What about Bickerstaff's friends?" I said, frowning. "Didn't Joplin say there was a whole gang of them?"

George nodded. "Yes, and I made progress there. One article gave the names of two of his supposed associates, people who were meant to have been at this final gathering at his house. They were young aristocrats named"—he consulted some notes for a moment—"Lady Mary Dulac and the Honorable Simon Wilberforce. Both were rich, with reputations of being interested in strange ideas. Anyway, get this—" George's eyes glinted. "From other references I've found, it seems Bickerstaff wasn't the *only* one to disappear in 1877. Dulac and Wilberforce *also vanished* around that same time."

"What, as in never-seen-again vanished?" I said.

"Right. Well, certainly in Wilberforce's case." He grinned at us. "Of course there were rewards offered, questions asked in parliament, but no one seems to have openly made the connection with Bickerstaff. Some people must have known, though. I think it was hushed up. Anyway, now we move on ten years, to the sudden reappearance of Mary Dulac. . . ." He rummaged in his stack of papers.

"Where is it? I'm sure I had it. Ah, here we go. I'll read it to you. It's from the *Daily Telegraph*, in the summer of 1886—a long time after the Bickerstaff affair:

MADWOMAN CAPTURED

The so-called 'Wild-woman of Chertsey Forest,' a scrawny vagabond whose demented howls have caused consternation in this wooded district for several weeks, has at last been apprehended by police. Under interrogation at the town hall, the lunatic, who gave her name as Mary or May Dulac, claimed to have been living like a beast for many years. Her ravings, matted hair, and hideous appearance disturbed several gentlemen present, and she was quickly removed to Chertsey Asylum."

A silence fell after George finished.

"Is it just me," Lockwood said, "or do bad things happen to people who have anything to do with Bickerstaff?"

"Let's hope that doesn't include us," I said.

"I haven't gotten to the bottom of the Dulac business yet," George added. "I want to go to Chertsey, check out the Records Office there. The asylum was shut down in 1904. Among the items listed as being removed from its library and taken to the Records Office at the time was something called *The Confessions of Mary Dulac*. To me, that sounds worth reading."

"It certainly does," Lockwood agreed. "Though I suppose being a madwoman's confessions, it might just be about eating bugs and things in the woods. Still, you never know. Well done, George. This is excellent."

"It's just a shame there's nothing about that mirror," George said. "It killed that guy Neddles in the cemetery, and it did something weird to me. I can't help wondering if it was involved in Bickerstaff's death as well. Anyway, I'll keep looking. The only other interesting thing I found out was about that hospital Bickerstaff worked at— Green Gates Sanatorium on Hampstead Heath."

"Joplin said it burned down, didn't he?" I said.

"Yeah. In 1908, with quite a loss of life. The site remained undeveloped for more than fifty years, until someone tried building a housing estate there."

Lockwood whistled. "What were they thinking? Who builds houses on the site of an old Victorian hospital that burned down in tragic circumstances?"

George nodded. "I know. It's almost the first rule of planning. As you'd expect, there were enough supernatural disturbances for the project to be shelved. But when I was looking at the plans, I discovered something. Most of the site's just grassland now: a few walls, overgrown ruins. But there *is* one building standing."

We looked at him. "You mean—"

"Turns out Bickerstaff's house was set slightly away from the main part of the hospital. It wasn't touched by the fire. It's still there."

"Used for what?" I said.

"Nothing. It's deserted, I think."

"As you'd expect, given its history. Who in their right mind would go there?" Lockwood sat back in his chair. "Great work, George. Tomorrow you nip down to Chertsey. Lucy and I will try to pick up Jack Carver's trail—though how we'll do that, I haven't a clue. He's well and truly disappeared. Right, I'm off upstairs. I'm totally bushed, plus it's high time I got out of these shorts."

He made to rise. At that moment there was a knock at the front door. Two knocks. A brisk *tap-tap*.

We looked at each other. One after another we slowly pushed our chairs back and went out into the hall.

The knocking came again.

"What time is it, George?" Lockwood didn't need to ask, really. There was a carriage clock on the mantelpiece, a grandfather clock in the corner, and, from his parents' collection, an African dream-catching timepiece that told the hour using ostrich feathers, cheetah bones, and a revolving nautilus shell. One way or another, we knew what time it was.

"Twenty minutes to midnight," George said. "Late."

Far too late for any mortal visitor. None of us actually *said* this, but it was what we were all thinking.

"You replaced that loose tile in the iron line, of course, Lucy," Lockwood said, as we looked down past the coats and the table with the crystal lantern. The only lights in the hall were the faint yellow spears spilling out from the kitchen. Various tribal totems hovered in the fuzzy half-dark; the door itself could not be seen.

"Almost," I said.

"Almost finished?"

"Almost got around to starting."

Another double knock sounded at the end of the hall.

"Why don't they ring the bell?" George said. "The notice clearly says you have to ring the bell."

"It's not going to be a Stone Knocker," I said slowly. "Or a Tom

O'Shadows. Even with the break in the iron line, they'd surely be too weak. . . ."

"That's right," Lockwood said. "It won't be a ghost. It's probably Barnes or Flo."

"That's it! Of course! Flo. It must be Flo. She goes out at night."

"Of course she does. We should let her in."

"Yes."

None of us moved along the hall.

"Where was that recent strangling case?" George said. "Where the ghost knocked on the window and killed the old lady?"

"George, that was a window! This is a door!"

"So what? They're both rectangular apertures! I can be strangled too!"

Another knock—a single one, a clashing reverberation on the wood.

"Oh, to hell with this," Lockwood snarled. He strode down the hall, switched on the crystal lantern, snatched up a rapier from the umbrella stand beside the coats. Bending close to the door, he spoke loudly through the wood. "Hello? Who is it?"

No answer came.

Lockwood ran a hand through his hair. He flicked the chains aside, undid the latch. Before opening the door, he looked back at George and me. "Got to be done," he said. "It might be someone who needs our—"

The door burst open, knocking into Lockwood; he was flung back hard against the shelves. Masks and gourds toppled, crashing to the floor. A hunched black shape careered into the hallway. I caught a glimpse of a white, contorted face, two madly staring eyes. Lockwood tried to bring his rapier around, but the shape was on him, clawing at his front. George and I sprang forward, came pelting down the hall. A horrid, gargling cry. The thing fell back, away from Lockwood, out into the lantern light. It was a living man, mouth open, gulping like a fish. His long, gingery hair was wet with sweat. He wore black jeans and jacket, a stained black T-shirt. Heavy lace-up boots stumbled on the floor.

George gasped. Realization hit me, too.

"Carver," I said. "That's Jack Carver. The one who stole the . . ."

The man's fingers scrabbled at his neck, as if he were trying to pull words loose from his throat. He took one step toward us and another—then, as if newly boneless, his legs gave way. He collapsed forward onto the parquet flooring, striking his face hard. Lockwood pushed himself away from the shelves; George and I halted, staring. All three of us gazed at the body laid out on the hall before us, at the twitching fingers, at the dark stain spreading out beneath him; most of all at the long, curved dagger driven deep into his back.

IV

Dead Men

Talking

Chapter 15

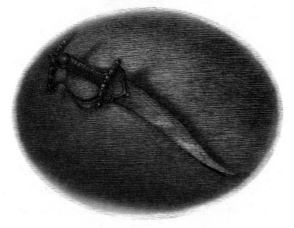

As always, Lockwood was fastest to react. "Lucy, take the rapier." He tossed it over. "Go to the door. Just a quick look, then barricade us in."

Cool night air swirled around me as I stepped between the body and the key table. I crossed the threshold and looked out into the street. Our tiled path was empty; the gate at the end hung open. The streetlight outside number 35 cast its bland apricot-pink radiance in a cone across the sidewalk. One porch was illuminated in a house opposite; another had an upstairs bathroom light on. Otherwise the houses were dark. From down the end of the road, I could hear the ghost-lamp's rumbling hum. It was off right now. Within the next two minutes it would come on again. I saw no one. Nothing moved.

Keeping the rapier in a guard position, I walked out a little farther, across the line of iron tiles. I peered down into the basement yard. Empty. I listened. Silence across the city. London slept. And while it slept, ghosts and murderers walked free. I stepped back into the house and closed the door, flipped the locks, and pulled the chain across.

Lockwood and George were crouching by the fallen body, George shuffling sideways to avoid the spreading pool of blood. Lockwood had his fingers on the man's neck.

"He's alive," he said. "Lucy—call a night-ambulance. DEPRAC, too. George, help me roll him over."

George frowned. "Shouldn't we leave him? If we move—"

"Look at him; he doesn't have long. Get him on his side."

While they did their business, I went into the library and made the calls.

When I got back they had him facing the shelves; he lay with his arm outstretched beneath his head, and his eyes half open. The pool of blood hadn't gotten any smaller. Lockwood, crouching low, bent close beside his face; George, pencil and paper in hand, kneeled at his back. I hovered close, near George.

"He's been trying to say something," George said. "But it's very faint. Something about bogeys."

"Shhh!" Lockwood hissed. "You misheard, I keep telling you. It was *bone glass*, clear as day. He means the thing he stole. Jack, Jack, can you hear me?"

"Bone glass?" I had a sudden flash of the little mirrored object, clasped across the corpse's breast. Its rim had been uneven, smooth and brown—I'd assumed it had been made of wood. Was it bone, then? And if so—what *kind* of bone? Or whose?

George leaned close. "Sounded very much like *bogeys* to me."

"Shut up, George!" Lockwood growled. "Jack—who did this? Can you tell me?"

The dying man just lay there. Strange to see him now, after all our searching. The fearsome, ruthless relic-man, Jack Carver. Flo had said that he wore the threat of violence around him like a cloak. That he was a killer. Perhaps so, but now that violence had been done to *him*, he wasn't at all how I'd imagined. Younger, to begin with, and scrawnier, too, with a gaunt, tight look around the cheekbones. There was something indefinably ill-fed about him, a look of constant desperation. His jacket hung loose around his thin, white neck, which had a patch of shaving rash under the jaw. His T-shirt was dirty; his jacket smelled bad, as if the leather hadn't been successfully cured.

"Who did this to you?" Lockwood said again.

A spasm of movement, shocking in its unexpectedness. The head reared up, the mouth opened and closed; milky eyes stared blindly out at nothing. George and I jerked back; George dropped his pencil. Noises came from the mouth, a string of sound.

"What was that?" I gasped. "What did he say?"

"I got it." Lockwood made an urgent gesture. "Write it down."

George was scrabbling on the floor. "The pencil . . . Oh god, it rolled under him."

"What he said was: *Seven from it. Seven, not one.* Got that? Wait, there's more."

"I'm not sticking my hand under *there*."

"Next bit: *You see such things. Such terrible things . . .*"

"Could you fetch the pencil, Luce?"

"*Will someone write it down?!*" Lockwood yelled.

In a frenzy of panic, George retrieved the pencil and scribbled down the words. We all bent close. The man was very still, his breathing wrenlike: tiny, frail, and fast.

"Where's the bone glass, Jack?" Lockwood said to him. "Has someone got it?"

The parched lips mumbled again.

George sat back with a cry. "Juice! He wants juice! Can we give him that? Are we allowed to give him juice?" He hesitated, frowning. "Have we actually *got* any?"

"*Julius!*" Lockwood growled. "He said *Julius*, George. As in Julius Winkman. Honestly, your ears." He bent in close again. "Winkman's got the bone glass, Jack?"

The faintest nod.

"Did Winkman do this to you?"

For unknown seconds, we waited. The man spoke again.

"Write it down, George," I said.

George looked at me. Lockwood glanced up, frowning. "Write down what, Luce?"

"What he just said."

"I didn't hear anything."

"He said: *Please come with me.* Clear as day."

Lockwood hesitated. "Didn't hear that. Write it anyway, George. And move back a bit. I'm watching his lips and you're blocking the light."

We shuffled aside and waited. We waited a long time.

"Lockwood," I said.

"What?"

"I think that might have been it."

None of us said anything. None of us moved.

Death is fugitive; even when you're watching for it, the actual instant somehow slips between your fingers. You don't get that sudden drop of the head that you see in movies. Instead you simply sit there, waiting for something to happen, and all at once you realize you've missed it. *Time to move along now, nothing to see.* Nothing to see there ever again.

We knelt beside the relic-man, as motionless as he was, holding our breaths, sharing the moment of transition. It was as if we were trying to stay with him, those first few seconds, wherever he was, wherever he was going.

It was the only thing we could do.

When it was obvious that he really *had* gone, life reclaimed us. We all sat back, one after the other, breathed deeply, coughed, rubbed our faces, scratched ourselves, did trivial stuff to prove that we were still capable and alive.

Between us was an object, just an empty, hollow thing.

"Will you *look* at this rug?" George said. "I've only just gotten out the stain from the cocoa we spilled the other night."

"What did the ambulance people say, Lucy?" Lockwood asked.

"The usual. They're waiting for protection. Barnes is arranging that."

"Okay. We've got ten, fifteen minutes. Time enough for what George has got to do."

George blinked. "What's that?"

"Search his pockets."

"Me? Why me?"

"You're the most light-fingered of us."

"Lucy's got smaller hands."

"She's also the best at drawing. Lucy, take the notebook. I want a sketch of the murder weapon, accurate as you can."

While George, white-faced, busied himself with the dead man's jacket, Lockwood and I moved along to the dagger sticking out of his back. My hands shook a little as I drew the rough shape of the hilt; I had to concentrate to keep the pencil firm. Funny how an actual death always hits you so hard. Visitors are *scarier*, sure, but they don't have quite that power to shock. Lockwood seemed as cool and in control as ever, though. Maybe deaths didn't have the same effect on him.

"It's a Mughal dagger," he was saying. "From India, maybe sixteenth century. The curved hilt's inlaid with ivory and gold. Grip's made of black cord, tightly wound around the metal. Lots of decorative pieces fixed to the pommel and at the end of the hand guard. Milky white stones, not sure what they are. Opals, you think, Lucy?"

"Not a clue. How on earth do you know this is a Mughal dagger?"

"My parents studied oriental traditions. Got whole books on this stuff. Ceremonial piece, I think. Is the blade thin and curved?"

"Can't see. It's mostly in him."

"Odd thing to kill someone with," Lockwood mused. "Who has one of these, outside a museum?"

"An antiques dealer might," I said. "Like Winkman."

He nodded. "How very true. Finish the sketch. What have you found there, George?"

"A lot of money, mainly. Look at this."

He held out a narrow brown envelope, stuffed almost to bursting with the quantity of bills inside. Lockwood riffled through it swiftly.

"All used twenties," he said. "Must be close to a thousand quid. Find anything else?"

"Coins, a pocketknife, a comb, and a crumpled note in your handwriting addressed to the Graveyard Fellowship. Also some tattoos, which have given me a lot to think about."

"The note in the café worked better than I expected," Lockwood said. "I'll take that. You can put the rest back. Yes, the money too. Then we'll put him on his front again. Barnes will soon be here. By the way, we don't let slip anything we've uncovered so far. I don't want Kipps getting hold of it."

George gave a sudden curse. "Barnes! The ghost-jar! I told Barnes I'd gotten rid of it."

"Oh, for heaven's sake. Go shut the oven door then, quickly. We haven't got much time."

Lockwood was right. We were just lowering Carver back down when we heard the ambulance crew arriving at the door.

It's never a massive pleasure to have Inspector Barnes and his DEPRAC forensic squad barging through the house, particularly when they're dealing with a dead man in your hall. For hours they stomped around in their work boots, taking photographs of body, knife, and bloodstain from every angle; emptying the corpse's pockets, photographing the contents and taking them away in little bags; and all this while we were confined to the living room to keep us out of the way.

What made it especially irritating was that Kipps had turned up too, together with several of his team. Barnes didn't seem to mind *them* interfering. Tall, shaggy-haired Ned Shaw stalked the ground floor, interrogating the medics, arguing with the cleanup crew, and generally being objectionable. Tiny Bobby Vernon loitered with his clipboard by the body, sketching the dagger just as we had. He watched the pocket-emptying closely, shaking his head and giving us hard looks through the living room door. Meanwhile humorless Kat Godwin tried listening for psychic traces that might have been left by the murdered man. She stood so long in a corner of the hall, eyes shut and frowning in sharp-chinned concentration, that I was tempted to creep up with one of George's jackets and use her as a coatrack.

The body was eventually zipped up in a bag and taken to the van outside. The rug was rolled up and removed. The forensic team used salt guns to cleanse the hall. One of the operatives, chewing methodically on his gum, stuck his head around the living room door. "That's all done," he said. "You want us to scatter iron?"

"No, thanks," Lockwood said. "We can do it."

The man made a face. "Murder victim. With murder victims, you've got a sixty-five percent chance of them coming back in the first year. Thirty-five percent after that. Fact."

"Yes, we know. It's okay. We can seal the ground. We're agents."

"First agent I've ever seen wearing shorts like that," the man said. He left.

"Me too," Barnes said. "And I've been in the business thirty years." He tapped his fingers on the sofa arm and glared at us for the umpteenth time. For half an hour now he'd been sitting there, giving us the third degree. Time and again he'd made us go over what had happened that evening, from the knock on the door to the ambulance crew's arrival. We'd been moderately truthful, as far as it went, though we hadn't mentioned what we'd heard Carver saying. The way we told it, he'd staggered in and dropped straight down dead, no whispered words on offer. Nor did we mention Lockwood's note.

Quill Kipps stood leaning on a sideboard behind him, arms folded, watching us through narrowed eyes. Godwin and Vernon sat on spare chairs. Ned Shaw skulked in the shadows like a hyena that had just learned to stand on its hind legs, glowering at Lockwood the while. It wasn't one of our usual merry living room gatherings. We didn't offer them tea.

"What I still fail to understand," Barnes said, "is why Carver came here to *you*." His mustache rippled as he spoke; his face was heavy with suspicion.

Lockwood, sitting in his chair, pulled negligently at his sleeve. It was hard to look elegant in his current outfit, but he was doing his best. "I assume he somehow heard we were investigating the theft. Perhaps he wanted to speak with someone competent, intelligent, and resourceful, in which case we were clearly the only option."

Kipps rolled his eyes. Barnes made an impatient exclamation. "But why should he come at all? Why break cover? He was a wanted man!"

"I can only think it had something to do with the Bickerstaff mirror," Lockwood said. "I think its powers appalled him. Don't forget, it killed his colleague Neddles before they left the cemetery. Who knows what else it did. He may have wanted to come clean about it, and tell us what it could do."

Barnes's scowl traveled the room. "This mirror has been gone less than forty-eight hours, and already the two men who stole it are dead! Think about it—it would probably have killed Cubbins here too if you hadn't covered it with the net."

"That's assuming his face wouldn't have cracked the glass first," Kipps said.

"It must be found!" Barnes clapped a fist into his palm. "Or this won't be the end of it. It's deadly! It kills wherever it goes!"

"The mirror didn't kill Carver," Lockwood said quietly.

"Ah, but it did. Because people are willing to commit murder to get it."

Lockwood shook his head. "Maybe, but whoever stabbed Carver doesn't have the mirror."

"How do you know that?"

"From the money he was carrying. He'd already sold it."

"That doesn't prove anything. They might have killed him to keep him quiet."

"If I'd given Carver a thousand pounds for the mirror and then murdered him, I might be inclined to take the money back," Lockwood said. "No, this was done by someone else. Someone with access to weird daggers. If I were you, Inspector, that's where I'd start."

Barnes grunted. "Whoever did it, my point still stands," he said. "This mirror is a menace. No one can consider himself safe until it's found. And so far I don't think much of either of your investigations. Kipps's ham-fisted arrests have filled every cell in London and achieved precisely nothing. Meanwhile the best lead we have turns up dead on Lockwood's carpet!" His voice rose several notches; the mustache jutted out like a windsock in a gale. "It's not good enough! I need action! I need results!"

From the chair where he perched like an eager schoolboy, Bobby Vernon spoke for the first time. "I'm making excellent progress at the Archives, sir," he trilled. "I feel sure I'll have a breakthrough for you very soon."

George sat slumped in the depths of the sofa. "Yeah, we're working on it too."

Kat Godwin had been staring at us in mounting irritation. "Inspector," she said suddenly, "Lockwood clearly hasn't told us the whole truth about tonight. Look how shifty Cubbins is; see the guilt in that girl's eyes!"

"I thought they always looked like that," Barnes said. He glanced up as a thin-faced DEPRAC agent appeared from the hall. "Well?"

"Just had word from Portland Mews, sir, around the corner. Number seven there heard an altercation on the street around half past eleven. Raised male voices, very angry. Some kind of argument. Sure enough, there's blood on the cobbles outside. It's where it happened."

"Many thanks, Dobbs. All right, we're moving out." Barnes rose stiffly. "I should warn all of you that it's an offense not to share information with other investigating agents. I expect cooperation between your teams. I expect results. Lockwood, Cubbins—don't forget to scatter iron in your hall."

The party broke up. Barnes and his men left first, then Kipps's team; I showed them out. Quill Kipps was the last to go.

He paused at the door. "Ms. Carlyle," he said, "a word with you."

"So you *do* know my name," I said.

Kipps gave a small smile, showing his neat white teeth. "Joking aside," he said softly, "I'd like to be serious for a moment. Don't worry, I don't want to know whatever little secret Lockwood's keeping from us. Fair's fair—this is a contest, after all. Although, incidentally"—he leaned slightly closer, so that I caught a lungful of some strong, flowery scent—"do you think it was exactly sporting of Lockwood to knock down poor Ned Shaw the other day? Wasn't that slightly against the rules?"

"Shaw started it," I said. "And Lockwood didn't really knock him down, he—"

Kipps made a dismissive gesture. "Be that as it may. Ms. Carlyle, you're clearly the most intelligent of your team. And you've some Talent, too, if everything I've heard is true. Surely you don't want to hang around with these losers any longer. You've got a career to think of. I know you had an interview with Fittes a while ago; I know they failed you, but in my opinion"—he smiled again—"they made a bad mistake. Now, I have a little influence within the organization. I can pull strings, get you a position within the company. Just think: instead of eking out a living here, you could be at Fittes House, with all its power at your disposal."

"Thank you," I said, trying to keep my voice calm. I couldn't remember when I'd been so angry. "I'm quite happy where I am."

"Well, think about it," Kipps said. "The offer's open."

"And I'll have you know we're not without influence at your organization already," I added, while closing the door. "Penelope Fittes has invited us to your anniversary party in a couple of days. Perhaps we'll see you there—*if* you've been invited. Good evening."

I shut the door in his face and stood against it, breathing deeply, trying to calm down. I walked up the hall, boots crunching through salt, to the kitchen. Lockwood and George were surveying the forgotten debris from our supper. It seemed a long while ago.

"All right, Luce?" George said.

"Yeah. I just remembered that Fittes party we were invited to. We still going to that?"

Lockwood nodded. "Of course. We'll have this case done by then, I hope. We've been discussing Barnes. He wants this mirror *so* badly. He knows what it does, or something important about it, mark my words."

"Well, we know a bit too, now," George said. "What did Carver say? 'You see such things, such terrible things.' He was talking about looking in the mirror. Take it from me."

Lockwood picked up a dried sandwich, inspected it, and returned it to the plate. "If it *is* a mirror," he said. "Carver called it a *bone glass*. If it's made from bones Bickerstaff pinched from the graveyards, then it presumably contains a Visitor—that's what gives it psychic power. Maybe that's what you see when you look deeply into it? The ghost, somehow."

"Or *ghosts*," I said. "'Seven from it, not one.'"

"Well, I saw *something* in it," George said softly. "It was terrible, but I wanted to see more. . . ." He stared toward the window.

"Whatever it is," I said, "it's so bad you die of fright if you see it properly. Like that relic-man Neddles did. I reckon Bickerstaff looked in too. Maybe what he saw made him go mad and shoot himself."

Lockwood shrugged. "Could be."

"No. That wasn't the way it happened."

Lockwood stretched. "We should get on and seal the hallway. It'll be dawn soon." He stared at me. I'd jerked suddenly upright. My heart was pounding, my skin felt like ice. I was looking all around. "Lucy?"

"I thought I heard something. A voice. . . ."

"Not Carver, surely. They doused the place pretty well."

I glanced toward the hallway. "Don't know. It's possible. . . ."

"So we've got a ghost free in our house now?" George said. "Fantastic. What a terrific night."

"Well, we'll fix him." Lockwood went to the shelf behind the door; he took a pack of iron filings and tore it open. George did the same. But I stood quite still, frozen in disbelief. A whispering voice had just spoken in my ear.

"Bickerstaff? No. That wasn't the way it happened at all."

I ran my tongue over dry lips. "How can you possibly know that?" I said.

Moving like a sleepwalker, I pushed between Lockwood and George, rounded the kitchen table, and crossed over to the oven. I put my hand on its door.

Lockwood spoke to me, his voice sharp and questioning. I didn't answer, just flung the oven open. A green glow spilled out into the room. The ghost jar gleamed in the shadows, the face a hazy, malevolent mask deep within the murk. It was motionless, watching me. The eyes were narrow slits.

"How can you say that?" I said again. "How can you know?"

I heard its spectral laughter bubbling in my mind.

"*Very simple. I was there.*"

Chapter 16

et's just freeze-frame that scene a moment: me, standing by the oven, staring at the jar. The ghost grinning back at me. Lockwood staring, George staring. Four sets of goggle-eyes, four mouths hanging open. Okay, the face in the jar is still the most disgusting, but for a second it was almost a tie. It was also precisely what I'd been hoping for all those long, frustrating months: my moment of vindication.

"It's talking!" I gasped. "I can hear it! It's just been talking now!"

"Right now?" This was either George or Lockwood—one of them, both of them, I couldn't tell which. They clustered at my side.

"Not just that! It claims it knows about Bickerstaff. It says it was there! That it knows how he died!"

"It says *what?*" Lockwood's face was pale and intense; his eyes glittered. He brushed past me, bent beside the oven. The greenish radiance fell upon him as he stared into the jar. The face glared hideously back. "No. That's impossible. . . ."

"*You're not the only one who has secrets,*" the ghost said.

Lockwood looked at me. "Did it speak? I couldn't hear the words, but I felt . . . something. A connection of some kind. My skin just crawled. What did it say to you?"

I cleared my throat. "It said . . . it said 'You're not the only one who has secrets.' Sorry."

He stared at me; for a moment I thought he was going to get angry. Instead he sprang upright with sudden energy. "Let's get it out onto the table," he said. "Quick, give me a hand here, George."

Together they wrested it free. As George took hold of the jar, the ghost's face adopted a series of repulsive grimaces, each more menacing than the last.

"*Torturer . . .*" it whispered. "*I'll suck the life from your bones.*"

"Something else?" Again Lockwood had caught the psychic disturbance, but none of the details.

"It, well, it doesn't like George, basically."

"And who can blame it? Clear a place, Luce—that's it, shove the plates aside. Right, George, set it down there. That's fine."

We stood back, looked at the ghost-jar. The plasm foamed this way and that, a violent green storm contained within the walls of glass. And the face was riding upon it, sliding up and down, rotating around, sometimes spinning upside down, but always fixing us with its horrid gaze. Its eyes were notches in the smoke, its nose a billowing spout. The lips were horizontal twists of rushing substance that split, drew apart, rejoined. They moved continuously. I heard the spectral laughter again, muffled and distorted, as if the sound came from deep underwater and I was helplessly dropping down to join it. My stomach turned.

"You think we can talk to it?" Lockwood said. "Ask it questions?"

I took a deep breath. "I don't know. It's never done anything like this before."

"We've *got* to try." George's body was rigid with excitement; he bent close to the glass, blinking through his spectacles at the face, which in response turned its eyeballs inside out, perhaps as a gesture of disdain. "Lucy," he said. "Do you know how remarkable you are? You're the first person since Marissa Fittes to categorically discover a Type Three. This is sensational. We *have* to communicate with it. Who knows what we might learn—about the secrets of Death, about the Other Side . . ."

"And about Bickerstaff, too," I said. "Assuming it's not lying."

Lockwood nodded. "Which it almost certainly is."

The face in the jar gaped in mock outrage. In my ear came a sibilant whisper: "*Oh, that's rich, coming from you.*"

"Lucy?" Again Lockwood sensed the contact. George hadn't felt a thing.

"It said: 'That's rich, coming from you.'" I beckoned to them both. "Listen, can I have a word?"

We retreated to the other side of the room, out of earshot of the jar.

"If we're going to talk to it, we have to be on our guard," I breathed. "No getting snippy with each other. It'll try to cause trouble. I know it will. It'll be rude to you both, like it was before. You'll hear the words from *my* mouth, but remember, I'm not the one insulting you."

Lockwood nodded. "Fine. We'll be careful."

"Like if it calls George fat again."

"Right."

"Or Specky Four-Eyes or something."

"Okay, okay," George scowled. "Thank you. We get the point."

"Just don't get mad at me. Are we ready, then? Let's go."

The room was dark: the light on the stove top was turned down low, the blinds closed fast against the coming dawn. The kitchen cabinets rose like columns in the shadows, and through the air came drifting scents of the night's first horror: iron, salt, the taint of blood. Green light spilled across the room. At its center, on the kitchen table, the ghost-jar sat like a terrible idol on an altar, glowing with spectral force. Swirling ichor pulsed and flowed within it, but the hideous face with its sightless eyes hung motionless beneath the glass.

George had found some salt-and-vinegar chips and tossed us each a bag. We assembled ourselves in chairs around the table.

Lockwood was calm, impassive, hands quietly folded in his lap. He surveyed the ghost-jar with a cool and skeptical gaze. George carried his notebook; he sat forward, almost doubled over in his eagerness. Me? As usual, I tried to follow Lockwood's lead, but it was tough. My heart was beating too fast.

What had Marissa Fittes recommended in such circumstances? *Be polite. Be calm. Be wary.* Spirits were deceitful, dangerous, and guileful, and they *did not have our interests at heart.* I could vouch for that. I cast a sidelong look at Lockwood. The last time this ghost had spoken, it had succeeded in driving all kinds of silly doubts into my mind. And now we were planning to talk to it together? It suddenly struck me what a perilous thing this was to do.

Marissa Fittes had also warned that prolonged communication with Visitors might drive a person mad.

"Hello, spirit," I said.

The eyes opened. The ghost in the jar gazed out at me.

"Do you wish to speak to us?"

"*Aren't we polite?*" the voice whispered. "*What, not planning to roast me at two hundred degrees today?*"

I repeated this word for word. "Three hundred degrees, actually," George said cheerfully. He was scribbling the response down.

The ghost's eyes flicked in his direction; to my ears came a sound like a hungry chomping of teeth.

"On behalf of Lockwood and Company," Lockwood said, "I humbly apologize for such discourtesy and welcome the opportunity to talk with a Visitor from the Other Side. Say that to it, Luce."

I knew perfectly well that the ghost could hear Lockwood just as well as me. It was the open valve in the jar's stopper that did it; somehow, sound could pass right through. Still, I was the official intermediary. I opened my mouth to speak—but before I could do so, the ghost gave its response. It was brief, pungent, and to the point.

I passed it on.

Lockwood started. "Charming! Hold on, was that from you or the ghost?"

"The ghost, of course."

George whistled. "I'm not sure I should write *that* down."

"There's no use being polite," I said. "Trust me. It's a foul thing and there's no point pretending otherwise. So you knew Bickerstaff, did you?" I said to the jar. "Why should we believe you?"

"*Yes,*" the whisper came. "*I knew him.*"

"He says he knew him. How? You were his friend?"

"*He was my master.*"

"He was his master."

"*Like Lockwood is yours.*"

"Like . . ." I halted. "Well, that's not worth reporting either."

"Come on, Luce," Lockwood said. "Spit it out."

George's pencil was hovering. "Yeah, got to record it all."

"Like Lockwood is my master. Happy now? I mean, this skull's an idiot." I scowled over at them; Lockwood was scratching his nose as if he hadn't heard, but George was grinning as he wrote. "George," I said tartly, "just remind me. What were the names of Bickerstaff's companions? Simon Wilberforce and . . ."

"Dulac. Mary Dulac."

"Spirit! Are you Mary Dulac? Or Simon Wilberforce? What is your name?"

A sudden burst of psychic energy made me jerk back in my chair. The plasm frothed; green light coursed around the room. The mouth contorted.

"*You think I might be a girl?*" the voice spat. "*What cheek. No! I'm neither of those fools.*"

"Neither of those fools, apparently," I said. "Then who?"

I waited. The voice was silent. In the jar, the apparition had become less distinct, the outlines of the face fainter; they merged with the swirling plasm.

George took a handful of chips. "If it's gone shy all of a sudden, ask it about the bone glass, about what Bickerstaff was doing. That's the important thing."

"Yes. For instance, was he actually a grave-robber?" Lockwood said. "If so, why? And how exactly did he die?"

I rubbed my face with my hands. "Give me a chance. I can't ask all that. Let's take it one step at a—"

"*No!*" The voice was urgent, intimate, as if whispering directly into my ear. "*Bickerstaff was no grave-robber! He was a great man. A visionary! He came to a sad end.*"

"What end? The rats?"

"Hold it, Lucy—" Lockwood touched my arm. "We didn't hear what it said."

"Oh, sorry. He was a great man who came to a sad end."

"*I said he was a visionary too. You forgot that bit.*"

"Oh yeah. And a visionary. Sorry." I blinked in annoyance, then glared at the skull. "Why am I apologizing to *you?* You're making some pretty big claims about a man who kept sacks of human bones in his basement."

"*Not in his basement. In a workroom behind a secret wall.*"

"It wasn't his basement. It was a workroom behind a secret wall. . . ." I looked at the others. "Did we know that?"

"Yes," Lockwood said. "We did. It overheard George telling us that earlier this evening. It's giving us nothing new or original, in other words. It's making all this up."

"*You know that the door on Lockwood's landing is lined with iron strips,*" the voice said suddenly. "*On the inside. Why do you think that is, Lucy? What do you think he's got in there?*"

There was a silence, in which I felt a rush of blood to my ears, and the room seemed to tilt. I noticed Lockwood and George watching me expectantly.

"Nothing," I said hastily. "It didn't say anything then."

"*Ooh, you little liar. Go on, tell them what I said.*"

I kept silent. The ghost's laughter rang in my ears.

"*Seems we're all at it now, aren't we?*" the whispering voice said. "*Well, believe me or not as you please, but yes, I saw the bone glass, though I never saw it used. The master wouldn't show me. It wasn't for my eyes, he said. I wept, for it was a wonderful thing.*"

I repeated this to the others as best I could; it was hard, for the voice had grown soft and wistful, and was difficult to hear.

"All very well," Lockwood said, "but what does the bone glass *do*?"

"*It gives knowledge,*" the voice said. "*It gives enlightenment. Ah, but I could have spied on him. I knew where he kept his precious notes, hidden under the floorboards of his study. See how I held the key to his secrets in my hand? I could have learned them all. But he was a great man. He trusted me. I was tempted, but I never looked.*" The eyes glinted at me from the depths of the jar. "*You know all about that, too—don't you, Lucy?*"

I didn't repeat that last bit; it was all I could do to remember the rest without getting distracted by unnecessary details.

"*He was a great man,*" the ghost said softly. "*And his legacy is with you today, though you're too blind to see it. All of you, too blind . . .*"

"Ask him his name again," Lockwood said, when I'd reported this. "All this counts for nothing unless we get some concrete details."

I asked the question. No answer came, and the pressure in my mind felt suddenly less acute. The face in the jar was scarcely detectable. The plasm moved more sluggishly, and the spectral light was fading.

"It's going," I said.

"Its *name*," Lockwood said again.

"No," George said. "Ask him about the Other Side! Quick, Luce—"

"Too blind . . ."

The whisper faded. The glass was clear; the ghost had gone.

An old brown skull sat clamped to the bottom of the jar.

George swore softly, took off his glasses, and rubbed his eyes. Lockwood clapped his hands on his knees and rolled his neck as if it hurt him. I realized that my back ached too, all over—it was a solid knot of tension. We sat staring at the jar.

"Well, I make that one murder victim, one police interrogation, and one conversation with a ghost," George said. "Now, that's what I call a busy evening."

Lockwood nodded. "To think some people just watch television."

Our encounter with the skull made it an all-nighter, of course. We couldn't go straight to bed after that. Despite our frustrations with its lack of cooperation, we were all too excited to rest, too pepped by the rarity of the event. According to George, this was indeed the first confirmed Type Three since Marissa Fittes had died. There'd been reports of others down the years, but the agents involved had all either died soon afterward or been certified insane, and sometimes both. Certainly no one had been able to provide a proper witness, as he and Lockwood had just done. I was unique, my gift was something to be prized, and it would make all our fortunes if we played our cards right. Lockwood was no less thrilled; he made us all a round of bacon sandwiches (an event almost as rare as chatting with Type Threes) and, while we ate them, talked about how we might proceed. The question was whether to go public straightaway, or try to get the skull to speak again, perhaps in front of other independent witnesses. He was sure many of our rivals would be reluctant to believe our story.

I didn't play too much part in the debate. I was pleased—of course—with my success, and with all the praise I was getting, but I felt exhausted, too. The effort of listening to the skull had quite worn me out. All I wanted to do was sleep. So I let the others talk, and when Lockwood moved on to discuss the one possible solid bit of information he felt we'd gotten from the ghost, I didn't join in that conversation either. But Lockwood and George read and re-read George's scribbled notes, and the more they read, the more energized and talkative they became.

The skull had mentioned something no one else knew, you see. Bickerstaff's hiding papers under the floorboards of his study. Secret papers.

Papers that might hold the key to the riddle of the bone glass.

Papers that might, conceivably, still be lying there, in the deserted house on the edge of Hampstead Heath.

Now, that *was* interesting.

As Lockwood said, the ghost was almost certainly fibbing. The chances of it truly having a close connection to Bickerstaff and the bone glass were not high. Even if it *was* telling the truth, those secret papers might well have disintegrated or even been eaten (how we laughed at this) by rats. But there *was* a chance. They *might* be there. He wondered if it was worth checking. George felt it was, and I was too tired to disagree. Before we went to bed (it was already dawn), we had our plans in place. The following day, assuming there were no other developments, we would mount an expedition.

The birds were singing outside the windows when I finally left the kitchen; it was going to be another lovely morning.

As I closed the door, I glanced back into the room. The ghost-jar still sat where we'd left it on the table—quiet and peaceful, the plasm almost translucent. . . .

The skull was grinning at me, as skulls do.

Chapter 17

When visiting a property with such a checkered history as the Bickerstaff ruin, you might think it is safest to stick to daylight hours. This (the sensible option) was sadly impractical for us, for a number of reasons. The first was that, after a night like we'd just had, we didn't get out of bed till noon, and it took much of the afternoon to prepare our supplies and call the appropriate authorities to get access to the deserted house. The second was George's insistence on dropping in to the Chertsey Records Office in search of *The Confessions of Mary Dulac*, that old document by one of Bickerstaff's associates. George wanted to do this as soon as possible; he hoped it might give us some insight into the horror that had taken place at Bickerstaff's place all those years ago. Also, he figured it was only a matter of time before Bobby Vernon read the same old newspapers he'd found, and made precisely the same connection.

The final (and most important) reason why we didn't get there until after sundown was me—or rather the question of my peculiar Talents. After our chat with the skull, Lockwood's faith in these was now sky-high. He told me as much as we worked in the office together, collecting equipment for the operation.

"There's no question about it, Luce," he said, setting out a neat row of salt-bombs along the floor, "your sensitivity is phenomenal, and we've got to give you every chance to use it. Who knows what you might pick up in the Bickerstaff house after dark? And I don't just mean by Listening—you could use your sense of Touch as well."

"Yeah," I said heavily. "Maybe." You might detect that I didn't speak with wild enthusiasm. It's true that I can sometimes pick up impressions of the past by touching objects that possess a psychic residue, but that doesn't mean it's always a pleasant thing to do. It was pretty clear that the Bickerstaff residence was unlikely to provide me with many jolly experiences, no matter how chirpy Lockwood might be right now.

I couldn't share much of his good humor that afternoon anyway. Once again the daylight had had the effect of lessening the thrill of the whispering skull's words, and I found myself increasingly uncomfortable that we were following a trail it had set for us. The first things I did when I came downstairs were to close the valve in the stopper and to cover the jar with a cloth. I didn't want the ghost to hear or see us unless we willed it. Even so, I couldn't help feeling the damage had already been done.

I finished emptying our work belts onto my desk, and began sorting through the thermometers and flashlights, the candles and matchboxes, the vials of lavender water, and all the rest, making sure everything was in working order. Lockwood was humming peaceably to himself as he set about restocking our supplies of iron. That was the other thing about the skull: almost in the same breath as mentioning Bickerstaff's secret papers, it had made new insinuations about Lockwood's room upstairs.

I turned to look out of the office window into the basement yard. Iron bands across the inside of the door? There was only one reason anyone might do that. . . . No, clearly the claim was ridiculous. Yet how could I take one of the ghost's comments on trust and disbelieve the other?

"Lucy," Lockwood said—it was almost as if he'd been reading my thoughts—"I've been thinking about our friend the skull. You're the one who talks to it. You've got a sense of its personality. Why do *you* think it's suddenly started speaking?"

I paused a moment before answering. "I really don't know. To be honest, I don't trust anything it says, but I *do* think there must be something about the Bickerstaff case that attracts it. You remember when it spoke, the first night—after we got back from the cemetery? I think we'd been talking about Bickerstaff, just as we were last night. It's overheard us talk about dozens of other cases these last few months, and it's never gotten involved before. Now it has, twice in three days. I don't think that's a coincidence."

Lockwood was filling up a canister of iron filings. He nodded slowly. "You're right. We've got to tread carefully until we understand what it wants. And there was one other thing it said. It claimed that Bickerstaff's mirror—this bone glass—gives you knowledge and enlightenment. What do you think *that* means?"

"Not a clue."

"It's just that George *has* looked in the glass. Only briefly, of course, but still. . . ." He glanced up at me. "How does he seem to you, Lucy? Do you think he's okay?"

"He seems a little distracted sometimes, but that's hardly new."

"Well, we'll keep an eye on him." Lockwood grinned; it was that warm smile that made everything seem simpler, ready to click perfectly into place. "With luck, he'll bring us some info on Bickerstaff today. Hopefully we'll hear from Flo soon as well. If we get word of Winkman's auction too, that'll *really* put the wind in our sails."

But Lockwood's optimism was misplaced. Flo Bones did not appear that day, and we had to wait till almost five o'clock before George returned, very weary and out of sorts.

"There's strange things going on in Chertsey," he said as he collapsed into a chair. "I went to the Records Office, and they confirmed that *The Confessions of Mary Dulac was* a real document from their archives. But when they went to get it—guess what? It was gone. Stolen. They can't say when, or how long ago. And there's no telling whether other copies even exist. Ah! It's *so* frustrating!"

"Was it little Bobby Vernon?" I asked. "Maybe he's ahead of you."

George scowled. "Wrong. *I'm* ahead of *him*—he's made an appointment in Chertsey for tomorrow. No, someone else thought it was worth stealing. . . . Well, we'll see. I called Albert Joplin on the way home, asked him if he had any ideas about where another copy might be. He's an excellent researcher. Might be able to help us here."

Lockwood frowned. "Joplin? You shouldn't let anyone know what we're up to. What if he tells Kipps?"

"Oh, Albert's all right. He likes me. Tell you what, though, he's fallen out with Mr. Saunders. Saunders is furious about all the trouble at Kensal Green; he's suspended operations, sent most of the night watch home without pay. Joplin's very annoyed about it. . . ." He adjusted his glasses and looked around at us. "So, that's my news. What's been going on back here?"

"I spoke to the Hampstead authorities," Lockwood said. "The site of the Green Gates Sanatorium is still derelict, cordoned off from the rest of the Heath, but accessible from a street called Whitestone Lane. Luce, you check the map book; we'll get the last bus before Curfew. Bickerstaff's house is on the edge of the site, open and unlocked. No keys ever required, because no one in their right mind goes there, apparently."

"Sounds just our kind of place," I said.

Lockwood got up; he stretched lazily. "Well, it's that time of the afternoon. I'm going to stick a sword into a straw woman. Then I'm off to rest. If half the stories we've heard about this house are true, it's going to be an active night."

Hampstead Hill, a leafy suburb in the north of London, is a pretty genteel sort of place, at least during the hours of daylight, and if our walk that evening was anything to go by, the streets on the western edge of Hampstead Heath are the cushiest of all. Wide avenues, lined with trees and rows of ghost-lamps, curved gently around the contours of the hill. Swanky properties, sprawling and detached, nestled in large gardens. Even the dusk that settled rapidly around us had a prosperous, well-fed feel.

This impression was maintained for most of the way along Whitestone Lane, a short, broad cul-de-sac of heavily built mid-Victorian villas lying right on the margins of the Heath. Well-kept lawns, verdant borders, rhododendrons as plump and bushy as a beggar's beard: the first few houses easily kept up the Hampstead standard. Toward the end of the road, however, things became shabbier, and the last two residences were empty and unoccupied. Beyond them the road ended at a pair of iron gates, high, rusted, and topped by rolls of barbed wire. Triangular DEPRAC warning posters, fringed with fluorescent orange, signaled it as a no-go zone. This was the entrance to the site of the Green Gates Sanatorium, burned down a century ago, and abandoned ever since.

A coil of rusted chain had been wound around the gates to secure them. There wasn't any padlock. There wasn't any need for one.

With gloved hands, Lockwood began to untie the chain; the links were stiff and fused. "You said they tried building a housing development here once, George," he said. "But they had to abandon it because of 'disturbances.' What was the story there?"

George had been staring through the gate bars into the darkness of the Heath. Despite the evening's warmth, he wore a wool hat and a pair of fingerless gloves. He also had on his dark night-jacket, jeans, and work boots; an extra strap, laden with canisters and salt-bombs, was looped across his torso. To my surprise, he had also opted for an extra large backpack, different from the one I'd prepared for him. It was clearly heavy; his face was lined with perspiration. "The usual," he said. "You know the kind of thing."

Lockwood pulled the chain free, pushed sharply on the metal. With a crack like bones breaking, the gates sprang open. One after another, we slipped through. George and I switched on our flash-lights. Almost directly beneath our feet, the road's fissured asphalt was swallowed under a layer of long, waving grass. Our lights danced and flitted over uneven, lumpy ground. Here and there tall beeches rose, and clumps of young oaks and silver birch. The line of the road curled away to the left among the trees.

"We follow the track to the site of the sanatorium," George said. "Half a mile, a bit higher on the hill."

Lockwood nodded. "Fine. We'll follow you."

We went in silence, single file, legs brushing through grasses. The last heat of the day still radiated from the earth. The moon had risen, and a cool silvered light bathed the undulating wasteland. Banks of white cloud towered like castles in the sky.

"When you say 'the usual,' George," I said finally, "you mean Shades?"

"Yeah, Shades and Glimmers, mainly. Half-seen presences, dim lights floating in the air. And the sanatorium's isolated on the hill, remember. No one wanted to stay up there."

"Nothing too dangerous, though?"

"Not in the sanatorium ruins itself. The Bickerstaff house is per-haps another matter."

We had climbed a little way along the contour of the hill. The lights of London stretched below us like a glittering neon sea. It was very silent. Curfew had already sounded, and the city had turned inward on itself, shutting out the night.

"Do you mind if we stop for a bit?" George said. "I need a breather."

He slung his backpack aside and collapsed upon the ground. It really *was* a monster pack, and the shape was odd—quite hard and curved; not blobby like you get with chains. "What exactly do you *have* in there, George?" I said.

"Oh, just some extra supplies. Don't worry about me. The exercise will do me good."

I stared at it, my frown deepening. "Since when have you cared about—?" And then I knew. I recognized the shape. I strode across and flicked open the backpack top, loosened the drawstring. I shone my flashlight on the plastic stopper, the smoothly curving sides of a familiar silver-glass jar.

"The *skull*?" I cried. "You brought the skull! You snuck it along with us!"

George looked pained. "*Snuck* makes it sound easy. It's quite an effort, actually. I know ectoplasm technically weighs nothing, but you wouldn't think so to feel this. My poor old back—"

"And you were going to tell me this *when*?"

"Hopefully never. It's just we don't know exactly where Bickerstaff's study is, do we? But the skull does. And if we couldn't figure it out, Lockwood thought—"

"*What?!*" I spun around on our leader, who had been doing a good impression of someone utterly fascinated by a nearby patch of nettles. "Lockwood! You knew about this?"

He cleared his throat. "Well—"

"He suggested it," George said promptly. "It was his idea. Which makes me think *he* should be doing some of the carrying, come to mention it. I've been lugging this since Marylebone, and my poor old back—"

"Will you shut up about your poor old back? This is crazy! You want me to talk with a dangerous Type Three ghost *inside* another haunted zone, with who knows what other Visitors around? Are you both mad? You expected me to agree to that?"

"No," George said. "We didn't. Which is why we didn't tell you."

I gave a cry of disgust. "Forget it! What happened to our treading carefully, Lockwood? I've a good mind to go back home."

"Please, Lucy," Lockwood said. "Don't overreact. It's not dangerous. We're keeping the jar in the pack; the stopper is closed—the ghost can't affect you, or communicate in any way. But we *do* have it as backup—if we're stuck and unable to find these papers."

"Papers that almost certainly don't exist," I growled. "Don't forget we're following a clue given to us by a malicious ghost-head in a jar. It's not reliable!"

"I'm not saying it is. But since it claims to have worked with Bickerstaff, taking it back to this house might be a good way of encouraging it to speak some more."

I didn't look at him; if I had, he would have given me the smile, and I wasn't in the mood for that. "You're taking me for granted," I said. "Me *and* this house."

"Terrible things happened up there," Lockwood said, "but that doesn't mean the place is haunted now. Bickerstaff's ghost was at the cemetery, remember? *He's* not here. The bone glass isn't here. Well, then! What's left to harm us?"

He knew better than that. We all did. Things were never that simple. I didn't answer, but just shouldered my pack and set off up the path, leaving the others to follow.

The trail cut in among the trees, leaving the London lights behind. The humps beneath the grass grew larger, and at last broke upward into stretches of crumbled wall, most low and tangled with moss and grass, some still rising to second-story height. It was the remains of the burned sanatorium. My instincts prickled; I sensed the presence of unwelcome things. Great pale moths fluttered lazily among the ruins. I looked at them with suspicion, but they seemed natural enough. We went on cautiously.

"I see death-glows," Lockwood said. "Faint ones in the ruins."

For a moment, when I listened, I thought I heard the faint crackling of flames, shouts, and distant screams. . . . Then the sounds faded. All I could hear was the wind sighing gently among the leaves.

We walked a little farther. As we passed close to the tallest remaining stretch of wall, a faint gray shape, only visible from the corner of the eye, appeared in the shadows of a broken doorway and stood there, watching us. I felt the cold brush of its attention.

"Type One," Lockwood said. "A Shade or Lurker. Nothing to worry about. What's that up there?" He stopped, pointed toward the crown of the hill.

"That'll be it," George said. "The Bickerstaff house."

The building rose stark and black against the silvered sky, distant from the tangled mess of ruins. It was set within its own little boundary wall, a large, ugly, raw-boned construction, made of awkward-looking bricks that seemed somehow out of proportion. In sunlight, I guessed they'd be dark gray. The roof had many chimneys, many steeply sloping planes of slate, some of which had fallen away. I could see roof beams jutting through like ribs. There were plenty of large windows, all empty, black, and watchful, the typical eyes of a deserted house. A gravel path led ruler-straight toward the door, up the incline of the hill. The garden was overgrown, the grass high as our thighs.

We stood at the gate, hands on rapier hilts, considering it coolly. George took a packet of mints from his pocket and passed them around.

"Well, I'll admit it *looks* pretty bad," Lockwood said, sucking on his mint. "But since when has a house's appearance meant anything? Remember that slaughterhouse in Deptford? That was a *terrible* looking place. But nothing happened there."

"Nothing happened to *you*," I corrected him. "Because you were upstairs hobnobbing with the owner. It was George and I who got jumped by a Limbless in the basement."

"Oh, yes. Maybe I'm thinking of somewhere else. What I *mean* is, we're not necessarily going to run into trouble here. Despite its history of violent death. Pass us another mint, would you, George?"

As reassuring speeches went, I'd heard better. Still, Lockwood & Co. hadn't earned its citywide reputation by dawdling outside haunted houses. That wasn't why Barnes had put us on this case, wasn't why we were going to beat Kipps to the solution. Come to think of it, it wasn't why Penelope Fittes had invited us to her party. Squaring our shoulders, we set off up the path.

"Just remember," Lockwood said, cheerfully breaking the night's silence and disturbing our morbid thoughts, "we've got two set objectives here. We look for those papers the skull mentioned. We try to pick up any psychic traces left by Bickerstaff and his friends. Simple, clean, efficient. We go straight in, we come straight out. Easy. There won't be any problems."

We halted at the end of the path. I contemplated the moldering steps, the crooked door, the shutters hanging askew against the broken windows, the little weather-beaten demons carved into the spiral pillars on either side of the porch. It has to be said I didn't *wholly* share his confidence.

There was a strong sweet scent coming from a climbing shrub that choked one wall. The air was warm and close. George had pattered up the steps; he squinted through the grimy bottle glass window beside the door. "Can't see anything," he said. "Who's going in first?"

"That'll be Lucy," Lockwood said.

I frowned. "Again? It's always me."

"No, it isn't. I was first for Mrs. Barrett. George did the iron coffin."

"Yes, but before that I—"

"No arguments, Luce. You're in the hot seat tonight. Don't worry, we'll be right behind you. Besides, like I say, with any luck there'll be nothing dangerous there. Just psychic memories and traces."

"Which is precisely what a Visitor *is*, Lockwood. An aggressive psychic memory. . . . Oh, very well. Why can't we ever do this at a more sensible time, like noon?"

I knew the answer to *that*, of course. It's only after dark you can detect the faint and hidden things. It's only after dark a house's memories begin to stir.

I pushed at the door, expecting it to be warped shut, or locked, or both. It was none of those. The door opened soundlessly, unleashing stale air and a pervasive smell of decay.

And I have to say my skin *did* crawl a little as I stood there, and the hairs on my neck *did* rise. Maybe Lockwood was right. Maybe the place would be free of actual Visitors. But this was a house where the previous proprietor had engaged in years of sinister occult research, where he'd probably tried to summon the spirits of the dead in a series of unsavory experiments, and where he'd suffered a mysterious and solitary death. Let's face it: we were talking trace memories that would need more than a squirt of air freshener to remove.

Still, I'm an agent, etcetera, etcetera. You know the deal.

Without (much) hesitation, I stepped inside.

Chapter 18

The good news was that nothing dead and wicked came rushing straight toward me down the darkened hallway. In our profession, that's a result. And when I listened, as I always do right off, I heard no psychic screams or voices. It was very quiet. The only sounds were the scrapes and shuffles of Lockwood and George as they squeezed in behind me and dumped their bags on the floor.

An empty chamber, cavernous and high. A strong smell of damp and mildew. I kept the flashlight off, as it's always wise to do, but it wasn't as dark inside as I expected, and my eyes began to see things. Shafts of moonlight shone down from holes in the roof somewhere far above, spearing into a staircase at the far end of the hall. It was a curved stair, dark with moisture and ruined by years of rain. In places, it was blocked with rubble; in places the wood had fallen away. Great pallid clumps of bracket fungus erupted from the balustrade, and thin knots of grass grew between skirting and wall. White crusts of mold flowered on the ceiling. Old brown leaves, blown in by countless autumn storms, lay in long piles across the hallway; papery and skeletal, they rustled as we moved.

I couldn't see any of the graffiti you'd expect in a long-deserted house: clear evidence of its dubious reputation. No furniture, no furnishings. A mahogany picture rail ran around the walls up near the ceiling. Flecks of wallpaper shivered in the warm draft we'd brought from outside. There were no light fixtures anywhere; ragged holes showed where they'd been torn away.

Somewhere in this rotting dereliction, Dr. Bickerstaff had worked with objects stolen from the local graveyards.

Somewhere here he had died. And then the rats—

No. It wasn't good to dwell on that story. I could feel my heartbeat quickening. Anxiety and stress are two emotions Visitors like to feed on. I shook my head clear and turned my attention to procedure, to the job at hand.

"Lockwood?" I said. He'd been gazing quietly into the dark.

"No death-glows here. You?"

"All very still."

He nodded. "Fine. What about you, George?"

"Temperature's sixty degrees, which is nice and normal. All fine so far."

"Okay." Lockwood walked a little farther into the room, shoes scuffling through the dry dead leaves. "We work quickly and quietly. We look for Bickerstaff's study, and we look for his laboratory or workroom, where his experiments took place. The newspaper said that was accessed from a living room—so that's probably downstairs. We don't know about the study. If we run across a psychic hot spot, Lucy has the option of taking readings—but that's up to her. And we don't bring out the skull unless she says so."

"That's right," I said.

"The main hot spot is likely to be upstairs," George said. His voice was curiously flat. Perhaps something in the feel of the place had affected him. "The room of the rats."

"If there *were* any rats," Lockwood said. "Anyway, we'll try to avoid that one."

We moved away along the hall and entered the nearest room. This too was quite empty—just bare boards and plaster, all picked out in silver moonlight. The ceiling was whole, the room dry. I ran my hand along the walls as I wandered past them, feeling for psychic currents. No, didn't find anything; it was just a dead, clean space.

We tried the room behind it, and that was similarly quiet. No temperature changes, no miasma or creeping fear. We tried a third, opposite the others across the hall. From its position and the ornate molding in the ceiling you'd guess it had been a formal reception room, where Bickerstaff and his guests took tea. Here even the wallpaper was missing; part of the wainscoting, too. There was nothing but moonlight, boards, and plaster. An uncomfortable thought occurred to me. As with Bickerstaff, so with the house. The whole place was a skeleton, stripped down to the bones.

As we returned to the hall, I caught a faint vibration; muffled, somehow familiar. "Lockwood, George," I whispered, "either of you get that?"

They listened. Lockwood shook his head. George shrugged.

"*I'm* hardly likely to, am I?" he said heavily. "My senses aren't nearly as sharp as—" He gave a sudden gasp of fright. "*What's that?*"

I'd seen it too. A traveling slit of darkness; a long, low, agile shape, moving through the shadows at the farthest margin of the room. It darted just below the wall, close to the window, but keeping out of the hazy pyramid of moonlight. It circled around toward us along the line of wainscoting.

Iron sang: Lockwood's rapier was out and ready. With his other hand he plucked his penlight from his belt. He stabbed it on, transfixing a tiny, black-brown huddling body in the circle of piercing light.

"Only a mouse," I breathed. "A tiny one. I thought—"

George exhaled loudly. "Me too. Thought it was bigger. Thought it was a rat."

Lockwood clicked off his penlight. The mouse—released as if from a spell—was gone; we sensed rather than saw its swift departure.

"Mustn't get rats on the brain," Lockwood said drily. "Everyone okay? Shall we go upstairs?"

But I was frowning at the far side of the room. "Hold on," I said. "When you turned your flashlight on just now, I thought I saw . . ." I took out mine, angled the beam at the far wall. Yes, caught there in the clean, bright circle, a thin black line cutting upward through the plaster. The telltale outline of a door.

When we drew close we could see the hinges embedded in the wall, and a small, rough hole where a key or handle must have sat. "Well done, Luce," Lockwood breathed. "Once this must have been covered with wallpaper, or with a fake bookcase, maybe. It would have been very hard to find."

"You think this is the way to Bickerstaff's workroom?"

"Must be. You can see where they forced it, years ago. It's hanging loose now. I think we can get in."

When he pulled at the door, it swung forward at an angle, for its upper part had rotted off the hinge. Beyond was a narrow passageway running deeper into the house. No light penetrated it. Lockwood switched on his penlight and took a brief survey. The corridor was narrow, empty, ending in another door. The smell of damp and mold was very strong.

All due caution had to be observed now. Before entering, we took systematic measurements, and jotted them down. Then, ducking low (the top of the door was below Lockwood's head), we started off along the little passage. Progress was slow and careful; every few yards we halted to use our Talents and take fresh readings. Nothing alarming happened. The temperature dropped, but only marginally. Lockwood saw no death-glows. Faint ripples of sound pulsed at the edge of my hearing, but I could make nothing of them. There were spiders here and there, on the ceiling and in the dust of the floor, but too few to be significant. Touch yielded no sensations.

George had become subdued. He moved slowly and spoke little, passing up several cast-iron opportunities for sarcastic or insulting remarks, which, frankly, was unlike him. At last, with him lagging behind us in the passage, I mentioned this to Lockwood. He'd noticed it too.

"What do you think?" I said. "Malaise?"

"Could be. But this is the first time he's entered a psychically charged location since he saw that bone glass. We'd better watch him carefully."

Of the four common signs of an imminent manifestation (the others being *chill*, *miasma*, and *creeping fear*), *malaise* is the most insidious. It's a feeling of soul-sapping heaviness and melancholy that can steal up on you so slowly you never notice it—until you have a ghost creeping toward you and you realize you don't have the willpower to run or raise your sword. At this extreme it becomes ghost-lock, and ghost-lock—being the opposite of life and happiness and laughter—is often fatal. This is why good agents always look out for each other, why we work in teams. Subtly, without drawing attention to ourselves, Lockwood and I moved so that George was between us. We protected him on either side.

We arrived at the door at the end of the passage. I put my fingers on the handle. A thrill of extreme cold speared up my hand and arm; I caught the on-off sound of voices—male ones, talking heatedly. I smelled cigar smoke and something sharper, an acrid chemical tang. Almost at once, the echo was gone.

"I'm getting traces," I said.

Lockwood's voice came from the back. "Everyone stand very still. Keep looking and listening. Don't open the door."

We waited in silence for a minute, maybe more.

At last Lockwood gave the all-clear. "Right," he said. "Ready when you are, Luce."

That was my cue. I took a deep breath, gripped the handle again, and stepped into the room.

Utter blackness enfolded me. I instantly sensed I was in a larger space. As always, it was tempting to switch on my flashlight, but I resisted the impulse and stood still, letting my mind open. Just behind me I could hear the door easing shut. Neither of the others spoke, but I could hear the quiet movement of their feet, feel their presence as they pressed beside me in the dark. They stood very close—closer than normal—but I didn't really blame them. In fact, I was grateful for it. It was so very, very dark in there.

I looked, but saw nothing. I listened, heard only the scantest ripples of sound, which swiftly faded. I waited for Lockwood to give the lights-on signal.

And waited. He was really taking his time.

"You both ready?" I asked finally. "I don't get anything. Do you?"

I became suddenly aware that I could no longer sense anyone on either side.

"You *ready*, Lockwood?" I said, my voice a little louder.

Nothing.

From somewhere across the room came a man's deep cough.

A surge of fear—strong, knife-thin—rose through me. I scrabbled at my belt, switched on my flashlight, swung it rapidly to and fro.

Just a room, another barren space: bare walls, dusty floorboards. A single window cavity, blocked with bricks. In the center of the room, a massive table with a metal top.

None of that interested me, because I was alone. Lockwood and George weren't there.

I spun around, wrenched open the door. My shaking flashlight picked out the pair of them a few steps away. They had their backs to me, their rapiers out; they were staring up the passage.

"What the hell are you doing out here?" I said.

"Didn't you hear it, Luce?" Lockwood hissed. "The scurrying?"

"Like rats," George whispered. "I thought it was coming toward us, but . . ." He seemed to notice me for the first time, standing in the door. "Oh, you've been inside."

"Of course I have." A finger of cold moved down my spine. "You came in too, right? You were in the room with me."

"No, we weren't. Watch where you're pointing that flashlight. The light's in my eyes."

"We thought you were with us here, Luce," Lockwood said.

"No, I went through the door, just like— Are you *sure* you didn't follow?" I remembered the soft shuffling sounds, the invisible presences pressing close. My voice grew tight and forced. "I felt you standing next to me. . . ."

"We didn't notice you go in, Luce. We got distracted by the scurrying."

"I'm surprised you didn't hear it," George said.

"Of *course* I didn't hear it!" I burst out. "If I'd heard it, do you think I would have left you behind and gone in there?!"

Lockwood touched my hand. "It's all right. Calm down. You need to calm down and tell us what's happened."

I took a long, deep breath to stop myself from trembling. "Come in through here and I'll tell you. From now on, we need to stay very close together. And please, let's none of us get distracted anymore."

The secret chamber, which we guessed had been Bickerstaff's workroom, displayed no other immediate psychic traces once we were all inside. Lockwood set a lantern on the sill beneath the bricked-up window; by its light George wandered around the perimeter, inspecting the wall. There was no other exit. Old gas lamp fixtures, rusty and sagging, extended from the bare plaster. The table in the center was the only furniture, its steel legs bolted to the floor. Its iron top was dirty with dust and plaster fragments. Deep grooves ran along the edges and opened into little spouts projecting over the floor.

Lockwood ran his finger along one groove. "Nice little channels," he said, "for the flow of blood. This is a dissection table. Mid-nineteenth century. I've seen examples at the Royal College of Surgeons. Looks like it was here that good old Dr. Bickerstaff experimented with body parts of the deceased. Pity it's made of iron, Luce, or you might have gotten some interesting psychic feedback from it."

I'd been drinking water from my backpack and was now chewing furiously on a piece of chocolate. I still felt shaken by my experiences at the door, but my fright had hardened into something stronger. If the presences here wanted to warn me off, they'd have to do better than that. I tossed the chocolate wrapper aside. "It was in this room they used to meet," I said. "A group of men, smoking and talking about their experiments. I know that much already, but I may get more. So hush up. I want to try something."

I moved to the opposite wall, far away from the iron surface of the table. There'd been a fireplace here; the grate was choked with birds' nests, rubble, fragments of wood and plaster. It seemed to me that this was the heart of the room, where Bickerstaff and his companions would have stood and smoked, discussing whatever lay upon the table. Here, if anywhere, the traces might be strong.

I put my fingertips against the plaster of the wall. Cool, damp, even oily to the touch. I closed my eyes, and lost myself. I *listened*. . . .

Sound welled up from the past. I grasped at it; it fell away.

It's strange how psychic echoes work. They come and go—first strong, then weak; waxing, then subsiding—like they're a beating heart or rhythmic pulse, deep in the substance of the house. It makes Touch a tricky, unreliable Talent. You can try the same spot five times and get nothing; on the sixth, you're knocked off your feet with the power of the psychic recall. I trailed my hand along the walls, tried the fireplace and the blocked-up window, and the only result was dirt-stained fingertips.

Time went by. I heard Lockwood shuffling his feet, George scratching somewhere unmentionable; otherwise they were silent. I had them both well trained.

I was just about to reach in my bag for my pocket pack of Agent's Wipes™ ("Ideal for removing soot, grave dirt, and ectoplasm stains") when I chanced to brush against the wall beside the door. A thin, sharp shock crackled out like sheet lightning across the back of my hand. I flinched away, and then—because I knew the sensation for what it was—deliberately placed my fingers back on the cold, rough plaster.

At once, as if I'd switched a radio on, I heard voices beside me in the room. I closed my eyes, turned to face the chamber, let my mind fill in the image that the sounds suggested.

A group of men, several of them, stood around the dissecting table. I picked up a general murmur of conversation, laughter, the smell of strong tobacco. There was something in the middle of the room: something on the table. One voice, louder, more assertive than the others, rose above the rest. The hubbub quietened, to be replaced by a solemn round of clinking glasses. The echoes faded.

And swelled again. This time I heard noise from a single throat— a busy, preoccupied whistling, as of someone deeply engaged in a pleasant task. He was sawing something; I heard the rasping of the blade. Silence fell . . . and now there was something else inside the room. I felt its presence in the horrible sense of spectral cold, in the sudden dread that made my teeth rattle in my gums. Also in a hateful sound I'd heard before: the burring wings of innumerable flies.

A voice sounded in the darkness.

"Try Wilberforce. He's eager. He'll do it."

Instantly the whistling and the sawing noise were gone. But the buzzing grew stronger, and now the terrible cold rose up to engulf me, just as it had three nights before, when I stood beside the Bickerstaff grave. I opened my mouth in pain. And as I did so there suddenly came a single cry from many throats, screamed directly in my ear.

"Give us back our bones!"

I jerked my hand from the wall. At once, like water sluicing down a drain, the deathly cold was sucked away, and I felt again the clammy warmth of the empty room.

George and Lockwood stood by the table, watching me.

I took my thermos from my bag and drank hot tea before telling them what I'd heard.

"The sound of the flies," I said at last, "the desperate cold . . . it was just the same as in the cemetery. Both have to do with the bone glass, I think. Bickerstaff definitely constructed it here."

Lockwood tapped the surface of the table. "To do *what*, though? That's the question. You look in the bone glass, and what do you see?"

"I don't know. But that idiot made something very bad."

"This voice you heard," George said. "Was it Bickerstaff, do you think?"

"Maybe. But actually I thought it sounded more like—"

It's never great when one of us breaks off halfway through a sentence like that. It's always bad news. Generally speaking, it means something's happened, or is very much *about* to happen, and we have to stop talking or die.

"Do you hear it?" I said.

Beyond the half-closed door: a little subtle scraping noise. A limping, shuffling, creeping *something* coming up the passage, and getting ever closer all the time.

"Turn the lantern low," Lockwood whispered.

George hit the switch; the room went almost black. Light enough to see by, dark enough for our psychic senses to stay strong. Without words we fanned out in the old Plan D positions: me to the right of the door, pressed close against the wall; George to its left, slightly farther out, so that he was clear if spectral forces smashed the door aside. Lockwood stood directly in front, ready to face the main attack. We each drew our rapiers. I wiped my left hand on my leggings, removing sudden perspiration. This is the worst part: when the Visitor's still concealed. When you know it's coming, but the full horror has yet to hit you. It's a time for the mind to play its tricks, for paralyzing fear to set in. To distract myself I ran my hand across the pouches in my belt, counting, memorizing, making sure everything was ready.

The soft, soft noises drew close. Through the crack in the door came a pale and spreading light. In its heart a shadow swelled and gathered.

Lockwood's arm moved back; the metal glinted. I raised my sword.

Chapter 19

A n unseen force struck the door, which was thrown violently back to hit George in the face. A fizz, a crack, a dark shape sprang into the room. Lockwood danced forward, swung his rapier. There was a strangled squawk of alarm.

For an instant, nothing moved; Lockwood seemed frozen. My rapier too hung halfway through its arc; my muscles had locked as soon as I heard the breaking canister and smelled the salt and iron scattered around me on the floor.

I plucked out my flashlight and switched it full on, illuminating Lockwood in mid attack position, the point of his rapier inches from Quill Kipps's throat. Kipps had one leg slightly raised; he was leaning backward with a goggling expression on his face, his chest going rapidly up and down. His own rapier tip was wobbling in midair a short distance from Lockwood's stomach.

Crowded in the doorway behind stood Kat Godwin, holding a night-lantern, and Ned Shaw, clasping another salt-bomb. Little Bobby Vernon's startled eyes peered from the darkness somewhere south of Shaw's left armpit. Each unlovely visage displayed mingled bafflement and terror.

Silence reigned, except for George's muffled swearing behind the door.

All at once Lockwood and Kipps jumped away from one another with exclamations of disgust.

"What the hell are *you* doing?" Kipps croaked.

"I might ask you the same thing."

"That's none of your business."

"It's *precisely* my business," Lockwood said. He ran his hand irritably through his hair. "It's *my* business that you're on. You're living dangerously, Kipps. You almost got a rapier in the neck there."

"Me? We thought you were a Visitor. If it wasn't for my bullet-speed reactions, I'd have completely disemboweled *you*."

Lockwood raised an eyebrow. "Hardly. It was only because I could already see that you saw who I was that I stopped myself driving the pommel of your own sword sharply back into your abdomen using the Baedecker-Flynn reverse-strike maneuver. Lucky for you that I did, and so didn't."

There was a pause. "Well," Kipps said, "if I understood what you were talking about, I'd no doubt have a neat retort." He returned his rapier to his belt. Lockwood stowed his, too. Ned Shaw, Bobby Vernon, and Kat Godwin loped scowlingly into the room. George emerged from behind the door, rubbing a nose that seemed even smaller and stubbier than before. For a while no one said much, but there was a great deal of assertive clinking as rapiers and other weapons were grudgingly put away.

"So," Lockwood said, "you've resorted to simply following us around, have you? That's pretty low."

"Following *you?*" Kipps gave a derisory laugh. "We, my friend, are following leads young Bobby Vernon here uncovered in the Archives. It wouldn't surprise me if you were following *us*."

"No need for that. George's research is doing us just fine."

Bobby Vernon tittered. "Really? After that display on Wimbledon Common, I'm surprised Cubbins still *has* a job."

Lockwood frowned. "It's going to be a pleasure to win this contest, Quill. By the way, your ad in the *Times* doesn't have to be *too* large. A plainly written half page admission of defeat will do absolutely fine."

"That's assuming Kipps *can* actually read and write," George said.

Ned Shaw stirred. "Careful what you say, Cubbins."

"I'm sorry. Let me rephrase it. I'll bet there are apes in the Borneo rain forests with a better grasp of literacy than him."

Shaw's eyes bulged; he fumbled at his belt. "Right, that's it—"

Lockwood flicked his coat aside, put his hand to his sword. At once Kipps, George, and Godwin did the same.

"Stop this!" I cried. "Stop this nonsense, all of you!"

Six faces turned to me.

I'd raised my voice. I'd clenched my fists. I may even have stamped a foot. I did what was necessary to snap them out of it. Their rage was escalating out of control, and with it, the danger hanging over us grew dark and palpable. Negative emotions in haunted places are never a good idea—and anger's probably the worst of all.

"Can't you feel it?" I hissed. "The atmosphere's changing. You're stirring up the energies in the house. You've got to shut up, *right now.*"

There was a silence. They were variously concerned, disgruntled, and embarrassed, but they did as I told them.

Lockwood took a deep breath. "Thanks, Luce," he said. "You're right."

The others nodded. "I know anger's out," George said. "But what about sarcasm? Is that a no-no too?"

"Hush."

We waited. Tension hung heavy in the air.

"Think we stopped it?" Quill Kipps said at last. "Think we were just in time?"

Even as he spoke, the element in Kat Godwin's night-lantern flickered, dwindled, flared again. George unclipped his thermometer and switched on the dial. "Temp's dropping. Fifty degrees now. It was fifty-seven in here when we came in."

"The air's getting thick," Bobby Vernon muttered. "There's a miasma building."

I nodded. "I'm getting aural phenomena. A rustling."

Kat Godwin could hear it too; her face was gray and drawn. "It sounds like, like—"

Like lots of little rushing things with scaly tails and scaly claws, hurrying through the house toward us. Brushing against walls, squeezing under doors, pattering through pipes and under floorboards, converging ever closer on that hateful airless room. That, to be frank, is what it sounded like. Kat Godwin didn't say this, and she didn't say the fateful word. She didn't need to. Everybody guessed.

"Chains out," Lockwood said. "Let's all think happy thoughts."

"Do it," Kipps said.

They may have had the social graces of hungry jackals, but give them their due: Fittes agents are well trained. They had their tool bags opened faster than we did, and a decent double circle of chains laid out in twenty seconds flat. Ned Shaw was still scowling at us, but the others were calm and matter-of-fact now. The priority was survival. We all squeezed in.

"This is cozy," George said. "Nice cologne, Kipps. I'm being genuine there."

"Thanks."

"Shut up now," I said. "We need to listen."

So we stood silent, seven agents squashed inside the circle. The lantern light continued to flicker wildly. I could see nothing, but the rustling, scraping, scampering sound grew nearer, nearer. . . . Now it was all around us, as if a terrible, pell-mell chase was going on, just out of eyeshot in the dark. From Kat Godwin's constricted breathing I knew she heard it; whether the others did, I couldn't tell. The tumult rose around me. It was as if the frantic chase continued up the walls. It kept on rising till it reached the ceiling. Claws skittered and slid on plaster just above our heads. Still it rose. The sound merged into the ceiling; the terrible rustling vanished away into the fabric of the house.

"It's gone," Kat Godwin said. "It's backed off. You think so too, Lucy?"

"Yeah, the air's clearing. . . . Wait, so *you* know my name as well."

"Temperature's back up to fifty-four," George said.

A general lessening of tension followed. Everyone suddenly realized how close we were all pressing. We scattered from the circle; the chains were put away.

The two groups stood looking at each other once again.

"Look, Quill," Lockwood said. "I've got a suggestion. This clearly isn't a place for an argument. Let's continue it later, somewhere else. Also, since none of us can stand the sight of each other, why don't we go our separate ways around the house? We'll all search where we like, and won't disturb the others. Sound fair enough?"

Kipps was pulling at his cuffs and brushing at his jacket, as if our recent forced proximity had made him worried about fleas. "Agreed, but don't make any sudden reappearances. I might take your head off next time."

Without further words, we steered past them and back down the passage. Once through the outer door, we retraced our steps to the main hall. Here Lockwood paused.

"Kipps showing up complicates things," he whispered. "They might spend a while in the workroom, taking readings, but they'll be creeping after us again very soon. And if those papers are there, I want to find them without any interference. Lucy, I know you don't want to use it, but this might be a good time to consult our friend, the skull."

I regarded George's bulging backpack without pleasure. "This still feels like a bad idea to me," I said. "But since we're running out of time . . ." I opened the pack, reached in, and turned the lever on the stopper. "Spirit," I said, bending close, "do you recognize this place? Where was your master's study? Can you tell us?"

The glass stayed cold and dark.

"Maybe you need to go in closer," Lockwood suggested.

"Any closer and I'll be tickling George's neck. Spirit, do you hear me? Do you hear me? Oh, I feel like such an *idiot* doing this. It's an utter waste of—"

"*Upstairs . . .*"

I jerked back; there'd been the briefest flash of green from the heart of the jar. Now it and the breathless voice were gone.

"It said upstairs," I said slowly. "It definitely said upstairs. But do we really—"

Lockwood was already halfway across the hall. "Then what are we waiting for? Quick! We haven't got much time!"

Negotiating those stairs, however, wasn't something we could do *too* quickly. Many of the treads were rotten and wouldn't support our weight. We had to step over slicks of tiles and splinters of fallen wood. High above, ragged patches of stars shone where the roof had been. Also we had to keep taking precautionary readings (much hastier than usual; we kept expecting our rivals to reappear below), which held us up still more. We picked up a slight decrease in temperature, and low-level noises (a faint crackling and whistling). Lockwood also saw some plasmic traces flitting through the dark. Then there was one final thing as we got to the top of the stairs.

"Look at the wainscoting," I said. "What are these dark stains running along it?"

George bent close and fixed them with his penlight. "Smudges and smears of grease," he said, "made by thousands of bristle marks. It's just the kind of stain that—" He hesitated.

"That *rats* make." Lockwood brushed past us impatiently,

took the last couple of steps in a single vigorous stride. "Forget it. Come on."

It was a big, square landing, ruined and half-open to the sky. Brown leaves and little twigs lay among the dirt and debris on the wooden floorboards, and the moonlight shone with cold assertion through gaping rents in the roof above. Behind us, a passage ran away deeper into the house, but this was half blocked by fallen rubble. The stairs had curved around on themselves during the ascent, so we were facing back toward the front of the house. Ahead of us were the open doorways to three rooms.

"*Yes. . . .*" the ghost's voice whispered in my ear. "*There. . . .*"

"We're close," I said. "Bickerstaff's study is one of those rooms."

The moment I said the name, there was a spike in the psychic sounds I heard; the distant crackling flared loud enough to make me flinch. A slight breeze blew through the empty house, moving leaves and curls of paper across the floor. A few fragments fell between the banisters and drifted away into the darkness of the void below.

"Might be worth going easy on that name up here," Lockwood said. "Temperature, George?"

"Forty-six degrees. Holding constant."

"Stay there and watch the stairs for Kipps. Lucy, come with me."

Soundlessly, we crossed the landing. I looked back, at George, who had taken up position by the banister, where he had a good view down over the curve of the staircase to a portion of the hall below. His mood seemed steady, his body language seemed okay. As far as I could tell, the malaise wasn't getting any worse.

His backpack hung open. I could see the top of the ghost-jar, faintly glowing green.

"*Yessss . . .*" the voice said. "*Good girl . . . You're getting closer. . . .*"

How eager the whisper sounded now.

"*The middle room . . . Under the floor . . .*"

"The middle one. It says that's it."

Lockwood approached the central doorway, started to pass through, and at once jumped back.

"Cold spot," he said. "Cuts straight through you."

I unclipped my thermometer and held it out beyond the door. At once I could feel the air's bitterness on my hand. "Forty-one degrees in, forty-six degrees out," I said. "That's serious chill."

"And not only that." Lockwood had taken his sunglasses from his coat and was hastily putting them on. "We've got spiders. And a death-glow—a real whopper. Over there, beneath the window."

I couldn't see it, but I wouldn't have expected to. To my eyes it was a fair-sized, squarish chamber, dominated by a large and empty window space. As with the rest of the ruined house, it was barren of furniture or decoration. I tried to imagine how it had looked in Bickerstaff's day: the study desk and chair, the portraits on the wall, maybe a bookcase or two, a carriage clock upon the mantelpiece. . . . No. I couldn't manage it. Too much time had passed, and the sense of menacing emptiness was just too strong.

A flood of moonlight shone through it, making everything glow a sleepy, hazy silver. The noise of static in my head buzzed loudly once or twice, then faded sharply, as if being squeezed out by the heavy silence emanating from that room.

Thick dusty layers of cobwebs hung in the corners of the ceiling.

This was it, the center of the haunting in that house. My heart beat painfully against my chest, and I could feel my teeth chattering. I forced the panic down. What had Joplin told us? The men had stood outside the house and seen movement in the window. "Lockwood," I whispered, "it's the room of the rats. It's where Bickerstaff died. We mustn't go in there."

"*Oh, don't be scared,*" the whispering voice said in my mind. "*You want the papers? Under a board in the middle of the floor. Just walk right in.*"

"A quick look only," Lockwood said, "and then we'll go." I couldn't see his eyes behind the glasses, but I could feel his wariness; he stood at the door and didn't step in.

"That's what the skull *wants* us to do," I pleaded. "But we can't trust it; you *know* we can't. Let's just leave it, Lockwood. Let's get out of here."

"After all this? Not likely. Besides, Kipps will be up here in a minute." He pulled his gloves higher on his wrists, and stepped through the door. Gritting my teeth, I followed.

The drop in temperature was brutal; even in my coat it made me shudder. There was an immediate hike in the static, too, as if someone had turned a dial the moment I went inside. The air was heavy with a peculiar sweet smell, not unlike the climbing shrub outside the window. It was thick, cloying, and somehow rotten. It had no obvious source.

It was not a room to remain in very long.

We walked slowly through drifting spears of moonlight, hands at our belts, surveying the floor. Most of the boards seemed held fast, stone-stiff and strong.

"It's in the middle somewhere," I said. "According to the skull."

"What a *very* helpful skull he is. . . . Ah, this one gave a little. Keep watch, Lucy."

In a moment he was on his knees, squatting by the floorboard, exploring its edges with his long fingers. I took my rapier from my belt and paced slowly around the room. I did not want to remain still there; somehow I needed to move.

I passed the door; across the landing, George was looking at me from his position by the banisters. He waved. The back of his backpack glowed a faintish green. I passed the window; from it I could see the slates of the entrance porch, the path leading down the hill, the tops of ragged trees. I passed an empty fireplace; on impulse I let my fingers touch the blackened tiles—

Sound looped out of the past; the room was warm, fire crackled in the grate.

"Here, my dear fellow. The boy's set it all up for you. We've chosen you for this great purpose. You are to be the pioneer!"

Another voice: "Just stand before it and take the cloth away. Tell us what you see."

"Have *you* not looked yet, Bickerstaff?" The speaker was querulous, prickly with fear. "Surely it should fall to you—"

"It is to be *your* honor, my good Wilberforce. This is your heart's desire, is it not? Come, man! Take a drop of wine for courage. . . . That's it! I stand ready to record your words. Now, there . . . We remove the veil. . . . So, look into it, Wilberforce! Look, and tell us—"

Appalling cold, a cry of terror—and with it, the buzzing of the flies. "No! I cannot!"

"I swear you shall! Hold him fast! Get him by the arms! Look, curse you—*look*! And talk to us! Tell us the marvels that you see!"

But the only answer was a scream—loud, loud, louder; and suddenly cut off.

My hand fell away from the wall. I stood rigid, eyes staring, frozen in shock at what I'd heard. The room was very still, as if the whole building held its breath. I could not move. I was engulfed by the echo of a dead man's fear. The terror subsided; blinking, gasping, I remembered where I was. In the center of the room, Lockwood crouched beside an uprooted floorboard. He was grinning at me broadly. He had several yellowed, crumpled papers in his hand.

"How's that, then?" he smiled. "The skull spoke truth!"

"No—" I lurched toward him, caught his arm. "Not about everything. Listen to me! *It wasn't Bickerstaff who died here.* It was Wilberforce. Bickerstaff forced him to look in the bone glass, right here in this room! The bone glass killed him. Lockwood—it was *Wilberforce* who died in this house, and I think his spirit's still here now. We need to get out. Don't talk, just leave."

Lockwood's face was pale. He rose; and at that moment George appeared beside us. His eyes shone. "Have you found them? You got the papers? What do they say?"

"Later," Lockwood said. "I thought I told you to watch the stairs."

"Oh, it'll be all right. It's quiet down there. Ooh, it's handwritten, and there are little pictures, too. This is fascinating. . . ."

"Get out!" I cried. A growing pressure beat against my ear. It seemed to me that the moonlight in the window was a little thicker than before.

"Yes," Lockwood said. "Let's go." We turned—and saw the hulking form of Ned Shaw standing in the doorway. He blocked the space. If you'd put a hinge on his backside and another on his elbow, he'd have made an ugly but effective swing door.

"George," I said, "how long has it been since you actually watched the stairs?"

"Well, I might have stepped over a moment or two ago to see what you were doing."

Shaw's little eyes gleamed with triumph and suspicion. "What have you got there, Lockwood?" he said. "What's that you're holding?"

"I don't yet know," Lockwood said truthfully. He bent, put the papers in his bag.

"Give them here," Shaw said.

"No. Let us pass, please."

Ned Shaw gave a chuckle; he leaned casually against the doorjamb. "Not until I see what you've got."

"This really isn't a place for an argument," I said. The temperature was dropping; the moonlight swirled and shifted in the room, as if slowly being stirred into life.

"Perhaps you're unaware," Lockwood began, "that this room—"

Shaw chuckled again. "Oh, I can see it all. The death-glow, the miasma forming. There's even a little ghost-fog. . . . Yeah, it's not a place to linger."

Lockwood's eyes narrowed. "In that case"—he drew his rapier—"you'll agree we can leave right now." He stepped toward him. Shaw hesitated, and then—it was almost as if those hinges I mentioned were in position and nicely oiled—swung back and let us through.

"Thanks," Lockwood said.

Whether it was the way he said it—lightly, but with amused disdain; whether it was my look of utter contempt, or the grin on George's face, or simply a pressure inside that could not be borne, Ned Shaw suddenly cracked. He ripped his rapier clear and, in the same movement, jabbed at Lockwood's back. I knew the move; it was a Komiyama Twist, used on Specters, Wraiths, and Fetches. Not on people.

My gasp as the sword was drawn half-warned Lockwood. He began to turn; the rapier point scratched at an angle along the fabric of his coat, caught against the threads, and penetrated the cloth. It caught him just beneath his left arm; he cried out and sprang away.

Red-faced, panting, Shaw plunged after him like a maddened bull. Reaching the center of the landing, Lockwood spun around, struck aside his enemy's outstretched rapier, and cut two parallel lines across the fabric of Shaw's sword arm, so that the jacket sleeve hung loose and limp. Shaw gave a bellow of fury.

Footsteps on the stairs. Kipps was taking them two at a time. Kat Godwin and little Bobby Vernon followed closely behind. All had their rapiers in their hands.

"Lockwood!" Kipps cried. "What's going on?"

"He started it!" Shaw cried, frantically warding off a series of remorseless blows as he retreated across the landing. "He attacked me! Help!"

"That's a lie!" I shouted. But Kipps was already hurtling to the attack. He advanced on Lockwood side-on. It was a position from which Lockwood would be unable to see him: sneaky and effective—a typical Fittes ploy. And then my *own* anger, which had been bubbling up since Shaw's treacherous assault, perhaps ever since that night on Wimbledon Common—overwhelmed me. I charged forward, rapier raised.

Before I could reach Kipps, Kat Godwin was upon me. Our blades met with a thin, high clash. The force of her first strike almost drove the weapon out of my hand, but I adjusted my wrist, absorbed the impact, and held firm. For a moment we were locked together; I could smell the lemony reek of her perfume, see the crisp stitching on her gray jacket. We broke apart, circled each other. Dust rose from our shuffling feet and hung sparkling in the silvery air. It was very cold. There was a ringing in my ears.

George had also made a beeline for Lockwood; he was defending him from Kipps and Vernon on the other side. Lockwood had removed a portion of Shaw's second sleeve. Bits of ragged cloth lay scattered across the moonlit floor.

Godwin brushed a flick of hair out of her eyes. Her face was so hard and set, she might have been made of marble. Maybe I looked the same. Part of my mind was yelling at me, telling me to stop and calm down. But it's hard in haunted houses—emotions get tugged and twisted out of proportion. I was furious, yes; we all were. But I wondered how far the atmosphere of the house was pulling us all toward extremes—George driving Vernon back with a series of ferocious jabs, then retreating as Kipps caught him on the thigh with a well-timed thrust; Lockwood, with cold, systematic precision, reducing Shaw's jacket ever closer to ribbons. Godwin—

Kat Godwin's next attack was twice as quick as the ones before.

White-faced, eyes staring, she swiped at my sword arm. The tip of the blade caught me neatly on the exposed skin between the wrist bones, just beyond the guard. It bit through the skin, making me cry out. I grasped my wrist. Flecks of blood showed between my fingers.

I looked up at her in shock—and then I looked beyond her. My mouth opened. I backed away.

"Giving up?" Godwin said.

I shook my head, pointing past her back toward the empty study.

In the center of the moonlight, in the spotlit patch below the window, a dark shape was rising from the floor.

A violent silence attended it. Moonbeams writhed and thickened; threads of ghost-fog thrashed and bucked close to the floor. Freezing air rolled out from the room, washing over us, plunging down the stairs. That foul miasma, that odious cloying sweetness, rose up to choke our lungs.

Kat Godwin made an incoherent noise; she'd turned and now stood slack-jawed at my side. The others had lowered their weapons and become similarly transfixed.

Up rose the shape.

"Oh God," someone said. "Bickerstaff."

Not Bickerstaff. I knew that now. Not Bickerstaff, but Wilberforce—the man who'd looked into the mirror. But even *that* was not the full horrible truth of the apparition that we saw.

It *was* vaguely man-shaped—that much was clear—but it was also somehow *wrong*. From certain angles, as it turned and twisted, it had the appearance of a tall gentleman, perhaps wearing some kind of frock coat. The line of the head was plain enough, bowed as if under some great weight, but I could not make sense of the rest. The arms were swollen, the chest and stomach undulating weirdly. Everything was held in shadow; I saw no details.

The figure rose into the light, swaying and shaking, as if responding to some frenzied internal music. The movement was foul; a terror radiated from it through the freezing air. Ghost-lock seized my muscles, I felt my bowels go slack; my rapier trembled in my hand.

Swaying like a drunken man, head lolling, body shifting, writhing with a horrid fluid grace, the figure rose, silhouetted against the moon. Little spreading nets of ice grew and fused on the windowpanes behind it. Still the head was bowed. The body's contortions—minute but somehow frenzied—redoubled, as if it sought to tear itself to pieces. The head jerked up, it turned toward us; it was a black void that sucked in light.

A desperate voice rang in my mind. *"Bickerstaff! No! Show me not the glass!"*

Someone—Godwin, I think—began to scream.

I didn't blame her. The figure was shaking itself apart.

Like a wet dog, it thrashed from side to side. And as it did so, pieces of its substance broke away. It was as if gobbets of flesh were shaking themselves loose, and falling to the floor. As each one landed, the lumps uncoiled, grew elongated, became low black forms that leaped and skittered out across the room, before circling around toward the door.

"Rats!" Lockwood cried. "Back to the stairs! Get out!"

His voice broke through our ghost-lock; one after another our training kicked in. But not before the first black forms were already upon us. Three, coal-black and shining, with yellow maddened eyes, came leaping, springing through the door. One launched itself at George, who met it with a wild swing of his rapier. The rat burst; a shower of bright blue ectoplasm spattered Vernon's jacket, making him squeal. Lockwood hurled a salt-bomb, igniting another rat; it burned with a livid flame. The third scrabbled away and up the wall.

Away by the window, in its nimbus of blue fire, the hellish figure hopped and capered, as if dancing with delight. Ribs shone, arm bones peeked from the whirling, disintegrating flesh. Fresh chunks and pieces tore themselves free; spectral rats scattered up the walls and across the ceiling. More came through the door.

"Back!" Lockwood cried again. He was walking backward slowly, methodically, slashing at the darting, clawing forms as they drew near. George and I were doing likewise; of the Fittes agents, Shaw and Godwin beat the most orderly retreat. Shaw scattered iron filings in a broad circle so that advancing rats fizzed and leaped and spun. Godwin tossed salt-bombs left and right.

Kipps? He'd already run off; I heard his boots beating out a cowardly fandango on the stairs. But Bobby Vernon seemed racked with panic, neither attacking nor retreating, his sword hanging limply, eyes locked on the bony, dancing thing.

It sensed his weakness. Visitors always do.

Rats converged upon him along the walls and ceiling. One dropped toward his head; Lockwood sprang close, long coat flapping. He swung his sword and, mid-fall, sliced the rat in two. Plasm fell like molten rain.

Vernon moaned; Lockwood grasped him by the collar, dragged him toward the stairs. From left, from right, the swift black forms came darting. I threw a salt-bomb, drove them shrieking back. The landing was awash with salt and iron; burning rats shrank and dwindled on all sides.

We reached the stairs; Lockwood flung Vernon ahead of him, jumped over a writhing rat that collided with the wainscoting, and clattered down. I was the last. I looked back into the empty room. In its livid fire, the thing by the window was almost reduced to bones. As I watched I saw it fall back, disintegrate entirely into a dozen darting forms that whirled around and around.

"*I beg you,*" roared the despairing, distant voice. "*Show me not the glass!*"

I pelted around the curve of the stairs, down along the hallway, toward the open door.

"*Not the glass . . .*"

I fell out of the front door, across the porch, and into the long, wet, moonlit grass. The summer night enfolded me; for the first time I realized how cold I'd been. Shaw and Godwin had already collapsed on the ground. Vernon was slumped against one of the pillars of the porch. George and Kipps had discarded their rapiers and were bent over almost double, gasping, hands clamped against their knees.

Lockwood was hardly out of breath. I looked up at the window overhead, where, lit by flickering blue other-light, the stick-thin figure and the rats could still be seen, dancing and capering. Rats leaped and bounded, ran up and down the walls and across the ceiling. They merged in and out of the figure, building it up to momentarily resemble a Victorian gentleman with swaying tail-coats, then stripping it back to the bones again.

The light winked out. The house was dark beneath the moon.

I turned away; and as I did so a brief, malevolent chuckling sounded in my mind. From the back of George's backpack a faint green glow flared once, then faded.

Now there was nothing but seven exhausted agents scattered wheezing on the quiet hill.

V
A Big
Night Out

Chapter 20

"Destroy it!" I cried. "That's the only option. We take it to the furnaces, and we burn the thing now!"

"Yes," Lockwood murmured, "but is that really practical?"

"Of course it isn't," George said. "We simply can't do it. It's too important for us—and for psychic science generally. And Luce, flicking marmalade at my head is really not a valid argument. You've got to calm down."

"I'll calm down," I snarled, "when this cursed skull is off the premises." I threw the marmalade spoon at the jar. It struck the side of the glass, bounced off with a ping, and landed in the butter.

"*Oh, dear. . . .*" A mocking whisper sounded in my head. "*Temper, temper. . . . This is such an exhibition.*"

"And *you* can shut up!" I said. "I don't need *you* to butt in too!"

Morning had come, which meant yet more crystal-clear skies,

another late breakfast, and—in my case at least—the releasing of a *lot* of pent-up rage. It hadn't come out on our long journey home from Hampstead, nor in my fitful sleep; it hadn't even stirred when I came into the kitchen and saw the ghost-jar on the counter. But when, as we discussed the night's events, I heard the ghost's hoarse chuckle cutting through my mind, my control finally snapped. I'd leaped at the jar, and it was all Lockwood could do to prevent me from smashing it right there and then.

"I keep telling you, it lured us to the house!" I said. "It knew about the horror in that room! It knew Wilberforce's ghost would be there! That's why it let slip about the papers in the first place; that's why it led us upstairs. It's vindictive and evil, and we were fools to listen to it. You should have heard it laughing at us last night, and now it's doing it again!"

"All the same," Lockwood said mildly, "we *do* have the papers. It didn't lie about that."

"That was just a way of trapping us, don't you see? It's preying on our weaknesses. And it does that by getting into my head! It's all right for you—you can't hear its horrid whispering."

"*Oh, how mean,*" the skull's voice said. "*Anyway, be consistent. Last thing I heard, you were begging me to speak. And I don't know why you're being so ungrateful, either. I got you the papers—and gave you a nice little workout, too. A pathetic little spirit like Wilberforce was never going to cause you any real trouble.*" It gave a fruity chuckle. "*Well? I'm waiting for a thank-you.*"

I stared across at the ghost-jar. Sunlight danced mutely on its glass sides, and there was no sign of the spectral face. But a door had suddenly opened in my mind, and a memory came sharply into focus. It was from last night, up at the house—one of the voices I'd heard echoing from the past:

"Try Wilberforce," the voice had said. "He's eager. He'll do it. . . ."

The tones had been familiar. I knew them all too well.

"It was him!" I pointed at the skull. "It was *him* talking to Bickerstaff in the workroom! So much for him not knowing about the mirror—he was there when it was made! Not just that, he actually suggested they make Wilberforce look in!"

The skull grinned back at me from the center of the plasm. *"Impressive,"* it whispered. *"You do have Talent. Yes, and it was such a shame that poor Wilberforce didn't have the strength to cope with what he saw. But now my master's mirror is back in the world again. Perhaps someone else will use it and be enlightened."*

I passed these words on to the others. Lockwood leaned forward. "Great—it's being talkative. Ask it what the mirror actually *does*, Luce."

"I don't want to ask this foul creature anything. Besides, there's no way it would ever tell us."

"Hold on," the ghost said. *"Try asking nicely. A little bit of courtesy might help."*

I looked at it. "Please tell us what the mirror does."

"Get lost! You haven't been very polite today, so you can all go boil your heads."

I felt its presence disappear. The plasm clouded, concealing the skull from view.

With gritted teeth, I repeated everything. Lockwood laughed. "It's certainly picked up a few choice phrases from its constant eavesdropping."

"There're a few more I'd like it to hear," I growled.

"Now, now. We've got to detach ourselves from it," Lockwood said. "You, Lucy, most of all. We mustn't let it wind us up." He crossed to the jar and closed the lever in the plastic seal, cutting any connection with the ghost. Then he covered it with a cloth. "He's slowly giving us what we want," he said, "but I think we could all do with a little privacy. Let's keep him quiet for now."

The phone rang, and Lockwood went to answer it. I left the kitchen too. My head felt numb, the echoes of the ghostly whispers still lingered in my ears. Thankful as I was to have some peace from the skull, it didn't make me feel much better. It was only a temporary respite. Soon they'd want me to talk to it again.

In the living room, I took a breather. I went over to the window and looked out into the street.

A spy was standing there.

It was our old friend, Ned Shaw. Gray, disheveled, and whey-faced with weariness, he stood like an ugly mailbox on the opposite side of the road, stolidly watching our front door. He'd clearly not been home; he wore the same jacket as the night before, half shredded by Lockwood's rapier. He had a take-out coffee in one hand and looked thoroughly miserable.

I went back to the kitchen, where Lockwood had just returned. George was busy doing the dishes. "They're still watching the house," I said.

Lockwood nodded. "Good. Shows how desperate they are. This

is Kipps's response to our seizure of the papers. He knows we've got something important, and he's terrified of missing out on what we do next."

"Ned Shaw's been there all morning now. I almost feel sorry for him."

"I don't. I can still feel where he spiked me. How's your cut doing, Lucy?"

I had a small bandage where Kat Godwin's blade had struck. "Fine."

"Speaking of sharp objects," Lockwood said, "that was Barnes on the phone. DEPRAC's done some research into the knife that killed Jack Carver. Remember I said it was an Indian Mughal dagger? I was right, though I got the century wrong. From the early 1700s, apparently. Surprised me."

"Where was it stolen from, though?" George said. "Which museum?"

"Oddly enough, no museum has reported it missing. We don't know where it's from. An almost identical one is kept in the Museum of London. It was found in the tomb of a British soldier in Maida Vale Cemetery a couple of years ago. The chap had served in India, and had all sorts of curios buried with him. They were dug up, checked by DEPRAC, and put on exhibit. But that dagger's still safely in its case, so where *this* one comes from is a mystery."

"I still think it comes from the Bloomsbury Antiques Emporium," I said. "And our friend Winkman."

"He *is* the most obvious suspect," Lockwood agreed. "But why didn't he take back his money? Hurry up with the dishes, George. I want to look at the papers we found."

"You could always give me a hand," George suggested. "Speed things up a little."

"Oh, well, you're almost done." Lockwood leaned casually against the counter, looking out at the old apple tree in the garden. "What do we know?" he said. "What do we actually *know* after last night? Have we made any progress with this case or not?"

"Precious little that might get us paid by Barnes," I said. "Winkman has the bone glass, and we still don't know what it's *for*."

"We know more than you think," Lockwood said. "Here's the way I see it. Edmund Bickerstaff—and it seems this chap in the jar here—made a mirror that has a very nasty effect on anyone who looks into it. It was supposed to do something else—the skull spoke of it giving you enlightenment—but they were happy to let others take the risk. Wilberforce looked in and paid the price. For unknown reasons—maybe because Bickerstaff panicked and fled—Wilberforce's body was left at the house; by the time it was discovered, the rats had done their work. But what happened to Bickerstaff? He was never seen again, but *somebody* buried him and the mirror in Kensal Green, with urgent instructions to leave them be."

"I think that somebody was Mary Dulac," George put in. "Which is why I want to find those *Confessions* of hers so badly."

Lockwood nodded. "Whoever did it, Bickerstaff was buried. We dug him up. His ghost was released, and it *nearly* got George."

"The mirror nearly got George too," I said. "Would have, if we hadn't blocked it so quickly."

"You say that," George said. He was staring out into the garden. "But who knows? Maybe I would have been okay. Perhaps I would have been strong enough to withstand the dangers and see what the mirror contained. . . ." He sighed. "Anyway, I'm finished. Pass me that towel."

Lockwood passed it. "The modern mystery," he said, "goes like this: somebody tipped off Carver and Neddles about the glass. Carver carried out the raid, though Neddles died. Carver sold the glass to someone—we assume Julius Winkman—for a lot of cash, but afterward was murdered, we don't know by whom. What we *think* we know is that Winkman has the bone glass, and *that's* the essential fact that is going to win us this case over Kipps and his idiot gang." He clapped his hands together. "There, am I right? How's that for a summary?"

"Very good." George and I were sitting at the table with an air of expectation. "I think we should look at the Bickerstaff papers now."

"Right." Lockwood settled himself beside us, and from his jacket drew forth the crumpled documents he had taken from the haunted room the night before. There were three pages, great sheets of parchment, mottled with the marks of decades of concealment—damp, dirt, and the nibbling of worms. Each sheet was covered on both sides with lines of spidery, inky handwriting—mostly tight-spaced, but here and there broken up by small drawings.

Lockwood tilted the papers toward the window, frowning.

"Drat," he said. "It's in Latin. Or is it Ancient Greek?"

George squinted at the writing over the top of his spectacles. "Obviously not Greek. Might possibly be some medieval form of Latin. . . . Looks a bit weird, though."

"What *is* it with mysterious documents and inscriptions that they always have to be in some old dead language?" I growled. "We had the same problem with the Fairfax locket, remember? And the St. Pancras headstone."

"You can't read any of this, I suppose, George?" Lockwood asked.

George shook his head. "No. I know someone who *can*, though. Albert Joplin's good with all sorts of historical stuff. He was telling me about a sixteenth-century Bible he found in one of their cemetery excavations; that was in Latin too, I think. I could show these papers to him and see if he'll translate. Swear him to secrecy, of course."

Lockwood pursed his lips; he tapped the table in indecision. "DEPRAC's got language experts, but they'd share everything with Barnes and, through him, Kipps as well. Okay, I don't much like it, but it may be we haven't got a choice. You can take them to Joplin. No—better still, see if he'll come here. We don't want Ned Shaw jumping you and stealing them the moment you step outside."

"What about those drawings?" I said. "We don't need an expert for them, do we?"

We spread the parchments out across the table and bent close to consider the little pictures. There were several, each done in pen-and-ink, each showing a distinct episode in a narrative. The art was rather crude, but very detailed. It was immediately obvious, from the style of the figures, from the clothes they wore, and from the general scenes, that the images were very old.

"They're not Victorian," George said. "I bet these originally come from a medieval manuscript. Maybe the text does too.

Bickerstaff found this somewhere, and copied it all out. I reckon this is where he got inspiration for his ideas."

The first illustration showed a man in long robes stooping beside a hole. It was night; there was a moon in the sky, suggestions of trees in the background. Inside the hole was a skeleton. The man appeared to be reaching into the hole and removing a long, white bone. With his other hand he held up a long, thin crucifix to ward off a faint pale figure that was rising beside him, half in, and half out of the ground.

"Grave-robbing," Lockwood said. "And using iron or silver to keep the ghost at bay."

"He's just as dumb as we are," I said. "It'd be *so* much simpler to do it during daylight."

"Maybe he *has* to do it at night," George said slowly. "Yeah . . . maybe he *has* to. What's the next picture show?"

The next one was another robed man, presumably the same person, standing beside a gallows on a hill. Again the moon was up, massed clouds banked across the sky. A decomposing corpse hung from the gallows tree, a thing of bones and rags. The man appeared to be in the process of cutting off one of the corpse's arms, using a long, curved knife. Once again he held the crucifix aloft, this time to keep at bay *two* spirits: one that hung vaporously behind the body on the gallows, the other standing ominously behind the gallows post. The man had an open sack beside him, in which the bone from the first picture could be seen.

"He's not making many friends, this fellow," Lockwood said. "That's two ghosts he has annoyed."

"That's just the point," George breathed. "He's *purposefully* seeking out bones that have a Visitor attached—he's seeking out Sources. What does he do next?"

He was doing more of the same, this time in some kind of brick-lined room. Alcoves or shelves in the walls were filled with piles of bones and skulls. With his sack lying open at his feet, the man was selecting a skull from the nearest shelf, while rather nonchalantly flourishing the crucifix behind him at *three* pale figures—the first two resentful ghosts, and a new one.

"It's a catacomb, or ossuary," Lockwood said. "Where they used to store bones when the old churchyards got too full. These three pictures show all the best places for finding a Source. And the fourth—" He turned the parchment over, and broke off.

"Oh," I said.

The fourth picture was different from the others. This one showed the man alone in a stone chamber, with the sun shining over fields beyond an open door. He stood at a wooden table, where he worked to construct something from several pieces of bone. He seemed to be somehow sewing the bones together, and attaching them to a small, round object.

A piece of glass.

"It's a guide," I said. "It tells you how to make the bone glass. And that idiot Bickerstaff followed the instructions. Is there a fifth picture?"

Lockwood picked up the last piece of parchment and turned it over.

There was.

In the center of the illustration was the bone glass, standing upright on the top of a low pillar or pedestal. Ivy wound around the pedestal, which was also decorated with large pale flowers. To the left side stood the man, stooping slightly as he faced the pedestal. One of his hands was cupped above his eyes, which gazed toward the glass with an expression of fixed intensity. Well might he do so, because on the opposite side of the pillar was what appeared to be a whole crowd of individuals in ragged robes and vestments. All were cadaverously thin. Some still had faces, with wisps of hair stuck to the back of their skulls; others were already skeletons. There were hints of bone beneath the robes, and bony legs and feet. In short, none of them looked too healthy. They all faced the bone glass as if looking back toward the man with as much interest as he was studying them.

We stared at the parchment, at the massed ranks of little figures. There was a deep silence in the sunny room.

"I still don't understand," I said at last. "What's the glass *for*?"

George cleared his throat, a harsh sound. "For looking through."

Lockwood nodded. "It's not a mirror. It's a window. A window to the 'Other Side.'"

Tap, tap.

It's not often something startles all three of us at once. Okay, the opening of Mrs. Barrett's tomb saw us all set personal high-jump records, but that was at night. In daytime? No. It never happens. Yet all it took this time was the sound of fingernails on glass and the shadow looming behind us at the kitchen window. We turned; a bony hand clawed at the pane. I glimpsed a scrawny neck and shoulders, pale wisps of hair fringing a weird, misshapen head. I leaped up from my stool; Lockwood's chair went crashing against the fridge. George jumped back so far he got entangled with the mops behind the door, and he started lashing out at them in fright.

For an instant none of us could speak. Then common sense intervened.

It *couldn't* be something dead. It was mid-morning. I looked again.

The sun was behind the figure, rendering it almost black. Then I made out the atrocious outline of the raggedy straw hat, the grimy, leering face.

"Oh," Lockwood said. "It's *Flo*."

George blinked. "Flo Bones? That's a girl?"

"We assume so. It's never been conclusively proved."

The face at the window moved from side to side. It seemed to be talking; at least, the mouth was making a series of alarming contortions. The hand waved violently, clawing against the glass.

George stared, agog. "You said she was quiet and refined."

"Did we? I don't remember." Lockwood was gesturing toward the back of the house; as the face disappeared from the window, he moved across to open the kitchen door. "This'll be about Winkman! Perfect! It's *just* what we need. I'm bringing her in. Luce—hide the papers. George, find sugar, put the kettle on."

George considered the greasy marks remaining on the window. "You think she'll want tea? She looked more a formaldehyde sort of girl."

"It's coffee," I said. "And a quick word of advice. No cheap comments at her expense. She's easily offended and would probably disembowel you."

"Story of my life," George said.

Outside, the summer birds had fallen silent, perhaps stunned by the figure stomping up the garden stairs. Lockwood stood aside; a moment later Flo Bones was bustling into the kitchen in her enormous boots, bringing with her the canvas sack, a frown, and the scent of low tide. She stood at the door and glared around at us silently.

In daylight her blue puffer jacket seemed lank and almost bleached of color, and it was difficult to tell where her hair stopped and the straw of her hat began. A great smear of gray mud ran across the front of her jeans, while seven shades of dirt decorated her round face. In other words, all the horrid implications of the night were fully realized. Yet her blue eyes looked doubtful, almost anxious, and she carried herself with less bluster than before, as if the daylight— and maybe her surroundings—intimidated her just a little.

"Welcome," Lockwood said, closing the door. "It's really good of you to come."

The relic-girl didn't answer; she was staring mutely around the kitchen, taking in the cabinets, the stacks of food, our piled supplies. All of a sudden I wondered where it was *she* ate, where she slept when not working by the river. . . . I cleared my throat. "Hey, Flo," I said. "We'll get some coffee on."

"Yeah, coffee would be good. . . . Not used to being up this time of day." Her voice was quieter, more reflective than I remembered it.

"It's quite a place you've got here, Locky. Even got a personal guard outside, I see."

"Oh, Ned Shaw?" Lockwood said. "You met him, did you?"

"I *saw* him, but he didn't see me. He was dozing into a newspaper. Still, I went around the back way, came over the garden wall, to keep things quiet-like. Wouldn't want word to leak out I've been socializing with the likes of you." She grinned, showing remarkably white teeth.

"That's quite right," Lockwood said. "Well done."

George was making the coffee. He cleared his throat meaningfully.

Lockwood frowned. "Oh, sorry. Introductions, yes. Flo, George. George, Flo. Now, Flo—what have you got for us? Hear anything about Julius Winkman?"

"I have," Flo said, "and the word is he's holding his auction tomorrow night." She paused to let the information sink in fully. "Now, that's *fast* for Winkman; he's only had this thing a couple of days, but he's already lined something up. 'Course, maybe it's because it's so valuable, but maybe he's trying to get rid of it as quickly as possible. Why? Because it's nasty. Oh, there's lots of rumors going around."

"Do some of those rumors say Winkman killed Jack Carver?" I said.

"I heard about *that* little incident," Flo said. "Died right here in your house, I understand. What is it with you, Locky? You're going to get a reputation. No, they don't say Winkman did it, though I'm sure he might have, but they *do* say that it's bad luck for anyone who comes into contact with that mirror. One of Winkman's men—he looked in it. No one was there to stop him. And he died. Yeah, I'll have a spot of sugar, thanks." George had handed her a coffee cup and saucer on a little tray.

"Give her a tablespoon with it," I said. "Saves time."

The blue eyes flicked toward me, but Flo said nothing as she dealt with her drink. "So, about the auction," she said. "There's a place near Blackfriars—north side of the Thames, mostly old warehouses for the shipping companies that used to operate there. Lot of them are empty now, and no one goes there at night, 'cept for wanderers like me. Well, Winkman's using one of these places tomorrow—the old Rostock Fisheries warehouse, right on the shoreline. He moves in, sets up his men, makes the sale, and melts away. All over in an hour or two. Happens very quick."

Lockwood was gazing at her fixedly. "What time's the auction?"

"Midnight. Selected customers only."

"He'll have security?"

"Oh yeah. There'll be heavies on watch."

"And you know this place, Flo?"

"Yeah, I know it. Do a bit of combing there."

"What height will the river be, midnight tomorrow?"

"Deep. Just past high tide." She scowled at me—I'd given a little gasp. "Well, what's wrong with *you*?"

"I've just remembered," I said. "Tomorrow night! It's the nineteenth—Saturday the nineteenth of June! It's the great Fittes party! I'd forgotten all about it."

"Me too," Lockwood said. "Well, I don't see why we can't do

both. Yes . . . why not? We'll make it a real night to remember." He strode to the table, swung a chair around. "George: kettle, Lucy: biscuits. Flo, why don't you please sit down?"

No one moved; all of us stared at him. "Do both what?" George asked.

"It's really very simple." Lockwood was grinning now; the radiance of his smile filled the room. "Tomorrow night we'll enjoy the party. Then we're going to steal the mirror back."

Chapter 21

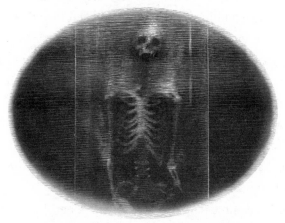

If there's one thing more stressful than being attacked by ravenous ghost-rats, it's finding that you're going to a fancy party and you haven't got a thing to wear. According to Lockwood, who subscribed to a magazine called *London Society*, the dress code for such occasions was tuxedos for men, and cocktail dresses for women. Agents were also permitted to wear agency uniforms, with rapiers, but since Lockwood & Co. *had* no uniform, that wasn't much help. It was true I had certain items in my wardrobe that could, at a stretch, be called *dresses*, but *cocktail* they most definitely were not. This fact, on the morning of the great Fittes anniversary party, sent me into a sudden panic. A frantic trip to the Regent's Street department stores ensued; by mid-morning I was back and breathless, laden with shopping bags and shoe boxes. I met Lockwood in the hall.

"I'm not sure any of this is right," I said, "but it'll have to do. What are you and George wearing?"

"I've got something somewhere. George wouldn't recognize a suit if it walked up and smacked him around the head. But he hasn't done anything about it; his friend Joplin's been here for the last two hours. They're looking at the manuscript."

Now that he mentioned it, I could hear the murmur of voices in the living room, talking over one another at great speed. "Can he translate it?"

"I don't know. He says it's very obscure. But he's mightily excited. He and George have been hooting over it like a couple of owls. Come and see. I want him off, anyway. We've got to get ready for tonight, and I need to go out and see Flo."

It had been three days since we'd seen Albert Joplin, and to be honest, I'd almost forgotten his existence. The little cemetery archivist was that kind of man. Last time I'd set eyes on him, shortly after the theft at Kensal Green, he'd been distressed and angry, loudly criticizing the lack of security on the site. His mood, clearly, had improved. When we went in, he and George were sitting on either side of the coffee table, talking and chuckling loudly as they stared down at the Bickerstaff papers laid out before them. Joplin was just as stoop-shouldered and tweedy as ever; light coatings of dandruff still iced his shoulders. But today his face shone, his eyes sparkled. If he'd been lucky enough to possess a chin, it would no doubt have been jutting with excitement. He was scribbling rapidly in a notepad as we entered.

"Oh, hello, Mr. Lockwood!" he called. "I have just finished transcribing the text. Thank you so much for showing it to me. It is such a remarkable find."

"Any luck with the translation?" Lockwood asked.

Joplin ran a hand through his mat of disordered hair; a small gray cloud of particles floated loose into the air. "Not yet, but I'll do my best. This seems to be some kind of medieval Italian dialect . . . it is rather obscure. I will work on it, and get back to you. Mr. Cubbins and I have had excellent discussions about it already. He's a lad after my own heart. A most intelligent, inquiring mind."

George looked like a cat that had not only got the cream but had been nicely stroked for doing so. "Mr. Joplin thinks the mirror may be uniquely important," he said.

"Yes, Edmund Bickerstaff was ahead of his time," Joplin said, rising. "Quite insane, of course, but a kind of pioneer." He gathered a mess of papers together and thrust them into a satchel. "I think it's tragic that the mirror has been stolen. Tragic too that if it's ever found, it would immediately be handed over to the DEPRAC scientists. They share nothing with those of us working on the outside. . . . Speaking of such problems, I told Mr. Cubbins that I haven't managed to find that other document you wanted—Mary Dulac's *Confessions*. I cannot think of another library that might have it—short of the Fittes Black Library, perhaps, which is also out of bounds."

"Ah well," Lockwood said. "Never mind."

"I wish you luck with all your investigations," Joplin said. He smiled at us; taking off his thick, round spectacles, he rubbed them contemplatively on a corner of his jacket. "If you have success, I wonder, perhaps you might give me a little glimpse of . . . No, I can see I've said too much. Forgive my impudence."

Lockwood spoke with studied coolness. "I can't comment about our work, and I'm sure George wouldn't do so either. I look forward to hearing what you make of the writing in due course, Mr. Joplin. Thank you for your time."

Bobbing and smiling, the little archivist made his departure. Lockwood was waiting for George when he came back up the hall.

"Kipps has stationed Kat Godwin outside our house today," George said. "I told Joplin not to talk to her, if she asks him anything."

"You two got along well again, I saw," Lockwood said.

"Yeah, Albert speaks a lot of sense. Especially about DEPRAC. Once they get a hold of something, it's never seen again. And this mirror could be something special. I mean—the idea that this might be some kind of window is extraordinary. We know that normal Sources somehow provide a hole or passage for ghosts to pass through. This thing is a *multiple* Source—made from *lots* of haunted bones—so just maybe that would make the hole big enough to look through. . . ." He glanced sidelong at us. "You know what, if we *do* get the mirror back tonight, there'll be no harm in checking it out ourselves before we hand it over. I could bring it back here, and we could try—"

"*Don't be an idiot, George!*" Lockwood's shout made both of us jump. "No harm? This mirror kills people!"

"It didn't kill me," George protested. "Yes, yes, I know I only saw it for a second. But maybe there's a way to view it safely."

"Is that what Joplin told you? Rubbish! He's a crank, and you're no better than he is if you even contemplate messing about with a thing like this. No, we get the mirror, we pass it on to Barnes. That's all there is to it. Understood?"

George rolled his eyes. "Yes."

"Another thing. What did you tell him about what we're doing tonight?"

"Nothing." George's face was as inexpressive as ever; two small spots of color showed on his cheeks. "I didn't tell him anything."

Lockwood stared at him. "I hope not. . . . Well, forget about it. We need to get ready, and there's a lot to do."

Indeed there was. The next few hours were a confusion of activity as we prepared for two separate, overlapping expeditions. Our duffel bags, stocked with an unusually high number of magnesium flares, were readied, together with our normal boots and work clothes. Lockwood and George, careful to avoid the watchful eyes of Kat Godwin in Portland Row, took these out the back way and were gone for several hours. Meanwhile, I polished our best rapiers, before spending ages trying on shoes and dresses in front of the mirror in the hall. I wasn't very happy about any of them, but I went for a dark-blue knee-length number with a scooped neck. It made my arms look fat and my feet look too big, and I wasn't convinced about the way it clung to my stomach. Other than that it was perfect. Plus it had a fabric belt to which I could fix my sword.

I wasn't the only one to have reservations about my dress. Someone had knocked the cloth off the ghost-jar, and the face had rematerialized. It pulled extravagant expressions of horror and disgust whenever I passed by.

The others got back late; evening was coming on. We ate; they got changed too. To my surprise, George conjured up a dinner jacket from the bowels of his bedroom. It was rather saggy under the arms and seat, and looked as if it had once belonged to an orangutan, but it *was* sort of passable. Lockwood strolled out of his room wearing the crispest, most dapper tuxedo and black bow tie I'd ever seen. His hair was combed back, his rapier sparkling; it hung at his side on a silver chain.

"Lucy, you look delightful," he said. "George, you'll have to do. Oh, here's something for you, Luce. Might go well with that excellent dress." He took my hand and placed in it a necklace of pretty silver links, with a small diamond suspended as a pendant. It was really very beautiful.

"What?" I stared at it. "Where'd you get this?"

"Just something I had. I suggest you close your mouth when you wear it—it's more elegant that way. Right, I can hear the taxi honking. We have to go."

Fittes House, headquarters of the estimable Fittes Agency, lies on the Strand just down from Trafalgar Square. We reached it shortly after eight p.m. For the occasion of the party, certain sections of the street had been blocked to normal traffic. Crowds had gathered near Charing Cross Station to watch the guests arrive.

At the marbled entrance, fires burned in open pits on either side of the doors. Illuminated banners, two stories long, hung from the walls. Each showed the rearing unicorn holding its radiant Lantern of Truth. Below, in silver letters, was emblazoned the simple proud motif: 50 YEARS.

A purple carpet of scattered lavender stalks covered the sidewalk between the doors and the road. This was roped off from the pressing knots of photographers and autograph hounds, and from the

TV cameras and their trailing worms of cable. A line of limousines waited in the center of the Strand, ready to disgorge their guests.

Our taxi chugged up, trailing little clouds of smoke. Lockwood swore under his breath. "I *knew* we should have come by tube. Well, we can't do anything about it now. Sure you've got your shirt tucked in, George?"

"Quit worrying. I even brushed my teeth as well."

"My God, you *have* made an effort. All right, here we go. Best behavior, everyone."

Out of the cab; a flurry of flashbulbs and snapping shutters (ceasing abruptly, since no one knew who we were); a few craning hands with autograph books outstretched; the soft and fragrant crush of lavender beneath my shoes; the brightness of the crane lights; the heat of the fires; then up the steps to the coolness of the portico, where a gray-suited doorman took our ticket and silently ushered us inside.

Twelve months had passed since I'd been in the foyer of Fittes House. Twelve months since I'd failed my interview. I remembered well the dimly-lit paneling, the soft gold light, the low, dark sofas, and the tables piled with brochures for the agency. I also remembered the distinctive scent of lavender polish and exclusivity. That time I hadn't even gotten past reception. I'd ended up ignored and tearful, slumped beneath an iron bust of Marissa Fittes at the far side of the room. The bust was still there in its alcove; stern-faced and schoolmistress-y, it watched as smiling Fittes kids led us off beyond the counter, across an echoing marbled floor, and under oil paintings dark with age.

So to more double doors, each marked with the rearing uni-corn. Silver-jacketed flunkies, identical down to the dimples in their chins, gave vigorous salutes; our approach had clearly made their lives worthwhile. With symmetrical flourishes they drew the doors aside and so unleashed upon us a riot of sound and genteel splendor.

It was a vast, broad reception room, lit by sparkling chande-liers. The high ceiling, decorated with stuccoed ornamental plaster swirls, featured panels on which were painted some of the most famous psychic achievements of the Fittes Agency. Marissa Fittes fighting the Smoke Wraith in the Bond Street bathhouse; Fittes and Tom Rotwell unbricking the skull of the Highgate Terror just as the clock on the wall struck midnight; the tragic death of poor Grace Peel, first martyr of the agency. . . . Legendary, heroic moments, familiar to us from our school days. This was the house where it had all originated, where psychic investigation had been raised to an art form; where the *Fittes Manual*, the foundation of our education, had been penned by the greatest operative of them all. . . .

I took a deep breath, set my shoulders back, and stepped forward, trying not to trip in my ridiculous high heels. Drinks were offered to me on a silver tray; with more eagerness than class I snatched an orange juice and looked around.

Early as it was, the place was already crowded, and I didn't need psychic Sight to tell at once that these were the Great and Good of London. Sleek-haired, sleek-faced men, wearing tuxedos as black and lustrous as panther pelts, stood conversing with bright-eyed, confident women, all glossy and bejeweled. I'd read somewhere that since the Problem started, female fashions had become more color-ful and revealing, and that was certainly the case here. Several of the fabrics on display would have blinded you if you'd looked at them too closely. The same was true of the plunging necklines; I noticed George rubbing his glasses even more assiduously than usual.

Aside from the show and glamour, the sight of this crowd was subtly disconcerting, and at first I couldn't figure out why. It took me a while to realize that I'd never seen so many *grown-ups* out at nighttime. Child waiters moved tactfully among the crowds, offering canapés of uncertain nature. A few young agents were present too; mostly from Fittes, but some from Rotwell's, recognizable by their wine-red jackets and haughty air. The rest were adults. It really *was* a special occasion.

Here and there across the room slender pillars of silver-glass rose to meet the ceiling. Each, lit by its own internal lamps, shone a different eerie color. These were the famous Relic Columns, which tourists paid to see. At present, their contents were hidden by the crowd. On a dais at the far side of the room, a string quartet played something jaunty, vigorous, and life enhancing. Melancholic music was banned after Curfew, in case it gave rise to oppressive thoughts. The chatter of the crowd was determinedly upbeat; laughter bullied the air. We walked through a sea of smiling masks.

Lockwood sipped his drink. He seemed relaxed, perfectly at ease. George (despite his efforts) retained a slightly rumpled look, as if he'd recently been trodden on. I was sure my face was flushed and my hair disarranged; certainly I was less pristine than the shiny women all around. "This is it, then," Lockwood said. "The center of it all."

"I feel *so* out of place."

"You look terrific, Luce. You might have been born to this.

Don't step back like that; you just prodded that lady's bottom with your sword."

"Oh, *no*. Did I?"

"And don't turn around so fast. You nearly cut that waiter in two."

George nodded. "Don't move, basically, that's my advice." He took a canapé from a passing kid and inspected it doubtfully. "Now that we're here, what are we going to do? Does anyone know what the hell this is? I'm guessing mushrooms and ectoplasm. It's all frothy."

"This is the ideal opportunity to take our minds off the later mission," Lockwood said. "We're meeting Flo at eleven forty-five, so we have plenty of time to relax and mingle. There'll be people here from government, from industry, from lots of important groups and companies. They're the ones who will be giving us all our future cases—*if* we do things right tonight. So we should circulate and get chatting to someone."

"Okay . . ." I said. "Where shall we start?"

Lockwood blew out his cheeks. "Don't really know."

We stood at the side of the room, watching the backs of the partygoers, the glitz and the jewelry and the slim necks go waltzing by. The sound of their laughter was a wall we could not get past. We drank our drinks.

"Who do you recognize, Lockwood?" I said. "You read the magazines."

"Well . . . that tall, fair-haired man with the beard and teeth is Steve Rotwell, head of Rotwell's, of course. And I *think* that's Josiah

Delawny, the lavender magnate, over there. The one with the red face and the sideburns. I'm not going to talk to *him*. He's famous for horse-whipping two Grimble agents after they smashed an heirloom during a ghost-hunt at one of his mansions. The woman chatting to him is, I believe, the new head of Fairfax Iron. Angeline Crawford. She's Fairfax's niece. Possibly another one not to make small talk with, seeing as we killed her uncle."

"She doesn't know that, does she?"

"No, but there's such a thing as good form."

"I can see Barnes," George said. Sure enough, not far away, the inspector was gloomily negotiating a champagne glass past his mustache. Like us, he stood alone, on the fringes of the crowd. "And Kipps! How did he get in? This party isn't as exclusive as they'd have us believe."

A knot of Fittes agents, Kipps among them, stalked past. Kipps pointed at us and made a comment. The others brayed with laughter; they minced away. I looked sourly at the chandeliers above us. "Can't believe you once worked here, George."

George nodded. "Yeah. You can tell I fit right in."

"Seems more like a stately home than an agency."

"These conference halls are the fancy bit, along with the Black Library. The rest of the offices aren't so swanky. But Kipps is pretty typical, unfortunately."

Lockwood gave a sudden exclamation; when I looked at him, his eyes were shining. "On second thought, we can scrap my last suggestion," he said. "Stuff the mingling. Who wants to do that? Boring. George—this library. Where is it?"

"Couple of rooms away. It won't be open. Only high-level agents have access."

"Do you think we could get in?"

"Why?"

"I was just remembering something Joplin said, about those *Confessions* that you're after. He said the Black Library was the one place where a copy might be. . . . Just wondering whether, since we're here—"

At that moment the crowds parted, and Lockwood stopped speaking. A very tall and beautiful woman was walking toward us. She wore a slim, silver-gray dress that shimmered subtly as she moved. She had silver bracelets on her slender wrists, and a silver choker at her throat. Her hair was long and black and lustrous, falling round her neck in merry curls. She had very fine cheekbones, attractive if rather high, and an imperious, full-lipped mouth. My first impression had been of a person scarcely older than me, but her dark and sober eyes had the flash of long-established power.

A muscular man with cropped gray hair and pale skin spoke at her shoulder. "Ms. Penelope Fittes."

I'd known who she was. We all did. But she surprised me, even so. Unlike her main rival, Steve Rotwell, the head of Fittes shunned publicity. I'd always imagined as her as a stocky, middle-aged businesswoman, as hatchet-faced as her famous grandmother. Not like this. She had the instant effect of reminding me how awkward I felt in my improvised dress and shoes. I could see the others instinctively drawing themselves up, trying to seem taller, more confident. Even Lockwood's face had flushed. I didn't look at George, but he'd almost certainly gone bright red.

"Anthony Lockwood, ma'am," Lockwood said, inclining his head. "And these are my associates—"

"Lucy Carlyle and George Cubbins," the lady said. "Yes. I'm very pleased to meet you." She had a deeper voice than I'd have expected. "I was impressed by your handling of the Combe Carey Haunting—and grateful that you recovered the body of my friend. If I can ever be of assistance, be sure to let me know." Her dark eyes lingered on each of us. I gave an affirmative smile; George emitted some kind of squeak.

"We're honored to be invited tonight," Lockwood said. "It's a remarkable room."

"Yes, it contains many treasures of the Fittes collection. Sources of the strongest power—all rendered harmless, of course, for our pillars are made of Sunrise silver-glass, and have iron pediments and bases. Come, let me show you. . . ."

She sashayed her way through the throng, which moved aside for us. In the nearest glass column, illuminated by pale-green light, a battered skeleton hung suspended on a metal frame. "This is perhaps the most famous artifact of all," Penelope Fittes said. "The remains of Long Hugh Hennratty, the highwayman whose ghost became famous as the Mud Lane Phantom. My grandmother and Tom Rotwell located the body at midnight on Midsummer Eve in 1962. Rotwell dug it up while Marissa kept the ghost at bay till dawn by frantically waving her iron spade." Our hostess gave a husky little laugh. "I've always said it's a good thing she was a keen tennis player, or else how would she have had the stamina or aim? But psychic investigation was in its infancy in those days—they didn't know *what* they were doing."

The skeleton was stained a muddy brown; the skull had few teeth and was missing its lower jaw. Aside from half of one femur, dangling beneath the pelvis, the legs and feet were gone. "Hugh Hennratty seems in rough shape," I said.

Penelope Fittes nodded. "They say wild dogs dug the body up and ate the legs. This may account for the ghost's anger."

"Chicken satay, anyone?" A young waiter materialized beside us with hors d'oeuvres on a golden tray. George took one; Lockwood and I politely declined.

"You must excuse me," Penelope Fittes said. "Circulation is the bane of a hostess's life! You can never stay long with anyone—no matter how fascinating they might be. . . ." She gave a twinkling smile at Lockwood, nodded dreamily at George and me, and drifted away. The crowd opened to receive her and the pale man, then closed fast, leaving us outside.

"Well. *She's* nicer than I expected," Lockwood said.

"She's all right," I said.

George, chewing on his satay stick, shrugged. "She wasn't as friendly as that when I was here. Ordinary agents never see her; she never comes down from her apartments. That gray-haired guy with her, though—her personal assistant—*he* used to get involved." His spectacles glittered resentfully. "He was the one who sacked me."

I looked into the crowd, but Penelope Fittes and her companion had gone. "He didn't seem to remember you."

"No. That's right. Probably forgotten all about me." George stuck the stick into the soil of a nearby potted fern, and hoisted his sagging trousers. A sudden fire of indignation burned in his eyes.

"You mentioned the Black Library just now, Lockwood. You know what, I don't see why we *shouldn't* take a little walk, see if we can peep in there."

He led the way slowly around the edge of the hall. Outside the windows the summer dusk was deepening. Colored spotlights cast strange effects of light and shadow across the moving crowd. Weird illuminations glowed inside the pillars—spectral mauves and blues and green. In several cases, ghosts appeared within the glass, staring sightlessly out, drifting ceaselessly around and around.

"Are we *sure* about this?" I asked. We were skulking in the shadows near a doorway, watching the throng, waiting for a chance to slip through. Not far away, Penelope Fittes talked animatedly to a handsome young man with a neat blond mustache. A woman with an incredible beehive hairdo shrieked at someone's joke. On the dais a jazz ensemble began to play a sharp but plaintive bluegrass melody. From the side doors a steady stream of waiters came, each bringing more wonderful dishes than the last.

"No one's paying attention," George said. "Now . . ."

We followed him through the door and into an echoing marble hall. It contained the doors to six elevators, five colored bronze, and one colored silver. The walls were lined with oil paintings of young agents—girls, boys, some smiling, others sad and serious—all beautifully depicted in their silver-gray jackets. Plinths beneath each one were decked with rapiers and wreaths of flowers.

"Hall of Fallen Heroes," George whispered. "I never wanted to end up here. See that silver elevator? That goes straight up to Penelope Fittes's rooms."

George led us along a series of interconnecting passages, progressively narrower and less splendid, stopping occasionally to listen. The sound of the party grew dim. Lockwood still had his drink glass; in his dinner suit, he moved as seamlessly as ever. I tottered along in my stupid dress and shoes.

At last George stopped at a heavy-looking wooden door. "We went the long way around," he said, "because I didn't want to bump into anyone. This is a service entrance to the Black Library. It *might* be open. The main doors are almost certainly locked at this time of night. It's got Marissa Fittes's own collection of books on Visitors, many rare items. You realize that it's utterly forbidden for us to go in? If we're caught, we'll be arrested and can wave our agency good-bye."

Lockwood took a sip of his drink. "What are the chances of anyone coming in?"

"Even when I worked here, I was never allowed more than a glimpse through the door. Only senior staff use it, and they'll be at the party. It's not a bad time. But we shouldn't stay long."

"Good enough," Lockwood said. "Just a quick look, and then we're done. Burglary's more fun than socializing, I always say. The door'll probably be locked, anyhow."

But it wasn't locked, and a moment later we were inside.

Chapter 22

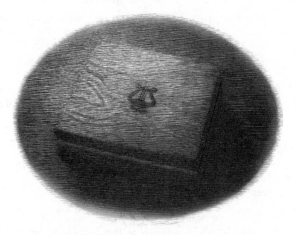

The Black Library of Fittes House proved to be a vast octagonal room, rising the height of two full floors toward a glass dome in the roof. It being night, the surface of the dome was dark, but lanterns beneath it shone warm light down into the center of the library. The walls were bookshelves, tier upon tier, with a metal balcony running around them at first-floor height. In two places, spiral stairs descended from this to the ground level, where we stood. The floor was made of wooden tiles, mostly of dark mahogany; but in the center, a design in paler woods depicted a rearing silver unicorn. The middle of the room was sparsely furnished; here and there were reading tables, and glass cabinets displaying books and other objects. Directly opposite us was a set of double doors, closed and locked. From somewhere came the hum of a generator; otherwise a great hush lay on the library. The air was cool and the light dim.

Inset lamps above each bookshelf glowed like hovering fireflies around the half-dark of the perimeter. The books themselves had been expensively bound in leather—purples, dark browns, and blacks. There must have been many hundreds on the ground floor alone.

"Impressive . . ." Lockwood breathed.

You might have expected George to be in his element here—along with chips and weird experiments, libraries are his thing—but he was twitchy, biting his lip as he scoped the balconies for signs of movement. "First we need the index to the collection," he said. "It'll probably be on one of the reading tables. Hurry up and help me. We mustn't stay long."

We followed him swiftly out into the bright center of the room. All around was watchful silence. Somewhere beyond the double doors I heard a murmuring: echoes of the party elsewhere on this floor.

The table nearest the door had a large leather book lying on it; George hauled it open with an eager cry. "This is the index! Now we just need to see if *The Confessions of Mary Dulac* is here."

While he turned the pages, I glanced at the nearest display cabinets. Lockwood was doing the same. "More relics," he said. "There's no end to their collection. Good lord, these are the knitting needles in the Chatham Puncture case."

I peered at the inky label on the side of my cabinet. "By the looks of it, I've got someone's pickled lungs."

George gave an agitated hiss. "Will you two stop messing about? This is no place—" He stopped short. "Yes! *Yes*, I don't believe it!

They *do* have the *Confessions*! It's listed here as book C/452. It's somewhere in this room."

Lockwood drained his glass decisively. "Very good. What are we looking for?"

"Check out the books. They should all have numbers written on the spines!"

I hurried to the shelves, inspected the volumes on them. Sure enough, each had its number in gold leaf, stamped into the leather. "Got the As here," I said.

Lockwood ran to the nearest stairs, vaulted the steps two at a time. His shoes tapped softly on the metal balcony. "B/53, B/54 . . . Nothing but Bs. . . . I'll check farther along."

"What was the number again?" I said.

"Shh!" George had suddenly stiffened where he stood. "Listen!"

Voices beyond the double doors; the rattling of a key in the lock.

I moved. I didn't see what the others were doing. I flung myself toward the nearest display cabinet, positioned between the shelves and the illuminated center of the room. Just as the door opened, I ducked down low behind it, scrunching up in high heels and party dress, bare knees pressed close to my chin.

A brief burst of party murmur, cut off by the firm closing of the door.

Then a woman's voice. Familiar, deeper than you'd have expected.

"It will be quieter here."

Penelope Fittes.

I squeezed my eyes tight shut, and pressed my teeth hard against the surface of my knee. That Lockwood! Yet another of his impulsive ideas had steered us toward disaster. This part of the evening was supposed to be relaxing—we were supposed to save the dangerous part for Winkman.

Footsteps on wood. They were walking into the center of the room, just where George had been a moment before. I waited for the inevitable outcry, the shock of disclosure.

"What was it you wished to say, Gabriel?" Penelope Fittes asked.

I opened my eyes; as I glanced to the side, my heart jumped. My rapier was sticking out beyond the edge of the cabinet. The tip of the silver blade gently sparkled in the light.

A man was speaking, polite and deferential. "The members are getting restless, Ms. Fittes. They feel that you are not helping them sufficiently with their work."

That same husky little laugh. "I'm providing every assistance. If they aren't up to the challenge, it's not my problem."

Very slowly I began to inch the rapier blade back in.

"You wish me to tell them this?" the man said.

"Certainly you must tell them. I'm not their nursemaid!"

"No, madam, but you *are* their inspiration— What's *that*?"

I froze, bit my lip. A trickle of sweat ran down the side of my face and pooled beneath my chin.

"The pickled lungs of Burrage the poisoner," Penelope Fittes said. "My grandmother had a great interest in crime. You would not *believe* the things she collected. Some of them have been of immense use over the years. Not these lungs, admittedly. They have no psychic charge at all."

"Odd choice of decoration for a library," the man said. "It would put me off my reading."

The laugh again. "Ah, it doesn't disturb those of us who come here. We have our minds on higher things."

The quality of their voices changed, became suddenly more muffled. I guessed they'd turned away from me. I rapidly pulled the remaining length of blade out of view; then, with infinite care, I leaned to the side, and peered around the edge of the cabinet.

Not fifteen feet away, I saw the backs of two people: Penelope Fittes conversing with a dumpy, middle-aged man. He wore the black tie and dinner jacket of a party guest; from what I could see, he had a rather thickset neck, a pinkish jowly face.

"Speaking of unusual artifacts," Penelope Fittes said, "I *do* have something to give you." She moved suddenly, and I ducked back into hiding. I could hear the points of her shoes clicking crisply on the dark wood floor. "Think of it as a token of my good will."

I couldn't tell where she was going, whether or not she was getting closer to me. I pressed myself tighter against the back of the cabinet.

Something made me look up. Lockwood was lying flat on his stomach on the surface of the balcony almost directly above. He was doing his best to merge with the metal and the darkness. The black tux jacket helped. His pale face didn't. I signaled at him to turn his head away.

"*Lucy!*" he mouthed.

"*What?*"

I couldn't make it out at first. He mouthed it several times. His eyes swiveled from me toward the center of the room. Then I realized what he was telling me: "*My glass.*"

I craned my head around the edge of the cabinet and, sure enough, my heart skipped another beat. There it was, his punch glass, sitting on top of the little display case in the center of the room. It was almost as if the spotlight was deliberately trained on it. How it sparkled. You could even see the little residue of red liquid at the bottom.

Penelope Fittes had crossed to that very cabinet. She was standing right beside it; the glass was at her shoulder. She had opened a drawer below the case, and was bringing something out.

All she had to do was glance up and focus on it, and she would see the glass right there.

But she didn't. Her mind was on other things. She closed the drawer and turned to her companion.

"We've repaired it," Penelope Fittes said. "And tested it. It works again splendidly. I hope the Orpheus Society make better use of it than before."

"You are very kind, madam, and they will be grateful. I'll be sure to pass on their thanks, and let you know how their experiments go."

"Very good. I suggest you don't rejoin the party. The box will be too noticeable. But you can go out this way."

The click-clack of her shoes sounded again—and to my horror I saw that the little door through which we'd entered the library was not far from me. They would pass right by my hiding place. After an instant's frozen indecision, I acted; I eased off my shoes—first one foot, then the other—then pressed my fingers to the floor and pushed myself up slightly, so that I could shuffle both feet backward. Now I no longer sat, but squatted on the balls of each foot, with my back still flat against the cabinet. With one hand I picked up my shoes; with the other I held my rapier steady, so that it wouldn't knock against anything and make a sound. I did all this faster than it takes to tell.

I waited. Up above, Lockwood had turned his head to face the wall; he had become a patch of shadow. The footsteps drew close, and now they passed by, a few feet beyond the cabinet, and I had a sudden waft of Penelope Fittes's flowery perfume. The man carried a wooden box under his arm. It was not very big, perhaps twelve inches square, and four or six deep. They paused beside the door, and I glimpsed the box clearly for an instant. Stamped in the center of its lid was an odd little symbol. It was a little like a harp, with three strings, bent sides, and a splayed base. Even in that extreme moment it made me frown; I had seen that symbol before.

Then the woman opened the door for him, and that was my chance to move. With two quick shuffles I was around the corner of the cabinet and hunching down again, so that I was out of sight when our hostess chose to turn around.

The door closed; the man must have departed without words. Penelope Fittes walked past the cabinet and away across the room. Once she had gone by, I shuffled back to my original position.

I listened to her cross the library, going at a brisk pace. When she reached the center, she stopped abruptly. I could imagine her looking around. I thought of George, of Lockwood's glass. . . . I squeezed my eyes shut tight. Then the footsteps resumed, there was the briefest swell and ebb of party noise, and the sound of keys turning in the door.

I exhaled properly for the first time.

"Nice moves, Luce," Lockwood said, pushing himself up from the balcony. "You were just like a sprightly crab. Where did George go?"

Yes, where *was* he? I surveyed the library's emptiness.

"Anyone care to help me?" a small voice called from under the reading table. "I'm stuck down here, and I think my bottom's wedged."

Back in the conference halls, the party was in full swing. The band played boisterously, the waiters filled glasses at ever greater speed; the guests, dancing with more enthusiasm than talent, were louder and more red-faced than before. We found a quiet place beside a unicorn-shaped chocolate fountain and took in some badly needed drinks.

"You should really join a circus, George," Lockwood said. "There are people who'd pay good money to see contortions like that."

"That'll be my next career." George took a long swig of punch. "Certain parts of me still feel folded. You've got the book?"

Lockwood patted his jacket pocket; after less than a minute's hasty searching, we'd discovered *The Confessions of Mary Dulac*, a thin pamphlet bound in black leather, on a high shelf on the upper level. "Safe and sound," he said.

George grinned. "Good. This has already been a successful night, and we haven't even come to the main event yet. Can we nip somewhere and read it now?"

"Afraid not," Lockwood said. "Better drink up. It's twenty to eleven. Time to go."

"Not leaving so soon, Mr. Lockwood?" Inspector Barnes materialized dourly at our elbows. It was hard to say what seemed more out of place: the pink cocktail in his hand, or the fountain spurting chocolate bubbles at his side. "I was hoping for a quiet word."

To our annoyance, Quill Kipps was lurking behind him, like a slim and baleful shadow. "That would be delightful," Lockwood said. "Have you enjoyed the party?"

"Kipps here tells me," Barnes said, "that you might have uncovered some interesting documents up in Hampstead. What are they, and why haven't you shared them?"

"I'd be delighted to do precisely that, Inspector," Lockwood said. "But it's been a long day and we're very weary. Could we visit you in the morning to explain?"

"Not now? Surely you could tell me this evening."

"It's not really a suitable location. Far too noisy. Tomorrow morning at Scotland Yard would be so much better. We could bring you the documents then too." Lockwood gave a warm, ingratiating smile; George took a half glance at his watch.

"You do seem in rather a hurry," Barnes said. His pouched blue eyes appraised us steadily. "Just off to bed now, are you?"

"Yes, George here turns into a pumpkin if he's out too late—as you can see, he's well on the way already."

"So you'll show me these documents tomorrow?"

"We will."

"All right, but I'll expect you bright and early. No excuses, no no-shows, or I'll come to find you myself."

"Thank you, Mr. Barnes. We very much hope to have good news for you then."

"That was bad timing," Lockwood said, as we crossed the reception area toward the outer doors of Fittes House. "Kipps will know we're up to something tonight."

I glanced behind me, just in time to see a willowy figure dart behind a pillar. "Yeah. He's following us right now."

"Subtle as ever," growled George.

"Okay, so we can't just go and pick up the supplies, as we discussed. We need to lose him. That means a night cab."

Exiting the building, we hurried down the purple carpet, past the smoking lavender fires, to the line of cars waiting at the sidewalk. All had the silver grilles and ostentatious iron ornaments of the official night-cab service. Behind us, at a discreet distance, came Kipps. When he saw us approach the taxi line, he abandoned attempts at subtlety, and joined us at the street.

"Don't mind me," he said, as we glared at him. "I'm going home early too."

The next taxi advanced. "Portland Row, please, driver," Lockwood said loudly. We got in; the car pulled away. Looking back, we could see Kipps getting in the cab behind. At once Lockwood leaned forward, spoke to the driver. "I'm going to give you fifty. I'd like you to drive to Portland Row, as I said. But when you leave Trafalgar Square, I want you to stop as soon as you're around the next corner. Just for a second. We're going to get out and I don't want the cab behind to see us do it. Okay?"

The driver blinked at us. "What, are you fugitives?"

"We're agents."

"Who's tailing you? The police?"

"No, they're agents too. Look, it's difficult to explain. Are you going to do what I asked, or do you want us to get out now without the fifty?"

The driver rubbed his nose. "If you want, I could wait till he gets really close, then stop so he crashes onto the sidewalk. Or I could double back, and ram him. For fifty I could do those things."

"No, no. Dropping us off quietly will be fine."

All went well; the car purred around the deserted expanse of Trafalgar Square. Kipps's taxi had been held up outside Fittes House by a departing limousine. It was fifteen, maybe twenty seconds behind us. We turned up Cockspur Street toward Haymarket and Piccadilly, past flashing ghost-lamps and smoldering lavender fires. As we rounded the corner of Pall Mall, the taxi slowed; George, Lockwood, and I bundled out and darted under the portico of the nearest building. The taxi roared away; an instant later, the second cab flashed by, with Kipps hunched forward in the backseat, no doubt giving instructions to the driver. We watched the cabs speed away into the night. Silence fell in the center of London.

We adjusted our rapiers and walked back the way we had come.

During the hours of darkness Charing Cross Station is deserted, but its concourse remains open. We retrieved our work supplies from the lockers where Lockwood and George had left them that afternoon, and changed clothes in the public restrooms. It felt good to get rid of the stupid dress, and particularly the shoes. I couldn't part with the little necklace Lockwood had given me, though; I kept it on under my T-shirt and light black jacket. All our clothes were black and as lightweight as possible; tonight we needed to move fast, and not be seen.

We walked swiftly east along the Embankment, following the Thames. Moonlight lay scattered on the surface like silver scales; the river was a serpent coiling beside us through the city. It was deep at that hour, as Flo had said. The water lapped high on the tide-wall, flicking against the stones.

With our change of clothes had come a change of mood, and we went in silence for the most part. This was the sharp end of the evening, its dangers very real. I could still sense the repulsive touch of Julius Winkman's hand on mine, from when we'd faced him in his little shop; his casual expressions of brutality still rang loudly in my head. He was not a man to cross, and what we were doing now was as risky in its way as any investigation of a haunting. Riskier, perhaps, since we relied on the cooperation of another if our intervention was to succeed.

"We're putting a lot of trust in Flo Bones," I said.

Lockwood nodded. "Don't worry. She'll be there."

We passed the Inns of Temple, where the lawyers work by day, and under Blackfriars Bridge. Now the riverside path ended abruptly at the side of an enormous brick building, its highest level protruding over the water. This was start of the old merchant district. Vast, abandoned warehouses stretched away like cliffs along the curl of the river, dark and empty, with pulley arms and gantries jutting out like the broken limbs of trees.

We climbed some steps to a cobbled lane beyond the warehouse, and continued through the darkness. There were no ghost-lamps here, and the air was cold. I sensed Visitors in that alley, but the night remained still and I saw nothing.

"Maybe I should come inside too," George said suddenly. "Maybe I need to be in there with you."

"We've gone over this," Lockwood said. "We all have our roles. You need to stay outside with Flo. You've got the equipment, George, and I'm relying on you."

George grunted. His backpack was very large, even more bulbous than when he'd had the ghost-jar. Lockwood and I carried no bags at all, and our belts were stocked differently. "I just think this is too serious for you to do it alone," George said. "What if you need help containing the mirror? What if Winkman has more than just a couple of enforcers? He might—"

"Shut up about it, George," Lockwood said. "It's too late to make a change."

We walked on in silence. The lane was a dark cleft between buildings, with a narrow stream of moonlight running down its center. At last, Lockwood slowed; he pointed. Ahead of us, an alley cut across to the left and right. On the right-hand side, we smelled the river. Farther on, the lane continued beside the silent walls of another warehouse. Its nearest windows were boarded up; far above, steep roofs and chimneys spiked the silvered sky.

Painted on the brick exterior of the building, in peeling and faded letters, were the words ROSTOCK FISHERIES. Lockwood, George, and I hung back, watching, listening. If this was the place of Winkman's auction, there was precious little sign of it. No lights, no movement; like so many areas of the city by night, this was a dead zone.

We started forward; at once the smell of mud and tidal water became strong. A thin white arm reached out from the shadows of the alley, grasped Lockwood by the coat, and pulled him sideways into the darkness.

"Not a step more," a voice hissed. "They're here."

Chapter 23

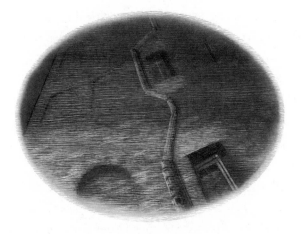

During our discussions with Flo Bones the day before, I'd repeatedly found myself doubting that she'd show up at all. It wasn't just that she was crazy, more that she was crazy in such a prickly and solitary way. Lockwood had promised her various generous pay-offs for her help—including money, licorice, and her pick of the relic trophies we kept down in the basement—but I still felt that joining us in this hazardous job would be the last thing she'd want to do. And yet here she was, in all her unwashed glory, leading us down the alley to a dark nook wedged between some trash cans, which, let's face it, rather suited her.

"Come in nice and tight," she whispered. "That's it. . . . We don't want them to notice nothing."

"Everything on schedule, Flo?" Lockwood asked. He checked his watch. "It's just half past eleven."

Her white teeth glinted in the shadows. "Yeah, Winkman arrived fifteen minutes back. Came in a van, and unloaded the merchandise. He's left two men outside the main doors; you'd have run into them if you'd walked a few more yards. Now he's gone inside with three other men, and a kid. They'll be securing the ground floor."

"A kid?" I whispered. "You mean his son?"

Flo nodded. "Yeah, it was that toad. They'll all bring psychic kids with them tonight. They're adults, ain't they? For this, they need young eyes and ears." She straightened. "If you're going ahead with it, Locky, you'll need to start climbing."

"Show us the place, then, Flo."

We followed as she flitted away along the side of the warehouse. Soon we heard the soft wash and sloop of the Thames, and the cobbles of the alley sloped steeply down to sand and shingle. Here, where the corner of the building rose from the river mud, a thick black iron drainpipe had been bolted to the mossy bricks. Flo pointed upward. "There's the pipe," she said. "See where it runs past that window? I reckon you could get in there."

"That window looks too small," I said.

"You're looking at the wrong one. I mean the one much farther up, almost out of sight."

"Oh . . . right."

"It's the way to get in, if you don't want 'em seeing you. They won't be thinking of upstairs."

I looked at the teetering drainpipe, zigzagging madly up the wall like a line drawn by an angry toddler. To be honest, I was trying not to think of upstairs either.

"Fine," Lockwood said. "We'll manage. What about you, Flo? You've got the boat?"

In response, she pointed out to the river, where a long, low black shape listed half in and half out of the water. Waves sloshed gently over the stern.

George leaned close. "That's her rowboat?" he breathed. "I thought it was a bit of rotten driftwood."

"It's almost certainly both."

I'd kept my voice down too, but Flo had sharp ears. "What's that? This here's little *Matilda*; I've sculled her safely from Brentford Sewage Works to Dagenham Tannery, and I won't hear a word said against her."

Lockwood patted Flo's shoulder, then surreptitiously wiped his hand on the back of his coat. "Quite right. It'll be an honor to sail in her. George, you understand the plan? You create the diversion, then wait with Flo in *Matilda*. If all goes well, we'll join you, or at least get you the mirror. If things don't work out so smoothly, it's Plan H: we make our ways separately back home."

George nodded. "Good luck. You too, Luce. Lockwood, here's your stuff. You'll need the masks and bag."

Setting his backpack down on the sand, he brought out a canvas bag, similar to but smaller than the one Flo used. A powerful odor of lavender came from it. Two black ski masks emerged next; we tucked them in our belts.

"Right," Lockwood said. "Set your watches. The auction starts in fifteen minutes, at twelve sharp. We'll want the diversion at twenty past, before they have a chance to do any kind of deal." He gestured to the pipe. "Lucy, you want to go first, or shall I?"

"This time," I said, "I'm *definitely* going after you."

It would be nice to say that climbing the drainpipe brought back happy memories from a country childhood, of spending warm summers swarming up trees in the company of other nimble friends. Unfortunately, since I never had a head for heights, the tallest thing I'd ever scaled was a jungle gym in the village playground, and I once barked my shin tumbling off *that*. So the next few minutes, as I inched my way torturously after Lockwood, were not the happiest of my career. The iron pipe was broad enough for me to lock my arms right around it, and the circular clasps that attached it to the wall made decent hand and footholds. In many ways it was like scaling a ladder. But it was rusty, too, and its flaking paint was prone to stabbing my palms, or coming away altogether in sudden shards. A strong wind was blowing up the Thames, whipping my hair into my face, and making the pipe shudder. And it was very high. I once made the mistake of looking down, where I saw Flo wading out to her little floating wreck, and George still standing by his backpack, staring up at me. They were as small as ants, and it made my hands sweat and my stomach feel as if it were already dropping; so I gritted my teeth and closed my eyes tight shut as I climbed, and I didn't open them again until the top of my head collided with the heels of Lockwood's boots.

He was leaning out above the dreadful drop, prying and tapping with his penknife at a pane of glass in the window at our side. The lead was old and soft, and soon the pane fell inward. Lockwood reached in; he fiddled with the metal clasp, cursing at its stiffness. With a final wrench, which made something in the pipe rattle alarmingly, the window swung open. A leap, a shimmy—and

Lockwood was through; a moment later he was stretching out to help me inside.

We stood in the shadows for a few minutes, taking sips of water, and in my case waiting for my arms and legs to stop shaking. There was a dusty smell in the building; not derelict like the Bickerstaff House, but mothball-y and unused.

"Time, Luce?"

"Five to twelve."

"I'd call that perfect, wouldn't you? And George will be well on his way to his position now, as long as he hasn't sunk."

I switched on my penlight and aimed it across the empty room. Once, perhaps, it had been a manager's office. Old bulletin boards with charts and figures hung silent on the walls. "When this is over," I said, "I think you need to have a word with George."

Lockwood was at the door, peering out into the passage. "What for? He's fine."

"I think he's feeling left out. It's always us that does this kind of job, isn't it, while he has to hang around outside."

"We've all got our talents," Lockwood said, "and George is simply less good at this stuff than you are. Can you imagine him climbing up here? That doesn't mean he hasn't got a vital role today. If he and Flo mess up their timing, if their boat capsizes, or they don't find the right windows or something, you and I are quite possibly going to die." He paused. "You know, this conversation's making me slightly nervous. Come on, we need to find our way downstairs."

This upper floor of the warehouse was a maze of office rooms and connecting passages; it took us longer than expected to discover the brick stairwell in the corner of the building. Time was against us now, but still we went carefully, stopping and listening at every corner. I counted the floors as we went, so as to be able to retrace our steps back to our open window. We'd gone down six full flights before we saw a faint glow extending up the bricks, heard the murmur of voices, and knew we were drawing close to the site of Winkman's auction.

"First things first," Lockwood whispered. "Masks on."

The ski masks were essential to protect our identities from the future attentions of a vengeful Winkman. They were hot, itchy, and hard to see out of, plus the wool covered our mouths and made it difficult to speak. Aside from that, it was a joy to wear them.

Pushing open a glass door, we found ourselves on a fenced catwalk overlooking an enormous space. It was the cavernous heart of the warehouse and probably stretched the entire length of the floor, though it was impossible to determine its dimensions. Only one small area was properly lit, and that was directly below us. Lockwood and I ducked low; we slunk forward to the catwalk edge to get a better view. From where we knelt, a steep row of metal steps led down to the warehouse floor. We were fairly safe for the moment, for no one within the light would easily be able to see out into the dark.

Winkman, it seemed, liked to keep things on schedule. We had arrived at precisely three minutes past midnight and the auction was already in progress.

Three tall lamps on metal stands had been set up at one end of the hall. They were positioned as if at the points of a triangle, and the area they lit functioned like a stage. Just on the edge was a row of six chairs facing the light. Three were occupied by adults, and three by children. Behind them, in the shadows, two largish, serious-looking men stood like ugly statues, staring out at nothing.

Two chairs had also been placed in the spotlit space between the lamps, and one of these was occupied by the boy from the antiques shop. He wore a gray jacket, and his oiled hair shone softly in the lamplight. He swung his fat little legs back and forth beneath the chair in a bored sort of way as he listened to his father.

Julius Winkman stood in the center of the stage.

Tonight, the black marketeer wore a wide-breasted gray suit and white shirt, open at the collar. Beside him was a long folding table, draped with a clean black cloth. With a hairy hand he made a delicate adjustment to the little golden pince-nez on his nose, as he indicated the silver-glass display box beside him.

"This first lot, friends," he said, "is a very pretty fancy. Gentleman's cigarette case, platinum, early twentieth century. Carried by Brigadier Horace Snell in his breast pocket the night he was shot dead by his rival in matters of the heart, Sergeant Bill Carruthers. Date: October 1913. Blood traces still present. Still contains a psychic charge from the event, I believe. Leopold can tell us more."

At once the son spoke up. "Strong psychic residue: gunshot echoes and screams upon Touching. No Visitor contained. Risk Level: low." He slumped back in the chair; his legs resumed their swinging.

"There you are, then," Winkman said. "Little sweetener before the main event. Do I hear any interest? Starting bid: three hundred pounds."

From our position high above, it was impossible to see the

contents of the little box, but there were two other cases on the table. The first, a tall rectangular glass cabinet, contained a rusted sword—and a ghost: even under the spotlights, I could see the eerie bluish glow, the soft tug and pull of moving plasm. The second, a much smaller case, held what looked like a pottery statue or icon, shaped like some four-legged beast. This too had a glimmer of other-light about it, faintly visible beneath the constraining glass.

Neither of these were what *I* was interested in, because to Winkman's *other* side was a small table, standing separate and alone, where the light from the three lanterns intersected. It was very bright, the focus of the entire room. A heavy black cloth covered the glass case on the table. Piled on the floor below it were heaps of iron chains, and rings of salt and iron filings in ostentatious protective display.

To my ears came a familiar hateful sound: the whirring buzz of flies.

I nudged Lockwood and pointed. He gave the briefest of nods.

There had been progress in the auction. One of the customers, a neat, prim-looking man in a pinstriped suit, had consulted with the small girl sitting next to him, and put in a bid. A second member of the audience, a bearded man in a rather shapeless raincoat, had topped that instantly, and the bids were now seesawing between them. The third of Winkman's three clients had remained entirely unmoved. He sat half turned away, negligently toying with the polished black walking cane he held. He was a young, slim man with a blond mustache and curly yellow hair. Sometimes he glanced at the glowing cases, and bent to ask questions of the boy at his side; but most often he stared at the black cloth on the table in the center of the room.

Something about the young man was familiar. Lockwood had been gazing at him too. He leaned close and mumbled something.

I bent closer. "What?" I breathed. "I can't make out what you're saying."

He rolled up the bottom of his mask. "Where did George get these things? Surely he could afford one with a mouth hole. . . . I said, that man nearest us—he was at the Fittes party. We saw him talking to Penelope Fittes, remember?"

Yes, I remembered him, glimpsed across the crowded room. The black tie at his neck could just be seen beneath his elegant brown coat.

"Winkman's clients must come from high society," Lockwood whispered. "Wonder who he is."

The first lot of the auction had been completed. The cigarette case had gone to the pinstriped man. Beaming and nodding, Winkman moved to the cabinet with the rusted sword, but before he could speak, the young blond-haired man raised a hand. He wore light brown gloves, clearly made of lambskin, or the hide of something else small and cute and dead. "The main event, please, Mr. Winkman. You know why we've come."

"So soon?" Winkman seemed dismayed. "This is a genuine Crusader blade, a French *estoc*, which we believe contains an actual ancient Specter or a Wraith, perhaps of one of the very Saracens it slew. Its rareness—"

"—does not interest me this evening," the young man said. "I have several similar pieces. Show us the mirror we've heard so much about, and let us move things along—unless the other gentlemen disagree?"

He glanced across. The bearded man nodded; the man in pin-stripes gave a curt wave of approval.

"You see, Winkman?" the young man said. "Come! Show us the prize."

The smile on Julius Winkman's face did not alter, but it seemed to me that his eyes had narrowed behind the flashing pince-nez. "Certainly, certainly! Always you speak your mind openly and honestly, my lord, which is why we so value your custom. Here then!" He swung his bulk across to the separate table, took hold of the black cloth. "May I present that unparalleled item, that extreme rarity that has so exercised the men at DEPRAC these past few days—friends, the bone glass of Edmund Bickerstaff!"

He pulled the black cloth away.

We had been so long in the pursuit of this object that it had acquired in my mind an almost mythic weight and dread. This was the thing that had slain poor Wilberforce, that had struck a relic-thief dead before he even left the cemetery, and killed one of Winkman's men. This was the glass that everyone wanted—Barnes, Kipps, Joplin, Lockwood, George, and I. People had murdered for it; people had died for it. It promised something strange and terrible. I had only caught a flash of it in Bickerstaff's coffin, but that shiny, crawling blackness remained imprinted on my mind. And now, finally, here it was: and it seemed so very small.

Winkman had arranged it like an artifact in a museum, propped up against a slanting velvet display board. It was in the center of a large, square, silver-glass case. From where we crouched, far above, its exact size was hard to judge, but I guessed it to be no more than six inches across, about the size of a saucer. The glass in the center seemed coarser than I'd expected, scuffed and uneven. Its rim was roughly circular, but brown and bumpy in outline. Many hard and narrow things had been tightly fused to make it. Many bones.

The buzzing sound rubbed at my ears. Two of the children in the audience made little whimpering noises. Everyone sat attentive and stiff, staring at the object in the case.

"I should point out that you're seeing it from the back," Julius Winkman said softly. "The glass on the reverse is highly polished; here it's rough, more like rock crystal."

"We need to see the other side," the shabby, bearded man said. "How can we possibly bid without seeing that? You're playing tricks with us here, Winkman."

Winkman's smile broadened. "Not so. As always, I have only the safety of my clients at heart. You know this object has a certain reputation. Otherwise, why would you be here? Why would you pay the minimum asking price, which I can tell you now is fifteen thousand pounds? Well, with that reputation comes dangers. You know there are risks attached to looking in the glass. Perhaps there are wonders, too—that is not for me to say—but this cannot be investigated until the item is sold."

"We can't buy on these terms," the bearded man grumbled. "We need to look at the viewing glass!"

"Look at the glass, by all means." Winkman smiled. "But not before you've paid."

"What else can you tell us?" the small man in pinstripes asked. "My backers require more solid information than you've given me so far."

Winkman glanced at his son. "Leopold, if you wouldn't mind?"

Up bounced the boy. "The item needs to be treated with extreme care. Quite apart from the dangers of the mirror itself, the bone fragments appear to be a Source for more than one apparition. At times I have counted at least six, perhaps seven faint figures hovering near the object. They project very strong psychic disturbances: much anger and agitation. The mirror surface itself gives off intense chill, and an attraction similar to fatal ghost-lock. Those who look in it are mesmerized, and find it hard—if not impossible—to drag their gaze away. Permanent disorientation may result. Risk levels: Very High."

"Well, gentlemen," Winkman said, after Leopold had plopped down, "that is our summary. Please—bring your assistants up and make a closer inspection."

One by one the audience rose and approached the case, the adults curiously, the children in fear and doubt. They surrounded it, whispering to each other.

Lockwood pulled up his mask and leaned in close. "It's twenty past. Get ready, and watch the windows."

High along the opposite wall, a row of great rectangular windows faced the night. Somewhere beneath them George and Flo would now be standing, George readying the contents of his bag. They would see the position of the light; they'd know the location of the auction. I shifted from one foot to another, felt the cold firmness of my rapier hilt.

Any moment now . . .

Down below, the crowd pressed closer around the case. The bearded man spoke peevishly: "There are two holes drilled through the bone here, near the base. What are they for?"

Winkman shrugged. "We don't know. We believe it may have been attached to a stand. No one would have wanted to hold it, I feel sure."

At my side, Lockwood gave a sudden soft exclamation. "That's it!" he whispered. "Remember those sticks I saw in the photo of Bickerstaff's coffin? I was right—they *were* some kind of stand: something to put the bone glass on."

"Winkman hasn't got it, then," I said.

"Of course *he* hasn't. Jack Carver didn't take the sticks, did he? No, someone *else* pinched them, after the photo was taken." He glanced at me sidelong. "I'd say it's fairly obvious *who*."

That's how Lockwood was sometimes: he liked to throw out tantalizing tidbits of information at the most inappropriate times. I would have questioned him right there (and thumped him if need be), but now Winkman was ushering his audience back to their seats. It seemed the bidding was about to start.

Lockwood looked at his watch. "Where *is* George? They ought to have started now."

"Gentlemen, gentlemen," Winkman said. "Have you conferred with your psychics? If you have no questions, time is pressing, and we must get to the main point of business. As I said, the starting price for this very unique item is—"

But the young man with the blond mustache had raised his hand again. "Wait. I do have a question."

Winkman cranked his smile wider. "Of course. Please."

"You have mentioned certain supernatural risks. What about the legal ones, rising from the murder of Jack Carver? Word is, Carver got you the glass, and a dagger in the back was what Carver got from you. We're not too particular about your methods, but this seems a little too public for anyone's good. DEPRAC is investigating this now, as are some of the agencies."

The edges of Winkman's mouth flicked downward, as if a switch had been thrown. "I'd like all you gentlemen to recall the previous business we've done together. Haven't I honored our agreements? Haven't you been satisfied with the items that I've sold? Let me tell you two things. First, I didn't commission Carver. He came out of the blue to see me. Second, I bought this item fair and square, and I left him in rare good health. I didn't kill him." Julius Winkman put a great hand on his chest. "All this I swear on the head of my dear little son, Leopold, what you see is as limber as a ferret here. As for DEPRAC or the agencies—" He spat sidelong onto the warehouse floor. "*That's* what I think of them. Still, anyone who's fearful is welcome to leave now, before the bidding takes place." He stood in the center of the stage with his arms spread wide. "Well?"

At that moment a white light bloomed beyond the window. None of the people on the warehouse floor noticed it, but we, in the shadows, saw it swell and grow, then fade into the dark again.

"That's our cue," Lockwood whispered. He pulled his mask down.

Down below, no one had answered Winkman. The young man had only shrugged; everyone remained seated.

Winkman nodded. "Right. Enough talking. Let's have your starting bids."

At once the man with the beard lifted an arm.

And the nearest window blew apart in an explosion of incandescent fire.

Chapter 24

W e'd known the first magnesium flare would explode the
moment it hit the glass, and we'd anticipated it would
shatter the pane it struck. What we didn't expect was
that the blast would be strong enough to break *all* the panes in that
huge warehouse window, and several in the windows on either side.
So the effect was even greater than we had hoped: a wall of glassy
shards toppling with the force and power of a melting ice shelf,
cutting straight through a pluming cloud of salt, iron, and white
magnesium flames.

Even before the shower of fragments burst to powder on the
ground, two more flares were spinning through the smoke above,
looping through the hole the first had blown.

And by the time *they* struck, Lockwood and I were already halfway down the steps, rapiers and flares in hand, hurtling toward the
warehouse floor.

The noise of the original explosion and the crack of ruptured glass had deafened us, even through our wool masks. And *we'd* been expecting it. The effect it had had on those directly below, to whom it came as an utter shock, could be seen in the swarm of figures milling within the tumbling silver smoke.

The child psychics were out of their chairs and running, screaming, into the dark. The guards blundered left and right, protecting their heads against the rain of salt and glass. Two of Winkman's clients had fallen forward onto their knees as if the end of days had come; the young blond man sat motionless in his seat as if paralyzed with shock. Winkman's son had leaped gibbering to his feet; Winkman himself stared left and right like a bewildered bull, fingers flexing, neck cords straining beneath the skin.

He caught sight of us as we clattered down the steps, and his black eyes opened wide.

Then George's second and third flares struck the ground. Two more eruptions of billowing white fire. Winkman was blown sideways; he crashed into the table that held the bone glass and fell heavily to the floor. Behind him one of the lanterns toppled, smashed, went out. Hot iron particles shot high, looped down in a glimmering red cascade.

It was a scene of carnage and confusion. The man in the pinstripes rolled onto his back, shouting, wisps of smoke rising from his suit. Winkman's son had fallen heavily against his chair, breaking it in pieces. The bearded man gave a cry of terror, stumbled to his feet and fled up the hall.

Still the young blond man sat immobile, staring straight ahead.

Lockwood and I were almost at the bottom of the steps. We'd

calculated on our distraction giving us several seconds' grace, and though George's work had exceeded our wildest hopes, we knew it wouldn't be enough. It was my job to maintain the distraction, while Lockwood snatched the mirror. I readied a fourth flare, lobbed it in the general direction of the flailing guards. Lockwood threw another, only *his* was directed firmly at the silver-glass case.

Two more explosions. One sent the guards scattering; the other shattered the case. Winkman, who'd been attempting to pull himself upright behind the table, disappeared in a blast of silvery fire.

Lockwood leaped over the protective chains and plunged into the smoke, trailing a scent of lavender; he had the canvas bag open in one hand.

When the silver-glass case had broken, the buzzing in my head had instantly grown louder. I looked into the fog and saw Lockwood's silhouette bending over the table, and—above him—shadowy rising forms. Many hollow voices spoke together: *"Give us back our bones."*

Then Lockwood opened the lavender bag, and with gloved hand swept the bone glass into it. The buzzing was stilled; the rising forms winked out. The voices were gone.

Lockwood turned, burst out of the smoke, came running back toward me.

Some yards away, the young man with the blond mustache got up. He reached for his polished cane, lying on the floor beside his chair. He twisted the handle sharply, tugged, drew forth a long and slender blade. He tossed the cane behind him, and started in our direction. I unclipped another flare, drew back my arm . . .

"Stop! Or I fire!"

Winkman had risen up behind the table, his face blackened, his hair blown back, pince-nez askew. Burned salt encrusted his face, his mouth hung open, and his jacket was peppered with smoldering holes. He had a black snub-nosed revolver in his hand.

I froze with my arm still back. Lockwood halted, facing me, almost alongside.

"You think you can run?" Winkman said. "You think you can rob me? I will kill you both."

Lockwood slowly raised his hands. He said something quietly at my side. His mask muffled it; I couldn't hear a word.

"First we will discover who you are," Winkman said, "and who sent you. We will do this at my leisure. Put down the canister, girl. You are surrounded now."

Sure enough, the guards had reemerged from the shadows; each also carried a gun. The young man, still immaculate in his soft brown coat, stood by, sword-stick glittering in the light.

Lockwood spoke again, urgently; once again I couldn't hear it.

"Put down the flare!" Winkman cried.

"What was that?" I muttered. "I can't hear you."

"Oh, for heaven's sake." Lockwood ripped up the bottom of his mask. "The other case! The one with the ghost! Do it!"

It was lucky I already had my arm in position; even so, it wasn't an easy shot. The glowing case with the rusted sword was several feet away, and half blocked by Winkman's head. Probably, if I'd thought about it, I'd have missed hitting it, five times out of six. But I didn't have time to think. I swiveled slightly, lobbed the canister high; then I ducked down low. At my side, Lockwood was already ducking too, so Winkman's bullets passed somewhere directly over us. Neither of us saw my canister hit the case, but the sound of breaking glass told us at once that my throw had been successful. That, and the screams of warning in the room.

I jerked my head up, saw a sudden alteration in the behavior of our enemies. None of them were any longer focused on us. From the ruins of the broken cabinet, where the sword now lolled at a drunken angle, a faint blue shape had issued, steaming and fizzing in the last flecks of tumbling salt and iron. It was slightly larger than man-sized, and blurry, as if a strong, firm silhouette had been partially dissolved. In places, it was utterly translucent; in the center of its torso it had no color or definition at all. Around its edges, scraps of detail could be seen, little twists and bumps that suggested clothes, and smoother places resembling dead skin. And up near the top—two shining pin-points of light glittering like frost? These were the eyes.

Cold air leaked from the Phantasm. It had no visible legs, but flowed toward the men as if on a rolling strip of cloud. The guards panicked; one fired a bullet straight through its body, the other turned and fled across the hall.

Winkman picked up a shard of silver-glass and sent it whizzing into the ghost. It cut through one outstretched arm with a fizz of plasm. I heard a spectral sigh of disapproval.

The young man held his sword-stick out, adopted an *en garde* posture. Slowly he moved toward the advancing shape.

Lockwood and I didn't stop to see more. We were running for the stairs. I reached them first, went clattering up.

A scream of rage. Out of the smoke behind Lockwood's shoulder the Winkman boy came charging, a shattered chair arm in his hand. Lockwood swiped backward with his rapier. The boy howled, clutched at his wrist; his club fell to the floor.

Up the stairs, three at a time. Behind came shouts, curses, the soft sighing of the ghost. I looked back down as we raced along the catwalk. The warehouse floor was almost invisible through the layers of silver smoke. A faint blue shape flexed and darted, seeking to get past the silvered flashing of the sword.

Somewhat closer, a great, barrel-chested figure was limping swiftly up the steps.

Through the glass doors; Lockwood slammed them shut. He shot two bolts into position and joined me, careening up the stairwell.

We'd climbed several flights when the hammering on the doors began.

"We need those bolts to hold a little longer," Lockwood gasped. "We need to be a long way down that drainpipe before they see us, or we'll be sitting ducks."

A bang, followed by a vast and tinkling crash, sounded from below.

"He's shot his way through," I said. "On the upside, that's one bullet less for us."

"How I love your optimism, Luce. What floor are we on now?"

"Oh, no . . . I forgot to count the flights. We needed to go up six."

"Well, how many have we done?"

"I think we need to go up a couple more. . . . Yes, this is our floor, I think—it's down along here."

As we left the stairwell, Lockwood checked the doors, but there were no more bolts to draw. We pelted down the corridor.

"Which office was it?"

"This one. . . . No, that's not right. They all look the same."

"It must be the one in the corner of the building. Here—look, there's the window."

"But it's not the right room. Lockwood—where are the bulletin boards?"

Lockwood had thrust open the window and was looking into the night. He craned his neck out. "We've come too far, I'm afraid—we're even higher than before. The pipe's here, but there's a nasty kink in it just beneath us, which I don't think we can climb past."

"Can we go back down?"

"We'll have to."

But when we ran back to the stairwell, we heard the thump of feet a flight or two below, and saw the first faint flashlight beam on the wall.

"Back again," Lockwood said. "And quickly."

We returned to the little office. Lockwood motioned to me to guard the door. I positioned myself flat against the wall, took my last canister of Greek Fire from my belt and waited.

Lockwood crossed to the window and leaned out. "George!" he called. "George!"

He listened to the night. I listened to the passage; it was very quiet, but it seemed to me that it was an attentive silence.

"George!" Lockwood called again.

Far below us, in the dark of the river, the hoped-for voice. "Here!"

Lockwood held the canvas sack up high. "Package coming down! Are you ready?"

"Yes!"

"Take it and then go!"

"What about you?"

"No time. We'll join you later. Plan H! It's Plan H now, don't forget!"

Lockwood threw the bag out into the night. He didn't wait for George's answering shout, but jumped back into the room and called to me.

"We're climbing up, Luce. That's the only option. We get to the roof and then see."

Stealthy, cautious footsteps sounded in the passage. I peered around the door. Winkman and two other men—one of the guards, and another I didn't recognize—were advancing along the corridor. As I moved my head back, something whined past and bit into the far wall. I tossed the flare around the corner and ran across to Lockwood. Behind me the floor shook; there was a silvery explosion, followed by assorted cries of woe.

"Put your feet on the sill," Lockwood said, "reach out, and swing yourself up. Quick now."

It was another of those occasions when if you think too hard, you're lost. So I didn't look at the gulf below or at the glinting river, or at the great expanse of moonlit sky that threatened to tilt and tumble before my dizzy eyes. I just stood on the sill, pulled myself out, and threw myself against the pipe, clutching it around, dropping only a little way before my feet found purchase and I was clinging safely to it. At once I began to climb.

In two ways this second ascent of the drainpipe was easier than the first. I was climbing for my life, so I didn't care so much about the wind, the flaking paint, or even the drop below me. Also it was shorter—I only had the equivalent of one floor to climb before I reached a rusty ledge of black gutter, and found myself clambering over it onto a flat expanse of leaded roof. In all, the whole thing probably took me just over a minute. I'd paused a single time, when I thought I heard a shrill shout of anger (or perhaps pain) some-where below. But I could not bear to look down; I could only pray that Lockwood was close behind. And sure enough, almost immedi-ately I heard a scratching noise below the gutter, and saw him haul himself up beside me.

"Are you all right?" I said. "I thought I heard—"

Lockwood pulled off his mask and smoothed his hair back. He had a small cut on the side of one cheek and was breathing heavily. "Yes. I don't know who he was, but I expect he deserved it. Unfor-tunately, when he fell out of the window, I lost my nice new Italian rapier."

We knelt side by side on the roof for a time, until our breathing slowed.

"The only good thing about being up here," Lockwood said finally, "is that I can't see Winkman clambering up after us. Aside from that . . ." He shrugged. "Well, let's see what our options are."

Our options, in short, were limited. We were on a long stretch of flat roof above the swollen Thames. To one side rose a sheer brick wall, belonging to a rooftop structure that had probably once enclosed the warehouse's power units. It ran the width of the roof, and we could not easily scale it. On the other side of us was the river. Far below us, moonlight glinted on water that was lapping at the joists and girders. It seemed a long way down.

I looked, but I couldn't see Flo or George, or their little rowboat at all.

"Good," Lockwood said. "That means they've hightailed it. Or sunk to the bottom, of course. Either way, the bone glass is out of Winkman's hands."

I nodded. "Nice view up here. The city looks quite pretty when you can't see all the ghosts." I glanced at him. "So . . ."

He grinned at me. "So . . ."

There was a scrabbling at the far end of the roof. Lockwood jammed his mask back over his face. Hands appeared on the parapet; a figure pulled itself swiftly up and into view. It was the blond-haired young man. His brown coat was missing, and his tuxedo jacket was lightly flecked with ectoplasm stains. Other than that, he seemed in fair condition. Like us, he had clambered up the pipe from the window below.

He got lithely to his feet and dusted himself off. Then he unclipped his sword-stick from his belt. "Well done," he said. "You've performed extremely well. That was an excellent chase, and I haven't had so much fun in ages. You know, I think your last spot of Greek Fire almost knocked Winkman right through the wall, which believe you me is not a bad thing. But this looks like the end of the line. May I have my seeing-glass now?"

"It's not yours," Lockwood said firmly.

The young man frowned. "Sorry? Didn't quite catch that."

I gave Lockwood a tactful nudge. "Your mask."

"Oh, yes." Lockwood pulled up the bottom of the wool. "Sorry.

I was saying that, strictly speaking, it *isn't* your glass. You haven't yet paid, or even bid for it."

The young man chuckled. He had very blue eyes and a pleasantly open countenance. "I appreciate the point, but Julius Winkman is raving and roaring down below. I believe he would tear you apart with his bare hands if he could. I am not nearly so crude; in fact, I see an opportunity that would be to both our advantages. Give me the glass now, and I promise to let you both go. I'll say you escaped with it. Then both of us win. You live, and I keep the glass, without having to pay that revolting troll Winkman."

"It's a good offer," Lockwood said. "And very amusing. I almost wish we could agree. Sadly, I don't have the glass."

"Why not? Where is it?"

"I threw it in the Thames."

"Oh," the young man said. "Then I really will have to kill you."

"You could let us go anyway, in a spirit of good sportsmanship," Lockwood suggested.

The young man laughed. "Sportsmanship only goes so far. That spirit-glass is something special, and I had my heart set on it. Anyway, I don't believe you *have* thrown the thing away. Maybe I'll kill you and get the girl to tell me where it is."

"Hey," I said, "I still have *my* rapier."

"However we do it," the young man said, "let's get this over with."

He walked swiftly toward us along the roof. We looked at each other.

"One of us *could* fight him," Lockwood said, "but then we'd still be in the same position." He looked over at the river. "Whereas . . ."

"Yeah," I said. "But, Lockwood, I really can't."

"It'll be all right. Flo's flaky, but we can trust her about some things. Water depth is one of them."

"We make *such* a habit of doing this," I said.

"I know. But it's the last time."

"Promise?"

But we were already running across the bumpy lead, building up as much speed as we could. Then we jumped out together, hand in hand.

Somewhere during the next six seconds I let go of Lockwood. Somewhere amid the screaming, rushing plunge, I let the rapier spin away. At the moment of jumping I had my eyes tightly closed, so I didn't see the stars take flight, or the city leap to meet us, as Lockwood afterward said he had. Only later, *much* later, maybe four or five seconds in, when I couldn't believe I wasn't already dead, and opened my eyes just to prove it, did I see the brightly sparkling waters of the Thames spread out in silent greeting beneath my rushing boots. I was in the process of remembering the rules about hitting the surface like an arrow so you didn't break *all* your bones when, with a whip-crack and a roaring, I was ten feet under in a cone of bubbles, and still going down.

At some point I hit equilibrium: I slowed, slowed . . . and hung suspended in the blackness, without thought, without emotion, without much attachment to life or living things. Then the current tore me up and sideways, and in a flurry of panic I recalled my life and name. I struggled, thrashed, and swallowed half the river—at which point it vomited me out.

I was whirling on an oily swell somewhere in the middle of the Thames. I lay back, coughing, gasping. Lockwood was at my side; he grasped my hand. Staring up toward the moon, I had a final glimpse of a slim figure standing silhouetted on a far-off rooftop, before the black waters swept us both away.

VI

Through the Looking Glass

Chapter 25

"Well," Lockwood said, "if you judge success by the number of enemies you make, that was a highly successful evening."

At two forty-five in the morning, the little kitchen at 35 Portland Row really comes into its own. We had eggs boiling, bread toasting, the kettle gently steaming on the side. It was a brightly lit and cozy scene, marred only by the presence of the ghost-jar on the counter. The skull was active, the horrid face grinning and winking at us from the center of the plasm. In our mood, however, this was easy to ignore.

Lockwood and I were feeling like ourselves again. This was faintly miraculous, since scarcely two hours had passed since we'd hauled ourselves out of the water onto the dirty shingle south of Tower Bridge. Our soggy walk back to Charing Cross Station had seemed to take forever, but once we'd changed back into dry clothes, things started to look up. By great good luck, we'd managed to snag a passing night cab. Now—showered, clean, and warm—we were agreed that we'd managed it very efficiently. We'd made it home quicker than George, anyway. He'd not yet returned.

"It's a success however you look at it," I said, patting the hot toast from hand to hand and spinning it onto the plate. "We've beaten Winkman! We got the Bickerstaff mirror! We can give it in to Barnes in the morning, and close the case. And Kipps loses his bet, which is best of all."

Lockwood was flicking through the pamphlet we'd stolen from the Fittes library just a few hours earlier—it seemed a lifetime ago. We'd left it in the Charing Cross lockers, so it had been spared a dunking in the Thames. "I notice Kipps and his team aren't lurking outside anymore," he said. "He must have given up when he realized we'd tricked him in the car. I only wish George would get back. He's taking his time."

"Probably couldn't find a taxi that would take him after being in that smelly old boat of Flo's," I said. "He must be having to walk. His station locker was empty, so we know he got away safely."

"True." Lockwood put down the pamphlet and got up to deal with the eggs. "I was right about these *Confessions of Mary Dulac*, by the way. They're mostly nonsense. Lots of babble about forbidden knowledge and seeking out the mysteries of creation. Anyway, they didn't do poor old Mary much good, since she apparently spent ten years living in a hollow tree. Want your egg in a cup or on the plate?"

"Cup, please. Lockwood, who do you think that man was—the one on the roof?"

"I don't know. But Winkman called him 'my lord,' so we can probably find out." He handed me my boiled egg. "He's some rich collector, or a modern version of Bickerstaff, prying into what doesn't concern him. Bickerstaff himself sounds like a monster, judging by what Mary Dulac says. Check it out—it's on the third or fourth page."

He busied himself with his supper. I picked up the *Confessions*. Despite the Fittes library's leather binding, it was very thin, scarcely more than a few pages long. It was more a collection of disjointed paragraphs than anything else. Someone had probably copied selections of the original, removing passages that were tedious or incoherent. As Lockwood had said, there was lots about the unhappy woman's life in the wilderness, and many philosophical rantings about death and the afterlife that I didn't understand. The part about Bickerstaff was meatier, though. I read it, between dabs at my egg.

Who was Bickerstaff, whose cursed shadow hangs over me these past ten years? Ah! He was a genius! And the wickedest man I ever knew! Yes, I killed him. Yes, we buried him deep and sealed him up with iron, yet still I see him in the darkness, whenever I close my eyes. Still I see him before me, swathed in his velvet cloak, performing his dark rituals. Still I see him, coming from his workroom, his butcher's knives all bloody in his hand. Still I hear that terrible voice, that soothing, persuasive instrument that made us all puppets of his will. Ah! Fools that we were to follow him! He promised us the world, promised us enlightenment! Yet he led us to ruin and the brink of madness. Because of him I have lost everything!

There followed a short digression about the varieties of bark and fungi that Mary Dulac had been forced to eat during her years living wild in Chertsey Forest. Then she returned to the subject in hand.

His darkness was in him always—in those staring wolf-like eyes, in that savage rage he unleashed at the merest slight. I cannot forget it—how he broke Lucan's arm when he dropped the candles, how he threw Mortimer down the stairs! I cannot forget. Yes, we hated and feared him. Yet his voice was honey. He mesmerized us all with talk of his great Project, of the wondrous Device that might be made if we had the stomach for the work. With the help of his servant, a most cunning and malignant Boy, whose eyes saw phantoms clearly, we went on expeditions to the churchyards, gathering materials for the Device. The Boy protected us from the vengeful Spirits, until we had them in the glass. It is the presence of these Spirits together, Bickerstaff says, that gives the Device its power. And what power! The mirror makes weak the fabric of the world, and offers the lucky few—Oh, horror! Oh, blasphemy!—a glimpse of Heaven.

I looked up at Lockwood. "Whatever it is you see through Bickerstaff's mirror," I said quietly, "I don't think it's Heaven."

He shook his head. "Nor do I. We were right, you know, Lucy. We were right about that bone glass. Bickerstaff's group was trying to see something that's forbidden to us all. They were trying to look beyond death, glimpse what happens next. Bickerstaff was

crazy—they all were. Including our friend over there." He jerked his head toward the face in the jar. Pinpoints of light glittered in its sockets as it gazed at us. The smile was broad and knowing.

"It seems in a very good mood tonight," I said. "It hasn't stopped grinning since we came in. Hey, I just thought of something . . . this evil servant boy Dulac goes on about. You don't suppose that . . . ?"

"Who can tell?" Lockwood scowled over at the skull. "It wouldn't surprise me at all." He sat back in his chair. "Well, thank goodness we've got the mirror, so no one else can take a chance with it. Bickerstaff didn't try looking himself, I bet—he just used others. It's no wonder his ghost was so horrid. I'm glad you tossed a sword through his head."

"When I heard his voice back in the cemetery," I said, "it *was* mesmeric, like Dulac says. It had a kind of hypnotic effect. It sort of made you want to do things, even though you knew you shouldn't. I think George and Joplin were affected by it, though they may not have consciously heard the voice. Remember how they stood frozen by the coffin?"

"Yes. Those idiots." Lockwood looked at his watch. "Luce, if George doesn't turn up soon, I'm going to start worrying. We might have to go and find Flo and see where she left him."

"He'll be here. You know how slowly he walks. Oh—look at this." I'd flipped to the end of the pamphlet. "It's what we wanted. Dulac's final confession."

Yes, (I read) *I killed a man. But murder? No! Should I one day stand in Judgment I shall claim it an act of self-defense— yea, a desperate act to save my very soul. Edmund Bickerstaff* was mad! He sought my life as openly as if he had put a knife to my throat. His blood is on my hands, but I have no guilt.

Wilberforce died. We all saw it; he looked in the Device and perished. Then came a great panicking. We fled in our carriages from that cursed place, vowing to reject Bickerstaff forever. Yet this the doctor would not allow. Within the hour, he and that silent Boy were at my house and he carried the Device with him. I feared them, yet I let them in. The doctor was agitated. Would I be quiet on the subject of poor Wilberforce? Could he trust me to keep my own counsel? Despite my assurances, he grew enraged. At last he denounced me; to prove my faith, I must look into the glass! In a moment the Boy had sprung behind me; he pinioned my arms. Out came the Device from the doctor's pocket. He held it before me; I had half a glimpse, half a glimpse only, and I felt my sanity shake loose, my limbs go cold.

So it would have ended, but for my father's service revolver on my table. I tore myself free and took up the gun. Covering my face, as Bickerstaff clawed at me and screamed, I shot— the bullet passed directly through his forehead. I fired also at the Boy, but like an eel he evaded my grasp, dived through the casement, and escaped. In some moments, God forgive me, this is my supreme regret. I wish that I had killed him, too.

I will not tell how we disposed of the doctor and his creation. Suffice it to say that we feared others might mimic our folly and seek out knowledge that isn't meant for Man. I only trust that we have constrained the Device as best we can, and that it may now lie forever undisturbed.

I closed the pamphlet and tossed it aside. "So that's it," I said. "That's how Bickerstaff died. Mary Dulac shot him, then she and her friends buried him secretly in Kensal Green. We've solved it. The case is closed." I picked up my plate, ready to carry it to the sink—and stopped suddenly, staring at the table.

Opposite me, Lockwood was nodding. "Dulac may have been crackers," he said, "but she got it spot on. *Everyone* wants the glass. Everyone's obsessed by what it might show, despite the fact that it seems to kill whoever looks in it. Those collectors last night would have paid thousands. Barnes is desperate too. Joplin's been hounding us to have a peek, and George is scarcely any better." He smiled ruefully. "George and Joplin are *so* similar, aren't they? They even clean their glasses the same way. Incidentally, did I tell you that I think Joplin was the one who pinched Bickerstaff's original stand from the coffin? He and Saunders are the only ones with access to the chapel where it was kept, you see. It's just the kind of thing that he . . ." He paused. "Lucy? What is it? What on earth's wrong?"

I was still staring at the table, at the thinking cloth with all its notes and scribbles. It's always right in front of us. Mostly, I never focus on what's written there. Now, quite by chance, I had—and if my blood hadn't drained from my face, it certainly *felt* like it. "Lockwood . . ." I said.

"What?"

"Was this here earlier?"

"Yes. That doodle's been there for months. I'm surprised you haven't noticed it. I keep telling George not to do that kind of stuff; it puts me off my breakfast. What, do you think we should replace the cloth?"

"Not the doodle. Shut up. This writing here. It says: *Gone to see a friend about the mirror. Back soon. G.*"

We stared at each other. "That *must've* been written days ago. . . ." Lockwood said.

"When?"

Lockwood hesitated. "Don't know."

"Look, here's the pen he wrote it with. Right next to it."

"But that would mean . . ." Lockwood blinked at me. "Surely not. He wouldn't."

"A *friend*," I said. "You know who that would be, don't you?"

"He wouldn't."

"He came back here, with the bone glass, and instead of waiting for us, he went straight out again. To see Joplin."

"He *wouldn't*!" Lockwood had half risen; he seemed uncertain what to do. "I can't believe it. I expressly told him not to."

A vibration in the room. It was faint and very muffled. I looked over at the ghost-jar. Poisonous green light gleamed within it; the face was laughing.

"The ghost knows!" I cried. "Of *course* he does—he was right here!" I shoved my chair back, sprang over to the glass. I turned the lever—and at once the foul cackles of the skull burst on my ear.

"*Missing someone?*" it jeered. "*Has the penny just dropped?*"

"Tell us!" I shouted. "What have you seen?"

"*I've been wondering how long it would take you to figure it out,*" the voice said. "*I guessed twenty minutes. Must've taken twice that. Two dim dormice would have sussed it out faster than you.*"

"What happened? Where did George go?"

"*You know, I think your little George is in a spot of trouble,*" the skull said gleefully. "*I think he's off doing something stupid. Well, I won't lose any sleep over it, after all the things he's done to me.*"

I could feel panic rising in my chest, my muscles freezing. I stammered out the ghost's words to Lockwood. All at once he was past me and grabbing the ghost-jar from the counter. He swung it over and crashed it down upon the table, sending the plates flying.

The face rolled against the inside of the jar, the nose pressed flat against the glass. "*Hey, careful. Watch it with the plasm.*"

Lockwood scraped his fingers back through his hair. "Tell it to talk. Say that if it doesn't tell us what it saw George do, we'll—"

"*You'll what?*" the ghost said. "*What can you do to me? I'm dead already.*"

I repeated the words, then flicked the glass with a finger. "We know you don't like heat," I snapped. "We can make things very uncomfortable for you."

"Yes," Lockwood added. "And we're not talking ovens now. We'll take you to the furnaces in Clerkenwell."

"*So?*" the ghost sneered. "*So you destroy me. How will that help you? And how do you know that's not exactly what I desire?*"

Lockwood, when I told him this, opened his mouth and then shut it again. The desires and dreams of a ghost are hard to fathom, and he didn't know what to say. But I did. All at once, I knew *precisely* what that ghost had always wanted—what had driven it in life, and what kept driving it in death. I felt it; I knew it as if the longing were my own. There *are* some advantages to sharing headspace with a phantom. Not many, but a few.

I bent my head close to the glass. "You like keeping little secrets from us, don't you? Your name, for instance, and who you once were. Well, we don't really care about that. See, I think we know enough already to understand what makes you tick. You were one of Bickerstaff's friends—maybe his servant, maybe not—and that means you shared *his* dreams. You helped him build that stupid bone mirror. You wanted to see it used. And why would you do that? Why did you have that mad desire to look past death and see what lies beyond? Because you were afraid. You wanted to be sure that something happened after it, that you wouldn't be alone."

The face in the jar yawned, showing appalling teeth. *"Really? Fascinating. Bring me a hot cocoa, and wake me when you're done."*

"Thing is," I went on implacably, "the same fear's driving you now. You *still* can't bear to be alone. That's why you're always yabbering at me, why you're always pulling faces. You're *desperate* for connection."

The ghost rolled its eyes so fast they looked like spinning tires. *"With you? Give me a break. I've got standards. If I wanted a proper conversation I'd find—"*

"You'd find *what*?" I sneered. "You'd find it *how*? You're a head in a jar. You're not going anywhere, and we're all you've got. So— we're not going to put you in the furnaces," I said. "We're not going to torture you. All we'll do, if you don't start cooperating, is shut your lever up, put you in a bag, and bury you in the ground somewhere. Nice and deep, so no one ever finds you. Just you, on your own, forever. How does that sound?"

"You wouldn't do that," the ghost said, but for the first time I

heard uncertainty in its voice. "*You need me, don't forget. I'm a Type Three. I'll make you rich. I'll make you famous.*"

"Stuff that. Our friend is more important. Last chance, skull. Spill the beans."

"*And here was I thinking Cubbins was the cruel one.*" The face drew back into the shadows of the plasm, where it glared at me with an expression of bloodcurdling malice. "*All right,*" it said slowly. "*Sure, I'll tell you. Don't think I'm giving in to your blackmail, mind. I just want to enjoy what's coming to you all.*"

"Get on with it," Lockwood said. I'd been muttering the ghost's words to him as best I could. He squeezed my arm. "Good work, Lucy."

"*Well, you're right, as it happens,*" the whispering voice said. "*Cubbins was here. He beat you home by almost an hour. He had the master's mirror in a dirty sack. And he hadn't been back long before someone else showed up. A little mousy fellow with spectacles and tousled hair.*"

I repeated this. Lockwood and I exchanged a glance. Joplin.

"*They didn't stay—there was just a short discussion, then they both went off together. They took the sack. I thought Cubbins seemed uneasy. He was unsure of what he was doing. At the last moment, he ran back in and left you that note. I'd say he was still fighting against my master, but the other fellow isn't. He's long gone.*"

"Still fighting against what?" It was as if a cold spear had pierced my side.

The teeth of the skull glinted beneath the ghost's smile. "*My master has been talking to them. You can see it in their eyes. Especially the other one—he's desperate to be enlightened. But Cubbins has the madness too. Did you not notice?"* A whispered chuckle. *"Perhaps you never look at him."*

I couldn't speak. Once again I saw the cowled phantom rising in the cemetery, towering over George. Once again I heard that soft and urgent voice: *"Look . . . look . . . I give you your heart's desire. . . ."* I thought of George and Joplin standing as if spellbound by the iron coffin. I thought of all George's little comments since then, his malaise at Bickerstaff's house, his distractedness, his wistful looks as he spoke about the mirror. The memories transfixed me in turn. I was frozen. It took Lockwood several tries before I could tell him what I'd heard.

"We knew he'd been affected by the mirror and the ghost," I said hoarsely. "We noticed, but we didn't pay attention. Poor George. . . . Lockwood, we've been so blind! He's desperate to investigate it. He's been obsessed with it all this time. And you just kept criticizing him, slapping him down."

"Yes, of course I did!" If my voice had risen, now Lockwood's did too. "Because George is *always* like that! He's always obsessed with relics and old stuff! It's just how he is! We couldn't possibly have known." Lockwood's face was ashen, his dark eyes hollow. His shoulders slumped. "You *really* think he's affected by the ghost?"

"By the ghost, by the mirror. He'd never normally do something like this, would he—go off, and leave us alone."

"No, of course not. But even so . . . Honestly, Luce, I'm going to kill him."

"That may not be necessary, if either of those idiots looks in the mirror."

Lockwood took a deep breath. "Okay. Think. Where'll they be? Where does Joplin live?"

"No idea, but he seems to spend most of his time at Kensal Green Cemetery."

He snapped his fingers. "Right! And not just the aboveground parts either. That gray stuff in his hair? It's not dandruff, put it that way." He bounded for the basement door, sprang through and down the stairs, feet clanging on the iron. "Come on!" he shouted. "Collect whatever supplies you can. Spare swords, flares, anything we've got! And ring for a night cab. We need to *move!*"

Ten minutes later, we were back in the kitchen, waiting for the taxi. We had our swords (old ones, taken from the rack in the training room), and two spare work belts, so ripped and burnt with plasm, they barely clipped together. Also a few bags of iron, two salt-bombs, and no magnesium flares. Everything else had been lost, used up, or soaked in our raid on Winkman.

Both of us were agitated; we stood at the table, checking and rechecking our supplies. The face in the ghost-jar watched us. It seemed amused.

"I wouldn't bother, personally," it said. *"I'd just go off to bed. You'll be too late to save him."*

"Shut up," I growled. "Lockwood, what were you saying about Joplin just now? About the gray stuff in his hair? You mean—"

He tapped his fingers impatiently on the counter. "It's grave dust, Luce. Grave dust from the catacombs beneath the chapel. Joplin's made it his business to go exploring down there, even though it's closed off and forbidden. He's been creeping around underground, poking and prying, looking for stuff, following his antiquarian obsessions. Anything odd he finds, he likes to keep. Like the stand from Bickerstaff's coffin, for example." He cursed. "Where *is* that wretched taxi?"

He continued pacing around the room. But I didn't. I'd gone quite still. Something he'd said had made a horrible connection in my mind.

Anything he finds, he likes to keep.

"Lockwood." My heart was hammering in my chest.

"Yes?"

"When Barnes phoned the other day, he mentioned that some museum had a Mughal dagger that was similar to the one buried in Jack Carver's back. So similar, they might almost have been a matching pair. You remember where that dagger was found?"

He nodded. "Maida Vale Cemetery, up in north London."

"Right. And when Saunders and Joplin first came here, they told us another place they'd worked in. Remember what it was?"

He stared at me. "It was . . . it was Maida Vale Cemetery. . . . Oh, *no*."

"I think Joplin found two daggers," I said. "I think he handed one in, but kept the other. And, recently"—I stared through the door to the rugless hallway, scattered with salt—"under the influence of Bickerstaff and the mirror, I'm afraid he put that second dagger to good use."

A cackle of laughter came from the jar. *"This is the best evening I've had since I was alive! Look at you both! Your faces are priceless."*

"I wouldn't have believed it was possible," Lockwood whispered. "George is in even more trouble than we thought."

The cab horn sounded in the street. I shouldered my bag.

"*Have fun, then,*" the ghost called. "*Give my regards to Cubbins, or whatever's left of him. He'll be— Wait, what are you doing?*"

Lockwood had snatched up a backpack from the corner of the kitchen and was stuffing it over the top of the jar.

"You needn't look so smug," he said. "You're coming too."

Chapter 26

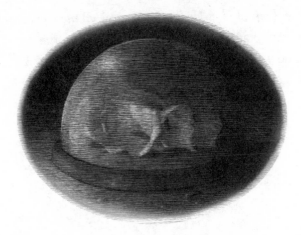

At Kensal Green Cemetery, the West Gate was open, the little watch-hut empty, and no lights showed as we approached the Anglican chapel through the trees. We were entering the final hour of darkness. Already the stars were paler; soon the horizon would blaze into light somewhere over the eastern docks, and the night's shadows be driven forth from London. But the birds were not yet singing.

Outside the chapel, the cabins of Sweet Dreams Excavations and Clearance were black and empty, the fire buckets cold. The mechanical diggers stood motionless, arms bent and bowed like the necks of sleeping herons. It was true, then: Mr. Saunders had suspended all activities and left the cemetery to its dead. But Lockwood and I strode swiftly across the abandoned camp, and pattered up the chapel stairs.

The lines of police tape had been torn away. Light gleamed in a razor-thin line beneath the door.

Lockwood held a finger to his lips. He'd been silent and grim-faced throughout the journey, scarcely uttering a word.

Which is more than I could say for my *other* companion.

"You'll be too late," a voice hissed in my ear. *"Cubbins won't have been able to resist taking a look. Peeped, choked, dead already: that's my prediction."*

"You'd better hope not," I breathed. "Or you know what we'll do to you."

Somewhere in the backpack I carried, I felt the indignant hum of churning plasm.

Since leaving the house, the ghost in the jar had kept up a whispered commentary, alternating wildly between threats, pleas, and expressions of false condolence. It was agitated, in other words; my threat to abandon it had left it deeply unsettled. Which didn't make it any less irritating. I'd have gladly hurled it into a bush, but we didn't have that option. The ghost knew Bickerstaff. The ghost knew the secrets of the mirror. We might need its help right now.

Lockwood glared at me for quiet; he reached for the great metal door handle. I readied myself, squinted in preparation for the transition from dark to light. With a sudden fluid movement, he turned it, pushed. The door squealed; brightness flooded our eyes. We both stepped in.

The interior of the chapel was much like we'd last seen it, on the morning after the theft: the desks of Mr. Saunders and Mr. Joplin, strewn with papers; the space heaters; the great black catafalque on its metal plate; the pulpit, the altar and its long, shiny altar rail. All was silent, all was still. There was no one to be found.

I listened for the telltale buzzing of the bone glass, heard nothing.

Lockwood touched the nearest heater. "Warm," he said. "Not hot. He's been here tonight, but not for a while."

I was looking at a familiar twisted shape in the near corner, swept aside amid piles of dirty salt and filings. "The iron coffin's still here, look. But Bickerstaff's body is gone."

"*My master is near,*" the ghost whispered suddenly. "*I feel his presence.*"

"Where?" I demanded. "How do we get to him?"

"*How can I tell? It's so hard in this jar. If you let me out, I'll sense far more.*"

"Not a chance."

Lockwood strode across to the wooden door behind the altar rail; he pushed and pulled, but the door remained firm. "The padlock's off," he said, "and the bolts are open. Someone's locked it from the inside."

"Are we *sure* he'll be in the catacombs?" I said. "It's not the sort of place *I'd* go."

"But that's just it!" Lockwood jumped back; he was staring wildly around the room. "Remember those illustrations in the Bickerstaff papers? The catacombs are exactly the sort of place where idiots like Joplin *do* hang out. It's a place to find stuff, it gives the right grisly ambience. And, crucially, it's private. You're not going to be disturbed down there." He cursed. "Ah, this is a nightmare! How can we get in?"

"*Blind as bats,*" the ghost said. "*Always looking, never seeing. Even if it's standing straight ahead of you.*"

I gave a snarl, thumping my fist into the side of the backpack. "Quiet, you, or I swear I'll—" Then I stopped dead, staring at the big, black marble plinth in the middle of the room. The catafalque. The Victorian device for lowering coffins into the catacombs below. I gasped. "The catafalque! Didn't Saunders say it was still working?"

Lockwood slapped his palm against his head. "Yes! He did! Of course! Hurry, Luce! Look everywhere! Cupboards, corners, over by the altar. . . . There must be a mechanism!"

"*Oh, you think?*" the skull scoffed. "*Honestly, this is pathetic. It's like teaching cats to read.*"

We rushed back and forth around the chapel, peering into every likely nook and shadow, but the walls were bare, and we could see no lever or button.

"We're missing something," Lockwood muttered. He turned on his heels, frowning. "It *must* be close."

"So we look again! Hurry!" I opened a small vestry cupboard, threw aside piles of moldy hymn books and service sheets. No lever there.

"*Hopeless,*" the skull whispered. "*I bet a five-year-old could figure this out.*"

"Shut *up.*"

"We've got to find it, Lucy. Heaven knows what Joplin's doing." Lockwood was tracing the far side of the wall, scanning high and low. "Ah, we've been so dumb! He's been right in front of us the whole time, and we didn't give him a moment's thought. He's been poking his nose into the case since before we opened the coffin. Barnes even told us that someone at the excavation site must have tipped off the relic-men about the mirror—otherwise they'd never have turned up so fast. Joplin was one of the few people who could have done that, but we never suspected him."

"There wasn't any reason to," I protested. "Remember how upset he was about the theft? I don't think he was acting."

"No, I don't either. But it never occurred to us that Joplin might have been genuinely upset, and yet *still* be guilty. You know what I think happened? He got Jack Carver to steal the mirror—just as Carver had stolen lots of stuff for him before. Saunders said there had been many thefts at his excavations over the years. That was all Joplin, pinching things he fancied. But this time, Carver double-crossed him. He realized the value of the mirror, and took it off to Winkman, who paid him well. Joplin was furious."

"Right," I said. I was racing along the wall—bare, white, without anywhere to hide a crack or cobweb, let alone a switch of any kind. "So furious he stabbed the relic-man with his fancy dagger."

"Exactly. Ordinarily, I bet Joplin would be too wimpy to hurt a fly. But if the skull's correct—if Joplin *has* been affected by the ghost of Edmund Bickerstaff, and is being driven mad . . ."

"*Yes,*" the skull whispered. "*That's what the master does. He takes the weak and feebleminded and bends them to his will. Like this, for example: Lucy, I order you! Smash my glass prison and set me free! Set me freeeee!*"

"Get lost," I said. "Lockwood—so do you really think that Joplin went after Carver?"

He was over in the far corner of the chapel, moving fast, speaking faster. "He did, and caught up with him when he was on his way to see us. They argued. When Carver revealed he'd sold the glass, Joplin went berserk. He stabbed Carver, who broke free and managed to get to us. Joplin, of course, would have thought he'd lost the glass forever. How wrong he was. Ever since then *we've* been searching for it, and kindly keeping him informed. And now George has actually brought him the glass, and Joplin's got his heart's desire, while we—we *can't find our stupid way down!*"

With a cry of frustration, Lockwood kicked the wall with a boot. We'd gone around the entire room without success. He was right. We were stymied; there *was* no way down.

"What about outside?" I said. "There might be another entrance on the grounds."

"I suppose, though how we'll find it in time, I don't know. All right," Lockwood said, "we'll look. Come on."

We ran to the doors, opened them—and stopped dead. There on the step, framed against the lightening sky, stood three familiar figures in silver-gray jackets. Bobby Vernon, Kat Godwin, big Ned Shaw: the small, blond, and menacing members of Quill Kipps's team. Not Kipps himself, though. They froze in the act of reaching for the door knocker. We gazed at them.

"Where's Quill?" Kat Godwin snapped. "What's going on?"

"What have you done with him?" Ned Shaw loomed in close. "No nonsense today, Lockwood. Speak up right now."

Lockwood shook his head. "Sorry, we haven't got time for this. It's an emergency. We think George is in trouble."

Kat Godwin's jaw clenched; there was doubt as well as hostility in her eyes. She spoke abruptly. "We think Kipps is too."

"He called us an hour ago," Bobby Vernon piped up, "to say he'd been following your friend Cubbins. He'd seen him go into the cemetery with someone. Told us to join him here. We've been looking everywhere, but there's no sign of him."

"Still spying on us, was he?" I sneered. "Shame."

"Better than skulking around with criminals, like you seem to be doing," Godwin spat.

"All that's irrelevant now," Lockwood said. "If Kipps is with George, they're both at risk. Kat, Bobby, Ned: we need your help, and you need ours, so let's get on with it." He spoke calmly and authoritatively; and though I saw Ned Shaw's fingers twitch, none of them challenged him. "We think they're in the catacombs under the chapel," Lockwood went on. "The access doors are locked, and we need to get down. Bobby, you'd know this sort of thing. Victorian catafalques, used for lowering bodies beneath the church. How were they operated? From above, from below?"

"From above," Vernon said. "The minister lowered the coffin during the service."

"Okay, so there *must* be a lever. We were right, Luce. So where—" He broke off, staring out across the twilit graveyard. "Kat, Ned—did you bring anyone else with you?"

"No," Ned Shaw scowled. "Why?"

Lockwood took a deep breath. "Because," he said slowly, "it looks like we've got company."

His eyes were better than mine; I hadn't noticed the little movements out among the gravestones, the swift dark shapes flitting up the grassy aisles. They converged upon the excavation camp, and now passed out into the gray open space between the sheds and diggers. A group of men, purposeful and silent; men used to being out at night. They carried sticks and clubs in their hands.

"*Hey, this is exciting,*" the skull's voice whispered in my ear. "*I'm so enjoying this night out. Now I get to see you all killed. We must do this more often.*"

"Not friends of yours, then, Lockwood?" Kat Godwin said.

"Acquaintances, perhaps. . . ." He looked sidelong at me. "Lucy, I think these fellows may have been sent by Winkman. That one on the end was at the auction, I'm almost sure. Lord knows how they've followed us, but I need you to do something for me now without arguing."

"Okay."

"Go back into the chapel, find the lever, go down and get George. I'll follow as soon as I can."

"Yes, but Lockwood—"

"Without arguing *would* be nice."

When he uses that tone, arguing with Lockwood isn't an option. I stepped backward into the chapel. The first men had reached the bottom of the steps. Between them they possessed a fair combination of features you wouldn't want to see approaching on a dark night: bald heads and broken noses, bared teeth and low-slung brows. . . . The clubs they held weren't too appealing either.

"What do we do?" Bobby Vernon stammered.

"Right now, Bobby," Lockwood said, "I think you need to draw your sword." He glanced back at me over his shoulder. "Lucy—*go!*"

Men came rushing up the steps; I slammed the door. From

outside came the sound of ringing steel, thuds, and crashing. Some-one screamed.

I ran into the center of the chapel, stood by the marble cata-falque. What had Vernon said? The minister would lower it down. Okay, so where would the minister have been standing? Where on earth would he be?

"Ooh, so tough," the whispering voice said. *"Shows how often you go to church."*

And then, all at once, I knew. The pulpit. The plain, wooden pulpit, its top carved in the shape of an opened book, standing quiet and forgotten a few feet from the catafalque. I strode across to it, try-ing to ignore the noises from outside. I stepped up onto its platform, looked down, and saw the hidden shelf cut into the wood just below the top.

There on the shelf: the simple metal switch.

I pressed it. At first I thought it had done nothing; then, smoothly and almost silently—there was only the faintest hum—the catafalque began to sink. The metal plate it rested on was descend-ing through the floor. I jumped down from the pulpit, ran across, and sprang onto the black stone.

Outside the chapel, something heavy thudded against the doors. I did not look up. I drew my rapier and stood ready, feet apart and breathing steadily. Past flagstones, away from light and into dark-ness, I was carried down into the earth.

"Don't be frightened." From the backpack, a wicked whispering brushed my ear. *"You're not alone. You've still got me."*

A shaft of brick had opened out into realms of solid space, and still I was going down. I could feel the gap around me, the sudden suck and cling of cold, dry air. Yet I could see nothing. I knew that I was spotlit in a column of light that deadened my senses and made me vulnerable. *Anything* could be waiting there, close by, and I would not know it until I landed right beside them. My hackles rose; all my instincts told me I needed to get away. The feeling of danger overwhelmed me. I tensed, ready to jump—

And the mechanism stopped.

With a hop and a scramble I was off the catafalque and out of that column of light. Then I forced myself to halt. I went very still; I stood in the dark and listened to the racing of my heart and beyond that, to the silence of this place.

But it was *not* silent, at least not to my inner senses. From unknown distances came little sounds—soft rustlings and sighings, faint peals of laughter that ended in a sudden sob. I heard whispering too, in cutoff snatches; and somewhere, most horribly, the stupid, repetitive clicking of somebody's wet tongue.

None of it came from mortal throats.

I was in the realm of the dead.

The psychic silence was also broken, more obviously, by a cheery whistling sound from the ghost-jar in my backpack. Occasionally it stopped, but only to start up a banal and tuneless hum.

"Will you pack that in?" I said. "I need to listen."

"Why? I'm happy. This is my kind of place."

"It's a place you'll stay forever, if you don't cooperate with me," I snarled. "I'll brick you up behind a wall."

The whistling abruptly ceased.

Always, when you're alone and vulnerable, emotions seek to undermine you. Mine went haywire now. I thought of Lockwood, fighting for his life upstairs. I thought of George—and the haunted, yearning expression on his face after glancing at the mirror five nights before. I thought about how easily everything I cared about could be destroyed. I thought of the emptiness of my work belt. I thought of Edmund Bickerstaff's terrible Specter rising high against the moon. . . .

I compressed those emotions. I boxed them in, and stored them in a cubbyhole in the attic of my mind. Time enough to open that box later. Right now I had to stay alert—and stay alive.

The ground was rough underfoot; I sensed bricks, worn and uneven, loose stones and pebbles, and untold years of dust. On all sides, soft, dry coldness stretched away. I could still see nothing at all. Around the shaft of light, everything was so black, I might have been in a narrow corridor or a massive void; there was no way of telling. It seemed inconceivable that anyone would deliberately come down here.

Then I caught the faintest whirring, the sound of buzzing flies.

Yes. The bone mirror. It was somewhere close.

Reluctantly—because electric light hinders your Talent, and also draws the attention of any watching eyes—I turned my penlight on, swiveling it to its lowest, haziest beam. I swept it up and around me in a slow, smooth arc, taking in my surroundings. There was the catafalque, resting on an exposed mechanism of giant metal levers, black and bent like insect legs. It sat in the center of a wide passage—its vaulted ceiling high, its floor strewn with debris. The walls—of stone and brick—were subdivided into shelves in many rows, and on most of these a lead coffin stood, pushed into its cavity to await eternity. Some shelves had been bricked up, some were empty; others were full of stones and rubble. Every twenty paces, side passages cut across the aisle.

Everything was laced with a coating of thin, gray dust. I thought of Joplin's hair.

Turning the flashlight off, I used my memory to advance in darkness, watching and listening all the time, trying to gauge the location of the mirror's buzzing. It wasn't easy, particularly since the ghost in the jar had stirred again.

"Can you feel them?" its voice said. "The others. They're all around you."

"Will you be quiet?"

"They hear your footsteps. They hear the frantic beating of your heart."

"That's it. You're going in one of these shelves, soon as I find George."

Silence. I adjusted the straps on the backpack savagely and tiptoed on.

As I drew level with the first cross-passage, I heard a shout echoing through the dark. The sound was distorted, bouncing brokenly between the walls. Was it George? Kipps? Joplin? Was it a living voice at all? I couldn't tell. But I guessed it came from somewhere to the right. Placing my hand on the bricks to guide me, I set off that way.

Instants later my hand touched something cold and smooth. I jumped back, switched on the flashlight: it was a dome of glass, placed on the shelf beside its coffin. Beneath the smudged dust where my fingers had passed, I saw a display of dried white lilies. For a moment I wondered how long they'd sat there in the dark, these memorial flowers, in perpetual bloom. Then I turned off the flashlight, went on again.

The passage was long and narrow, and itself crisscrossed with other, nearly identical side routes, all lined with coffins. I stopped at each intersection, then continued on. As much as possible I went in darkness, hoping to see Visitors as easily as they saw me.

Because Visitors *were* there.

Once, at an unknown distance down a passage to the left, I saw a faintly glowing form. It was a young man, wearing a suit with a high, stiff collar. He stood motionless, with his back to me, one of his shoulders much higher than the other. For some reason I was very glad that he did not turn around.

From down another aisle came an urgent tapping. When I looked, I saw one of the lowest shelves aglow with other-light, the tapping coming most distinctly from its very small lead coffin.

"*This is jolly,*" the skull said. "*But these wisps are nothing. My master is here too.*"

"Up ahead?"

"*Oh, yes, I think you're getting closer.*" It chuckled softly. "*Remember that shout just now? Want to bet that was Cubbins looking in the bone glass?*"

With difficulty, I swallowed my rage. If the ghost was talkative, perhaps it could give me information. "Tell me about the mirror," I said. "How many bones did Bickerstaff use to make it? How many ghosts did it take?"

"*Seven bones and seven spirits, if I recall.*"

"What do you see if you look in the glass?"

"*Oh, I took care never to do that.*"

"What about Bickerstaff? Did he ever look himself?"

"*He may have been mad,*" the ghost said simply, "*but he wasn't stupid. Of course he didn't. The risks were too great. Tell me, don't you think Cubbins may be busy dying? Aren't you wasting time?*"

Hurrying on, I came at last to what seemed to be an outermost aisle of the catacomb, onto which all the side passages opened. And now another burst of noise sounded up ahead: angry voices, cries of pain. I sped up, stumbling on the uneven ground. My boot caught on a loose brick. I tripped, reached out to correct myself, and my hand knocked a piece of stone or mortar from the shelf alongside. It fell, clinked and clattered briefly in the darkness. I stood motionless, listening.

"*It's all right. No one heard,*" the ghost said. It left a dramatic pause. "*Or DID they . . . ?*"

All seemed still, except for the painful thudding of my pulse. I continued, going slowly. Soon the passage began to bend around to the right, and here I saw flickering lantern light stretching across the bricks, picking out the blackened pockmarks of the empty shelves. The noise of the mirror was louder now, and it was very cold—the temperature dropped lower with each step.

"*Careful,*" the skull whispered. "*Careful . . . Bickerstaff is near.*"

Crouching low, pressing close to the wall, I slipped near the edge of the light and peeped around the corner of the passage. After the darkness, the faint glow blinded me. It took my eyes a few moments to adjust. Then they did, and I saw what was in the room.

My legs felt weak. I supported myself against the wall.

"Oh, *George*," I breathed. "Oh, *no*."

Chapter 27

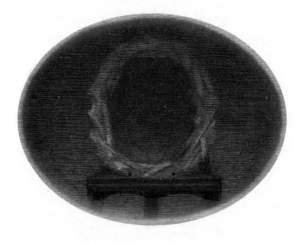

I'd been wrong about the light. It wasn't a lantern at all. A flickering gas lamp *did* sit on a table, but its fragile beams scarcely reached the cobwebbed ceiling high above, let alone filled the rest of the room. But other things were there. Other things that glimmered with a very different kind of radiance.

Bad things.

A narrow circle of iron chains had been laid in the center of the chamber, and inside this space rose a tall, thin, three-legged stand—a tripod of black wood. At its top, slotted neatly into a narrow groove, was something small and roughly circular, covered by a gentleman's silk handkerchief. From it came the familiar dark buzzing, and a wave of vicious cold that made me shiver even where I crouched across the room. Occasionally the handkerchief shifted slightly, as if blown by invisible currents in the air.

The bone mirror—in position on its original stand. Ready to be used.

The mirror wasn't alone inside the circle. A group of faint gray shapes hung there, surrounded by a pulsing cloud of other-light. It was very hard to see them; they were clearest when you looked away. They were human forms, clothed in drapes and shapeless garments, and pressed so close together they actually overlapped. Their faces were blurry and indistinct—smeared gray blotches replaced the eyes and mouths. Without counting, I knew there were seven of them, for they were the spirits trapped in the making of the mirror. Their anger and their sorrow beat upon me; and from far off I heard their ceaseless calling:

"*Our bones . . .*" they pleaded. "*Give us back our bones. . . .*"

On another occasion, the spirits and the bone glass would have been enough to transfix me with horror. I would have been unable to tear my gaze away.

But not today. For in front of the circle was George.

He sat on a wooden chair, directly facing the shrouded mirror. His hands had been tightly lashed to the chair back. His head was lowered, slumped against his breast, his glasses at an angle. His eyes were shut. To my extreme relief, he was still alive; his chest heaved up and down.

Across the room stood another chair, turned toward George. Here, to my brief surprise—I'd almost forgotten my encounter with the Fittes team—sat Quill Kipps. Like George, his hands were tied behind him. But he was awake, his hair streaked with cobwebs, his thin face gray with grave dust. His jacket was askew, and his shirt torn at the collar. He looked as if he'd had a rough time, suffered a few indignities. Mostly, though, he just looked deeply annoyed. His eyes glittered as he gazed around.

There was no sign of Albert Joplin anywhere.

But there *was* something else in the little chamber and, of all the bad things there, this was surely the worst of all. I didn't notice it at first, for it was beyond Kipps, and fainter than the ghosts beside the mirror. But then my eyes were drawn to the dark mass lying on the floor, and to the shadow rising high above it. My hands shook, my mouth went dry.

"*Master!*" the skull whispered at my back, and I could feel the thrill and terror quivering in its voice. "*The master is here!*"

The ghost of Edmund Bickerstaff stood at the far end of the room.

On the dirt of the floor the doctor's body lay: the foul, part-mummified corpse from the iron coffin, with its ragged black suit and spray of glassy hair. It was as stiff as a twisted branch, as shiny and dark as polished mahogany. Its shriveled, teeth-baring monkey's face stared sightlessly up at nothing.

But from the center of its chest rose the same terrible, wispy apparition that I'd seen at the grave site five days earlier. Eight feet tall it was, eight feet tall and taller; a thin, robed shape with a drooping hood that kept the face in shadow. It towered so high it seemed it might break through the brickwork vaults and disappear into the ground above. It hung there, almost motionless, minutely waving from side to side, in the manner of a rearing snake. The eyes were hidden, but I could see the bone-white chin, the heavy, brutish mouth.

For a moment I could not understand why the Visitor did not

plunge down upon Kipps, who was seated just in front of it. Then I saw that another iron chain had been slung across the floor, cordoning off Bickerstaff's body. The ghost was trapped inside.

Even so, its wickedness filled the room. I could sense the dark intensity of its desire. Right now, its attention was concentrated on the mirror—and on George. It wasn't aware of me. But that would change the instant I stepped into the chamber. The thought made me feel ill.

Yet I had to act, and do it fast. Joplin was nowhere to be seen. Now was the time to rescue George, and for that I needed to be light of foot. Crouching in the darkness, as soundlessly as possible, I began to pull the backpack off my back.

"You can see he's trying to recreate original experiments," the skull was saying. *"Got the mirror set up nicely on its stand. There are the seven spirits, still as feeble as ever. Always moaning, never actually doing anything. And he's even got the master standing by. It's almost like the old days, back again. Hold on—why are you putting me down?"*

I shoved the backpack into a vacant shelf. "You're too heavy," I whispered. "You stay here."

"No!" The skull spoke urgently. *"I must be part of this. I wish to see the master! Take me to him!"*

"Sorry, you're staying put." I loosened the top of the rucksack, and pulled the fabric down a little, revealing the top few inches of the jar. The plasm had flared bright green; I glimpsed the distorted face, whirling around and around. "If I need you," I said, "I'll come and get you—and you'd better help when asked, or you'll stay here permanently."

"*Curse you, Lucy!*" the skull cried. "*Why don't you obey me?*" It gave a sudden shout. "*Master! It's me! Welcome back!*"

Over in the corner, the cowled figure stood silent. It did not respond.

"*Master . . .*" The plaintive whisper was filled with fear and yearning. "*Over here! It's me!*"

The figure didn't stir. All its intentness was on the bone glass, and on George.

"*Yes,*" the skull said irritably. "*Well, he's not what he was.*"

Of course he wasn't. Like most Type One and Type Two Visitors, the ghost of Edmund Bickerstaff was locked into a fixed pattern of behavior, obsessively repeating what had gone before. Its consciousness was paper-thin, a fragment of what it had been. But I didn't have time to point this out to the skull. Stealing forward on noiseless feet, I emerged into the chamber, scanning all around. Shadowy aisles of brick and concrete stretched away on every side. Everything was silent; I could not see Joplin.

As soon as I broke cover, Quill Kipps noticed me. He gave a start of surprise, then began frantically beckoning me with little jerks of his head. The grimaces he made were quite ridiculous; on another occasion I could have watched for hours. Instead I ignored him altogether, and tiptoed over to George.

Close up, his face looked puffy; one cheek was bruised. He didn't move when I touched him.

"George!" I whispered. "*George!*"

"Don't bother! He's out cold!" Kipps's whisper was desperate. His head was waggling overtime. "Come here and set me free!"

I crossed over in a couple of strides, trying not to look at the phantom looming just beyond the strip of chains. Stubby tentacles of plasm flexed and probed against the margins of the circle. The cowled head twisted, and I felt a sudden heaviness, a cold weight on my spirits. It saw me. It knew I was there.

I shrugged the feeling off. "Kipps, are you all right?"

He rolled his eyes. "What, me? Tied up by a madman and left in a haunted catacomb in the company of Cubbins? Oh, I'm just peachy. Can't you tell?"

"Oh, that's good," I said, beaming.

"I was being sarcastic."

My beam turned to a scowl. "Yeah, so was I." I ducked behind him, readying my sword. To my dismay, his hands were tied with chains and secured with a padlock. I couldn't cut him free.

"You're chained up," I whispered. "I need the key."

Kipps groaned. "That glazed-eyed fool will have it."

"Joplin? Where is he?"

"Gone off somewhere. He heard a noise, went to investigate. He'll be back any moment. What are you going to do to get me out of here?"

"I don't know. Shut up." I was finding it hard to think. Psychic noises buffeted my head—the mirror's buzzing, the plaintive calling of the seven spirits, even some distant insults from the irate skull. And—above all—the presence of the hooded figure bore down on me. What would Lockwood do if he were here? My mind was blank. I didn't know.

"Can I just say," Kipps growled, "that when I get out of this, I'm going to kick your idiot friend's backside from here to Marylebone?"

"Let's face it," I said, "you shouldn't have been spying on us. But yes, so will I. Wait—would Joplin have put the key on that table?" I crossed quickly, rounding the edge of the mirror circle, where the pale spirits turned to follow me. The table was piled high with a confusion of objects—dusty pots, ornaments, jewelry, and many, many books and papers. If the key was there, I couldn't see it. I threw my hands up in despair. What could I do? *Think.*

"*Watch out, Lucy. . . .*"

That was the skull's whisper, echoing faintly from the passage. I froze—then began reaching for my belt. Even as I did so, someone stepped from the darkness behind me. A sharp point pricked the back of my neck. The skull gave a chuckle. "*Oops. Maybe I waited a little too long to warn you there.*"

"Please don't do anything annoying, Miss Carlyle." It was Albert Joplin's bleating voice. "You feel the knife? Very well. Take off your belt and rapier."

I stood frozen, rigid with panic. The knife tip prodded me gently.

"Quickly, now. I get jumpy when I'm cross. My hand slips. Do as I say."

No choice. . . . I unclipped the belt, and let it and my rapier drop to the floor.

"Now, walk back across to Kipps. Don't try anything. I will be right behind you."

Slowly, stiffly, I obeyed. In its circle, the hooded phantom moved closer to the iron. I saw the grinning mouth, its snaggle-teeth; its hungry eagerness crackled through the room.

Kipps was gazing bleakly at me from the chair. "Yes, this is just about the efficiency I'd expect from Lockwood and Company," he said. "What next? Lockwood comes in, trips over, and impales himself on his sword?"

Albert Joplin said, "Stand beside Kipps, put your hands against the back of the chair. Wrists together. Now, I have one more piece of cord, which . . . No—you do what you're told!" I'd tried to turn; the knife jabbed me, making me cry out in pain. "That's better," Joplin said. With a series of quick movements, he bound my hands to the chair. I stood beside Kipps, neck stinging, as Joplin walked away.

He looked as rumpled as ever, his jacket laced with grave dust, his hair a storm-tossed crow's nest. He still moved in the same stooped manner, shoulders hunched inward, spindly-legged and pigeon-toed. He was circling back to George. There was a short, stubby knife in one hand; in the other a notebook. A pen was tucked behind one ear. He hummed softly to himself as he went. When he glanced back, I saw that his nose was red and swollen-looking, and he had a bruise on his chin.

But it was his eyes that really shocked me. They were dark and sunken, the pupils very wide. He seemed to be staring intently at something far away. His head was cocked, as if listening.

In its circle, the Bickerstaff ghost swayed from side to side.

"Yes, yes . . . in a moment." Joplin talked absently, as if to himself. When he got to George, he bent down and squinted toward the shrouded mirror, perhaps comparing heights. What he saw seemed to satisfy him. He straightened, and slapped George sharply twice around the face. George gave a croak, and stared wildly all around.

"That's it, my boy. Time to wake up." Joplin patted his shoulder. Taking his pen from his ear, he made a mark in his notebook. "We must make haste with our experiment as agreed."

Quill Kipps uttered a curse. "Agreement, my foot," he muttered. "I don't know what Cubbins thought he was up to, coming here in the first place, but they had some kind of argument in the church upstairs. One minute they were talking; all at once they were coming to blows." He shook his head. "It was pathetic. The worst fight ever. They knocked one another's glasses off, and spent half the time crawling around trying to find them. I'm surprised they didn't pull each other's hair."

"And you didn't go to help George?" I said icily. I pulled at my cords. No, they were tight; I could scarcely move my hands.

"To my lasting regret," Kipps said, "I did. I'm sorry to say Joplin put that knife to Cubbins's throat and forced me to throw down my rapier. When we got down to the catacombs, Cubbins tried to escape, and was knocked out for his trouble. Joplin's been setting up this ridiculous contraption for the last half hour. He's out of his mind."

"Yes, he is. More than you know."

One glance at the mirror, and George had been affected; one brief moment of exposure to Bickerstaff's ghost, and its influence had remained. But how long had *Joplin* been exposed to it since then—how many nights had he been near the body in the chapel, with the ghost's silent, baleful energies directed upon him? He probably couldn't even *see* the phantom clearly. He probably didn't know what it was doing to him.

"Mr. Joplin," I called. Knife in hand, the little archivist was waiting beside George, who was slowly rousing groggily. "You're not thinking straight. This experiment will never work—"

Joplin adjusted his spectacles. "No, no. Don't worry. We won't be disturbed. The entrance stairs are locked, and I've shut off the catafalque mechanism from below. No one can get down, unless they want to jump twenty feet into a pitch-black hole. And who would be prepared to do that?"

There was one person I knew who might. But he was busy up above, and I couldn't rely on him. "That's not what I mean," I said. "The mirror is deadly, and Bickerstaff's phantom is influencing you. We need to stop this now!"

Joplin cocked his head to one side; he was gazing toward the circle where the ghost stood. It was as if he hadn't heard. "This is a remarkable opportunity," he said thickly. "My heart's desire. This mirror is a window on another world. There are marvels there! And George will have the honor of seeing them! It just remains for me to get the pole. . . ."

With his shuffling, round-shouldered gait, he pootled over to the table. My head reeled; he was using almost the same words as Bickerstaff had, when he forced Wilberforce to look into the mirror all those years before.

Behind its chains, the hooded phantom watched Joplin go.

"Lucy . . ." George called. "Is that you?"

"George! Are you all right?"

Well, he didn't *look* so hot, all puffy faced, and red about the eyes. His glasses were still wonky, and he wouldn't meet my gaze. "Surprisingly comfortable, Luce. Chair's a bit hard. I could do with a cushion."

"I'm so angry with you, I could burst."

"I know. I'm really sorry."

"What did you think you were doing?"

He sighed, rocking forward in the chair. "It just seemed . . . I can't explain it, Luce. When I left Flo, when I got the mirror in my hands, I just felt this desire. . . . I *had* to look at it again. Part of me knew it was wrong, I knew I had to wait for you—but somehow all that seemed unimportant. I might even have taken the thing out of the bag right away, only I wanted to show Joplin. And when he came, he said we should do it properly. . . ." He shook his head. "I went along with it, but when we got to the chapel, and I saw the empty coffin . . . all at once, it was like my eyes had cleared. I realized I was doing something mad. Then I tried to get away, but Joplin wouldn't let me."

"Quite right too." Joplin was back. He had a long pole, with a hook fixed to the end. "I showed you the error of your ways. I must say, you've disappointed me, Cubbins. You had such promise. Still, at least we sorted out our little disagreement, man to man." He fingered his swollen nose.

"Man to man, my eye," Kipps snorted. "It was like seeing two schoolgirls squabbling over a scented pencil. You should have heard the squeals."

"Now, hush," Joplin said. "We have things to do." He flinched; a worried look crossed his face, as if someone had spoken sharply him. "Yes, yes, I know. I'm doing my best."

"But, Mr. Joplin," I cried, "it's a death sentence to look in the mirror! It doesn't show you marvels. If you'd read Mary Dulac's *Confessions*, you'd understand exactly what I'm talking about. The guy Wilberforce dropped dead as soon as—"

"Oh, you've read them too?" For a moment his blank look vanished, and he looked keenly interested. "You *did* find another copy? Well done! You must tell me how. But of course *I've* read the *Confessions*! Who do you think stole it from Chertsey Library in the first place? I have it on my table there. It was very interesting, though it was Bickerstaff's notes, which Cubbins kindly showed me, that were the icing on the cake." He gestured at the mirror in its circle. "I couldn't have reconstructed the layout otherwise."

I tugged at the ropes around my wrists. The knots chafed me. To my right, I could sense Kipps doing the same. "I thought those notes were in medieval Italian," I said.

Joplin gave a complacent smile. "Indeed. And I'm fluent in it. It was quite amusing watching George puzzle over it while I quietly copied the whole thing."

George kicked out at Joplin and missed. "You betrayed me! I trusted you!"

Joplin chuckled; he gave George an indulgent pat on the shoulder. "Here's a tip: it's always wise to keep your cards close to your chest. Secrecy is crucial! No, Miss Carlyle, I'm well aware of the risks of looking in the mirror, which is why my good friend George is going to do it for me—*now*."

So saying, Joplin turned to the iron circle in the center of the room. Reaching in with the pole—and oblivious to the seven faint figures that hovered there—he flipped the cloth away from the top of the stand.

"George!" I shouted. "Don't look!"

From where I stood, I couldn't see the surface of the mirror. I only saw the roughened back of the glass, and the tightly woven rim of bone. But the buzzing noise was louder, and even the seven spirits in the circle shrank away, as if afraid. Behind its chains, the

Bickerstaff ghost rose still taller. I sensed its eagerness; I heard its cold hypnotic voice in my mind. *"Look . . ."* it said. *"Look . . ."* This is what it had desired in life; in death, through Joplin, it desired the same.

George had screwed his eyes tight closed.

Joplin had been careful to stand with his back to the tripod. His hunched shoulders were rigid with fear, his pale face tight with tension. "Open your eyes, Mr. Cubbins," he said. "You know you want to."

And George did. Part of him, the part that had been snared by the mirror days before, desperately wanted to look. I could see him shaking, struggling with himself to resist. He had his head turned away; he was biting on his lip.

I wrenched at my bonds. "Ignore him, George!"

"Look. . . . Look. . . ."

"Mr. Cubbins—" Joplin had taken out his pen and pad in readiness to record what happened. He tapped the pen irritably against his teeth. He looked peeved; under the cloak of madness, he was still a fussy little academic, anxious to carry out an experiment that interested him. He might have been observing the behavior of fruit flies or the mating rituals of worms. "Mr. Cubbins, you will do as I ask! Otherwise . . ." I felt a wave of malice radiate from the cowled figure in the circle. Joplin flinched again, and nodded. "Otherwise," he said harshly, "I will take this knife and cut the throats of your friends."

Silence in the catacombs.

"Ooh." That was the skull's voice, faint from down the passage. *"Good options! This is a win-win situation for me."*

George sat bolt upright in the chair. "Okay," he said. "Okay, I'll do it."

"No, George," I said. "You're absolutely not to."

"Well, he *could* take a little peek," Kipps said.

"Don't give in to it!" I cried. "He's bluffing!"

"Bluffing?" Joplin inspected the point of his knife. "You know, I believe poor Jack Carver thought the exact same thing. . . ."

"It's no good, Luce," George said dully. It was as if the malaise was back; there was profound weariness in his voice. "I'm going to have to do it. I can't help myself anyhow. I've *got* to look. The mirror's tugging at me—I can't resist."

He'd opened his eyes. His head was lowered; he stared down at his chest.

"No!" I tugged at my wrists, so that Kipps's chair rattled on the dirty brick floor. Tears filled my eyes. "If you do this, George Cubbins, I'm going to be *so* mad."

"It's all right, Luce," he said. He smiled sadly. "All this mess is my own fault. And after all, it's what I've always wanted, isn't it? To uncover mysteries—to do something no one else has ever done."

"Well spoken!" Joplin said. "I'm proud of you, young man. Now, I stand ready to record your words. Don't stop to think—speak fast and clear! Tell me what you see."

Another echo from the past. Bickerstaff's words to Wilberforce, one hundred thirty years before. It might almost have been the same person talking. Perhaps it was—how much was Bickerstaff, how much was Joplin?

"Please, George . . ."

Kipps groaned. "She's right, Cubbins! Don't give the madman the satisfaction."

Joplin stamped his foot. "Will everyone *please* be silent!"

"Lucy," George said suddenly, "about all this. I know I was weak, and what I did was wrong. I'm sorry for it. Tell Lockwood for me, okay?"

With that, he lifted his head and looked into the mirror.

"George . . . !"

"*Look. . . .*" the hooded shape above me murmured. "*I give you your heart's desire.*"

George looked. He stared straight through his little round spectacles into the glass. There was nothing I could do to stop him.

Joplin swallowed eagerly. His pen hung quivering above the page. "So, tell me, Cubbins, what is it that you see?"

"George?"

"Speak, boy!"

"*Your heart's desire . . .*"

George's face had tightened, the eyes grown wide. A terrible happiness shone from him. "I see things . . . beautiful things. . . ."

"Yes? *Yes?* Go on—"

But George's muscles had suddenly grown slack. The skin slumped, his mouth slowly opened like a drawbridge lowered on a chain. The fierce joy that had spread across his face remained, but all the intelligence in it, all the sparky life and stubbornness, began to slip away.

I jerked forward, wrenching at my bonds. "George!" I shrieked. "Look at me now!"

"Talk!" Joplin shouted. "Quick!"

It was no good. As I watched in horror, George's jaw sagged wide. He let out a long, harsh, rattling sigh. His eyelids drooped; his body shuddered once, twice, and fell still. His head twitched, then slid slowly sideways. It came to rest. His mouth hung open; his eyes stared out at nothing. A few threads of pale hair drooped loose across his waxy brow.

"Well," Albert Joplin said, with feeling. "What an infernal nuisance. He might have told me something useful before he died."

Chapter 28

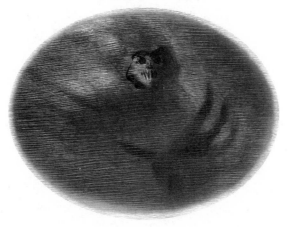

I stared at George's body. I too seemed to have stopped breathing.

"I mean, what use is 'beautiful things'?" Joplin complained. "That's not scientific, is it? And now that dawn's here, I'm not sure it's even worth trying another test!" He stamped a foot in irritation. "Honestly, what a *nuisance*."

He continued muttering to himself, but I scarcely heard him. His voice was far away. All sounds were hushed to me. I was alone in the numbness of my mind.

"George!" I said softly. "Wake up!"

"It's no good, Carlyle—" This was Kipps. "He's gone."

"Oh no, he always looks like that. . . ." I said. "You should see him in the mornings. He's just a bit sleepy, aren't you, George? George, come *on* . . ."

George didn't answer. He was slumped like an old coat tossed across the chair. His mouth was open. His hands hung limp. I thought of Jack Carver lying on our rug, of the stupid emptiness of death. I gave a little moan.

Joplin's gaze flicked up at me. He had been studying his watch; now he looked across at me with narrowed eyes. Where had the amiability gone, the foolish fluttering of the timorous archivist? The appraisal he gave me was hard and cold.

Something else was watching too. At the moment George looked into the mirror, the ghost of Edmund Bickerstaff had swelled to fill its circle. I'd felt the cold satisfaction of its triumph, its glee at seeing George succumb. Now it switched its attention to a new victim. The draped form twisted; the hooded head loomed over me. I glimpsed the shrouded face—the grinning mouth with sharp, bared teeth, the bone-white skin, eyes like black coins.

When I looked back at Joplin, his eyes looked just the same.

Kipps, being adult, could not truly see the ghost—but he felt its presence all right. I sensed him shrink back in his chair. Me? I drew myself up. I clenched my fists. Something slammed shut inside me, closing off my grief behind stony walls. My mind grew calm. My hatred was a winter lake—icy, clear, and stretching out forever. . . . I sat and gazed at Joplin.

"Perhaps," he was saying to himself, "perhaps we *could* have another try. Yes. All we need to do is put her in the chair. Where's the harm, where's the difficulty? Maybe she'll survive, where the boy has failed."

With birdlike steps, he moved toward me, knife in hand.

"Keep away from her," Kipps said.

"Your turn," Joplin said, "will come presently. Meanwhile be silent, or I'll set the master on you."

He did not approach head-on, despite my bound hands. Instead he walked behind me, knife outstretched. With a single slice, he cut the cords; once again the knife was at my neck. I stood silent, massaging my chafed wrists.

"Walk to the other chair," Joplin said.

I did so, forcing myself to breathe slowly, deliberately calming down. "You'll be making a mistake if you make me look into the mirror," I said. "I talk with ghosts. They talk to me. I can tell you many secrets. There's no use in me dying."

"Walk forward. I don't believe you, I'm afraid. Who has that Talent?"

"I do. I have a Type Three with me. Its Source is in my bag close by. Bickerstaff is nothing compared to it. Let me show you."

Away in the darkness, I could sense the ghost in the jar give a start. *"Hey, why bring me into this? He'll be as bad as Cubbins. Weird experiments, odd habits. . . . Next thing you know, he'll have me with him in the bath."*

Joplin had paused; now the knife's pressure resumed. "I still don't believe you."

"Good!"

"But if you have a relic with you, I shall examine it closely later."

"Oh, great. Thanks for nothing."

It took only a few steps to cross to George's chair, under the gaze of Bickerstaff's ghost. In the central circle, the seven spirits of the mirror clustered above the ebony stand. As before, they were quite motionless; their plaintive voices echoed faintly in the air. The skull had been right—they didn't *do* much. They seemed quite passive, obsessed only with the fate of their lost bones.

But the mirror was another matter. I kept my eyes away from it, but could still see it out of the corner of my eyes. The bone rim gleamed dully, but the glass was a jet-black hole. The buzzing noise was fearfully loud. I sensed movement in the glass, a coiling adjustment in its blackness. And with that came a sudden powerful urge to look properly upon it. The desire rose up within me like a scream. I shook the sensation away, but neither could I bear to look at George. I stared fixedly at the ground, fingers digging into my palms.

A small push. Joplin thrust me forward, slightly away from him. I glanced back, saw him bending behind the chair, cutting the ropes that bound George's limp hands. I turned, but the knife was up again, warding me off.

"Don't try it," Joplin said. He was staring up at me, head lowered, yellowed teeth bared. "Pull the body out and sit in the chair."

"I'm not going to do that."

"You haven't any choice."

"Wrong. I'm going to collect my rapier, from where I dropped it. Then, Mr. Joplin, I'm going to kill you."

The Bickerstaff ghost, in the circle behind Joplin, made a sudden urgent movement. As if he had been shoved between the shoulder blades, Joplin stumbled forward. His eyes were voids; with a snarl, he raised the knife and started for me.

I readied myself to move.

And at that moment George got up from the chair.

I screamed. Somewhere behind me I heard Kipps gasp in fear. Joplin made a weird noise somewhere between a wail and a growl; the knife fell from his hand.

From the ghost-jar in the passage came an indignant curse. *"Alive? Oh, that's typical. It was all going so well."*

Face blank, glasses askew, George jumped forward and grabbed Joplin around the waist. He swung him sideways and, with a mighty heave, sent him tumbling back over the iron chains. Joplin fell, colliding with the tripod legs; the stand swayed and toppled. The mirror broke loose and went crashing to the ground.

George stood upright, brushed the hair away from his eyes, and winked at me.

I still stared at him, dumbfounded.

"George . . ." I stammered. "How—?"

"Bit busy," he said. "Ask me later." He flung himself at Joplin.

Squealing, thrashing in his panic, the archivist had been fighting clear of the fallen tripod. Above his head the seven spirits hovered; to my surprise—though he was inside their circle—they made no attempt to touch him. As George drew close, Joplin caught hold of the fallen tripod and swung it frantically. It missed George by miles, slipped out of Joplin's grasp, and clattered away across the floor to strike against the *other* loop of iron chains, the ones surrounding the Bickerstaff ghost. They were dislodged—a small gap opened where the ends had met.

At once, there was a thump of air, a sudden roaring. A cold breeze burst out across the room, sending clouds of grave dust ballooning away into the catacombs. The chains jerked and rattled as if they were alive—the gap was blown apart. The hooded figure turned its shrouded head to me.

It bent and flexed, squeezing thin as smoke as it passed out through the hole. Behind it coiled a growing trail of wispy ectoplasm, looping back to the body on the floor. The shape stretched up, high as the ceiling. It drifted forward. Its robes split apart; two arms emerged, white and skinny, with knobbly, grasping hands.

The Bickerstaff ghost was free.

Quill Kipps could sense it. Eyes popping, sinews straining, he jerked and rattled in his chair. "Lucy!" he croaked. "Help me!"

There wasn't time to find my rapier. That was over at the table, beyond where George and Joplin were rolling on the floor in a frenzy of slaps and curses. If I went to get it, Kipps would die.

But I had no other weapon. Except . . .

I ran toward Kipps, toward the ghost. As I did so, I bent down and grabbed one of the lengths of iron chain that had been scattered by Joplin's fall. I picked it up, went on without breaking stride. Even as I reached the chair, I was already swinging it in front of me.

I met the ghost of Dr. Bickerstaff head on.

It was looming over Kipps, arms outstretched as if to swaddle him. Two see-through hands reached down. With a war cry that was half screech, half gurgle, I spun the chain in a wild circle, slicing through the tips of the bone-white fingers, turning them into fizzing curls of mist. The ghost reared back. I thrust myself between it and the chair, whirling the iron high and low.

"Careful!" Kipps ducked frantically as the chain whistled past him.

"Not efficient enough for you?" I gasped. "Want me to leave?"

"No, no. You're doing great—Ahh!" That was the chain passing through his hair.

Back across the floor, great quantities of plasm were oozing from the center of the corpse. The ghost grew longer and more serpent-like. Its head and torso were far above me, swinging from side to side, making little darts and feints in an effort to get beyond the chain. The arms jabbed inward, to be cut in two; instantly they re-formed. Showers of plasm fell around us, peppering our clothes.

And all the while we fought, the voice of Edmund Bickerstaff was calling, calling in my mind—urging me to look, promising me my heart's desire. It was the same old message. He had no other. And though his ghost was very terrible, though its madness and its malice made it strong, I found myself growing ever calmer and more confident. I stood there, dirty, tired, and (because of the plasm) gently steaming, protecting my rival from death. And as I stared at the apparition, I saw that the cowl had drawn back, leaving the doctor's face exposed. Yes, it was hideous and snarling; yes, the teeth were sharp and the eyes were like black coins, but—with the hood off—it was just a man's face, after all. A stupid, obsessive man, who, to make himself feel important, had liked to dress in eerie robes. Who had sought answers to things he shouldn't know, but had been too scared to look himself. Who had used others—both in life, and now in death. Was his voice hypnotic? Perhaps to some, but not to me.

I'd had enough of him.

I changed my posture from defense to attack. As the ghost recoiled from a high swing of the iron, I stepped in close, adjusted my arms, and brought the chain up and over my head like a fisherman casting his line. The iron cut straight down through the center of Bickerstaff, from hood to floor, slicing him neatly in two.

A sigh, a gasp—the apparition vanished. A thread of plasm whipped across the floor and was sucked back into the body. With a snap of air, it was gone.

Steam rose from the tip of the iron chains. I let them drop. Kipps was sitting rigid in the chair, with a slightly harrowed look on his face.

"I've driven it back," I said. "Shouldn't re-form for a while."

"Right," he said. He moistened his lips. "Thanks. Though you didn't need to give me a buzz cut too. Now, set me free."

"Not yet." I looked across the room. "There's one more thing to finish."

While I'd faced the ghost, the fight between George and Joplin had also been resolved. Having rolled and tumbled their way across the chamber, they had ended up in a flailing heap beside a pile of empty coffins. Joplin was on top; with a cry, he tore himself from George's grasp, and tottered to his feet. George could not respond, but collapsed, exhausted, against the wall.

Joplin's shirt was ripped, his jacket half off; he seemed entirely dazed. Yet still there was only one thing on his mind. He stared back across the floor, to where the bone mirror lay, facedown. He started staggering toward it.

No. No way. It was time to end this.

Even in my weary state I was faster than the archivist. I walked across, I reached the mirror. Seven figures still hovered above it, faint and mournful. I bent down, picked it up, and then—ignoring the clustering spirits, ignoring Joplin's shout—carried it over to the table.

It was icy cold in my hand. The bones felt smooth; they tingled to the touch. The buzzing noise was very loud. I took care to hold the disc with the mirror side down. When I looked up, the group of shapes were all around me—near, but also distant. They were focused on the mirror. I felt no threat from them. Their faces were blank and smudged, like photos left out in the rain.

All around me their faint cries sounded: "Give us back our bones. . . ."

"Okay, okay," I said. "I'll see what I can do."

The first thing I did, when I got to the table, was pick my rapier off the floor. Then I scanned the mess scattered across the tabletop, noting certain tools belonging to Joplin: crowbar, chisel, mallet. I didn't like to think what he had used them for.

Joplin had come to a halt on the other side of the table. He had the same look of dull intensity in his eyes. "No!" he croaked. "It's mine! Don't!"

I ignored him. I looked back toward the catacombs, to the passage I'd entered from. A faint green glow could just be seen there, a grumpy face peering from my backpack.

"Skull!" I said. "Now's the time! I have the mirror here. Talk."

The faint voice was uneasy. "Talk about what?"

"You were there when it was made. Tell me how to destroy it. I want to free these poor trapped spirits here."

"Who cares about them? They're useless. Look at them—they could ghost-touch you in seconds, yet all they do is float around, groaning. They're rubbish. They deserve to be trapped. Now, as for me—"

"Speak! Remember what I'll do to you if you don't!"

Across the table, Joplin suddenly lurched toward me. I raised my rapier and warded him off. But as I did so, my grip on the mirror loosened. It slipped in my other hand and twisted, so that I caught a flash of the jet-black glass. . . .

Too late, I slammed it facedown on the table and squeezed my eyes tight shut. A sudden appalling pain speared through my gut; I felt as if I were slowly being turned inside out. And with that pain came a burning desire to look in the glass again. It was an overwhelming urge. Suddenly I knew that the mirror would solve everything. It would give me bliss. My body was parched, but the glass would quench my thirst. I was famished, but the glass would give me food. Everything outside the mirror was dull and worthless—nothing was of consequence but the shimmering, gleaming blackness. I could see it, I could join it, if only I turned the mirror over and gave myself up to it. It was laughably easy. I set my rapier down, began to move my hand . . .

"*Poor stupid Lucy. . . .*" It was the skull's voice, breaking harshly through my dream. "*A fool like all the rest. Can't take her eyes away, when all she has to do is smash the glass.*"

Smash it . . . ? And then the one tiny piece of me that remained wedded to life and light and living things recoiled in horror.

I snatched up the mallet, and drove it down on the back of the mirror.

There was a terrific crack; a burst of released air, and the buzzing noise—which had remained constant in my ears all this time—suddenly cut out. From the seven spirits came a sighing—a sound almost of ecstasy. They blurred, shuddered, and vanished from sight. Beneath my hands, the mirror was a wonky mess of bones and twine; flakes of black glass lay across the table. I felt no more pain or desire.

For a moment, in that silent chamber, no one moved.

"Right," I said. "That's that."

Joplin had been transfixed; now he gave a hollow groan. "How *dare* you?" he cried. "That was invaluable! That was *mine!*" Darting forward, he rummaged on the tabletop and drew out an enormous flintlock pistol, rusted, cumbersome, with hammers raised.

He pointed the gun at me.

A polite cough sounded beside us. I looked up; Joplin turned.

Anthony Lockwood stood there. He was covered in grave dust, and there were cobwebs on his collar and in his hair. His trousers were torn at the knees, his fingers bleeding. He'd looked neater in his time, but I can't say he'd ever looked better to me. He held his rapier casually in one hand.

"Step back!" Joplin cried. "I'm armed!"

"Hi, Lucy," Lockwood said. "Hello, George. Sorry I've taken a while."

"That's all right."

"Have I missed anything?"

"Step back, I say!"

"Not much. I rescued George—or, I should say, he rescued me. Kipps is here too. I've got the bone mirror—or what's left of it. Mr. Joplin was just threatening me with this antique gun thing."

"Looks like a mid-eighteenth-century British army pistol," Lockwood said. "Two bullets, flintlock action. Quite a rare model, I think. They phased it out after two years."

I stared at him. "How do you *know* these things?"

"Just sort of do. The point is, it's not a very accurate weapon. Also, it needs to be kept somewhere dry, not in a damp old catacomb."

"Silence! If you don't do what I ask—"

"Shouldn't think it'll work. Let's see, shall we?" With that, Lockwood moved toward Joplin.

From the direction of the archivist came a hiss of fury and the forlorn clicking of an antique pistol. With a curse, he threw the gun at our feet, turned, and stumbled away across the room. Directly toward the Bickerstaff body on the floor.

"Mr. Joplin," I shouted, "stop! It's not yet safe!"

Lockwood started after him, but Joplin paid no heed. Like a thin, bespectacled rat, he skidded and veered from side to side, panic-stricken, helpless, tripping on chains, skidding on debris, unsure where to go.

The answer was decided for him.

As he passed the mummified body, a hooded figure rose from the bricks. The ghost was very faint now, wispy even to my eyes, and Joplin walked right into it. White, translucent arms enfolded him. He slowed and stopped; his head fell back, his body jerked and twitched. He made a sighing sound. And then he toppled gently forward, through the fading figure, onto the brick floor.

It was over in seconds. By the time we got there, the ghost had vanished. Joplin was already turning blue.

Lockwood kicked the chains closed around the Bickerstaff body to seal the Source. I ran over to George. He was still sitting sprawled in a corner. His eyes were closed, but he opened them as I drew near.

"Joplin?" he asked.

"Dead. Bickerstaff got him."

"And the mirror?"

"Afraid I broke it."

"Oh. Okay." He gave a sigh. "Probably just as well."

"I think so."

My legs were feeling wobbly. I sat down next to him. Over on the other side, Lockwood was leaning, gray-faced, against the wall. None of us said anything. No one had the energy.

"Hey," Kipps's voice echoed across the room. "After you've had your little rest, could someone please untie me?"

Chapter 29

The sun was up over Kensal Green; it wasn't yet six a.m., but already it was pleasant to be out. Trees glistened, the grass shone; there were probably plenty of bees and butterflies drifting around, if I'd had the energy to notice. As it was, the only samples of wildlife I could see were the dozen or so DEPRAC officers who'd taken up residence in the excavators' camp. I sat on the chapel steps above them, letting the fresh warmth play on my skin.

They'd brought vans in, and were using the site as a temporary incident room. Beside one vehicle, Inspector Barnes stood in animated conference with Lockwood. I could almost see his mustache bristling from afar. Outside another van, a group of medics treated George—and also Kat Godwin, Bobby Vernon, and Ned Shaw, who stood together in a ragged line. As for Quill Kipps, he'd already been patched up. He sat a few steps below me; together we watched a procession of officers entering the chapel. They carried iron, silver, and all manner of protective boxes, to make safe the contents of the catacombs.

Here and there on the ground below the chapel, white-coated officers picked over scraps of clothing, blood, and fallen weapons—relics of the great fight that had taken place an hour or two before.

As Lockwood told it (and as reported by many of the newspapers afterward), the battle with Winkman's thugs had been a desperate affair. No fewer than six assailants—each armed with club or bludgeon—had taken part in the attack. Lockwood and the three Fittes agents had been fighting for their lives. It had been cudgel against sword, weight of numbers against superior fighting skill. The battle raged up and down the chapel steps, and at first, the sheer ferocity of the attackers had threatened to triumph. Gradually, however, the operatives' swordplay turned the tide. As dawn broke over the cemetery, the thugs were driven back across the camp, and out among the graves. According to Lockwood, he himself had seriously wounded three of the men; Shaw and Godwin had accounted for two others. The sixth had thrown away his baton and fled. In the end, five captives had lain helpless on the ground beside the cabins, with Kat Godwin standing guard.

Victory, however, had come at a cost. Everyone had been hurt—Lockwood and Godwin with little more than scratches, while Ned Shaw had suffered a broken arm. Bobby Vernon had been badly struck about the head, and could not stand. It was left to Lockwood to force entry into the nearest work cabin; then, leaving Shaw to find its phone and call Barnes, he had sprinted into the chapel, where he found the open shaft of the catafalque. As I'd expected, he lost no time dropping into darkness, before hastening in search of George and me.

Getting out was easier than getting in. We'd eventually located the keys to the catacomb doors (and to Kipps's chains) in Joplin's pocket, and so were able to leave by way of the stairs. We reached the surface, going slowly, just as DEPRAC's team arrived.

Inspector Barnes had come bounding up the steps to meet us. Before listening to either Lockwood or Kipps, both of whom vied to get his attention, he had demanded the mirror; it was the only thing on his mind. Lockwood presented its pieces with a flourish. Judging by the droop of Barnes's mustache, its condition disappointed him. Nevertheless, he at once summoned medics to help us, before organizing a wider search of the catacombs. He wanted to see what else Joplin might have hidden there.

There was one artifact, however, that his officers didn't find. I had my backpack—and, in it, the silent ghost-jar. Arguably, the skull had saved me. I would decide its fate when I got back home.

After an early conversation with Barnes, Kipps had been largely ignored. For some time he had been sitting on the chapel steps, gray-faced, a dusty, haggard shadow of his usual strutting self.

On impulse, I cleared my throat. "I want to thank you," I said. "For what you did—in supporting me back there. And for going after George. I'm surprised, actually. After seeing you hightail it from the rats in Bickerstaff's house, I wouldn't have guessed you'd have the guts to do any of that."

Kipps gave a mirthless laugh; I waited for the inevitable acid retort. Instead, after a pause, he said quietly, "It's easy to judge me now. But you don't yet know what it's like, the day your Talent starts to fade. You'll still sense ghosts—you'll know they're present. But you won't see or hear them properly anymore. You'll get all the terror, without being able to do anything about it. Sometimes nerves will simply overwhelm you."

He broke off then, and stood, his face hardening. Lockwood was walking toward us over the sunlit grass.

"So, are we all arrested?" I asked, as he drew near. I could think of several reasons why Barnes might be mad with us just now, my smashing the bone glass being only one of them.

Lockwood grinned. "Not at all. Why shouldn't Mr. Barnes be pleased? Yes, we broke the mirror. Yes, we killed the main suspect. But the danger to London's over, which is how he sold the case to us in the first place. He can't deny we've succeeded, can he? At least, that's what I told him. Anyway, he's got the mirror, even if it is broken, and he's got whatever else Joplin stashed in here. Also, the crooks we caught might well testify against Julius Winkman. All in all, he's happy, in a grudging sort of way. And so am I. How about you, Quill?"

"You gave the thing to Barnes, then," Kipps said shortly.

"I did."

"And he's awarded you the case?"

"He has."

"Full commission?"

"Actually, no. Since we did all the legwork, but you and your team were there to help us in the final act," Lockwood said, "I suggested we split it seventy/thirty. I hope that's satisfactory."

Kipps didn't answer at first. He breathed hard through his nose. "It's . . . acceptable," he said at last.

"Good." Lockwood's eyes glittered. "And so we come to the matter of our bet. The deal, as I recall, was that whoever lost this case should put an ad in the *Times*, praising the winners to the skies and doing some general groveling. I think you'll agree that since *we* located the mirror, *we* homed in on Joplin, and Barnes has declared *us* the official winners, those losers must surely be you and your team. What do you say?"

Kipps bit his lip; his tired eyes searched left and right, hunting for an answer. At last, as forced, tiny, and reluctant as an earwig being extracted from a crack, the answer came: "All right."

"Fine!" Lockwood said heartily. "That's all I wanted to hear. Of course, I can't make you do it, and frankly I wouldn't even *want* to, after fighting hard alongside your team today. Also, I know how you tried to help George and Lucy—and I won't forget that. So don't worry. The forfeit isn't necessary."

"The ad?"

"Forget it; it was a silly idea."

Conflicting emotions crossed Kipps's face; he seemed about to speak. All at once, he gave a single curt nod. He drew himself up. Trailing small clouds of grave dust, he stalked off down the steps toward his team.

"That was a nice gesture," I said, watching him go. "And I think it was the right thing to do. But . . ."

Lockwood scratched his nose. "Yes, I'm not *sure* he's too grateful. Ah, well—what can you do? And here comes George."

George's injuries had been treated. Aside from a few bruises, and some puffiness around the eyes, he looked in surprisingly good shape. Still, he seemed sheepish; he approached on hesitant steps. It was the first time we'd been alone with him that morning.

"If you're going to kill me," he said, "do you mind doing it quickly? I'm asleep on my feet here."

"We all are," Lockwood said. "We can do it another time."

"I'm sorry for causing this trouble. Shouldn't have gone off like that."

"True." Lockwood cleared his throat. "Still, I should probably apologize too."

"Personally," I said, "I'm not apologizing to anyone. At least, not until after a nap."

"I've been snappy with you, George," Lockwood said. "I haven't properly taken into account your excellent contributions to the team. And I'm aware that your actions today were almost certainly affected by your exposure to the mirror, and to Bickerstaff's ghost. You weren't quite yourself, I understand that."

He waited. George said nothing.

"Just a little opportunity there for you to apologize some more," Lockwood said.

"I think he's dozing off," I said. George's eyelids were drooping. I nudged him; his head jerked up. "Hey," I said, "one thing. One thing I've got to ask you now. When you looked into the mirror—"

George nodded sleepily. "I know what you're going to say. The answer's nothing. I didn't see anything there."

I frowned. "Yeah, but listen—I almost got caught too. I felt the tug, just with a single glance. It was all I could do to pull away. And you looked right into it. Not only that, you said to Joplin that you saw—"

"'Beautiful things?' Oh, I was making that up. I was telling Joplin what he wanted to hear." He grinned at us. "The whole thing was an act."

Lockwood stared at him. "But I don't understand. If you looked into the glass—"

"He *did*," I insisted. "I watched him do it."

"Then how did you survive when Wilberforce and Neddles— and everyone else who looked into it—ended up dying of fright?"

For answer, George slowly took off his glasses. He lowered them, as if to clean them on his sweater, and put his finger up against the lens. He pushed; instead of hitting glass, his finger went right through. He wiggled it from side to side.

"When I had my scrap with Joplin earlier," he said, "we each knocked our specs clean off. Mine hit a stone or something, and both lenses fell out. I lost them on the floor. Joplin didn't notice, and you can be sure I wasn't going to tell him. So whatever was in that mirror could have been dancing a hornpipe for all I knew or cared. Didn't bother me at all."

"You mean, when you looked at it—"

"Exactly." He tucked his empty frames neatly in his pocket. "At that distance, I'm totally blind. I couldn't see a thing."

Chapter 30

SECRETS OF THE CATACOMBS!

BLACK MARKET RING EXPOSED

HORRORS OF THE MADMAN'S HOARD

INSIDE TODAY: A. J. LOCKWOOD REVEALS ALL

For several years, the *Times of London* has speculated on the existence of a sinister black market trade dealing in dangerous objects related to the Problem. Accusations and rumors have been rife, but hard evidence has been scanty—until now.

Following yesterday's news of several arrests in Kensal Green and Bloomsbury, we are now able to report that agents from Lockwood & Co. have discovered and broken up a ring of thieves operating in the respectable heart of the city. In a special interview, Anthony Lockwood, Esq. reveals how his intrepid team, aided by several assistants from the Fittes

Agency, fought pitched battles with dangerous criminals, and uncovered a hoard of stolen artifacts in a haunted catacomb.

Today Mr. Lockwood discusses the full paranormal terrors of this epic investigation, including the horrifying Rat-ghost of Hampstead and the Terror of the Iron Coffin. He also traces the web of clues that led to the exposure and death of Mr. Albert Joplin, a well-known archivist, who has since been implicated in at least one murder. "He was a man too fascinated by the past," Mr. Lockwood says. "He spent too long rooting in the dark corners of our history. Finally, his obsessions corrupted him and took his sanity. In this troubled age we live in, perhaps this is a lesson for us all."

Full Lockwood Interview: see pages 4–5
"House of the Rats" clippable floor plan and photos: see pages 6–7
Can Cemeteries Ever Be Made Safe?: see page 25

Three days after the final events beneath the chapel, we gathered for elevenses in the basement office at 35 Portland Row. We were in cheerful spirits. We'd had a lot of sleep, and we'd had plenty of attention. The great Fittes fiftieth-anniversary party was still the most popular subject in the daily papers, but our adventures were a close second. Not only that, our check from DEPRAC—signed by Inspector Barnes himself—had just cleared in the bank. And it was yet another sunny morning.

Lockwood sat behind his desk, with an enormous mug of coffee at his elbow, sifting through the mail. Steam coiled slowly from the mug. He was relaxed, his collar unbuttoned; his jacket hung on the suit of armor we'd been given by a grateful client the month before. Over in the corner, George had taken down the big black leather casebook and, with a silver pen, was beginning to write up his account of the Missing Mirror. He had a healthy stack of press clippings, and a pot of glue.

"Lot of good stuff to stick in for this one," he said. "Better than the Wimbledon Wraiths, anyway."

I set aside the *Times*. "Great interview, Lockwood," I said, "though I'm not sure Kipps is going to be super chuffed at being labeled your *assistant*."

Lockwood looked wounded. "I think he gets quite a decent write-up, all things considered. I'm quite complimentary. He could have been not mentioned at all."

"One thing I see you definitely *don't* mention is the mirror," I said. "You talk about Bickerstaff, but only because it was his phantom in the iron coffin. There's nothing about the bone glass, or what Joplin was really up to."

"Well, you can thank Barnes for that." Lockwood helped himself to one of the homemade chocolate flapjacks George had rustled up that morning. He was doing a lot of cooking, George, making us all our favorite things as a way of saying sorry. He didn't have to, really, but neither Lockwood nor I had gotten around to telling him yet. "Barnes expressly forbade me to talk about the mirror," Lockwood continued, "or about anything it might have done. So, for the press, we had to focus on the whole black market thing— you know, Winkman and all that. Joplin's going to be portrayed as a mad eccentric." He chewed his flapjack. "Which he was, I suppose."

"'His obsessions corrupted him,'" I said, quoting the interview. "Like they corrupted Bickerstaff all those years ago."

"Yes, just people getting over-curious," Lockwood said. "Happens all the time. . . ." He glanced at George, who was busy sticking something in the book. "Of course, in this case, there *was* something extra going on. The mirror exerted a powerful attraction on anyone exposed to it. Bickerstaff's ghost did too. Between them, someone like Joplin, who was weak, greedy, and fascinated by such things anyway, was easily driven mad."

"But here's the real question," I said. "What's the truth about the mirror? Did it do what Bickerstaff claimed? Could it actually have been a window onto what happens after death? A window on another world?"

Lockwood shook his head. "That's the paradox about all this. You can't find out the truth without looking in the mirror, and looking in the mirror tends to kill you." He shrugged. "I guess one way or another it *does* show you the other side."

"I think it *was* a window." George looked up at us from his work. The bruises on his face were still obvious, but the sparkle had returned to his eyes. He had a new pair of glasses on. "To me, Bickerstaff's theory makes a weird kind of sense. Ghosts come into this world via a weak spot. We call that the Source. If you put enough Sources together, just maybe you'll create a big enough hole to see through. It's a fascinating idea that—" He broke off, realizing we were staring at him. "Um, that I'm not interested in anymore. Who wants another flapjack?"

"It's all irrelevant, anyway," I said, "since I broke the mirror. It's useless now."

"Is it, though?" George flashed us a dark glance. "DEPRAC has the pieces. Maybe they'll try to put it back together. We don't know *what* goes on in Scotland Yard. Or at Fittes House, for that matter. Did you *see* all those books in that library? They even had Mary Dulac's pamphlet—and how obscure was that? There could be *so* much hidden knowledge in that room."

"*George*," I said.

"I know. I'll shut up now. I'm only talking. I know the mirror was a horrible thing."

"Speaking of horrible objects," I said, "what are we going to do about *this* one?" The ghost-jar was on the corner of my desk, covered with a wool tea cozy. It had been there for three days. Since the events at Kensal Green, the ghost had stubbornly refused to appear; no face, no voice, not even the slightest plasmic glow. The skull sat clamped at the base of the jar, staring out with vacant sockets. There was no sign of the malignant spirit; all the same, for reasons of privacy, we kept the lever on the top tightly closed.

"Yes," Lockwood said. "We need to make a decision about that. It actually helped you in the catacombs, you said?"

"Yeah. . . ." I glared at the silent cozy. It was a striped orange one that had been knitted by George's mother and given to Lockwood as a present. It covered the jar quite well. "The skull spent half the time cheering because we were about to die," I said. "But on several occasions it did seem to be vaguely helpful. And right at the end—when the mirror had me, and I could feel myself slipping away—it spoke and snapped me out of it." I frowned. "Don't know if it really meant to. If it did, it was probably only because of all the threats I made. We know what a twisted thing it is. In Hampstead it almost got us killed."

"So what do we do with it?" Lockwood said.

"It's a Type Three," George put in; he spoke almost apologetically. "I know I shouldn't say this, but it's too important to be destroyed."

Lockwood sat back in his chair. "It's up to Lucy. She's the one most affected by it. George is right: the skull may yet be valuable, and we had big ideas about revealing it to the world. But is it truly worth the hassle and the risk?"

I pulled the cozy up and stared into the jar for a moment. "If I'm honest," I said, "the last thing I'd want now is to tell anyone about my connection with this ghost. What would happen? It would be like with Bickerstaff's mirror, only worse. Everyone would go crazy. DEPRAC would take me off and do endless experiments, trying to find out stuff from the skull. It would be hell. I'd never get any peace. So if you don't mind, can we keep it quiet for now?"

"Of course we can," Lockwood said. "No problem."

"As for destroying it," I went on, "I'm not sure that we should. When I was in the catacombs, I heard the voices of the spirits trapped inside the mirror. *They* weren't wicked—just very sad. They weren't talking to me like the skull does, but they communicated with me, even so. That's why I broke the thing: it's what they wanted. What I'm saying is, I'm getting better at understanding my Talent; I think it may be getting stronger. And I've definitely never had as strong a connection with any other spirit as I have with this skull. So, for better or for worse, even though it's a nasty, conniving, deceitful thing that mixes truth and lies in everything it says, I think we have to keep it here. For the moment. Maybe it'll be properly useful to us all one day."

After my little speech we were quiet for a time. George took up his pen. I did some paperwork. Lockwood sat staring at the window, deep in thought.

"There's a picture here of that warehouse where Julius Winkman held his auction," George said, holding up a clipping. "You didn't tell me the roof was that high."

"Yep," I said. "Our jump was even scarier than Flo Bones's boat. What time is Flo coming over this evening, Lockwood?"

"Six. I still think it's a bit dangerous inviting her to dinner, but we owe her lots of favors. We'd better get in a ton of licorice, too. By the way, did I tell you I found out how Winkman's men traced us? Winkman had an informer working at DEPRAC. When Lucy and I got caught at his shop, that first time, he made inquiries and learned which agents had been put on the case. So after the auction, he already had a good idea who we were. He sent men after us, and they tailed us to the cemetery."

"It's not very nice to think that Winkman knows our names," George said.

"Hopefully he'll be a bit too busy to worry about that for a while."

"There *is* one other thing," I said. It had been at the back of my mind for days, but only now, in the calm and dappled sunlight, did it find space to come forward. "When we were in the Fittes Black Library, and we saw Penelope Fittes talking with that man . . . she gave him something—a box; I don't know if either of you saw."

"Not me," Lockwood said. "My head was turned away."

"I was contorted into an impossibly small space under the table," George said. "You don't want to know what I was looking at."

"Well, I've no idea what was in that box," I went on, "but it had a symbol printed on the outside. George—you remember those goggles you pinched from Fairfax at Combe Carey Hall?"

"I not only remember"—George ferreted in a particularly messy corner of his desk—"I have them here." He held up the goggles: thick and rubbery, with crystal eyepieces. We'd studied them a bit over recent months, but we'd been unable to make much of them.

"Look at your desk!" I chided. "You are *so* like Joplin. . . . Yes, there—see the little harp design on the lens? That symbol was stamped on Ms. Fittes's box, too."

Lockwood and George regarded it. "Curious. It's not a logo of any company I know," Lockwood said. "Think it's some internal department of the Fittes Agency, George?"

"No. Not an official one, anyway. Come to think of it, the whole meeting was a bit odd. What was it that Ms. Fittes and that bloke were discussing? Some group or other? Couldn't hear too well; my knees were against my ears." He took off his new spectacles and lowered them to his sweater, then thought better of it and self-consciously raised them to his nose again.

"It's all right," I remarked. "You're allowed to rub your glasses. You're not at all like Joplin really."

Lockwood, busy selecting another flapjack, nodded. "Nothing like him. He was a weird, friendless sociopath with a morbid death-obsession, while you . . ." He picked up the plate. "Flapjack, Luce?"

"Thanks."

"While I . . ." George prompted.

Lockwood grinned. "Well . . . you have at least two friends, haven't you?" He passed the plate across. "And that brings me to something I've been wanting to say."

George looked at me. "He's going to tell me off some more."

"I think he's going to boast about the Winkman fight again. The fight we didn't see."

"Yeah, he'll have fought off *four* blokes single-handedly now."

Lockwood held up his hand. "No, it's still three, though one of them *was* quite big and hairy. The thing is," he said, "I've been thinking about this case. All through it, everyone's been obsessed with the secrets of the mirror. Joplin, Kipps, us; we all got snared by it. Barnes, too. Winkman's actually the only one with any sense. He didn't care about the glass, did he? He just tried to sell it. He understood that it was the mystery about it that made it valuable." He looked down at the table, as if marshaling his thoughts. "Anyway, to keep things brief—"

"If you wouldn't mind," I said. I winked at George, and crunched the flapjack.

"To keep things brief, I've decided secrets cause nothing but trouble. There's a darn sight too many of them, and they make things worse, not better. So, I've come to a decision. I want to show you both something."

I stopped crunching.

"Oh God, you haven't got some dodgy tattoos, have you?" George said. "I've only just gotten over Carver's."

"No, it's not tattoos," Lockwood said. He smiled, but there was sadness in it. "If you're not doing anything, I could show you now."

He got up, and crossed the room toward the arched doorway. George and I, suddenly quiet, rose and followed him. George's eyes scanned mine. I realized that my hands were shaking.

We left the office, with its desks and streams of sunlight. We spiraled up the iron steps, above the washing baskets and strings of drying laundry; came out into the kitchen, where last night's dishes lay undone. We went out into the hall, where a brand new Arabian rug stretched toward the door. We walked below the hanging masks and ghost-catchers, turned at the foot of the stairs, and began to climb again. The messy coatrack, the living room, the open library door . . . My senses were alive to it all. We passed through all the clutter of the house we shared—ordinary things, familiar things, that might in moments have their meanings changed, subtly and forever, by whatever it was we were about to see.

The landing, which only has one narrow window, was as dim and shady as ever. The bedroom doors were closed. As usual, one of George's damp bath towels was draped unpleasantly over a radiator. From an open window somewhere came birdsong, very beautiful, very loud.

Lockwood stopped outside the forbidden door. He put his hands in his pockets. "Here we are," he said. "It's been a while since I gave you both your tours, and . . . well, we never exactly completed them, did we? I thought you might like to see in here."

We stared at the ordinary door, its faded label mark no different from before. "Well, yeah . . ." I began, "but only if you . . ."

He nodded. "Just turn the handle, walk right in."

"Hasn't it got some kind of secret lock?" George said. "I always assumed there might be some clever mantrap built into it, maybe a guillotine thing that shoots down as you step through? No? Was I overthinking it?"

"I'm afraid you were. There's nothing. I trusted you both, of course."

We stared at the door.

"Yes, but Lockwood," I said suddenly, "all that stuff about secrets works both ways. So what if we're curious? If you're not comfortable with it, there's no reason why we have to know."

It was the old Lockwood smile again; the landing grew much brighter. "It's fine. I've been thinking about doing this for a while now. Somehow, I never got around to it. But when the skull started whispering to you about it, I knew the time had come. Anyway, let me do the honors for you."

The skull, in so many things, was a liar and a cheat, but it could speak the truth, too. It had told us the location of the Bickerstaff papers, casually forgetting to mention the ghost that waited there. At Kensal Green it had helped me access the catacombs, then crowed with delight when I almost died. Its truths, in other words, carried dangers. And it had told the truth about this room.

As Lockwood pulled open the door, we saw that its inner side was thickly lined with strips of iron, carefully nailed into the wood. They were there to block the psychic radiance that now burst out from inside.

A heavy curtain spanned the window opposite, muffling the daylight, keeping the bedroom dark. The air was close and strong, and smelled heavily of lavender.

At first it was difficult to make out anything at all. But as George and I stood there in the doorway, we began to see the glint of silver charms hanging on the walls.

Our eyes adjusted; we gazed at what was in the room. And then I felt the floor pitch under me, as if we were suddenly at sea. George cleared his throat. I put out my hand to clench his arm.

Lockwood stood slightly behind us, waiting.

"Your parents?" I was the first to find my voice.

"Close," Anthony Lockwood said. "My sister."

Glossary

* indicates a Type One ghost
** indicates a Type Two ghost

Agency, Psychic Investigation—A business specializing in the containment and destruction of **ghosts**. There are more than a dozen agencies in London alone. The largest two (the Fittes Agency and the Rotwell Agency) have hundreds of employees; the smallest (Lockwood & Co.) has three. Most agencies are run by adult supervisors, but all rely heavily on children with strong psychic **Talent**.

Apparition—The shape formed by a **ghost** during a **manifestation**. Apparitions usually mimic the shape of a dead person, but animals and objects are also seen. Some can be quite unusual. The **Specter** in the recent Limehouse Docks case manifested as a greenly glowing king cobra, while the infamous Bell Street Horror took the guise of a patchwork doll. Powerful or weak, most ghosts do not (or cannot) alter their appearance.

Aura—The radiance surrounding many **apparitions**. Most auras are fairly faint, and are seen best out of the corner of the eye. Strong, bright auras are known as **other-light**. A few ghosts radiate black auras that are darker than the night around them.

Catacomb—An underground chamber used for burials. Never common in London, the few existing catacombs have fallen entirely into disuse since the outbreak of the **Problem**.

Catafalque—A hydraulic mechanism used to lower coffins into a **catacomb**.

Chain net—A net made of finely spun **silver** chains; a versatile variety of **seal**.

Chill—The sharp drop in temperature that occurs when a ghost is near. One of the four usual indicators of an imminent **manifestation**, the others being **malaise, miasma,** and **creeping fear.** Chill may extend over a wide area, or be concentrated in specific cold spots.

Cluster—A group of **ghosts** occupying a small area.

Cold Maiden*—A gray, misty female form, often wearing old-fashioned dress, seen indistinctly at a distance. Cold Maidens radiate powerful feelings of melancholy and **malaise.** As a rule, they rarely draw close to the living, but exceptions *have* been known. *See also* **Floating Bride.**

Creeping fear—A sense of inexplicable dread often experienced in the build-up to a **manifestation.** Often accompanied by **chill, miasma,** and **malaise.**

Curfew—In response to the **Problem,** the British government enforces nightly curfews in many inhabited areas. During curfew, which begins shortly after dusk and finishes at dawn, ordinary people are encouraged to remain indoors, safe behind their home **defenses.**

Dark Specter **—A frightening variety of **Type Two ghost** that manifests as a moving patch of darkness. Sometimes the **apparition** at the center of the darkness is dimly visible; at other times the black cloud is fluid and formless, perhaps shrinking to the size of a pulsing heart, or expanding at speed to engulf a room.

Death-glow—An energy trace left at the exact spot where a death took place. The more violent the death, the brighter the glow. Strong glows may persist for many years.

Defenses against ghosts—The three principal defenses, in order of effectiveness, are **silver, iron,** and **salt. Lavender** also affords some protection, as do bright light and running **water.**

DEPRAC—The Department of Psychic Research and Control. A government organization devoted to tackling the **Problem.** DEPRAC investigates the nature of **ghosts,** seeks to destroy the most dangerous ones, and monitors the activities of the many competing **agencies.**

Ectoplasm—A strange, variable substance from which **ghosts** are formed. In its concentrated state, ectoplasm is very harmful to the living. *See also* **ichor.**

Fetch**—A rare and unnerving class of **ghost** that appears in the shape of a living person, usually someone known to the onlooker. Fetches are seldom aggressive, but the fear and disorientation they evoke is so strong that most experts classify them as **Type Two** spirits, to be treated with extreme caution.

Fittes Manual—A famous book of instruction for ghost-hunters written by Marissa Fittes, the founder of Britain's first psychic investigation **agency**.

Floating Bride*—A female **Type One ghost**, a variety of **Cold Maiden**. Floating Brides are generally headless, or missing another part of their anatomy. Some search for their missing extremity; others cradle it or hold it mournfully aloft. Named after the ghosts of two royal brides, beheaded at Hampton Court Palace.

Gallows mark—A stone used to support a gallows post. Often this stone remains at the execution site long after the wooden frame has rotted away.

Gallows Wraith**—A malignant subtype of **Wraith**, found at former places of execution. "Old Crack-neck," which killed three agents in Tyburn Fields, is the most famous gallows Wraith of all.

Ghost—The spirit of a dead person. Ghosts have existed throughout history, but—for unclear reasons—are now increasingly common. There are many varieties; broadly speaking, however, they can be organized into three main groups (*See* **Type One, Type Two, Type Three**). Ghosts always linger near a **Source**, which is often the place of their death. They are at their strongest after dark, and most particularly, between the hours of midnight and two a.m. Most are unaware or uninterested in the living. A few are actively hostile.

Ghost cult—A group of people who, for a variety of reasons, share an unhealthy interest in the returning dead.

Ghost-fog—A thin, greenish-white mist, occasionally produced during a **manifestation**. Possibly formed of **ectoplasm**, it is cold and unpleasant, but not itself dangerous to the touch.

Ghost-jar—A **silver-glass** receptacle used to constrain an active **Source**.

Ghost-lamp—An electrically powered streetlight that sends out strong white beams to discourage **ghosts**. Most ghost-lamps have shutters fixed over their glass lenses; these snap on and off at intervals throughout the night.

Ghost-lock—A dangerous power displayed by **Type Two ghosts**, possibly an extension of **malaise**. Victims are sapped of their willpower, and overcome by a feeling of terrible despair. Their muscles seem as heavy as lead, and they can no longer think or move freely. In most cases, they end up transfixed, waiting helplessly as the hungry ghost glides closer and closer. . . .

Ghost-touch—The effect of bodily contact with an **apparition**, and the most deadly power of an aggressive **ghost**. Beginning with a sensation of sharp, overwhelming cold, ghost-touch swiftly spreads an icy numbness through the body. One after another, vital organs fail; soon the body burns bluish and starts to swell. Without swift medical intervention, ghost-touch is usually fatal.

Glimmer*—The faintest perceptible **Type One** ghost. Glimmers manifest only as flecks of **other-light** flitting through the air. They can be touched or walked through without harm.

Greek Fire—Another name for **magnesium flares**. Early weapons of this kind were apparently used against **ghosts** during the days of the Byzantine (or Greek) Empire, a thousand years ago.

Haunting—*See* **Manifestation**

Ichor—**Ectoplasm** in its thickest, most concentrated form. It burns many materials, and is safely constrained only by **silver-glass**.

Iron—An ancient and important protection against **ghosts** of all kinds. Ordinary people fortify their homes with iron decorations, and carry it on their persons in the form of **wards**. Agents carry iron **rapiers** and chains, and so rely on it for both attack and defense.

Lavender—The strong sweet smell of this plant is thought to discourage evil spirits. As a result, many people wear dried sprigs of lavender, or burn it to release the pungent smoke. Agents sometimes carry vials of lavender water to use against weak **Type Ones**.

Limbless**—A swollen, misshapen variety of **Type Two ghost**, with a generally human head and torso, but lacking recognizable arms and legs. With **Wraiths** and **Raw-bones**, one of the least pleasing **apparitions**. Often accompanied by strong sensations of **miasma** and **creeping fear**.

Listening—One of the three main categories of psychic **Talent**. **Sensitives** with this ability are able to hear the voices of the dead, echoes of past events, and other unnatural sounds associated with **manifestations**.

Lurker*—A variety of **Type One ghost** that hangs back in the shadows, rarely moving, never approaching the living, but spreading strong feelings of anxiety and **creeping fear**.

Magnesium flare—A metal canister with a breakable glass seal, containing magnesium, iron, salt, gunpowder, and an igniting device. An important agency weapon against aggressive **ghosts**.

Malaise—A feeling of despondent lethargy often experienced when a **ghost** is approaching. In extreme cases this can deepen into dangerous **ghost-lock**.

Manifestation—A ghostly occurrence. May involve all kinds of supernatural phenomena, including sounds, smells, odd sensations, moving objects, drops in temperature, and the glimpse of **apparitions**.

Miasma—An unpleasant atmosphere, often including disagreeable tastes and smells, experienced in the run-up to a **manifestation**. Regularly accompanied by **creeping fear**, **malaise**, and **chill**.

Night watch—Groups of children, usually working for large companies and local government councils, who guard factories, offices, and public areas after dark. Though not allowed to use **rapiers**, night-watch children have long **iron**-tipped spears to keep **apparitions** at bay.

Operative—Another name for a psychic investigation agent.

Other-light—An eerie, unnatural light radiating from some **apparitions**.

Pale Stench*—A **Type One ghost** that spreads a dreadful **miasma**, a smell of noxious decay. Best confronted by burning many sticks of **lavender**.

Phantasm**—Any **Type Two ghost** that maintains an airy, delicate, and see-through form. A Phantasm may be almost invisible, aside from its faint outline and a few wispy details of its face and features. Despite its insubstantial appearance, it is no less aggressive than the more solid-seeming **Specter**, and all the more dangerous for being harder to see.

Phantom—Another general name for a **ghost**.

Plasm—*See* **Ectoplasm**

Poltergeist**—A powerful and destructive class of **Type Two ghost**. Poltergeists release strong bursts of supernatural energy that can lift even heavy objects into the air. They do not form **apparitions**.

Problem, the—The epidemic of hauntings currently affecting Britain.

Rapier—The official weapon of all psychic investigation agents. The tips of the **iron** blades are sometimes coated with **silver**.

Raw-bones**—A rare and unpleasant kind of **ghost**, which manifests as a bloody, skinless corpse with goggling eyes and grinning teeth. Not popular with agents. Many authorities regard it as a variety of **Wraith**.

Relic-man/relic-woman—Someone who locates **Sources** and other psychic artifacts and sells them on the black market.

Salt—A commonly used defense against **Type One ghosts**. Less effective than **iron** and **silver**, salt is cheaper than both, and used in many household deterrents.

Salt-bomb—A small plastic throwing-globe filled with **salt**. Shatters on impact, spreading salt in all directions. Used by agents to drive back weaker **ghosts**. Less effective against stronger entities.

Salt-gun—A device that projects a fine spray of salty water across a wide area. A useful weapon against **Type One ghosts**. Increasingly employed by larger **agencies**.

Sanatorium—A hospital for patients with chronic illnesses.

Seal—An object, usually **silver** or **iron**, designed to enclose or cover a **Source**, and prevent escape of its **ghost**.

Sensitive, a—Someone born with unusually good psychic **Talent**. Most sensitives join **agencies** or the **night watch**; others provide psychic services without actually confronting **Visitors**.

Shade*—The standard **Type One ghost**, and possibly the most common kind of **Visitor**. Shades may appear quite solid, in the manner of **Specters**, or be insubstantial and wispy, like **Phantasms**; however, they entirely lack the dangerous intelligence of either. Shades seem unaware of the presence of the living, and are usually bound into a fixed pattern of behavior. They project feelings of grief and loss, but seldom display anger or any stronger emotion. They almost always appear in human form.

Shining Boy**—A deceptively beautiful variety of **Type Two ghost** that manifests as a young boy (or, more rarely, girl) walking in the center of cold, blazing **other-light**.

Sight—The psychic ability to see **apparitions** and other ghostly phenomena, such as **death-glows**. One of the three main varieties of psychic **Talent**.

Silver—An important and potent **defense** against **ghosts**. Worn by many people as **wards** in the form of jewelry. Agents use it to coat their **rapiers**, and as a crucial component of their **seals**.

Silver-glass—A special "ghost-proof" glass used to encase **Sources**.

Source—The object or place through which a **ghost** enters the world.

Specter**—The most commonly encountered **Type Two ghost**. A Specter always forms a clear, detailed **apparition**, which may in some cases seem almost solid. It is usually an accurate visual echo of the deceased as they were when alive or newly dead. Specters are less nebulous than **Phantasms** and less hideous than **Wraiths**, but equally varied in behavior. Many are neutral or benign in their dealings with the living—perhaps returning to reveal a secret, or make right an ancient wrong. Some, however, are actively hostile, and hungry for human contact. These ghosts should be avoided at all costs.

Stalker*—A **Type One ghost** that seems drawn to living people, following them at a distance, but never venturing close. Agents who are skilled at **Listening** often detect the slow shuffling of its bony feet, and its desolate sighs and groans.

Stone Knocker*—A desperately uninteresting **Type One ghost**, which does precious little apart from tap.

Talent—The ability to see, hear, or otherwise detect **ghosts**. Many children, though not all, are born with a degree of psychic Talent. This skill tends to fade toward adulthood, though it still lingers in some grown-ups. Children with better-than-average Talent join the **night watch**. Exceptionally gifted children usually join the **agencies**. The three main categories of Talent are **Sight**, **Listening**, and **Touch**.

Tom O'Shadows*—A London term for a **Lurker** or **Shade** that lingers in doorways, arches, or alleyways. An everyday urban **ghost**.

Touch—The ability to detect psychic echoes from objects that have been closely associated with death or a supernatural **manifestation**. Such echoes take the form of visual images, sounds, and other sense impressions. One of the three main varieties of **Talent**.

Type One—The weakest, most common, and least dangerous grade of **ghost**. Type Ones are scarcely aware of their surroundings, and often locked into a single, repetitive pattern of behavior. Commonly encountered examples include: **Shades**, **Lurkers**, and **Stalkers**. *See also* **Cold Maiden**, **Floating Bride**, **Glimmer**, **Pale Stench**, **Stone Knocker**, and **Tom O'Shadows**.

Type Two—The most dangerous commonly occurring grade of **ghost**. Type Twos are stronger than **Type Ones**, and possess some kind of residual intelligence. They are aware of the living, and may attempt to do them harm. The most common Type Twos, in order, are: **Specters**, **Phantasms**, and **Wraiths**. *See also* **Dark Specter**, **Fetch**, **Limbless**, **Poltergeist**, **Raw-bones**, and **Shining Boy**.

Type Three—A very rare grade of **ghost**, first reported by Marissa Fittes, and the subject of much controversy ever since. Allegedly able to communicate fully with the living.

Visitor—A **ghost**.

Ward—An object, usually of **iron** or **silver**, used to keep **ghosts** away. Small wards may be worn as jewelry on the person; larger ones, hung up around the house, are often equally decorative.

Water, running—It was observed in ancient times that **ghosts** dislike crossing running water. In modern Britain this knowledge is sometimes used against them. In central London a net of artificial channels, or runnels, protects the main shopping district. On a smaller scale, some home-owners build open channels outside their front doors and divert the rainwater along them.

Wraith**—A dangerous **Type Two ghost**. Wraiths are similar to **Specters** in strength and patterns of behavior, but are far more horrible to look at. Their **apparitions** show the deceased in his or her dead state: gaunt and shrunken, horribly thin, sometimes rotten and wormy. Wraiths often appear as skeletons. They radiate a powerful **ghost-lock**. *See also* **Gallows Wraith, Raw-bones**.

PRAISE FOR

The Screaming Staircase

LOCKWOOD & CO. BOOK 1

"Stroud (the Bartimaeus series) shows his customary flair for blending deadpan humor with thrilling action, and the fiery interplay among the three agents of Lockwood & Co. invigorates the story (along with no shortage of creepy moments). Stroud plays with ghost story conventions along the way, while laying intriguing groundwork that suggests that the Problem isn't the only problem these young agents will face in books to come—the living can be dangerous, too."
— *Publishers Weekly*

"Authentically spooky events occur in an engagingly crafted, believable world, populated by distinct, colorful personalities. The genuinely likable members of Lockwood & Co. persevere through the evil machinations of the living and the dead and manage to come out with their skins, and their senses of humor, intact. This smart, fast-paced ghostly adventure promises future chills."
— *School Library Journal*

"Three young ghost trappers take on deadly wraiths and solve an old murder case in the bargain to kick off Stroud's new post-Bartimaeus series . . . A heartily satisfying string of entertaining near-catastrophes, replete with narrow squeaks and spectral howls."
— *Kirkus Reviews*

"Stroud brings the seemingly disparate plot points together with his usual combination of thrilling adventure and snarky humor. . . . all members of this spirit-smashing trio get in their fair share of zingers, providing a comedic balance to the many narrow escapes, false leads, and shape-shifting specters that otherwise occupy Lockwood & Co."

—*Bulletin of the Center for Children's Books*

A 2013 *Los Angeles Times* Book Prize Finalist
for Young Adult Literature

2013 Cybil Award for Speculative Fiction

CCBC Choices List

2014 Edgar Award Nominee

A Junior Library Guild Selection

PRAISE FOR THE BARTIMAEUS BOOKS
by Jonathan Stroud

THE AMULET OF SAMARKAND

★"A darkly tantalizing tale."
—*Publishers Weekly*

★"One of the liveliest and most inventive
fantasies of recent years."
—*Booklist*

THE GOLEM'S EYE

"Fast-paced excitement."
—*Kirkus Reviews*

"A must-purchase for all fantasy collections."
—*School Library Journal*

"The top of the class of the currently popular fantasy series."
—*The New York Times Book Review*

PTOLEMY'S GATE

★"[A] potent ending that is at once
unexpected and wholly earned."
—*Publishers Weekly*

★"The trilogy wraps up with excitement, adventure
and an unexpected wallop of heart and soul."
—*Kirkus Reviews*

★"[T]he best yet . . . a stunning ending to
a justly acclaimed trilogy."

—The Horn Book

THE RING OF SOLOMON

★"A riveting adventure for Bartimaeus fans, old and new."
—Booklist

★"So rarely do humor and plot come together in such equally
strong measures that we can only hope for more adventures."
—The Horn Book

★". . . this is a superior fantasy that should have fans
racing back to those [Bartimaeus] books."
—Publishers Weekly

★"Definitely a must-purchase."
—School Library Journal